GEOMETRIES OF THE MIND

Geometries of the Mind

Norman Erik Keller

Writers Club Press
San Jose New York Lincoln Shanghai

Geometries of the Mind

Writers Club Press
an imprint of iUniverse.com, Inc.

For information address:
iUniverse.com, Inc.
5220 S 16th, Ste. 200
Lincoln, NE 68512
www.iuniverse.com

ISBN: 0-595-15465-4

Printed in the United States of America

For my wife, Darlene, who has put up with much throughout so many years.

Chapter 1

▼

The Convictions of Change

Wednesday, April 12, 1995, was a crisp, sunny, early spring day—*the* day Lasky had looked forward to for twelve years. This was the day his resignation as Chief Engineer took effect. He would finally get to say good riddance to an industry he hated, and a corporate world into which he would never fit. As he cleaned out his desk, he looked around his small, smoky office. The tile-covered cement floor, flanked by the seemingly ancient yellowing walls, and the single, double-paned window that opened into the industrial nightmare he had found himself in for the past near decade, served to hurry him along in the joyful task at hand.

"A twelve-by-twelve foot cell old boy, and you've been in it for all these years," he thought. "How the hell did this happen to you, anyway? You were far from the dumbest in college...a lot of promise, a lot of ideas. And to have been reduced to this! A goddamn steel industry where you were chief electrical engineer, quality control engineer, wire tester, inspector, meeting minutes taker, and whatever else they could devise for you! Remember your boss telling you to make coffee for those damn QC meetings, while the foreman laughed at you for having a young hotshot college graduate wait on them?

"Those bastards, Tom Ferley, Marv Eltmann, Walter Cotters, Frank Ketterman, and all those bastard foreman! And don't even think about those common lackey laborers, Calvin and Stu, and the shit they used to give you! Them, of all people! And yet their boss covered for them! You, old boy, were never that lucky! Well, forget it now, Mier, it's over, and the sooner you get your ass out of this pathetic place and get on with your special work, the better! Get your ass moving and finish packing. This is one trip down memory lane you don't need!"

In reality, an onlooker would have rightly thought Lasky had a good job. He was an important member of management, was paid extremely well, and despite the 'lackey duties' of his early days in that industry, was a credit to himself and his company. Somehow though, his personality interpreted anything that could be thought of as lowly work to be a purposely designed insult for him. Yet he was not of the Yuppie mentality. Nor was he a vain man, at least, not in the characteristic sense. He was aware of this, as were those he worked with daily. But he did have an ego problem, and from his private study of psychology and psychoanalysis, he had zeroed in on it. Somehow though, the application of this knowledge to his deepest resentments always eluded him. Application was his problem.

That same onlooker would have seen those lackey duties as part of the course for anyone who was new to management. An initiation into the upper levels of the working world, so to speak. An unfairness perhaps, but a mechanism of the world, nevertheless. The fact that the Chairman of the Board paid him a visit in an effort to have him stay with the corporation didn't matter to Lasky. Neither did the extra $10,000 per year salary increase the executive had offered him to reconsider. No, Lasky's mind was made up. He had *had enough*, a phrase he repeatedly muttered to himself since handing in his letter of resignation three months earlier.

The farewell parties corporate threw for him, the salary increase, the promise of a new office, more men for his department, all passed by him—respectfully acknowledged, but ultimately unknown...or unapplied. It was as though some part of him was bent toward seeing only the bad and the negative, never the good of his own situation. He never considered his three years at that multibillion dollar engineering corporation, or the two years in that small magnetic heads industry either, as having been stepping stones to the position of responsibility and authority he was now leaving. Instead, he looked back on all of it and all of *them* as blemished years of abject failure—doing work that he detested, and having to interact with people that he considered worthless.

The six boxes of his personal engineering, scientific, and math books were stacked on top of each other, blocking any access to the door of his office. His job was now finished. The packing was done. As he stood there reflecting on the daily duties he discharged from this room, an atmosphere of quiet overtook the quonset hut that housed his office. Slowly, almost unknowingly, he felt a sadness creep gently into his heart. Seventeen years of industrial effort in all, a way of life he had come to know, was about to slam shut. And that fact finally hit him hard.

Without being aware, he sat down behind his desk for the last time. It was then that the anger and natural hostility of his mind subsided, being silenced by the memories of genuine good that now poured into his heart. But the mind willed out, and Lasky was a man of the mind. Snapping himself out of what could have become an understandable melancholy for anyone in similar circumstances, he started to rise from his chair, when a voice shattered the now fading, yet still numbing silence of his office cell.

"Hey Mier, are you in there?" came a slow drawl from behind the stacked boxes.

"Come on in, John, it's good to see you! I didn't know if you'd come by before I left."

"No! I couldn't let you go by yourself, Mier! I know how you feel about this place and all. Everyone does. But we don't feel that way about you, leastwise me and the guys in the mills." John's old face smiled from beneath his graying hair, as he put his hands into his pocket, like a small boy who forgot how to say to good-bye…or never learned how to.

Lasky looked softly at John, one of the technicians in his engineering department, and the one man he truly liked. At thirty-eight years, Lasky realized that "Old John," as he fondly thought of him, was something of a father figure to him. And why not? John, sixty-six, had demonstrated fatherly feelings toward Lasky many times, by helping his boss over the all too frequent hard times that were characterized by the latter's outbursts at the "unfairness and stupidity of the bastards in this company!" Despite, or maybe because of his small town background and personality, Lasky had made a position for him in his department, thereby rescuing the older man from his own personal horror: enforced retirement.

As in many days past, the two men talked quietly in Lasky's office. The atmosphere was calm between them, each understanding the other in ways that pass beyond the words they used, each facing the fact that the end of their mutual effort was at hand.

"Still plan to go into that retirement of yours to work on those science ideas, Mier? I know it's not my place to tell anyone what to do or not do, but ya know, you're leavin' a good job! It's got a rock solid future, ya know! Take it from me. I wish I had the chance to go to college and make something more of myself than I did. You did, and now you're giving it up. Twelve years in one company is a lot to throw away. Maybe everyone doesn't like you here, but I think a lot of them do. You're one of the old timers now, ya know, and that counts for somethin', 'specially in Steel! Ever think of that?

"What if you run out of money? It can't last forever, and you've gotta live, ya know! And don't forget, you may not care for other people in general, but you're damn well gonna miss 'em, even if you bitch about 'em! There's a lot to not having a job, 'specially a good one like you got…or had. And do ya know somethin' else, Mier? I'll bet there's a lot more to bein' your own boss, too. Things that you don't suspect now, and won't till yer callin' yer own shots." John's habit of stuffing several thoughts into one long-winded fashion was well known to Lasky. But he liked this compressed way of communicating, or maybe, he liked it because it was Old John's way.

"John, I know everyone thinks I'm making a mistake. I don't! My finances are fine, and will carry me a long way. I've made certain of that. Besides, John, as far as this place goes, you know I don't fit in here. They know it too, and so do I. It just doesn't work, at least, not the way I wanted, or expected it to. And anyway, this project of mine means everything to me. It's the most important thing I have in my life. It kept me going all these years. I worked hard, saved, did without, invested, the whole nine yards. And now I can do what I want."

"Nooowww, yer not gonna make some kind of Frankenstein monster or do something crazy, are you?" John snickered, meaning no ill. But perhaps in that little laugh, Lasky sensed a concealed curiosity, and maybe, caught a dark glimpse of the parallel events he was about to unfold.

This set the engineer off, without his thinking that he was talking to an old friend. He was always secretive of his private work in science, his "Project" as he called it when, on those rare occasions, he did mention his personal life at all. Maintaining this behavior concerning his private life and affairs in general did create a conspicuous void. The type of void that sets people to wondering and talking, especially in a small town with a big industry. But Lasky was adamant that his life and affairs were none of anyone's business, other than his own.

"Dammit, John, don't talk like an ass. What the hell is wrong with you! My life doesn't consist of sitting with the 'good old boys,' guzzling booze and trying to make every skirt in the bar! Just because I keep to myself, people go off on tangents! Listen. What I do, John, is **none** of **anyone's** business! Got that?" He flashed a grim, cold stare at his friend, and finished with, "Is it any wonder I don't get involved with people?!"

John caught the way Lasky said *anyone*, loud and clear. And he knew it included him. His feelings were hurt, but the older man knew something of the arrogance of younger people in general, and of Lasky's volatile temper in particular.

"Sorry, Mier. Just kidding," John replied in a low, repentant voice.

"Forgive me, John. This is no way for friends like us to part. It's just
that the attitude and behavior of the people in this town remind me of the
coal region I grew up in. They don't have a goddamn better thing to do
than to mind each others' business, and start rumors. It infuriates me so
much, that sometimes I feel like I'll explode! I didn't mean you, John, in
that last remark of mine. I meant all of those bastards with their left-
handed remarks I caught over the years, you know what I mean, from the
guys in the mills, and in the office.

"Those cracks about me, that I thought I was too good to pal around
with them after work, especially since the Plant Superintendent and my
boss, the VP of engineering, bowls and golfs with some of them. Add that
to my refusal to talk about my private life, and couple this with those few
remarks I made over the years about my 'scientific studies,' and, well, it
didn't take them long to concoct stupid speculations. They just can't get it
through their heads that I don't care for their company during work,
much less for socializing with them off the job. And golf and bowling?
FORGET IT!

"So after taking enough of those cracks throughout the years, it just
pisses me off whenever I hear anything that reminds me of them, even
remotely. OK? I *am* sorry I lashed out at you, John. I really didn't mean it."

John smiled understandingly, and let the matter drop.

Together, the two men loaded Lasky's private possessions from his former office into the engineer's new car, an Elantra, to which he had treated
himself. It was a going-away gift from himself, to himself, to mark his
departure from industry, and the beginning of his new life of private scientific research.

Old John and Lasky stood by the car for some time, exchanging those
final few pleasantries that mark the parting of the ways of good friends.

Those needless words that hang on the lips when an end has come, and neither knows how to say good-bye.

"Well, Mier, are ya gonna come back and see us every now and then? You live only 'bout thirty-five miles away, so ya got no excuse!" John said in a joking, yet low, probing voice.

"My friend, you know what I said a thousand times before. When I leave a place, I don't return. It's been my policy as far back as I can remember. I never even attended my undergraduate or graduate schools' reunions. When something ends, it ends. Like a book. Close the covers, and go on to the next volume."

Suddenly, a quiet broke out between them. It was only a few moments by the tick of the clock, but for Old John it seemed to last much longer. He was looking at Lasky, yet looking through him, into another image of the younger man that was forming right before his eyes. Old John shook his head slightly and blinked his eyes, with the type of bodily gesture one usually uses to pull oneself out of a daydream state.

But the transformation continued. He saw his former boss fading in and out of their present reality. In this reality-shift, the younger man was dressed differently, and almost unrecognizable in appearance. As in some vision, Old John saw Lasky as a withering shell of his normal self, a phantom, desperately trying to cling to life and sanity. He felt a terrible chill run through him, as though somehow, this was a portends of things to come.

John's face became grim and rigid…and sheet-white. Suddenly, he sensed he was seeing a reality not yet created. One that he did not understand, but which struck a terror in him to the last shred of his being. It died away after those few seconds, but left an unmistakable and lingering foreboding in him. Lasky wondered what was happening with his friend. He noticed his friend's radical change in demeanor and the slight shaking, but let it pass. After all, it was a final parting as far as Lasky was concerned, and people do react to these times differently.

"Ya know somethin', Mier? I got a feeling yer not done here yet. No, yer not gonna come back to work or anything like that, but because of…well…I don't know what, but I think yer just not done with things back here. I feel bad, *real bad* about the 'why' behind it all. Like something in a pitch black corner that's hidin' and waitin' to bring all of this about. But ya know, somehow, I just *know*—you, this plant, and this town 'ya despise so much, are gonna meet head on…one more time."

"Tell you what, John. You're welcomed over my home anytime. You know that. So this doesn't have to be a final good-bye between you and me. Give me a ring if you ever want to come over. It would be good to see you again."

Both men knew this was a manifestation of that damn lie that is told a thousand times each day by people who truly suspect that they are parting for good. The "don't worry, I'll write" or "call" or, "oh, we'll get together again, you know that!"

As Mier opened the door of his car, he swung around, and extended his right hand to Old John. The older man's hand was already extended, like a vine searching for a rock face to cling to. Both men now became abrupt, in an effort to end what was to end?

"Take care, John."

"You do the same."

With that, Lasky got into his car, started the engine, and slowly drove through the company's large parking lot, until he came to the exit. He was alone now, and automatically defaulted to his normal, verbal self-dialogue.

"Well, old boy, that's it. Seventeen goddamn years in three different industries. It's true. Seen one, and you've seen them all! Just a different product, different faces. The political garbage, the posturing for the boss and the executives, their Yes! men, and all of those little kingdoms each department builds and defends at the expense of getting the job done. They're all the same. One is as bad as the other, and you've finally rid yourself of the lot of them! There were times I never thought you would! Ever!"

Turning out of the company driveway onto the public road, he noticed the street sign: *Steel Court Lane.* "Bye to you too! Damn! It feels **good!**"

Feeling like a kid who just got out of school for summer vacation, he let out a yelp of excitement. He realized that the dawn of a new life—*his* new life, one that he struggled and sacrificed for so long, had finally broken. All of the wonder of this uncharted frontier seemed to be reflected in the road on which he now drove to his home. To Lasky, this was the first forty-five minutes of the rest of his life.

"You are now leaving Sunnberry. A community of friendly folk, enjoying commercial and industrial prosperity, and a town where good people still help each other. Population: 150,000, and still growing.," the last town marker read on the way out. Lasky noticed it as he did a thousand times before, and as all those other times, simply remarked in a vindictive voice, "Yea...Right!"

Lasky did not have a genuinely cold nature, not like those who extolled 'understanding' and 'tolerance' as virtues, while secretly destroying the lives of those they hated. Having traveled extensively throughout Europe during his three weeks of vacation each year, and being required to live in many different cities throughout the States in his seventeen years of service to corporate America, he simply became callous to the ways at which things are never as they appear or as they are said to be. He caught himself reviewing this self-generated dialogue and abruptly cut it short. He had more important things to do now than slinging insults at a city that nevertheless, he thought, had provided him with an industry that had given him a good living for the past twelve years.

He used the driving time to ruminate, and recalled the steps that were necessary in bringing about his newly won freedom. Everything was in place now. He had transferred his savings and investments from his former bank in Sunnberry, to a different, more progressive one, closer to his home in Pleasant Corners. The town's motto was a "Genuinely friendly little town with only *some* big ideas."

It was easy for this well educated and traveled engineer to see that the people there wanted life only a little better, but not too much. Not at the expense of becoming another Sunnberry or worse, with all of the noise, pollution, crime, and activity of 'city life.' The "Towne Fathers" as the councilmen called themselves, were descendants of the original settlers of some 300 years ago. For generations, they saw change occurring around them, and while taking of the fruits of that change—cautiously, shrewdly, and from a distance—they and their constituency preferred to keep the vine at bay. Somehow they always managed to legislate away big business and less friendly people.

Even the Branstrome Bank and Investment Corporation, whose parent company was located on Wall Street, reflected the town's attitude. Its own greeting poster proudly displayed in its lobby read, "25,000 people, give or take a few, is enough for any sensible community these days." This attitude suited Lasky to a tee. It was an ideal situation. A town small enough to bank in, with a facility that provided federal security for their client's funds and financial investments, while extending those added courtesies to premium clients that are typically found only at institutions in large cities. Yet the actual population of 26,000 made it large enough for him to maintain whatever degree of anonymity he chose. He smiled to himself at having had the good fortune in finding this little paradise so close to the ever widening Hell Mouth he considered Sunnberry to be.

Money was no longer a problem for him. He recalled how his father's sudden death in 1981 left him an unexpected insurance policy inheritance of $650,000. Even at the age of twenty-four however, he realized that if he retired from his then three year engineering career, the money would be gone in no time. Youth, even his youth, still had its lures of good times, parties, and frivolous spending. Besides, he recalled, he was in his last semester of night school at the University of Maryland, completing his M.Sc. degree in Physics, and was formulating the ideas for his "Project." Should he divert from it then, he knew he would never finish that degree, or his Project.

As the road wound silently in front of him, he smiled, musing over his reasoning back then, and how right that reasoning was. He only thought then, but knew now, that most other young men of that age would have just had one hell of a good time, however short, with the money. Instead, he recollected thinking that he should put his inheritance to work.

He had made some shrewd investments during those hay days of seventeen percent interest for those with money to invest: short term T-bills, medium to high-risk money markets, CDs, and some well-chosen stock in utilities, along with venture capital in the emerging computer giants. Then there was also the small fortune he made by investing $50,000 into a high-risk commodity deal involving Soya, and another in resurrecting a South African gold mine that was believed to be on its last legs. Both of these highly speculative gambles paid off beyond anyone's expectations—including his.

It turned out that he discovered he had a nose for smelling money. But since money was only a tool to him, he never considered this talent in any depth, a talent that most Wall Street brokers would kill for. No, Lasky's interests were purely scientific. Everything else was simply a 'necessary nuisance,' as he termed other activities when he did discuss the mundane aspects of daily existence.

"Well, you've got a little over $950,000 tied up in investments now, and enough in dividend income to net you a retired $76,000 a year. The bastards can't tax those investments you're rolling over the dividends on, and the principle is safe. And you certainly won't starve due to the normal taxes on your retirement dividends, either. The house is paid for...damn good buy for $95,000, what with four acres of land...and you squeezed out all of your scientific equipment over the past six years, to boot, from your salary in the steel company. Boy, **that** was **tough**! But you did it! You're in damn good shape, old boy, mighty damn good shape! And all this at thirty-eight!"

As he drove through the mountainous Pennsylvania countryside en route to his home, the impact of his newly earned carefree life began to set in hard—very hard. Surprisingly though, it passed from a feeling of pride, to a sense of humility. Perhaps it arose from some moral source deep within him. At this moment, he was not the private, arrogant, and sometimes excessively confident man who had just finished patting himself on the back for a job well done. Nor was he the man who more often than not held a not-so-secret contempt for people or circumstances that stood in his way of accomplishing what he wanted.

Instead, as he passed the fresh early spring growth of the woods and the small hamlets, and saw the cars pulling into the driveways, he realized that these people, returning from earning their daily bread, would continue this ritual for the rest of their lives. They would never be able to come and go, buy and enjoy, do and not do almost without care, as he was now able to. Instead, he thought, they would live "lives of quiet desperation." A very real sense of sadness enveloped him. Somewhere within, under the thick veneer of social coldness that he justified by convenient self-concern, he did have a compassion for others, a sympathetic bond created by his membership in the human race. This awareness and its emotions continued with him throughout most of his drive home.

The warm reddish-orange glow of the setting sun was calming and friendly. Its mellowing rays at last snapped him out of what had become a despondency brought on by his normally hidden care for others.

"Well, Mier, looks like life holds surprises at every turn, doesn't it? I can't remember when you last had a caring thought for the plight of other people. You're not really a bad guy, just one wrapped up in his own world, like everyone else. Oh well. It doesn't make you right or wrong, or them for that matter, either. It's just the way it is." He was returning to his usual objective state, and began to consider the first in his series of first-things-first.

"What to do, Mier? What do you do *now*, starting this moment? *Where* do you start? *How* do you start? There's no job to go to tomorrow. Should you take the rest of this week and the weekend off, and start the experimental work of Project TAAC on Monday? Celebrate these next few days? Get started in the lab tonight? You thought you had it all planned out.

Sure, all of the generalized details of devoting your retirement to the Project, and the specifics of getting prepared for your retirement. But now that your retirement has arrived, you realize you never considered the day-to-day details of handling the very purpose of your independence: TAAC."

Suddenly Lasky felt a twinge of fear. But in reality, it was more than a twinge. Like nearly everyone else, he was a product of the regimen of social commitment and responsibility—a job, traveling to and from work, daily interaction with other people, set times for lunch, dinner, sleep, etc. Maybe Old John was right after all. Maybe there was more to "…callin' 'yer own shots" than he realized. Being a bachelor as well didn't seem to help here either, although he never really considered the pros and cons of the marital arrangement. Now he saw that he would indeed be alone most of the time. No daily interaction with other people. How would this affect him?

But wait a minute. He didn't like other people as a rule, or did he, and was he only now coming to suspect this? Maybe his daily interaction with people he thought so little of was, in fact, the wellspring of his motivation to be 'better' than them? Maybe. His thoughts started to become confused, and his eyes began to water. His head was pounding. He just couldn't get a mental handle on these stray thoughts or the day-to-day mechanics of his new life situation. John was right. There was "a lot more to bein' 'yer own boss."

He caught sight of his house off to the left, as he cruised down the small two lane highway that passed in front of it. It was a typical split-level structure, built in the mid-fifties, before the 'new' construction materials were in vogue. All of those 'miracles of modern technology' that were supposed to make homes nearly maintenance free, but which in reality keep the home improvement centers buzzing to the present day.

Its dark red brick exterior and simple white aluminum siding offset the serious tone generated by the jet-black shutters attached to each window. The large bay window in the living room was one of his favorites, giving a cheerful view of the front of his nestled 'estate' as he jokingly called his home and land. As he approached his property, he again realized how the forty-foot high cone-shaped 'cemetery trees' lining the driveway hid his house almost completely from view, while the three enormous blue spruce trees and assorted sizes of crab apple trees broke up the flat contour of his large front lawn.

That the house was built halfway in on the four acre lot pleased him. It afforded a comfortable distance from the highway, lending a quieter environment from what little traffic noise this particular highway produced. At the same time, this landscaping plan allowed for a large backyard, which guaranteed him the added privacy he desired. He was finally beginning to feel like himself again, and was quickly regaining that sense of relief and freedom that he enjoyed earlier in the day.

As he neared the driveway, he caught sight of a small silver car parked in the visitor's macadam parking wing to the left of the two-car garage. For a brief moment, he couldn't figure out who was parked on his property. After all, it was Wednesday, and he did not expect anyone. Besides, no one ever visited him, except for K…. His thoughts were stopped short by his anticipation, as he pulled into the entrance of the drive. Standing in front of the garage doors was Kate, pristinely poised, motionless. Her great smile said, "Welcome home, Mier!" in a gentle and loving way. As with the infectiousness reaction of a yawn, he returned the smile automatically, and wondered what was in the large white box adorned with the bright red ribbon she was holding.

As Lasky drove slowly toward her, he saw her long auburn hair being tossed about her shoulders and face by the recently arrived warm spring breeze. The innocence of this scene did her justice. Her five foot, eight inches height and slender, well-built figure, was extremely well complimented by a quaintly shy and reserved personality; something Lasky thought all females in her twenty-five year old age bracket were devoid of—until he met her. His smile broadened, replacing the last traces of his typically serious and cynical demeanor, as he saw her light complexion face stare out from behind the shocking mass of now swirling hair.

"She really is a beautiful woman, Lasky, and a very loving one." He grinned broadly, as he continued his now completely mental self-dialogue. "Despite her Irish ancestry, she has a quiet disposition. Something you need, old boy, and she knows it! I wonder if anything permanent will come out of our relationship. It's been three years since she came to this area after finishing college, and two years since you met and started dating. It seems so comfortable of an arrangement. She never pushed for a commitment as anyone would normally expect. Probably that bad, brief marriage which she was so fortunate to get out of alive."

The smile on his face now turned to stone, and a hate filled his eyes to such a degree, that he no longer saw Kate in front of him. A blackness which only Death itself could appreciate took control of his mind and senses.

"If I ever meet that son-of-a-bitch of a former husband of hers, they'll take his goddamn pieces out in a body bag, and I don't mean maybe!"

This unheard self-talk brought Lasky dangerously close to violence. The fury that arose at the thought of her being so badly beaten by that 'subhuman' as he called her ex, made him feel like smashing the steering column of his new vehicle with his fist. There were a number of attitudes and injustices as he called them, which brought out an almost uncontrollable rage in him, and of all of them, the worst was the physical or emotional abuse of a woman by a man. He began to verbalize to himself again, and oscillate between his thought and this self-talk.

"Like that underaged little prick in Arizona, who hit his probably sixteen year old wife! Damn lucky you nailed that little bastard at one in the morning, and that supermarket manager was as understanding as he was. If he hadn't told you to "disappear, fast!" before he called the cops, you'd have been arrested for sure! Arizona!! And a few minutes ago you were starting to feel nostalgic about your old job! Are you nuts ?!

"If you hadn't been sent all over the country to set up the circuits in those wire drawing machines, you probably wouldn't have hardened as much as you did. Two months here, three months there, six somewhere else. No, it wasn't easy when you get right down to it! You *earned* your retirement Mier. **No one** gave it to you, or made it easy for you, by any stretch of the imagination!"

He caught himself after a split second of this recollection. All the time the mind needs to pass through a thousand-and-one thoughts and feelings. His attention was now focused on current reality.

Their age difference was never an issue to them, jointly or individually. Kathleen Noel Murphy dated heavily until she married the "bastard," as she called her ex. After completing her Bachelor's degree in Graphic Arts at twenty-one, she felt that her Mike would make her happy for the rest of her life. She thought she had the finest gentlemen she could ever get, only to find a sick and dangerous personality hidden behind the 'state-of-the-art dating bullshit' devised by her generation, as Lasky termed the current dating process. After that experience, she paled at the thought of ever becoming seriously involved with a man again. Then she met Mier Erik Lasky, a year after moving to Centreland County, Pennsylvania.

They chanced upon each other at the Penns University main library, while he was doing research for his Project. Its eleven mile proximity to his home made it convenient for his research at times, but was in fact a school he did not care to visit too often. In actuality, its grossly over exaggerated academic self-image was about one hundred times the size of its scientific libraries and their usefulness. Still, it was all the part of a backwoods 'charm' that he wisely kept at a distance while securing his own lifestyle.

That cold night in January 1993 found Kate there too, still trying to uncover the economic details of the area in order to start her own graphics design business. "Certainly," she had reasoned, "a small industrial city like Sunnberry in the middle of nowhere would have room for a business which offered people in such a cloistered place something the established businesses probably never heard of—competition, based on a new service and product at a fair price." And how right her assumption turned out to be.

In that chance meeting in the Reference Room, Lasky was stopped dead in his tracks by the sight of this beautiful, auburn hair young woman. While it was indeed her looks that first caught his attention, it was her presence and bearing that sealed his interest, and prompted him to smile at her, but this, only after his skirmish with the Director of Reference. Maybe it was his tactical approach to the difficult little man, coupled with his natural strength of self in handling the encounter, that attracted her to him. Still, many times he thought of how she surprised herself by returning his smile, and how easily they next struck up a nothing conversation, and then left for coffee together. Within a few days, they lunched together, after that, dinner, and then...all in a few short months.

It was Lasky who went out of his way to help her during those first uncertain months of final preparation and launching of her business, by filling her in on the "real workings of hick towns like Sunnberry." It made no difference to him that she established her business there. He felt it was time that supposed 'city' had a good dose of progress, and most importantly, *genuine* competition, something that was inconceivable to the old businesses there, still dealing in the products and services of a generation past. To his mind, its lack of accelerated enterprising spirit placed it and its inhabitants in the same rank and file of the people in the coal region in which he was raised. His cynicism was unrelenting.

He explained and showed her the way those hicks operate. Little gems of operational truth as he called them, that would never be found in their Chamber of Commerce bulletins. It was a real eye-opener for Kate. Having been raised in Albany, New York, and educated at the University of Michigan, Ann Arbor, she was familiar only with city ways, not the subculture and characteristics of "nice small town people who'll put the shaft to you with one hand, while holding their Bible fervently in the other," as Lasky bluntly told her. Unknown to her however, he wanted to help in other, more concrete ways.

Perhaps it was because of both her beauty and nonpretentious personality. Or perhaps because she was so young and on her own. Maybe it was her quiet, seeming self-confident poise, a posture which nevertheless gave way at unguarded moments to a genuinely frightened young lady, who had nowhere to turn in a strange new place. Or just perhaps it was really that Lasky felt something for her. Something which he consciously denied. A constellation of thoughts and an attendant set of emotions which he forbid himself to indulge in, owing to a past troubled relationship. The reason was not important to him at the time, even though he considered it carefully. What was important was what he did for her next.

After knowing her only three months, he introduced her to Alphonse Chinelli, the Operations officer of Branstrome's. She was stunned to find that this financial institution which she had heard of in Albany, was eager to loan her the $275,000 she needed to start her somewhat risky *Say It With Pictures* graphics business. She joyfully told Lasky that a loan of this size without collateral was unheard of in the cities. "Perhaps," she thought, "he was being too hard on the 'hicks' in the area. It just might be that they were becoming an understanding and progressive lot, after all."

When she voiced this speculation to him, he surprisingly admitted the possibility, for both of their sakes. "Maybe their ways are changing, but I was not mistaken in the way they used to be," he said jokingly, keeping a secret to himself. After all, he was older, and knew when to back off an issue with a woman he was obviously feeling something for.

Little did Kate know of Lasky's secret in this matter. The day before their joint meeting at Branstrome's, Lasky spoke to Chinelli, and underwrote Kate's loan from his private funds held by Branstrome's. He told the Operations officer that Kate was not to know. His anonymity in this assistance was obvious to him, or so he thought.

He had known other women, and always something would happen to end it abruptly. But now, he wanted no sense of duty or obligation on Kate's part to create a strain between them. He also flatly rejected that self-gratifying sense of playing savior, which he knew would inevitably arise within him if his intercession in this matter was common knowledge between them. Lasky understood all too well the operational mechanisms of the ego in general, and of his own in particular, and there were a few that he learned to consciously control.

Besides, he had confidence in her business. And if worse came to worse, he'd lose $275,000. "So what?" his mercenary side concluded, "It'll be one hell of a tax write-off!" By this reasoning he calmed himself, reassuring his initial hesitations that he would still come out way ahead. Besides, since he lived on very little for long periods while amassing the funds he now drew on, he was confident that he could survive on the remaining $675,000, and the yearly $52,000 stipend it would provide him.

His final consideration was that there was something he wanted here. Not a profit of financial gain, but rather, well…who knew? He did not permit his mind to answer this question, or even speculate beyond this point, although he secretly knew the answer lied beyond simple sex. This mental maelstrom was Lasky.

Kate watched him slowly pull up the drive, and set to her own recall of this strange man. She remembered returning his smile in the library. Why? Here was an obviously older man. His six foot, two inches height and 225 pound size should have caused her fear, owing to her ex-husband's similar size. But she didn't sense an instinctive fear when she looked at him. Maybe it was because Lasky, while not extremely muscular, had a big frame, unlike her somewhat dumpy ex. Lasky's giant chest conveyed a tense, vibrating strength, which she felt he was very capable of using, should the need arise. But it did not strike her as an aggressive strength. At least, not one that this man would direct toward a woman. His bodily gait and facial demeanor seemed to project this summary clearly to anyone who saw him. But there was more.

In all of that mass, she sensed an overwhelming gentleness, a more bark than bite personality. But God help the one who aroused the bite side of this man whom she immediately came to think of as the Jekyll-Hyde type. Unknown to Lasky, she noticed him as soon as he walked through the doors of the busy university reference room. She could feel his dawning presence immediately change the atmosphere of the room, and the mood of those there, as he stormed through the two large glass doors in a highly focused, almost goose step fashion.

She remembered thinking how this massive figure's stepping stride seemed to say, "I'm here to work. Get me what I need, and don't bother me!" There was a genuine and overwhelmingly frightening grimness to his manner of movement, and in his large, somewhat bony face. He used his eyes to project the sum total of his presence, like lenses magnifying rays of light to a highly directed focus. They were not set too deeply into his skull, but the deep ridges of his eyebrows gave them a dark foreboding appearance, and a gaze which was very penetrating. She later realized that even in broad daylight, it was somehow hard to see them clearly, unless he focused them on you. There was a coldness in those eyes, dark brown infinities of purpose, determination, and mistrust.

She could also sense he was not a ladies' man. Early in their relationship she found that he had no use for the noun lady, nor its use as an adjective in describing the currently reigning social phenomena relegated to its universal use. He had explained it to her.

"In my opinion, ERA and women libbers want the privileges of men, but don't want to participate in the ruthless struggles and primal maneuverings that spring up daily in the outer and inner worldly conflicts of men. Nor do they understand the isolation and brutality of the biologically determined world of men, and in which we are, to whatever extent, comfortable. And certainly, they want nothing to do with the lack of caring and understanding in men, which Nature invested in their gender.

"To them, the socialized and industrial warfare, whose tactics differ only from those of the bush and the weapons used, are primitive and unnecessary. That they are primitive, yes. That they are unnecessary, no. No more than the same genetic impulses which cause us to explore any frontier—from a continent, to space.

"Of course women have a critical role in all of this, and should—must—share in it to whatever extent they want to, and are mentally, emotionally, and physically capable of, but not at the expense of legislation and laws designed to turn men into female personalities with a male sex organ. All of their posturing inevitably ends in this final scenario: a male body with female emotions. And we will have *nothing* to do with that, or with those who demand such a nightmare of equality."

This was how Lasky very clearly defined his feelings to her on the male and female roles, over their coffee, that first night they met. She remembered how she flinched at his definition of the sexes and their roles, when he answered her query on this matter. She also remembered how quickly she found that however hard his views were on this issue, he meant what he said, and lived it.

But she also rapidly became aware that he was not a male chauvinist, not by any stretch of the imagination. He did want to see womens' roles expand to their full limit, just as those of his own sex had to expand theirs in order to survive. She recalled other men she knew, especially the bastard, and how fervently they professed a belief in anything of interest to a woman they have designs on, especially ERA and women's' rights. This recollection brought up its immediate counterpart: what they were secretly like. "They'll agree with anything you say in order to get you into bed," she mused to herself. The bastard was the most perfect example of this, she thought.

She was quick to understand that Lasky simply saw each gender as having its own particular strengths and weaknesses, virtues and vices, all dictated by the genetic basis of Life. A natural, physical life-code, that was as unrelenting and unforgiving as was the necessary brutality of the Law of Survival of the Fittest. His view was that society's tampering with this biological code of life, as he called it, was as violent and obscene as were those "Bastions who propagated their one-sided Ethic of Equality." He vigorously opposed them and their "spew of venom," whenever he encountered it.

This too was Lasky, a part of what made him who and what he was. She came to understand that his social philosophy and masculine identity were forged in the fires of contemporary society, and in the coldness of his mental caverns of pragmatism and reason; all under the umbrella of his personal experience in life. All these things raced through Kate's mind as his Elantra rolled slowly up the drive.

Her memory of that night continued.

She had watched and compared his movements to those of the other men in the reference room, on that frigid, snow-covered January night of two years ago. Bent unnaturally over computer keyboards situated somewhere between waist and knee level, the others worked at the terminals, which were supported by child-sized shelves. They unquestionably accepted the situation, boldly reinforced by a large sign placed above each computer station: "DO NOT ADJUST THE KEYBOARD SHELVES!", an order from the director.

The director was a seedy little man, who apparently thought that that room and its contents were his personal possessions. In such a hick area as Lasky tauntingly defined it, this abysmal excuse for a modern university allowed such tiny people their reign of pseudoself-importance at the expense of the student, and an adult patronizing public that chose not to make waves. Not Lasky. Loosening the control knobs on the sides of the height adjustment bars, he pulled the keyboard support shelf of his workstation up to waist level, making it comfortable for his height as he stood typing in his electronic database inquiries.

Kate's smile broadened as his car continued its slow roll up the driveway. She was mentally concluding the events in the reference room that night, and how they led to the opening of their relationship. Her smile broadened even wider as she thought of how the director cleared his voice in his squeak-box fashion, in an attempt to attract Lasky's attention, and how she coyly watched, as women do, unseen, waiting for this minidrama to start...or finish.

From the disapproving grimace on the little man's face, it was clear that this rearrangement of a member of his kingdom was completely unacceptable. It was equally clear to him that he would have to inform the ignorant man who had the temerity to disturb the order which he, the Director, had established as a Law!

After three unsuccessful guttural attempts to attract Lasky's attention, the Dictator of Reference strutted out from behind his large, circular desk. He crossed the room in a prancing, almost whirlwind fashion, and in an indignant tone of voice, loud enough for everyone to hear regardless of their position in that large arena, began to chastise the stranger for his rearranging efforts. At first, Lasky treated the unwanted and unwarranted intrusion in the same manner one would treat a pesky insect that decided to make its presence known. He ignored the little man and his ravings, and continued his search inquiry of the database.

Finally, the director grabbed Lasky by his right shoulder, and virtually screamed at him, "I'M TRYING TO GET YOUR ATTENTION! ARE YOU DEAF AS WELL AS IGNORANT, OR ARE YOU SIMPLY STUPID?!"

A deadly, deafening silence fell throughout the room. Kate knew that everyone had read Lasky's presence, and was wondering if he would physically thump the director: a default mechanism of the hicks of the area in solving such social problems. Instead, Lasky turned around and fixed his gaze upon the little form that was now in front of him. He moved a step closer to the director and made direct face-to-face and dead center-to-center eye contact with him. Kate's heartbeat had quickened, as she realized that not half of an inch separated Lasky's huge face from the small, gaunt, rigid mask-like face of the director.

"What did you say?!" came Lasky's normal volumed, but resonant voice.

There was a frightening quality in that voice, but not necessarily one of physical violence. Rather, it had some unknown quality she never experienced before, one that moved outward from the words themselves, like some unknown power arising from the darkest depths of his psyche. That dark quality also conveyed an unnatural authority to Lasky, an authority that was welling up from uncharted recesses within the researcher, from realms whose gates were about to be flung opened at his command, and unleash…God only knew what. Her mind cut itself off at this point, not wanting to answer its own question.

There was a very real terror unfolding that she could feel, and which she sensed others in the room could also perceive. A genuine danger burst forth in those few short words of his. She lifted her head from the book she was now only pretending to be reading, unaware that her camouflage was lost in the process. But the move went undetected by Lasky. He was involved in a battle. His insect had became bothersome, and it was time to snuff out its influence one way, or another, permanently.

The director stood motionless. Everyone in the room now had their attention fixed upon the events developing before them. The rustling of pages stopped. The sound of books being laid down ceased. The scratching of the sides of volumes as they were removed from or replaced on the shelves ended. Only that deadly, deafening silence, marked now by a tension of the type which precedes a violent eruption of Nature, could be felt to penetrate the Reference Room, and everyone in it.

Lasky's darkness lashed out in a merciless fashion, as he looked seemingly deeper into the dilating pupils of the now sweating and visibly shrinking Director. With a vengeance, the engineer delivered his final blow, in a voice level that now equaled the Director's in his initial attack:

"I ASKED YOU A QUESTION! WHHAAAT DID YOU SAY?!"

The once cocksure little librarian, whose arrogance stemmed from ordering around young students and older people marking time until their retirement, was now little more than a two dimensional, transparent figure. His pseudoauthoritarian rule, derived from the threat of firing the obedient workers in his kingdom, showed itself for what it was—a vain delusion. It was now being ruthlessly shattered. A low level reply seemed to sneak past his thick, meaty lips.

"Uhhh, nothing, sir, no problem," came the fainting answer.

Lasky was not content to knock the disrupting insect to the ground. A permanent solution was called for to eliminate further distractions in his future visits to this "Reference Swamp," as he would refer to that room from now on.

"Make sure you didn't, and make damn sure it stays that way!" came Lasky's final blow, which sent the insect into oblivion. The giggles, snickers, and outright laughter that came from both students and staff alike, added to the rebellious mood that now permeated Reference. With an air of the arrogance of monarchy, Lasky sneered at the *plane* figure, turned back to his workstation, and continued with his work. It was abundantly clear to all present. He had just dismissed the former Dictator of Reference, as his own employees called him behind his back. The breathing transparency slid away from the open area of confrontation, and sunk below eye level of his circular bunker.

It was after this battle that he stared directly at her across the short distance where she was sitting, and smiled at her. It was a great, friendly, warm smile. It was the Dr. Jekyll in him now emerging. To her amazement, she caught herself returning his smile. It was as though she were on automatic pilot, and didn't have control over her facial muscles. Somehow, between the interval of his smile and her reply, she found him standing in front of her, asking if he could join her at her study table. Still on automatic pilot, she heard the words, "Of course!" come cheerily and somewhat tauntingly out of her own mouth. It was only a few short minutes after that, that she found herself walking out of the library with him, on the way for a cup of coffee and some conversation.

Between those first unsure moves when a man and woman first meet, and the steaming wisps of hot coffee that swirled up from their cups in the restaurant, she became aware of his unease. His manner now seemed completely different from that of the man who smiled at her so intensely, and made the first gesture of friendship less than an hour ago in that Reference Room. It was not the type of uneasiness that stems from a false, overt intent interest in the woman as a person. No, this was more on the order of an uneasiness due to an uncertainty that suddenly reared its cautious, ugly head. An uncertainty about her specifically, and of women generally, owing to his past relationships with them.

This is how she read him. She sensed that he had been a player in this type of scenario, perhaps many times before, and obviously had a poor review each time. Was he divorced? Did he have children? Perhaps he never married? If so, why not? All the typical questions and ponderings any woman brings to a new, potentially emotional and serious relationship encounter. What was more important she recalled, was her wondering why she asked herself those questions. These pertinent questions about a man she knew nothing about, in a situation she couldn't fathom herself getting involved in again, had made her uneasy as well. Still, two days later, they met in Sunnberry for lunch, one that lasted for three hours. It was then that she had the answers to her questions, and began to understand why she was attracted to this older and somewhat strange man.

For some reason, as he drove slowly up his driveway, Lasky reviewed the same events of their first meeting, that austere night in January, that were occupying Kate's mind at that very moment. But to him, it seemed like it was long ago, certainly much longer than two years. He wondered about her internal dialogue on this matter, and just what it was about him, specifically, that led her into this developing relationship. Maybe, somewhere in his mind, he feared that this situation with her was too good to be true. Over the years, she explained that she was attracted to him not only simply because of his demeanor and bearing, but because of the consideration and care for her that he expressed during their evenings out, and her extended stays at his home for the weekends and special celebrations, as in the case of each other's birthdays, as well as the usual holidays. She also carefully pointed out to him that the gentleness he expressed during their lovemaking was something that was extremely important to her, owing to her experiences with "the Bastard."

All he could think of now was their first lunch in Sunnberry. He had pulled into the parking lot of the Gargoyle Inn, a quiet, secluded businessman's bar and lounge that attracted its clientele as much for its rustic Medieval decor and trappings, as it did for its excellent cuisine. He recalled the bitter cold of that day in January, and had wondered if this woman would keep their appointment. He had looked down at his wristwatch as he came to a stop in a convenient parking stall, and noticed it was two in the afternoon, the time they had agreed to meet.

Such a late time for lunch was very convenient. He calculated that by then most of the business lunches would be over, and he and Kate would not only have the privacy of his favorite booth that he had reserved, but that the lack of conversational chatter that abounds during the lunch hours, would make their meeting more intimate. He wanted to find out, quickly, if he should continue to see this young lady, and determined the sooner he found out all that he could about her, the better it would be for him.

In order to show her that he was intent on discovering the meaning of their attraction for each other, he resolved to be candid with her about his private life. In doing this, he felt certain she would reciprocate, and open her personal history to him. He knew he was intensely interested in her, and he knew why, although he forbid himself to consciously think his feelings through. There was too much distance yet between them, after all, they had only just met. Then again he had considered, this distance between them might never be resolved. Yet, he had a peculiar feeling for her, and a powerful longing he had never experienced as intensely before.

While these thoughts had been racing through his mind, he had begun to look for her car. He suddenly realized that he didn't know what it looked like! After their coffee that first night, he had walked her back to the library, and they parted from there. He recalled how he had begun to panic. The thought of her not showing up had seized him. He had also suddenly realized that he didn't even know her last name. Despite the low temperature, he had begun to sweat. It was becoming apparent to him just how important this stranger was to him after all, when suddenly Kate disturbed him by knocking on the passenger side window of his car.

He remembered how the rapid pounding of his heart instantly calmed as he saw her broad, warm, almost loving smile peer at him through the frosted window. Her long auburn hair was swirling erratically across her right shoulder and face, giving her a frozen, ice-palace like, angelic appearance. Lasky felt relieved. But that was not all he felt. He felt a very real weakening sensation inside, and a comfortable, queasy feeling in the pit of his stomach. It was a long time since he had experienced anything that came close to this.

By the time he opened the car door and stepped out, Kate was standing on his side of the car, laughing at him. "Do you always talk to yourself like that?" she laughed. "The expression on your face was one of pure fear. What did you forget, a credit card or something?" She really didn't know the reason for his self-talk and panic, but apparently his anxiety was easily readable.

He started to make up an excuse to cover his embarrassment, but then remembered his resolve to be candid with her. "No. I suddenly remembered I didn't know what kind of car you were driving, or your last name. It occurred to me that maybe you...."

Kate broke in laughing again, beginning to understand the situation and his emotions clearly. "Ohhhhh, I wouldn't do something like that. I always keep my appointments once I make them." Her laughter flowed into a sensual smile, the kind Lasky saw on other women when they were flirting. Her light complexion turned deathly white in that ice cold wind, but Lasky was unaware of this at first. He was caught up in the radiant glow that flowed through her presence.

He had realized then he must have stood there, staring at her, silently, for a full minute or so before she finally spoke. "Are we going inside? I'm freezing out here!" her face breaking out into another broad smile. He heard her words as though they were coming at him through a tunnel from far away.

The glaze of winter over her eyes had made her look like a small child desperately trying to convince her parent she needed the warmth of a blazing fireplace, and something good to eat. Lasky's trance was finally broken by these last words, but only after he became aware of a surge of emotion he was experiencing for her. He was overwhelmed by a caring passion that demanded he take her in his arms, and they blend into each other in a reverie of physical and emotional ecstasy, then and there—a totality of union that consumed each other in its fires, the human fires of abandon and total surrender.

But he pulled himself back to reality. "Sure, Kate. Let's go inside and relax. It's cold out here, and I wouldn't want you getting sick." Together they had made their way across the ice and snow covered, silver and white blanket of the parking lot, and into the Gargoyle.

Once inside she started laughing again, but she would not say why. He thought he had made a fool of himself, but Kate was not privy to his internal dialogue. She whirled around, and with a very gentle and understanding smile, stroked his left cheek once with her right hand in a slow, delicate fashion, and said, "I really like you!" The sincerity in her voice convinced him, and the softness in her glazed eyes, magnified by the cold air in the coat room of the Gargoyle, told him she was not patronizing him. She felt something for him too, and this eased his tension. His self-berating instantly stopped.

As the maitre d' escorted them to their booth, Lasky carefully noticed Kate's attire. Her slightly above the knee length, onyx black velvet dress, cast alternating silver shimmering patterns of light across its fabric, while its tastefully low cut front complimented by a thin, red velvet choker around her neck, made Lasky feel his temperature rise somewhat. He could also feel the pounding of his blood pressure in his throat and ears, and heard himself whispering to his bachelor-hood, "Oh, no," but was cut short by the maitre d's interruption as they reached the booth.

"Your waiter will be here shortly, Mr. Lasky. Please let me know if there is anything I can do for you," and with a smile, left them to their own devices.

"They know you here, Mier. Do you come here often?" Kate asked.

"Yes. We frequently use this place for business lunches, this and the *Whale's Wharf* across the river. They're good places to get an inside track on the customers you're doing business with. You know how it is. People loosen up in places like this." He immediately realized what he just said, and how it must have sounded. And from Kate's giggle he knew how it did indeed sound, that he was using these tactics on her.

Lasky was right though. The relaxed atmosphere and tastefully decorated interior, did put them at ease. The dim electric wall candlelights, and dark mahogany paneled walls, set off by thick, dark red shag carpeting, all offset by the heavy, upholstered black cloth soft chairs, made for a very cordial and warm setting. The heavy floor length, dark red velvet curtains, drawn in order to separate them from the main dining area, gave both of them a strong sense of social presence, yet privacy. They exchanged their telephone numbers and addresses, and finally, their last names.

All of Lasky's misgivings had dissolved in that dark, silent romantic setting. He had let his guard down. He had asked Kate about herself, and specifically, about her childhood and early adult background, parents, and the many questions that each partner eventually needs to know about the other. Kate did likewise for him.

She told him that she was alone in the world. Her parents were killed in a boating accident when she was fourteen, along with her older brother. Her final three years before going to college were spent in her mother's sister's care. She felt she owed much to this aunt. Kate was of pure Irish ancestry, as far back as she knew, but aside from a historical fact, it really meant nothing to her. She considered herself an American. She told him of her love of art, literature, and music, mostly of the classical schools, but that she did enjoy contemporary works of fiction from such authors as Tolkien and Steven King.

Due to her love of art and her passion for independence, she majored in Graphic Arts at the University of Michigan, so that she could earn a good living doing what she liked, which she considered a necessity in life. She hoped to go on to graduate school to learn advanced techniques that would enable her to secure an art post, perhaps at a well known gallery in New York or Chicago, or perhaps even an associate professorship in the field at a university. She explained how her academic advisor had told her that a masters would qualify her for either direction.

However, as she and other graduating seniors discovered during a career day at her university, positions in the Graphic Arts field in general were as scarce as hen's teeth these days. The advice she and her friends had received was far from a realistic interpretation of the market's opportunities, or society's value of this new area of combined art and technological endeavor.

She had searched out and soon met others in the general art field. There were many unemployed Ph.D.s in Art History, and masters in Graphic Arts and Theater. From their conversations, she determined that the best solution to her dilemma was for her to express herself in a graphics business of her own, targeting businesses and industries that were slow to change, but which were being pushed into modern, computer-based advertising techniques that relied heavily on the new area of graphics design. Here, those employing this specialized field were doing thriving businesses in printing, advertising, and publishing.

The problem, she explained, was the capital investment required to open such a business. Typically, the firms that were doing so well were old, established businesses that were forced to adapt to the computer revolution if they were to remain competitive. These firms functioned by simply hiring individuals in her field at reasonable salaries, to do the work for them while they made the huge profits. As a consequence, she would wind up doing someone else's work, developing their ideas, for their profit. She couldn't see herself doing this for a lifetime.

Then, she had met "The Bastard" a month after graduation, during the one interview she did manage for the position of assistant director of a small art gallery off Broadway and 42nd Street in New York City. Since this was her original choice over her option of forming her own business, she considered it. After all, this position could open the doors for her to bigger and better things. But it didn't work out that way.

He was the characteristic Wall Street yuppie type, twenty-eight, tall, and a broker with a large and reputable Wall Street brokerage house. He was someone going places, as he told her many times. He was a good looking young man, but somewhat plump due to a lack of regular exercise. Nevertheless, he was handsome, intelligent, and seemed to have an instinctual handle on the matters of life. He dressed very well, and this, combined with his shrewd, big city ways, gave the appearance that he was more than his reality could justify. Taken together though, he did seem to have all of the answers. Three short months would show her however, that while he thought he had the answers, he had none of the solutions…to his problems, or hers.

She would never forgive herself for allowing him to sweep her off her feet. They were soon married, with her filing for divorce three months later. The photos of the beatings she endured at his hands were taken by the attending hospital's legal department, and submitted in evidence on behalf of her suit for divorce: a matter of procedure under New York state's law in cases of marital abuse. The grounds of the divorce, spousal abuse, brought Mr. Michael Runnion more than the yuppie bargained for— thirty days in the Nassau county jail and a public record for assault and battery. Again, a matter of New York state law, when the evidence is supplied by an independent agency, such as a hospital, and charges are pressed by the abused spouse.

It was after this that she fell back on her original plans, and decided to go for broke on the idea of a business of her own in the graphic arts. After a couple of weeks of reviewing the information on this business venture, that she had uncovered before her marriage, she followed through with some additional investigation into the structure and supply and demand aspect of her field in the national market. She decided that the most reasonable thing for her to do was to take up residence in a small area that had several large, well established, prospering industries, coupled with a strong local business character, and heavy in the services industry. Perhaps here, she thought, after establishing residency, she would qualify for a loan, and could begin her own enterprise. So she had moved to this area in Pennsylvania, since its profile fit her evaluation perfectly.

She made numerous attempts to find out all she could about the makeup of the business community and the industrial demands of the area, but continually hit the proverbial brick wall. Every merchant and local businessman or woman treated her as a potential threat. Result? She received no help from them. She then tried researching state and local government publications, trying to make an inroad, but found the information highly idealized, as she put it, and not at all accurate as to what little she found out actually did exist.

In the meantime, she lived off the remainder of her trust fund left her by her parents. But this source of revenue was dwindling to nothing fast, regardless of how frugal she was with her expenses. She told him she could manage on the trust for the rest of the year, but after that, she would be just another unemployed college graduate with a degree in a field that would, at best, provide her with an average living in a big city—something she did not want.

If worse came to worse she told him, she was going to get a government loan, go back to school in Michigan, and get an accounting degree. She could open an accounting office, and in time, if this business was successful, she envisioned opening her own graphics arts business from the profits of this more salable profession, and then build the type of life she always wanted.

Lasky listened attentively. He had heard such dreams a thousand times before, and knew that most ended in failure, for one reason or another. He was among this high casualty rate, having wanted to go straight through school and get a doctorate in engineering physics. He secretly considered how fortunate he was though. It wasn't many who were able to resurrect their dream in some fashion, through the legacy of a sizable inheritance.

He had paid special attention to the intensity and stubbornness in her eyes and taut facial muscles, as she shared her resolve with him. It had been perfectly obvious to him that she was not looking for a meal-ticket. She was not that kind of woman. Perhaps because of this, and those emotional feelings he felt for her that were pounding at the walls of his heart, he decided then and there that he would help her. But not before he had that private discussion with Chinelli.

Now it was his turn. He recalled that if he had not decided to be forthright with her in advance, he would have objected vigorously to her probing, whether she was open with him about her own past, or not. But his mind was made up on this issue in advance. So after finally placing their orders, he went ahead with his story.

He explained that he was the only child of a middle class businessman, and was raised in a small coal mining area in eastern Pennsylvania. His childhood was uneventful, due to his mostly having stayed by himself. The entertainment he made for himself consisted of hiking in the deep mountains that encircled the valley of his home town of Kulpsville, and reading. His great passion, astronomy, was discovered early, but owing to its basis in physics, and the need for a doctorate in that field in order to do meaningful research, he opted for electrical engineering instead, after giving up his more practical dream of getting a doctorate in engineering physics.

"It was the way things unfolded," he said. "If I had had the financial where-with-all earlier than when I came into it, I would have gone on to get the doctorate. But I didn't, and so I changed course."

He told her how he prepared for college as best he could in a pathetically inadequate local school system. He was accepted at several universities, but the government loans would not pay for what was even then an expensive tuition. This, coupled with the interference from his mother, forced him into a job at Westinghouse in Maryland instead, after graduating high school. Neither she nor his father could see the need for an engineering education, wanting him to enter the family jewelry business, and run one of their three stores in another town.

His own will was not developed sufficiently at seventeen, but he did his best in fighting their ideas and the paternal pressure they brought to bare on him every step of the way. He took the Westinghouse job, he explained, and during that year at Westinghouse, he grew up, and as he stressed it, began to bring his *will* under his own direct and conscious control. During that first year away from home, he then told his parents to go to hell, reapplied to the University of Maryland, got his student loans, and saved every penny from his technician job at Westinghouse. Through these avenues he was able to finance his first year at that university.

It worked. In three years of intensive work, summer school included, he graduated with his B.Sc. in Electrical Engineering, having done very well in his studies. From there he returned to Westinghouse as an Electrical Engineer, and worked there for nearly three years, dealing primarily with Nuclear Regulatory Agency and Navy Defense Departments contracts. But he was very unhappy in this monopoly-sized corporation. He was simply one of a thousand engineers, each not knowing what the final purpose the circuit element they were individually assigned to work on was for. Since the work was "Top Secret," none of them could discuss their individual assignments with the others.

Realizing how his life would be if he remained there, he immediately decided to get his M.Sc. in Physics, Theoretical Electrodynamics specifically, at the night school division of the University of Maryland. His graduate education began one week after starting for Westinghouse as an degreed engineer, he recounted. He had some ideas he had been working on for the four years he was in undergraduate school. They involve, he explained, "high voltage and high frequency electricity, but with a new twist, so to speak. I call it simply, the Project."

After getting his masters in a little over two and one-half years of very intense night school work, he left Westinghouse. He thought that he should get some experience in practical application of magnetism, a tool he intended to use in the Project. Certainly there would be no better place to do this than in an industry that made magnetic heads, those devices which make ATMs, VCRs, and many other necessities and conveniences of everyday life a reality. So, he went to Combe Magnetics, a small, somewhat struggling firm, where he thought he could not only learn about magnetism, but perhaps make a difference, and even wind up becoming an executive.

Such was not to be. The political vendettas, subterfuge, and kingdom building efforts to run each department virtually as a feudal state, apart from all other departments, was as bad as it was at Westinghouse. All he got for his troubles at the end of two years, was a request to resign from a former older friend who had become the Vice President of engineering there. He left their employ immediately, and took a job he hated—an electrical and quality control engineering job in the steel industry.

He had explained to Kate that his father's death had left him with a substantial nest egg, but having invested it for an early retirement, he had to earn a living in the meantime. The market was bad for engineers, especially electrical, and so he took what he could find. Luckily, it was in the same town as Combe Magnetics, Sunnberry, and so he did not have to finance another move. Here he had stayed until his investments, gelled, nicely, allowing him the early retirement he desired.

Kate had looked at him quizzically, a soft, very feminine smile overtook the graceful features of her face. She knew he was aware that she wanted to know all about him. She had been completely open with him, and she expected the same. Was he the type to hold back, she wondered? Did he have this personality defect as her Mike had, more subtly but just as deadly? Was it over before it began? She did feel something for him that she never knew before. She didn't want it to be over before it began.

He recalled how he had picked up her reservations and misgivings immediately, and how, in reply, he extended his large hands across the red linen tablecloth, and took her somewhat pale, slender hands in his. He had looked at her in as loving and gentle fashion that his personality would allow in order to assure her he was not another Mike.

Suddenly, he caught himself in that ever present moment of now and focused on Kate, who moved to the left side of the garage as the bay door opened. Lasky pulled to a screeching halt inside, threw the car door opened, and jumped out. He was smiling like a child expecting a long awaited present. He became aware of a softness in his heart, and a gladdening in his soul. His melodramatic nature likened him to a medieval knight who had just returned from a long and successful campaign, to find his Lady waiting for him. Such was the flavor of the thought metaphors that Lasky privately entertained.

He hurriedly walked the short distance to the spot where Kate was frozen in place, gently moved the strands of auburn fire from her face, cupped his hands around her shoulders and said, "Kate! This is some surprise! I didn't expect you to...."

She interrupted the flow of what she knew would be a broken train of thank you's and replied, "Now, Mier! After all! This is a big day for you! You finally got wanted you wanted! Now you're on your own!"

Chapter 2

▼

An Uncertain Reality

They climbed the three steps that led to the front door landing. As Lasky opened the door, he turned to Kate and said, "Well, what's in the box? Not something to wear, I hope! I hate new clothes! The damn things take too long to break in!"

Kate smiled wryly, laughed, shook her head and replied, "You'll never change, Mier! You're just a big kid in oversized shoes who wants toys of one kind or another! Well, I have a real surprise for you. Something I think you'll like."

As they climbed the short flight of stairs that separated the top level from the basement of the split level house, Lasky kept tickling her in the ribs, trying to pry the secret of the box from her before they reached the summit that opened into the living room. "Come on, what's in it? Come on, come on, gotta tell me!" was all Kate heard until they reached the living room.

Still laughing together, she looked at him and said in a soft, almost flowing way, "Here, Mier. I hope you will use this. It is something I think you needed for a long time," as she handed him the box.

Lasky placed it on the coffee table in front of them, its contents sloshing from side to side, as he greedily tore off the top. As he looked inside, his actions slowed down, first into a state of slow motion, and then into a series of mechanical, jerky movements as he reached into the opened vessel. As he removed his present, he looked at Kate, bewildered, and removed the object of so much joking only a few moments ago.

"Are you kidding me? A cat?! What am I going to do with a cat?!"

Kate laughed as he had never heard her laugh before. Through watering eyes, he heard her say, "No, you idiot, it's not a cat! It's a female *kitten*! Someone you can raise and talk to when I'm not here, and when you get down…which is pretty often from what I've seen!

"You'll be surprised what a difference a little creature like this will make in your life. It will get you out of yourself somewhat, and make you feel better, a lot better. More than you can imagine right now. You brood too much, get too wrapped up with your self-created anxieties over nothing, and go off on too many emotional tangents. Instead of wasting so much of your life in worry, Mier, this little guy will help you find more of yourself, more often than you would believe at this moment."

Lasky lifted the tiny animal out of the box, and lifted it up to eye level. The kitten was completely black, with a temper to match. Its first action was to nip his finger as he touched its nose. Its coal black eyes were unusual, and in them, Lasky saw a determination for self-assertion that he could relate to.

He laughed and said to Kate, "He has a bad temper. We're sure to get along famously," and put the animal on the floor. Its tiny eight week old size made it look like a toy. As the kitten scurried away, intent on exploring its new home, Lasky was about to voice the problems of owing an animal, but she cut him off.

"No, don't worry. I bought him a week ago. He is litter box trained, and all of the paraphernalia he needs is in the back of my car. Food included."

He knew he was damned to ownership at last. "OK, that does it then. I guess I got me a little critter for a pal. Thanks, Kate, you may be right. It is just the thing I need." As he said this, he put his arms around her, and surrendering to her thoughtfulness, gave her a long, gentle kiss.

"Now that's more like it, Mier. You're welcome."

"I hope you can stay the night, Kate. I could use the company. I have a lot on my mind now, and some diversion might allow the mind to order itself, without my interfering with more anxieties. You know, it's one thing to *want* something, it's another thing entirely to actually *get* it!"

Kate realized he did not understand what he just said, and shook her head at his thoughtless, self-centered concern. Instead of pointing his callousness out to him, she replied, "Is that all you can use? Company?"

His self-absorption was shattered, as he realized what she meant.

"I didn't mean it the way it sounded. I need you very much. Would you please stay the night?"

"Of course I will. I intended to. Feel better now?"

Somewhere in this short exchange he felt he said something inappropriate, but dismissed his concern. Instead, his double-edged nature made him pleased with himself for at least sensing that his comments were off the mark. "Thanks much," was his only reply.

While Kate brought the kitten's assorted paraphernalia and food into the house and set it up in a far corner of the kitchen, Lasky began to prepare them dinner. His years of bachelorhood forced him to become a decent cook, the only alternative to eating out daily and spending large amounts of money for what he termed second rate fare at first rate prices.

As they ate their steak, potato, and salad dinner, Kate noticed how his conversation decreased, and his attention drifted. He was introverting again, worrying over something. Half way through dessert, she determined to break through his cage of what was quickly becoming a melancholy.

"You're just lost now. It will take time to realize you're the only one you have to account to for anything from now on. I was scared too when I started my business. Don't forget, I not only had no management experience, I saw that I was in debt up to my eyeballs, and the panic that took hold of me almost made me close the shop and return the money to Branstrome's. It's nothing either to worry about or be afraid of. I got the hang of it, and so will you. OK?"

Her ability to see into those aspects of his nature that he considered hidden, was something Lasky knew he needed desperately. In a moment of her finishing her encouraging dialogue, he snapped the bars of the cage closed and came back to the present.

"You're right, Kate. All of this 'what-iffing' that's going on in my head is silly. Sometimes I act like such a fool, worse than a fool. Like a complete ass, making substance out of shadows, and reacting to them as though they were real conditions and events."

Kate smiled at the characteristic lopsided manner of his speech, and dismissed the entire episode, as was her tactics in successfully dealing with Lasky's shifting emotional and mental storms.

"Let's clear this mess up, Mr. Lasky, get the dishes out of the way, and…we shall see what we shall see," she said teasingly, as she arose from the table.

As they worked, a quiet overtook them. When they finished their task, they settled on the large couch in the living room, a pensive mood being shared between them. As Lasky placed his right arm around her, Kate nestled her head under his chin, and against his chest.

Finally, the silence was broken by Kate's question. "You're worried about your work, aren't you? I mean, there is something about it that is really upsetting you, isn't there?"

Normally, she would not have stirred the issue. She understood that for some reason, Lasky would not discuss his "project" with anyone, not even with her. She respected this attitude, but an air of secrecy breeds curiosity that sooner or later attracts attention. Kate did not feel she was prying. Rather, her concern got the better of her, as she could see that the achievement of his dream of early retirement so he could work on his Project full time was making him intensely unhappy and more melancholy than usual.

Lasky remained quiet for longer than is usual for someone trying to ward off peaked interest in a private matter. He realized though, that their relationship had grown to that point where trust was the next commodity to be brought into the relationship. Either that, or have the relationship thin, and eventually die—something he did not want.

It was more than the convenience of having a beautiful and desirable sexual partner. More than the idea of having someone with whom he could share other matters and concerns. More than the secure feeling of knowing that he would see her several times a week. Lasky knew that he was in love with her, and she with him. But for their pasts, they would have made the arrangement legal with wedding vows. But such could not be for either of them he reasoned, at least, not at this time.

Yet, there was this issue of trust that clearly needed to be extended to her. And why not? She helped him resolve so many other personal shades cast upon the screen of his mind which she removed with the clear light of understanding and the fresh perspective she had given him. Why not here too? But how far to go? How much to tell? This Project is serious and bizarre, he reminded himself. If she knew too much, perhaps she would think him unbalanced in the end, and walk away from this "sick" scenario as she had done from the "bastard." She had misjudged Mike also, for far too long a time. Maybe she would view him in the same way?

"You're right, Kate. It is my work that has me bothered. My "project" as I call it. I know I have kept you in the dark about it, but I have my reasons. Honestly, it is a weird idea I am working on. So weird, that if I told you all about it, I'm positive you'd think I was completely unbalanced, and simply walk away. I don't want to lose you. I feel I'm in a lose-lose situation.

"If I do tell you all about it, I'm afraid you'll walk away for the reason I already gave. If I *don't* confide in you, at least somewhat, I suspect you'll still walk, because you'll think I don't really trust you. No relationship can last without that all important quality of trust. Even I know that! That's what's stopping me from getting this insanity off my chest...well, not the insanity of the project...that is not insane...but the insanity of worrying

that I'll lose you either way. *Then* comes the worry about what you will do
if I do tell you however much I decide I should tell you, and you find out
what the project is about."

Kate starred at the wall across the room from where they were sitting,
wondering for a brief moment, if he wasn't unbalanced after all. After she
thought she knew him so well, Lasky just went off on a tirade of compressed worries, illogic, and child-like confused thinking that made her
wonder. But her mind was quick and analytical, without the neurotically-
driven emotional storms that plagued his thinking so much.

After a split second of evaluation-analysis-conclusion and decision, she
whispered to him, "Mier, I know you're not crazy. Sometimes you act as
though you are, but that's simply because you react to your fears and
imaginings as though they were real. We discussed that more than once,
remember? You're not the only one in the whole world who's this way.
Believe me, I could tell you stories.

"The point is, I'm here if you want to talk. I don't judge you as you
judge yourself. But I have to tell you, that if anything makes me mad, it's
that you project your fears onto me and decide according to them and in
advance, just what I will or won't do. *That's* unfair and plain *wrong*. And I
can prove it to you. How many times did I disappoint you in acting opposite of the way you were afraid I would act? And how many times did your
fears that I would act this way or that come about? You like baseball. Well,
tell me. What's your batting average here?"

She was right, and Lasky finally realized it. For a brief moment, Mier
Lasky saw through the blinding haze of his self-defeating neuroses. With
an unconscious exertion of his will, he mentally seized the crippling emotional inner forces that continually acted upon him. He jumped up from
the couch without warning, sending Kate crashing sideways onto the
couch, began pacing toward the center of the room, turned about in an
overly dramatic fashion, looked squarely at Kate, and began.

"This is wrong, Kate! I haven't been fair to either you or myself all
along. I need someone I can confide in. Someone more balanced than me

who can help me through this darkness I feel inside, or at least, let me vent the pent-up feelings that are tearing me apart. OK. Let me start at the beginning.

"When I was about 10 years old, I saw a movie on television that did something to me. As time went on, I came to realize that the topic of that show became the single driving force in my life. It's really stupid if you think of it. A sci-fi movie from the mid-50's determining the direction and actions a person's life would take. Anyway, it did. I can't even remember the title of it, but it was about this old physics professor who had the idea of amplifying his thoughts in order to turn it into a force that could be used as any other force is used.

"From his private research and experimentation, he found that the forces that either made up thought or along which thought traveled through the brain were electromagnetic in nature, and that the chemical basis of thought—which science was beginning to become aware of at the time the movie was made—acted only as so many wires or conduits that simply allowed the electromagnetic nature of thought to flow more rapidly through the brain. In other words, he rejected the idea that is still held today by modern science, that the chemical nature of brain secretions are responsible for thought, and are in fact, the very thought itself. And Kate, if you study the current literature of neuropsychiatry and neurology, you'll see that while it doesn't actually claim that the phenomenon of thought is simply due to chemicals flowing in the brain, it is implying that, and it doesn't take a genius to see through their wording.

"This professor began his experiments by taping a series of electrodes to the front and back of his skull, since conscious thought occurs in the frontal region, with the back of the brain also generating a lot of electrical brain activity. This is what they do today in medicine to measure the brain's state. You know, 'EEG brain wave measurement' they call it. The medical profession uses it to diagnosis sleep disorders, and as a test for possible brain tumors.

"Then, he began to detect the electromagnetic signals that are associated with all thought, whether conscious or unconscious. Once he could pick up these signals, he devised a way to tap the electromagnetic radiation from an 'atomic reactor power station' as they called it in those days, that was on the property next to his. He siphoned it off, and through a series of antennas and power amplifiers, *amplified* the *intent* contained within a given thought, in order to reproduce that force out here, in our four-dimensional world."

Kate interrupted. "Intent in a thought? The intent being a force? Can you be a little more clear?"

"Let me give you an example. He kept concentrating on turning a page in a large book he had. You might say the 'thought' was about the page, and 'turning it' was the intent within that thought. Once he picked up the brain wave electrical signal and amplified the thought, he automatically amplified the intent that was contained in the thought. After a lot of trial and error, he succeeded in turning the page, but it nearly killed him. There was something about the original thought being amplified that had a feedback effect on him.

"But he kept experimenting, siphoning off more and more energy from the power station until directing the intent of his thought outward into the world became a normal event for him. In short, he was able to move simple objects around in his laboratory. Then something happened. There was a power surge at the reactor site. The surge was so great—at least that's how the unscientific screenwriter explained it—that his brain and nervous system became replicated many, many times over. Not inside his own head, but as external, living creatures with the ability to move and jump short distances through the air. They were also equipped with two tentacle-like projections.

"Their purpose, as the screenwriter put it, was to survive by attaching themselves to the neck of living people, and sucking the brain and nervous system out of their hosts. In short, they would suck the brain and nervous system of a person out through the back of the head where they attached themselves, liquefy the brain and stem by this drawing action, and use it as their nourishment. Of course, the poor bastard they attached themselves to died a slow and agonizing death. But then, that was just the horror part of the horror film. I found the so called scientific details interesting even at that age, and never forgot it."

Kate sat motionless throughout Lasky's explanation, sizing him up as he went along. She was relieved that the issue of his concern was only something bizarre, almost like a childhood fixation that had somehow carried itself over into his adult life. She heard and read of such things before. As she considered his dialogue and the intensity of his delivery however, she found herself thinking that his concern and even self-absorption seemed timid when compared to the real nightmares of crime and violence that could be found on nearly any city block in every part of the country.

As he continued, Kate became aware that he was really talking to himself, as though presenting a summary of his own history for self-examination. It also became clear to her that he took this subject very seriously. She began to realize that it was not some fixation left over from childhood, but something for which he apparently found a scientific basis. Separating the sci-fi and horror from the underlying motivations of the film that were driving him, she found herself listening more intently, and beginning to form questions that she expected him to answer.

"I have some questions, Mier. What about…."

"In a minute. Let me finish. Remember what I said about him amplifying the *intent* contained within a given thought, and that it was this 'essence' *in* the thought that reproduced the force in our four-dimensional world? You remember how he kept concentrating on turning a page in a book, while amplifying the intent to do so, and that after a lot of trial and error succeeded in turning the page? Well, that wasn't actually in the movie. The old professor didn't differentiate the thought from the intent. That is what I somehow gleaned from it as a kid seeing it for the first time, and that was what I carried with me throughout the years. As I got older and became interested in electricity and physics, I began to realize that there was a scientific basis for what I took from the movie."

"You mean that physics or electrical studies allows such a thing?"

"Not exactly. But physics gives us an understanding of the way Nature works. Electricity—in this case electrical engineering—is nothing more than the specific application of those laws to a given problem. That's the rationale."

"Go on. You have me interested. I have some more questions, but I'll hold them till you're done."

"After I got my degree in electrical engineering, I wanted to learn more about electromagnetism, but not just from the physics standpoint. And I didn't want to learn more of it exclusively from the long-hair physics point of view, either. I needed to learn more of both, but combined in a way that I could possibly use it to further my ideas on this subject. Then, I lucked out and found a program at the University of Maryland, in engineering physics, and designed my own curriculum with 'acceptable' subjects so I could get the degree, but still get the specialized knowledge my undergraduate work told me I needed.

"My thesis was entitled "Electromagnetic Fields, Interactions, and Harmonics, and Their Relationship to Brainwave Analysis." This way, I was able to put it all together, and without telling any of my profs what I was up to, find out if my ideas were at least "physically sound" as they say. If they weren't, the profs would have shot it down, simply because it was impossible, and they would know this from having much more knowledge of the field."

Kate interrupted. "You're losing me, Mier. What does all of this have to do with you being so upset and depressed? Sounds like you should be happy you got so far with such a, well, unusual idea."

"You wanted to know what my problem is. Well, I'm trying to tell you. But I can only do it one way, because that's how I think. I can't pick up something in midstream, and zigzag this way and that, back up, whatever. I gotta do it this way. OK?!"

Kate realized he was losing his composure. She had seen this before. It was his way of reacting when he felt he was about to be rejected, or if he would be questioned about something he was afraid would be proven wrong by someone asking a question he never anticipated—a question that would utterly destroy something he held dear.

"I'm sorry. I just want to know more, fast. It's like a good novel. You want to read as fast as you can to get to the end, because the suspense is killing you!" Her designed laughter that followed broke the spell of his nervousness. He continued.

"As a result of the studies and lab work I did for my master's degree, I figured out several working hypotheses which came close to what I originally extracted from that movie. Should I go on?"

Kate moved forward on the couch, being intent on hearing more of what Lasky had to say. "Go on, Mier. But please, explain don't spare any detail that will give me a very clear picture of just where you are heading."

"Fine. These are the three premises I came up with.

"One. That the chemicals associated with human thought are as the old professor in the movie suspected. They are merely conduits that enable thought to move through the brain in paths that were determined and designed by Nature, over millions of years of evolution. Thoughts of a specific kind have specific pathways, which in turn have specific brain chemicals associated with them. In short, Nature chose the shortest distance between two points, so to speak, when it came to the mechanisms that govern thought: its pathways; its associations; and its intents. Nature devised the brain chemicals as the means to keep thoughts fixed to those pathways."

Kate couldn't help herself at this point, and simply cut into his lecture. "Wait a minute! Can you be more specific? I need an example of what you're talking about."

"OK. When you think of, say, a cow, what do you associate with it? Milk, grass, fields, barns, farmers, and so on. Now think of a squirrel. Bet you don't have the same *natural* associations with this animal that you do with the cow. Now you think of trees, nuts, leaves, and so on. This is what I mean. The chemicals are associated with pathways for given thoughts, their natural associations, and consequently, the *intents* within them! It prevents them from overlapping, and allows us to have memory and to think. Sure, you can force the natural associations into unnatural ones, but not for long. Try it. You wind up getting…a headache."

Now Kate was very interested. All she said was, "Go on!"

"Two. Thought itself is composed of what is termed in electrical engineering, a fundamental frequency. That's the frequency at which any signal is generated, according to what's generating it. Like with house current. It has a frequency of sixty hertz, or cycles per second, meaning that it reverses direction that many times each second. But for every frequency, there are other frequencies mixed in with the fundamental frequency. These are called harmonic frequencies. They can be filtered out, used, whatever. The point is, they're there by Nature's design. Other frequencies, those that are called radio frequency, have one million or more hertz to them as their fundamental frequency, and are said to be rich in harmonics. In other words, they have many, many other frequencies, both above and below the fundamental frequency. With human thought though, we're dealing with fundamental frequencies of only one to fourteen hertz. Yet, they're loaded with harmonics too."

He gave a tense pause, trying to find the right words to continue. At that moment, however, he was more concerned with getting the stress caused by his unknown nagging concern out of his system, than he was at having Kate understand him. Even in this emotionally contradictory state however, he knew that if he wasn't clear in explaining his ideas it would only lead to more internal tension. Kate sat quietly, waiting for him to continue, and began petting the kitten that had jumped on the couch next to her.

"I became convinced that thought itself is like an envelope, and consists of the fundamental frequency. But the *intent* within a thought is actually composed of *one or more* of those harmonic frequencies combined. Since the voltages of thought are only thousands or millionths of a volt, well, the guy who wrote the story that movie was based on either had some medical background, or did some good research of the medical and electronic material available at the time.

"Three. That intent—due to the harmonics—can be filtered out, electronically, and then, as with any electrical signal of whatever frequency, amplified. When this is done, and the voltage is increased a thousand or million times, the intent contained in the thought will manifest in our four-dimensional world as whatever force is in accord with its nature. In other words, the intent of turning a page in a book, or moving a pencil, or a chair across a room for that matter, will be accomplished in reality. It will just be a matter of filtering and of power amplification.

"Imagine what a new field of science this will create!! And then...." But he cut himself off abruptly, suddenly seeming to come out from behind his own eyes. He realized he got carried away, and caught himself just in time. He would not divulge to her the fourth and last part of his idea. It was just too strange even for him to think about for longer than a few minutes at a time.

Kate read him easily. "You're holding back on something, aren't you?"

Lasky stood motionless for a few moments, trying desperately to ward off what he felt was her disappointment in him not fully trusting her.

Rather than push him any further, she said, "That's all right Mier. You explained a lot, and I am very happy that you found it in you to trust me so much. I promise, not a word of this to anyone from me. When you feel like telling me the rest, I'll be ready to hear it, because honestly, if I had a technical background, I'd love to work on this idea with you. It is extremely fascinating to me!"

Lasky was self-absorbed again, worrying about what he had told her, yet suddenly feeling as though he should tell her the rest of what he had succeeded in doing along experimental lines so far, and even the final part of what he intended to do, or at least, try to do. As a sound coming from a great distance away, he became aware of her words, and was snapped out of his introspection by her words "I'd love to work on this idea with you!" He felt better emotionally at that moment than he had felt in years.

Kate patted the section of the couch next to her, motioning for him to sit down. The kitten had curled up into a tiny black ball in her lap, and was fast asleep. "I can't very well move now, Mier, so you'd better come here. Someone didn't find your lecture as interesting as I did, and decided to go to kitty dreamland." Like a small, obedient child, Lasky walked over to the couch, and sat down next to her.

"Well, Kate, now you know," he whispered, as someone might who had just finished some strenuous labor.

"You mean, now I know *almost* all of it."

"Yes."

Before Kate could finish saying what was on her mind, the kitten shot out of her lap, hooked its claws into Lasky's shirt, and began rock-climbing maneuvers up his shirt, trying to reach his face. Its meowing and purring, coupled with a look of sheer desperation and determination on its tiny face at scaling the height, made both of them laugh. Lasky's serious spell was broken. He grabbed the animal gently in his left hand, held it up, and looked at it. The kitten, as though sensing he needed some comic relief, adopted an utterly ridiculous expression that made it seem as though he was grinning at Lasky, while barring its teeth at the same time. When Lasky touched its black nose with his finger, he received a harder nip than the first time, breaking the finger's skin.

"Dammit, cat, what's wrong with you?! Are you going to do that every time I try to play with you?"

But the kitten just maintained the strange grin, and hung suspended in midair like an oversized 8-ball. Kate laughed loudly and uncontrollably at the comical scene, silently sizing it up. Two lunatic-type personalities alone together in the same house. "I wonder which one will kill the other first," she thought, and continued to laugh out loud.

Pointing his finger at the kitten for the third time, Lasky coolly said, "Look cat, I'm the boss here, and things are run *my* way, get it? And one of the rules is, **no biting!**"

No sooner had he delivered this ultimatum to the kitten, then it bit him again, this time drawing a little blood. "Ow!" Lasky snorted, dropping the animal on the couch next to Kate, who was holding her sides due to her laughing so hard. When the kitten hit the couch, it disappeared from sight, crawled up the back of the couch, and in a few seconds wound up on the back of Lasky's neck, where it inflicted another stinging bite. Lasky jumped up, grabbing his neck with one hand, the kitten with the other. Even though Kate was laughing hysterically from the chain of events, she worried that Lasky might unintentionally squeeze the tiny animal too hard, and harm it.

Before she could coherently object, Lasky smiled, laughed at the animal, and said, "You know, you have the same type of determination and stubbornness that I have. But you're sneaky, and hit unexpectedly. So I hereby name you 'A-Bomb the Terrible,' or just 'A-Bomb' for short."

The kitten purred loudly, and once again, adopted what became know as the stupid grin, something that would bring much needed relief and humor into Lasky's self-occupied and anxious life.

The tension in the room, initially broken by Lasky's explanation, and the light-hearted mood brought on by the antics of A-Bomb, suddenly shot up again. Kate knew he was having an anxiety attack, probably brought on by overcoming a personal taboo of telling her of his secret work, which violated some unconscious barrier of the distrust of others, in which she was apparently still included. Or perhaps, she thought, he overcame some ritual neurosis by explaining his closely guarded secret—a deeply seated neurosis whose roots lie in the need to control outside events through mental gymnastics, and well placed inner barriers built up from rigid thought.

Kate decided to break the frozen moment. "Mier, I think I'll get ready for bed. Wanna play?!"

Lasky's introversion crumbled rapidly, but in stages: the sound of her voice; the awareness of her shapely figure bearing back hard into the couch; the shortness of her skirt riding up further as she now began to slowly lean forward, while exposing her legs; the sultry, devilish smile on her face. All of which Lasky was pleasurably and painfully becoming aware.

"What, *me*? Bed? Damn right! That's more like it! All of this soul purging makes me sick! I've had enough for one night! Let's play!"

Kate stood up slowly, her short, full-bottomed skirt riding teasingly even higher, exposing the sheen of her hose against the flesh of her taut, firm thighs. Lasky felt his pulse quicken. As she moved with a purposeful and feminine, yet dignified rhythm toward him, he began to feel his heart, now pounding in his throat. In a moment, she was upon him, smoothly sliding her arms around his neck.

As she pressed her heated body strongly against his, her hot, moist breath pulsated on Lasky's neck as she kissed it, setting his strong body into a quiver, one that set up a powerful inner vibration within him. His body responded fully. The pounding of his heart was now in his ears, and the heightened excitement of the love-making that was unraveling, set up an orgasmic thumping in him that surged through every cell and fiber of his body.

Without a word, she kissed him passionately, her right hand moving slowly down his chest at the same time. Lasky's anticipation rose to a level of biological tension that was at the same time near ecstasy, yet unbearable to maintain for any length of time.

"Give me a few minutes," Kate whispered in his beet-red ear. "I'll be in the bedroom."

As some shape-shifting phantom, she seemed to glide out of sight, around the corner, and into the hallway, disappearing into some unknown region. Such was Lasky's appraisal of her thoroughly seductive exit. As she moved through the hallway however, she became aware that her physical movement through space had an emotional shadow. She found herself admitting the unthinkable. She had fallen in love with Mier

Lasky. Her silent vow of never entertaining this state of serious involve-
ment again with another man after her bitter experience with the bastard,
was suddenly shattered.

She heard a sharp snapping in her ears, as though some barrier in her
mind had snapped like a rubber band. In that moment, she crossed the
emotional line between understanding her feelings, and accepting them.
With all of his faults at self-preoccupation and mental bogeymen, he had
a child-like quality that gave him a reality and character she needed. And
now, she not only admitted it to herself, but accepted it.

After what seemed to him to be an agonizing blur of time, Lasky heard
the click of the light switch in the master bedroom, and bolted toward the
hallway. In a moment, he was there. Kate stood motionless, silhouetted
against a small, dimmed night-light. The bulb's flickering element gave a
strobe light appearance to Kate's form, and made it seem to shift subtly
through her black negligee. The negligee's red, complicated trim enhanced
it, lending an aura of intense mystery at what lied within, while projecting
a serious feminine outline needing completion.

She looked at him as though seeing him for the first time since their
meeting in the Reference Room. There was a difference this time. Now
she saw him as a part of 'we.' Her self-defense of emotional separateness,
shattered by the recent self-acceptance of her feelings for him, communi-
cated something to Lasky. It was these same emotions he too was wrestling
with at the fringes of his conscious thought. The love he was feeling for
her, and his final acceptance of that same 'we,' was something he still
struggled to suppress from his awareness.

But in that moment it no longer mattered. The two of them were
now new and unique to each other, and to themselves. In the dawning of
this silent tempest they came together, and dissolved into a single oblivion of union.

Chapter 3

▼

The Moment of Truth

It was only 7:30 A.M., but Kate was already finishing the last of her makeup, and preparing to leave for *Say it With Pictures.* Lasky was in a dead sleep. After she left the bathroom and quietly closed the door, she moved to the master bedroom and peeked in at him. She wondered if the grin on his sleeping face was the result of their lovemaking the night before, or if A-Bomb's silliness was already beginning to wear off on him.

She smiled at this thought, gave a muffled laugh, blew a kiss at him, and quietly said, "I'm leaving you a note honey, in a place you're sure to find it. See you tomorrow." With that, she gently closed the door of the master bedroom, and walked down the long hallway toward the kitchen. Lasky remained sound asleep, and missed all of it.

In the kitchen, she quickly wrote him the intended note:

Darling:

I decided to leave a bit early this morning. We have a big opportunity coming from the new cannery that opened outside of Sunnberry, and I want to make sure everything is just right. Their advertising big shot is coming to see us today, and he might arrive early. He wants to discuss the details of our handling their account, and to give us their first test job. I was going to tell you last night, but well, we got onto other things. (smile) Have a good day. Do whatever you feel like. After all, it is your first day of retirement. I'll be waiting for your usual Monday call at noon. Hope I have some good news for you about this new account. Tell you all about next weekend.

All my love,

Kate

She paused and considered the "All my love" closing of her note. In the past, she always ended such notes to him with "Yours," or "Love, Kate," the type of ending that has the ring of a close friendship to it, instead of the more serious overtones this ending clearly contained. She hesitated at leaving the closing as she wrote it, but finally let it stand. She knew he would read these thoughts into it also, and realized that she wanted him to. "After last night, something happened between us that never did before. Something *more* than the sex. I know he felt it too, and I want him to know I felt the same thing. Not push, but maybe…well, I want him to know it too."

She stuck the note to the refrigerator door with one of the ladybug magnetic note holders she bought for him for this purpose, and quickly but quietly ran down the stairs to the landing of the split-level. In a few moments she was out the door, in her car, and rolling down the long driveway to the road that ran past Lasky's house. Within a minute she was headed toward Sunnberry, and what she hoped would be the first big break for her company—landing the permanent advertising representation of the "Tom Thumb's Pride" canned goods account.

Lasky lay motionless in bed, staring at the ceiling. It was 9:43 A.M., and he had just woken after a blissful night's sleep filled with romantic dreams of Kate. His first thought as his head cleared from sleep, was that it was unusual such dreams lacked at least one erotic element. Instead, they were filled with images and emotions that mirrored the first stages of puppy love, so well known to teenagers as their bodies began producing the relevant hormones that trigger puberty.

He was aware of the pleasant, sinking feeling in the pit of his stomach, and the queasiness that rippled delightfully through every nerve of his body. His verbal self-dialogue began again. "Well, Mier, I think you are in love with that lady! You're too old for puppy love, and after last night, any puppy love would have dissolved in the fires of the moment. Nope, I think you got it for her good, and you're going to have to do something about it. You know it can't continue like this forever; this 'convenience' as you like to think of it. You hate ties...or at least you did...but this is something different. It just ain't gonna keep workin' the way it is now! But there's time for all that, now that you're...."

"Retired" would have been his next word. But his self-generated discussion was abruptly broken by a black mass falling squarely on his face, covering his eyes completely, and stunning his nose from its impact. He sprang to a sitting position in bed, terrified by what had just happened. Waking from sleep, engrossed in a nearly alien idea, not yet oriented to the new day, and having such a shock to his system caused his heart to flutter, and for him to lose his breath.

"What the hell...!" Looking down on the blankets covering his legs he saw his new nemesis, A-Bomb, the Terrible, pulling at the covers with its tiny claws, tail straight up in the air, giving him that same stupid grin of the night before. Within moments a steady stream of meows followed.

"You lunatic!" Mier screamed. "What are you doing! Trying to give me a fatal heart attack on the first day of my retirement? Dammit, cat, if you're going to live here you'd better get the rules straight! And the first rule is never, and I mean *never*, come into this bedroom uninvited!"

The cat simply continued to claw the blankets, spin this way and that, looked at him again, and gave him a seemingly even more stupid grin. Lasky started laughing, half embarrassed from being shocked by his new tiny pet, and half amused by its complete innocence. As he began to pet it, the animal purred loudly, a much louder sound of contentment than he had ever heard from any other cat he previously encountered. "Quite a motor you got there, huh, little lady?"

Several minutes passed before he realized that he was playing with the kitten and having a good time, laughing, getting a tiny bite here and a little nip there from the pocket-size little life. "Well, time to move," he muttered, and with that, slung the blankets to one side, sending the kitten reeling inside the mass.

After washing and dressing, he walked down the hallway, on the way to the kitchen. A breakfast of scrambled eggs, sausage, pancakes, hash browns and toast was on his mind. The more he thought about them, the faster he walked the distance separating him from the "best room in any house," as he always referred to the kitchen. After he passed the master bedroom door, he heard a muffled dragging sound. Somewhat unnerved, he whisked around, only to meet the blankets that were formerly on the bed and were now following him.

"What?!" Then he remembered. "Cat, you're gonna be a lot of trouble, I can see that!" and laughing, bent down, unraveled the black terror from the blankets, and carried her into the best room in any house. "I know. You're hungry too. Well, let's see what we can do about it."

After a leisurely breakfast, Lasky left the counterbar cluttered with dishes. He rarely used the eloquent dinette situated in the east corner, preferring to eat at the counterbar that nearly divided the spacious kitchen into two parts: the food handling and preparation area, and the dining area proper. It didn't remind him of the one requirement of bachelorhood that goes with the territory—eating alone.

For a moment he thought about it, and realized that he and Kate only ate at the dinette, even for quick snacks of coffee, never at the bar. He then realized that he designed this ritual so as to offset the lonely meals, by somehow having the dinette act as a buffer, reminding him that she would come back, and they would once again be together. He started to realize further how much she meant to him. He considered how he unconsciously devised this ritual-plan in order to maintain a bachelor-hood status, but one that was rapidly losing its appeal.

With another ritual, he brought himself back to the present by shaking his frame vigorously, while waving both hands violently and rotating both wrists while shaking his fingers hard. "There! That's better! There'll be time for all that contemplating later. Right now, I think it's time for the moment of truth!" With that, he walked out of the kitchen and into the living room, and headed for the stairs to the lower level, and his laboratory.

On the landing he paused. Something shot through him, causing him to freeze to the spot. An apprehension began looming up from some deep, black pool of the unconscious, flooding his senses with streams of mounting, masked anxieties. His heart began to pound hard, causing the skin on his chest to pulsate visibly. Beads of cold sweat, microscopic at first, broke through the pores of his skin, building up until they rolled down his body, dampening his clothing. His mouth went dry as he became lightheaded. Only the throbbing in his eyes snapped him out of the swoon he was rapidly falling into, on his way to a complete blackout.

"What the hell's the matter with you, old boy?! *What's wrong?!*" He began to breathe deeply and slowly, using a mental relaxation technique he learned years ago to regain command of his physical form. As the pounding in his chest subsided, and moisture began to return to his mouth, he sat down on the first step of the second flight of stairs that led to the lower level of the house, and to his laboratory. He continued his mentally-induced state of complete relaxation, until his body went limp and collapsed against the stairway wall. The ice cold sweat was gone, leaving his clothing with an uncomfortable wetness.

"They'll dry out. It'll just take a few minutes. Your body temperature is returning to normal." After an additional five minutes of the deep, rhythmic breathing and mental visualization exercise, he was himself again. "God, what is it that's doing this to you?! It's something you remember—or wish you did—something that's connected with T.A.A.C., but what?!

"You can feel it, it's trying to come up in your mind, but dammit, it just won't! I'll tell you, old boy, you'd better either get a hold on yourself, or dredge up from inside whatever it is that is at the root of this, or you'll never get this work done! You'll be stopped dead in your tracks! And with the voltages and current levels you'll be working with for the Final Phase of the Project, one slip and you could literally kill yourself! Imagine poor Kate finding you dead on the floor, looking like a crisp piece of overdone charcoal!

"Think, dammit, think! What's it going to be?! Dig up the repressed memory, or learn to control yourself, like you just did! The answer's obvious, isn't it? You don't have years to spend on some shrink's couch, pouring your guts out to him, let alone discussing this Project with him. So you'd better just get a hold of yourself, and learn to control these goddamn anxiety attacks. You've done it before, and you can do it as the need arises!"

His self-reassuring dialogue brought back his mental strength and control. After one more deep, rhythmic breath, he picked himself up from the step, and proceeded to descend into the dimly lit bottom level of the house. Once there, he turned right, and walked another twelve feet. In front of him was a four-by-seven foot steel door, manufactured with a dark walnut stain, which gave it the appearance of wood.

Directly above the bronze door knob was a bright white, thirty-six key, keypad. Its twenty-six alphabetical letters and ten numbers allowed him to change the combination to almost any conceivable sequence he chose. This guaranteed that no one but him could gain access to his private laboratory.

"One of the best inventions I saw in years," he muttered to himself under his breath, "best idea for a keyless lock I ever saw," and with that, pressed U-N-I-O-N-1-0-9-8. There was an almost imperceptible series of clicks, as the multibolt latch assembly rotated its tumblers, pulling the bolt mechanism back into its housing. Lasky turned the door knob, and pulled hard. The door swung opened, exposing a dead blackness inside.

He walked inside and flipped the light switch on. The room was large, thirty-five-by-forty feet, with a seven and one-half foot white drop ceiling.

The walls were covered with a medium dark mahogany paneling, flat in texture, so as not to reflect any glare from the overhanging fluorescent lighting that ran through the length of the room.

Lasky stood for a few moments, looking at the equipment the laboratory housed. Four modern, high speed computers, one situated in each direction of the compass, sat poised on large benches that jutted out at a distance of thirty inches from all four walls, those against the east and north walls running the full length of the walls. In the east, the bench was littered with an assortment of electronic components housed in over a hundred wallrack, labeled tray cases.

There were resistors of every conceivable wattage, tolerance, and resistance; capacitors of every voltage, capacitance, size and color; inductors of different values, winding descriptions, and makes; diodes ranging from a few milliamps to several amps current-carrying capacity for both rectifying and avalanche use; thyristor, silicone controlled rectifiers; transistors; integrated circuits; spools of insulated hook-up wire; soldering irons and guns of different wattages; along with coil winding jigs; ceramic and mylar insulating posts; and small digital test multimeters.

The bench itself was littered with coils of wire and electronic components strewn here and there, giving it the appearance of a television repair shop in a state of chaos. The bench against the south wall had been cut in two, the last half of it having been removed. This allowed Lasky access to the second half of the wall, on which hung a huge blackboard, covered with mathematics, electronic design notes, circuit drawings, and notes to himself entitled "T.A.A.C.: Thought Amplification and Control—Notes."

The remaining half of the bench was really a large desk, strewn with books on electromagnetism, quantum mechanics, electrical and electronic engineering, and radio frequency theory and circuit design; numerous handwritten papers; and photocopies of articles from engineering and scientific journals. Above this section of the bench hung a three shelf bookrack containing the books he most frequently used in his work. The north wall's bench was filled with electronic test, measurement, and signal equipment of the type he needed: analog and digital oscilloscopes; multi-meters; clip-on current ammeters; radio frequency generators and ampli-fiers; signal generators; test probes; and three different design and evacuation range vacuum pumps.

He stood in the middle of the room, and began his self-dialogue, "You've come a long way, Lasky. My God, from some crazy sci-fi show of the '50's to this! And to think, man, there *is* a basis to all of this after all. The damn thing can work, and by God, you're going to *make* it work!" He turned to the west wall, and walked toward it.

"This is it. This is where you're going to succeed, and it's all gonna hap-pen on this spot. I can't believe you've come this far, but you have, and you did it by yourself, in this homemade lab. Screw the big universities and their bullshit funding and their 'you're-gonna-jump-through-my-hoop' attitude! You were **right** in your theoretical work, and in the experimental. You don't need any of them!" As he now only whispered these words of self-praise in an arrogant tone to himself, he looked hard at what lay in front of him.

The workbench against the west wall was sixteen feet long, and situated against the center of the wall. The eight and one-half foot space on either side of the bench housed an enormous six and one-half foot high, sixteen inch diameter Tesla coil, with banks of high voltage, high current capacity, oil-filled capacitors connected in parallel to each apparatus. Power cables ran from a 220 volt AC, 50 amp source current to two transformers wired in parallel, that were used to drive each of the Tesla coils—huge 50,000 volt AC transformers rated at 10 amps each.

When activated, the transformers powered the primary coil of each Tesla assembly, shorting the charge build-up through an electrode open air-gap once the transformer's output built up to the level Lasky wanted. The resulting power, then delivered to the Tesla's tall, wide secondary coil, produced an output of over five million volts at radio frequency current levels that were extraordinarily powerful for such a coil, and which were virtually lethal if an active part of the coil assembly were accidentally touched.

On the bench were several frequency generators, radio frequency power amplifiers, two multichannel frequency counters, a few signal generators, a control panel that was hard wired to the instruments on the bench, and a twenty-four inch diameter, thirty-six inch tall, Pyrex heavy wall glass chamber shaped like a cylinder—his 'Thought Chamber'—attached to a removable twenty-eight inch square of Pyrex glass plate. The hole in the center of the glass plate, and the metal tubing emerging from it, formed a right angle to the bench top, and ran under the bench and back up through its surface. This made it easy for Lasky to lock the chamber down to the glass plate, and connect the glass assembly to a vacuum pump.

Directly behind the chamber was a twelve inch long, six inch diameter, metallic case shaped like a cake decoration dispenser, its two pointed caps being hard wired into the instruments on the bench. This 'fluid condenser' was Lasky's own design, originating from his new research in the field of thought studies. In the center of the chamber were two heavy gauge tungsten electrodes, placed at forty-five degree angles to its wall, pointing downward toward the glass plate. A series of shiny magnetic wire coils were wrapped around different sections of the cylinder's outer surface, each being connected to either a frequency generator, signal generator, or power amplifier, all connected with the multichannel frequency counters according to Lasky's design.

He looked carefully at the discharge electrode assembly jutting out of the top of each Tesla coil. These assemblies were a huge, white ceramic insulating post supporting the pointed, heavy gauge steel electrode itself. The electrode from each coil was tapped with solid wire, high voltage insulated Belden hookup wires, itself encased in a coaxial cable designed specifically for transmitting high voltage, high current, high frequency electrical discharges. As he looked at them, he started to laugh.

"Can you imagine if you didn't tap their output like that? You'd have fifteen foot or longer lightning discharges running through this lab and lighting up the whole house! The damn display would probably be seen for miles, even without windows down here! It would ionize the air in and outside the house, and the whole building would glow like an electric eel in a black box!" He laughed hard for a few seconds, and then regained his composure. "All right, enough is enough. Let's get down to work!"

There were two separate zones on the plate, each marked off by a white circle. In the one zone, a thick physics textbook lay open. The second zone was empty, except for a one inch diameter white dot painted on its center. Lasky moved the Pyrex chamber over the center of the glass plate, added a coating of high vacuum grease to the rim of the cylinder, and sealed it to the plate with a large circular aluminum clamp fitted with a suction ring around its wall and bottom, and clamped the cylinder down onto the glass plate.

After inspecting the arrangement, he rechecked all electrical connections between the Tesla coils' primary and secondary coils, their spark gaps, the capacitor bank connections, their discharge electrodes, and their direct connections to the power radio frequency amplifiers, and finally, their connections to the signal and frequency generators and the frequency counters. The last check insured that the output of these connections was properly made to the multiswitch, multidial control panel.

As the last act of preparation, Lasky connected a two foot length of vacuum tubing to the end of the copper tube evacuation line emerging through the bench's surface to the vacuum pump inlet, examined the pump's connection to the control panel, and checked the vacuum gauge. Everything was ready.

The mental and physical effort Lasky expended in readying the apparatus sobered him. He became nervous. "I wonder if you're worried about something going wrong, or if you're going to find out that the Final Phase simply won't work. God, it's **got** to work! So many years, so much struggle, so many bridge-burning decisions. What if it doesn't work? Goddamn it, I can see it now. The rest of your life spent trying to make the bastard work, and winding up in the grave a failure!"

He started to break out in a cold sweat again, and sat down in the chair at his study desk against the south wall. "Think, think, goddamn it, get hold of yourself! Get back to the relaxation response and rhythmic breathing! Get hold of yourself!" The anxiety attack had grown into a full blown panic attack, one that robbed him first of his ability to breathe normally, and then his ability to see. His eyesight began to go, and a hysterical blindness came over him.

"Oh, no, not again! Not blind again! This has been going on since you were fourteen, you son-of-a-bitch, and each time it's worse than the last! Twenty to thirty minutes in a nightmarish pit of blackness, and now I can't breathe!"

Suddenly, he heard a faint rustling, as though something was sliding gently through the loose papers on his desk. Unable to see, he felt the desk, grabbing at books and papers, finding nothing. Then the dizziness set in, and he froze to the seat of the chair. For nearly a half hour he remained blind, sweating, unable to breathe evenly, choking, gasping for air at intervals, terrified that there was something else in the room with him. Something which was sitting in a corner, waiting to jump on him and tear him to pieces. As imagination ran wild, he could feel his blood pressure rising dangerously high, his heart now thumping, rapidly, loudly and hard, as though his body had dissolved, and he was simply a single, beating muscle about to explode.

Finally, as his eyesight returned, he was able to trigger the relaxation response and rhythmic breath. In ten minutes he had control of his body and mind again, got up, lit a cigarette, and began to puff on it slowly and deeply. Coming to his senses fully, his first thought was to look for whatever made the sound that terrified him so badly during his minutes of helplessness. Instead, he broke into a self-assuring, "Look. That was part of the hysteria. You probably rustled the papers on the desk yourself, and flew into a panic because you were spaced out, and couldn't remember what happened only a few moments before. Snap out of it!"

Dismissing the incident, in a moment he was pacing up and down the length of the lab, a physical device used by so many to sort out their thoughts. "Okay, let's go through it again, one more time, and then get on with it. Let's take it step-by-step.

"One. You're going to fire up the apparatus. Use the check list to be sure you don't screw something up. Check each item off as you do it.

"Two. Attach the electrode band, and be certain you have it positioned properly over the cortex region of your brain. The front two electrodes should dig into the front of your skull just enough to lower the skin's resistance across these points, so they pick up your brainwave signal with as much current as they can, and with the least distortion coming from the electrical signals generated by cells in the skin over the front of your skull. This way, you'll pick up the maximum signal strength of the thought 'envelope' and have its fundamental frequency locked in to the TAAC fluid condenser.

"Three. Bring the Tesla coils' voltage up to one-eighth of the maximum power output, balance the two Tesla outputs, and combine the *intent* of the thought contained in the harmonics of the fundamental frequency that are now stored in the fluid condenser, and 'mix' them with the Tesla high voltages.

"Four. Concentrate on repeating the 'Prof. 1' experiment in Zone 1 of the chamber. Keep it up for at least one minute.

"Five. Bring the Tesla power up to one-quarter power. Repeat the 'Sphere' experiment in Zone 2. Keep it up for at least two minutes, and use it to focus your concentration, and to steady your mind on one, single idea.

"Six. Terminate the 'Sphere' experiment instantaneously. Make your mind blank. "Seven. Increase power to one-third max.

"Eight. Move on to the Final Phase. This is it! Actually try the Final Phase for the first time. Increase power as much as you have to, but slowly, until something occurs, or you run out of power. Okay. That does it. Let's go." With that, Lasky walked back to the west wall, took a deep breath, and began. A fleeting thought of how he wished he could live a normal life shot through his mind, but it disappeared into a mental vortex of grim determination.

He sat down in the specially insulated chair that was part of the experimental bench arrangement. In the event of an accident, an ordinary chair resting on the tiled cement floor would conduct electricity to ground, killing him instantly. His self-talk resumed.

"One. Fire up the apparatus." Turning to the control panel on his left, he threw the toggle switch that turned on the vacuum pump. In less than a minute, the soft, even hum of its motor quickly turned into a hard-sounding, dragging, laboring noise, as its gauge dropped to 30 inches of mercury, indicating all the air had been evacuated.

"Good. You don't need high vacuum. This rough vacuum is good enough." After the vacuum gauge pegged and stabilized at 30 inches, Lasky flipped the switch off. A deafening, eerie silence penetrated the laboratory, as the lone figure lost all awareness of his surroundings and continued.

"Two. Attach the electrode band." Having said that, he picked up a two inch wide, light tan, leather band whose inside was fitted with two cone-like metal projections, and placed them over his head, bringing the two electrodes to a position directly above the center of his eyebrows, and over the center of his forehead, and fastened it around his head. He adjusted the strap on the side of the band, until the two cone-like projections caused a slight discomfort to his forehead.

He smiled to himself, knowing that this action decreased his skin resistance, allowing him to pick up the maximum amplitude of his brainwaves. "Three. Bring the Tesla coils up to one-eighth power, and balance their outputs." As though obeying the command from another, Lasky threw two large, high current switches on the control panel, and adjusted two dials, one with either hand, until the AC voltage delivered to the primary winding of each power transformer was only 28 volts. The spark gap of each Tesla coil began to snap, as lethal voltage and current jumped across them, charging the capacitor banks, and delivering an induced current into the massive six foot coils of each Tesla unit.

No sound came from the two massive coils, indicating that the insulation on the extremely small diameter magnet wires they were made of, was not breaking down. The coaxial cable assemblies began to hum, as they delivered nearly one million volts of balanced, pure, raw radio frequency energy to the power amplifiers, combining and boosting the electrical harmonics of the intent of his thought that was now stored in the fluid condenser. The thought-intent, now filtered and boosted a million times, passed through into the remaining apparatus assembled on the experimental bench, directing it into Zone 1 of the Thought Chamber.

The closed textbook in Zone 1 lay motionless, as he continued to concentrate. At first, it seemed that the hard cover of the book lifted up, but immediately and silently it collapsed back to its original position. In a few more seconds, as Lasky's mental image of the cover opening up became clearer in his mind, the cover moved upward, held its position for several seconds, and then slammed down hard against the plate glass, sending a vibration through the workbench.

"Good! The same as last time! Now, keep going!" With that, he began to see in his mind, pages moving, turning, lifting from their position on the right-hand side of the text, to the left side. Instantly, they began to move, back and forth, shifting, wrinkling, turning with a speed no human hand could duplicate. He sat there with a wide smile on his face, watching the action in the Thought Chamber. He was obviously thoroughly proud of his achievement.

When he finally glanced at the wall clock behind the apparatus, he realized he had been sitting there for seventeen minutes instead of the one minute he planned, turning pages, and becoming hypnotized by the process. "Time to move on to the 'Sphere' experiment."

As his attention shifted away from the book and its moving pages to the white circle in Zone 2 of the Thought Chamber, the motion of the pages decreased drastically. In a second all of them lay motionless. The only evidence that the experiment was successful at all, was the cover of the book that still remained opened. He forgot about the ozone buildup in the room, the product of so much electrical activity. Becoming aware of its strong odor, he threw two switches on the control panel, sending two exhaust fans, one directly above each Tesla coil into motion, evacuating the toxic gas buildup in the laboratory.

Lasky then increased the power to the transformers, bringing them up to one-quarter of their maximum input voltage. The voltage meters connected to each of the two power transformers now read 55 volts, and like the coaxial cable assemblies, they too began to hum. The sparking across the open-air gap became more violent, and the coaxial cables feeding from the Tesla coils' electrodes into the equipment on the workbench, started to vibrate and move visibly, their output now somewhere in the two million volt range. He then concentrated all of his conscious attention on the one inch diameter white dot in Zone 2 of the chamber.

As he fixed his gaze upon it, he visualized it turning into a solid white sphere, one that began to rotate rapidly, and revolve in a small orbit in the Zone. Within seconds, the white dot disappeared, just as he visualized. In its place, a white sphere had come into being, spinning rapidly at first, and then moving to the left, stopping, and finally taking up a circular orbit about ten inches in diameter. He watched with amazement as the sphere continued to orbit and rotate, first slower, then faster, until it became only a solid white blur, all according to his mental visualizations. Beyond excitement now, he entered the eighth step, and the Final Phase of the experiment.

He sobered himself, and continued. In a few moments, he lost all awareness of his surroundings. Kate, his life, his past, his present; all dissolved in a Zen-like state of *now*. He was neither watching a process nor working at one, but rather, he *became* the process himself. He abruptly shut down the spinning sphere in his imagination. Its counterpart in Zone 2 immediately disappeared, resuming its reality state of being nothing more than a simple one inch diameter white dot.

Immediately, he adjusted the control panel dials to one-third power input. Seventy-three volts surged into the transformers, driving the open-air spark gaps even harder, and sending the coaxial cables into a rhythmic, swinging motion. The hum coming from them and the transformers was loud now, yet Lasky was aware of none of it. An independent observer, standing behind the scene, would have seen something that appeared to be taken from some horror or fiction story. Here was an oblivious emotionally driven man, perhaps on the verge of insanity, but certainly consumed by an unreal obsession, sitting in a maze of weird, buzzing, sparking, lethal equipment, testing the extent of Nature's laws, and pushing Providence to the limit.

"This is it," his now nearly silent self-talk informed him. "If you're right, the only difference between the sphere being a mental image and it having a reality of its own, is the power needed to bring its molecules into order. It's got to be only the level of power that is needed to do this. If it exists in your mind, Lasky, then it has a molecular structure that corresponds to its real-world counterpart; and that structure **must** be contained in the intent, in your mental image of it, and therefore in the harmonics of thought that represents it in your imagination. It's **got** to be only a matter of power!"

With that, Lasky gazed at Zone 2 intently, and concentrated all of his thought on the predetermined object he now tried to bring into physical existence: an ordinary, everyday, No. 2 Ticonderoga pencil. Against the white background of the zone, an outline, fuzzy at first, began to take form. In seconds, its outline was clear, sharp, and solid. Yet, when he willed it to move, it moved with the same ease and continuous motion with which the sphere moved. He knew from previous experiments, that this meant it was nothing more than the sphere. A mental creation, one without real-world substance.

Locked into his Zen state of immersion, he began to boost the power input dials to the next, predetermined power level of one-half full power. But in the time it takes for one thought to melt and another one to form, his anxiety took over, and the compulsiveness of his nature set up in him a blinding ambition to test his apparatus to the full extent. In an overwhelming burst of pure passion, his hands turned the dials to deliver full power to the transformers, and into the entire TAAC assembly. The power gauges on the control panel now registered one hundred percent of the transformer's input voltage. 220 volts were sent pulsing through them. He heard them hum and buzz ominously, as they had never done before.

The room lit up. A surreal, bluish-white light, generated by the open-air spark gaps, extended in cone-like fashion clear to the east wall at the back of the laboratory, the space between them seemingly filled with a dark violet haze. The Tesla coils themselves now hummed even more erratically, threatening a breakdown of their insulation, with a bluish-white hue surrounding their full height, while blue-violet streamers began to leak from their electrode-coaxial cable connections.

The transformers now gave off a loud, high pitch vibration, as they rocked back and forth on their wooden platforms, while even the signal generators and the fluid condenser showed signs of breaking down, with the strong smell of heat coming from them. Lasky was oblivious to everything, except the image of the Ticonderoga pencil in Zone 2, and what was happening. It began to fade in and out, as though it was a shadow, not quite decided on becoming a body. Yellow and brown fibers then appeared, as though he was able to see into the pencil's structure, and watch it pass from a mental image into a thing with its own solid reality.

As he continued to watch, he sank deeper into a state of complete absorption with the events unfolding before him. Ozone now filled the room, reaching dangerous levels, while the lightshow grew in intensity as the streamers from the Tesla coils and their coaxial cables jumped and hummed violently, giving evidence of their breaking down as well. Lasky heard none of this, as he witnessed the creation of the first man-made thought-object. The pencil had formed solidly in Zone 2, and fell with a characteristic faint thud on the Pyrex glass surface. As he willed it to roll, he saw its irregular motion, and heard the faint wraps its side edges made as the object rolled faster and faster, according to his willed efforts.

It worked! He had brought an object from his mind into reality! But he was too deep in the process to understand just what he had accomplished. Too deep in the blood-fever of success and self-absorption to realize that another thought was breaking the borders of his consciousness, and beginning to move around the edges of his mind. He was too deep in his process to have noticed this, or that the soft, scuffling of papers on his desk had resumed.

The Ticonderoga No. 2 pencil came to a rest in Zone 2. In a mesmerized state, Lasky began to think of it. His mind automatically made quick associations. He associated its use in daily writing, in signing checkbooks, credit cards receipts and money transactions, as though the invention of the pencil was *the* bridge between what people had and what they wanted. A bridge to a better life, to freedom, to the means of accumulating wealth, to investments…**investments**…advisors, and the "**bastard.**" Kate's ex. The thought of him froze Lasky's body to his chair.

Lost in a scene, now composed of nine-tenths fantasy and one-tenth of what was left of his hold on reality, the apparatus continued to buzz, hum, shake, vibrate, and glow with a fury that was only equaled by the rage that had imperceptibly but completely taken over Lasky's mind. As he saw him beating Kate in his mind, he felt something surging up from undefined and uncharted recesses within his being, a something that seemed to pulse in his solar plexus and then skyrocket upward into his brain and consciousness.

He was lost in a different a black blood fever now, one whose essence was that of pure hate, and whose only reality was that of mindless and total destruction. This was an inner force of an evil combined with a justice that unparalleled any similar feeling he had ever known throughout his still young life. He was aware that something had freed itself from the deepest pits of his unconscious.

Suddenly, he was wrenched into a fleeting awareness of the outside world by a shadow moving silently yet inevitably toward the open-air gap discharge of the transformer powering the Tesla coil near the south wall.

He did not hear the last rustle of a stray sheet of paper the tiny kitten had knocked off his desk and onto the floor as it jumped down, attracted by the bright light and crackling of the open-air discharge. In the time between heartbeats, A-Bomb pounced forward toward the discharge, sending sheer panic throughout Lasky's mind and body.

He realized somewhere in between his normal absent-mindedness and his not being used to having the kitten, that he had left the laboratory door opened, and the tiny creature had followed him in. Yet he was unable to move, still frozen by the raging inferno of hate that was still consuming him. Overcome by its innocence and natural curiosity, the little animal playfully passed its right front paw through the discharge. A deafening crack reverberated throughout the laboratory. The kitten was thrown sideways against the wall with terrible force, its mass of black fur smoldering and burning, as its now lifeless body slumped to the floor.

The kitten's actions had shorted out the transformer of the Tesla coil, causing the transformer to explode violently, sending pieces of deadly shrapnel in all directions throughout the room. Before several of the lethal projectiles pierced the second Tesla's towering six foot coil, destroying it, the imbalance in its five million volts of radio frequency energy output caused by the first Tesla's destruction, sent a large feedback current flowing in the apparatus on the workbench, and through the headband electrode Lasky was wearing. As the current hit his skull, waves of red, black and yellow energy filled the insides of his eyes, causing his body to feel as though it were plunging into a lake of fire and brimstone.

He then felt an agonizing searing sensation in his head, as though every cell in his brain were burning with a white hot brilliance, much like fireflies whose light had accelerated from yellow to white. As he collapsed into darkness, his last thoughts were still riveted on his pain, and…on the "bastard."

Mike Runnion leaned against the front wall of the shower stall, slowly moving his head sideways through the pulsating streams of hot water. He delighted in all forms of sensuality, much, much more so than most other men. His was a world of carefully calculated cruelty that masked itself with a handsome face, a good physique, fine clothing, and a profession that was admired by many, respected by most, and feared by all.

He had the knowledge and connections to help someone he might like to use, or to break; someone he instantly disliked, or feared. It all fit perfectly for him. He knew it, and reveled in it every waking hour of his life. Watching a client, or would-be client, or perhaps a 'friend,' try to placate and exalt him in order to gain his knowledgeable investment advice and direction, gave him the feeling of very real, worldly, sensate power. This was a power to create or destroy, and that was all he needed.

For an ever so fleeting moment, the thought flashed across the screen of his mind that in another setting, he might have been a serial killer, entering orgasmic states of pleasure as he held control of life or death over his victim. At least, that what the experts in criminology today now think of his type, he mused. But he quickly extinguished this fainting glimmer of conscience. Such social devices, meant to keep the average Joe and the weak in the social places the big boys predetermined for them, didn't apply to him. It couldn't. Yet, somewhere inside....

His yuppie lifestyle suited him to a tee, and his position at the Wall Street brokerage house even seemed to be enhanced by his trendy police record and divorce. "Sort of like paying dues to an exclusive club of heavy-hitters and world-shakers and makers" he thought, as the smile on his face turned into a sinister grin.

"Ah, well, you'll have such tidbits in life, Mike! Just another price you paid for not being one of the sheep. Besides, that silly bitch got what she deserved! Trying to make you the homey type, and dictate to you! Who the hell was *she* to tell *you* how to run your life, what time to come home, ask you to account for your time, and oh! your favorite of all, try to handle your money...to *buy a house in the suburbs*?! Away from the city and all the action?! Man, she's lucky she didn't get more of a thumping than you gave her!

"Silly bitch, Kate, she got what she deserved, and you're lucky you caught the situation in time! Yea, she was a good lay, but nothing you can't get anytime you want, and a hell of a lot less better than some of the recent ones…like Magda! Man, you did yourself a favor by getting rid of that whore!"

The thoughts ended on a sour note though, as somewhere within him, he knew he was a liar of the worst kind. One who lies to himself while degrading others in the process of self-justification.

"What's wrong with you! Dredging up thoughts over the bitch! Look at Magda! Man, that little slut gave you one hell of a ride tonight, and she'll do it over, and over, and over again, for the investment advice-bone you throw her every once in awhile! I *love* it! Wine her, get pumped up, dine her, get even more pumped up, screw her till she can't breathe right, and then dismiss her, just like you did tonight! As that commercial says, 'Boys, it doesn't get any better than this!'" The bastard's malignant grin widened until a laugh fell out of his mouth, one of those nervous, empty sounds that came from the throat, instead of the belly.

He stepped out of the shower with a spring in his step, temporarily bolstered by the night's events, and hummed "I Gotta Be Me" loudly as he toweled himself off. Putting on his Sach's *Knight's Armour* robe and *Boot* slippers, he tripped forward into the living room, trying to walk before the last one was firmly on his foot. His Central Park apartment was luxurious and well protected, as would be expected of any high rent district in any city. Protection was important to him, others protecting him, that is. The quiet of that twenty-third hour of the day reminded him of this, and how snug he was amid the horror and struggle for survival that was going on at that instant in nearly any alley or side street in the same city.

"Safe and secure in the life you want," he thought. "Let the asshole cops risk their lives guarding you! That's what the stupid sons-of-a-bitches deserve, a hand-to-mouth salary and the chance to play 'tough guy.' They can push the small fry around all they like. Use them like they'd use you, if they had the chance. Bunch of losers and slobs anyway, buutttt, they do give you what you need. No use losing your valuable life over daily shit. That's *thhheeeiiirrr* job! Besides, someday, and that someday will be *soon*, you'll have a Penthouse. Think of the security and protection you'll have then! Think of the money and power that will make a life of total control possible! If there's one thing you gotta do, it's watch your ass and get to the big time! Baby, you're gonna go all the way!"

As he entered the living room, his decorator furniture, and Persian rugs slung casually yet stylishly over the darkly-stained hardwood floors, made him feel at ease. They were symbols of his growing control over his own life, and over the lives of others. He reflected how the insider tracks he developed in the Market were paying off, with only more promise of paying even bigger dividends in a time just around the corner.

"Your portfolio is beyond impressive for a thirty-four year old broker. Maybe you're playing it close to the vest with your insider track, but it's worth it! Even if you get caught, a year at a country club pen will only magnify your reputation in this business, aaannnddd, you'll still have your loot boot! Remember: the only 'justice' is for them boys with the money; all the others get the *shaft* of justice, and nothing more. Remember that!" His mental pep-talk was unexpectedly interrupted by a 'ssssshhhhhh' sound that came from some point in front of him. His reactions became frozen. His emotions began searching furiously for an answer. They did not know whether to raise the panic alarm in him at the thought of an intruder somehow gaining entrance to his apartment, or if the sound was just a night noise he had not heard before. He finally turned to the multibolt dead lock on the front door. Even though the room's light dimmer was set for soft glow, he could see that the bolt knobs were still in their horizontal position, indicating the locks were still in place. And the two chain-latches still supported their heavy gauge links, insuring no trespasser made his way past their defenses. His emotional alarm calmed down immediately.

"Getting the jitters, uh? Afraid of losing what you got, uh? Mike, baby, you should know better than that! It ain't gonna happen. Not to you. You got it too much together!" As he turned to walk into the kitchen for a near-midnight snack, the 'ssssshhhhhh' returned.

Irritation, rather than fear, pulled his attention back to the wall from where the sound was coming. "What the…" he said loudly, as he looked at the couch. The sight of the expensive furnishing soothed him for a moment, and the exorbitantly priced copy of Van Gogh's *Irises* above it, calmed him almost immediately. "Rats, maybe?" he thought. "Rats?! **Rats**?! Up here?! On the fourteenth floor?! Give me a break! Probably something settling out in that damn wall. Place has got to be over a hundred years old. Yea, that's it, something settling, falling down behind the wall. What a wimp, Mikie, getting uptight over some shit like that, especially after the Magda-ride tonight! What-a-wimp!" Finally dismissing the sound, he turned back to the kitchen.

Two steps later, another 'ssssshhhhhh.' "Goddamn it!" he screamed, heading toward the couch now, being propelled by a blind fear/anger emotional mixture. "I'll settle this fu…" This time, one, two, and then three 'ssssshhhhhh's' emerged from behind the couch, each from a different position. The emerging power of Wall Street stopped short, his heart now beating in the center of his head.

Where the glow of the dim light failed into shadow, what looked to him to be the corner of some object, poked out from behind the right arm of the couch, making the 'ssssshhhhhh' sound as it did. It was a something with a soft, fuzzy reddish glare to it. It pulled back behind the couch arm, and then popped out a little further, each time making the sound that he was becoming used to.

Mike Runnion stood and stared at the thing, in an almost emotionless, thoughtless state. The situation was completely outside of his everyday experience. Being such, his mind and emotions struggled automatically and unconsciously to make something of this new event. It had to be labeled in order to be understood. Even the basic responses of fright, flight or fight were outside of his possibility, until the thing was identified.

Whatever it was changed, not its position, but its depth. The corner of the thing that stuck out from the behind the couch wavered, moving in and out a little, back and forth just a bit, but not giving an inch from where it stood. Shortly, he heard another 'ssssshhhhhh,' this one coming from directly behind the couch. After two more 'ssssshhhhhh's,' a yellow corner poked its edge up, wavering, moving in and out, just as its reddish companion did.

The bastard was now somewhere between fascination, fear, curiosity, and anger. None of these emotions, or combination of them, took hold of him long enough for him to be able to act. The two corners continued to pop in and out in a rhythmic motion, as though they were moving to some unheard tune. The bastard watched for what seemed to him to be several minutes, unable to move from his spot. The cadence of the objects' motions was then destroyed by a third 'ssssshhhhhh,' this one coming from behind the left arm of the couch. As with the other two, it finally thrust a single, wavering corner up into a different area where the edge of the dimmed room light ended in shadow.

This one was different. Its color was an indigo black, which made a contrast with the surrounding blackness of shadow in the room, thereby giving it visible form. Its faintly glowing darker black color against the flat blackness of the room's shadow gave it a surreal appearance, much like an afterimage. Within seconds, the three corners took up a new cadence, one popping up, another pulling back, with the third being somewhere in between these other two motions. Mikie's mind was now completely empty. He simply stared at the trio, unable to label them or the experience he was now in.

Finally, the trio slowly rose from their positions, and floated up into the air. The yellow one took up a position directly over the *Irises*, with the other two flanking it. He was now able to see them completely. Each retained its color and wavering in-and-out movement, but now, Mikie saw that each one was changing its shape as well, changing within their basic rectangle design, into different geometrical forms, while yet maintaining what appeared to him to be an overall size of about three feet long and two feet wide. They looked like hollow rectangles, holograms, projected harmlessly from some hidden point, producing a light show for his entertainment. A wave of bone-deep relief crested though him.

"What the hell…is this some kinda joke?! What is this?! Looks like those Windows *Mystique* screensaver images on my PC!" He spun around and walked quickly to the front door, determined to find out if someone had gotten in after all. "Maybe a couple of my Market buddies trying to punish me for my success on the Street and with the ladies! All right you bastards, where the hell are you?!" he yelled, now half out of relief, half out of anger.

When he got to the door, he found that it was as he thought earlier— fully secured from the inside. No one had gotten in. He turned from the door and walked back quickly into the living room, determined to find their hiding place. After searching the living room and closets, he searched the three other large rooms, the kitchen, and even the patio, while the 'screensavers' remained fixed in place, silently wavering, moving in and out. He returned to the living room, ranting and raving from the mental turmoil and frustration that overtook him. His rational world had collapsed again, not having found the trio's source.

"You sons-of-bitches! Whatever you are, you goddamn bastards, I'll fix you for good!" Having screamed at them, he picked up a coffeetable display book, "Your Life Is What You Make It," and hurled it as hard as he could at the reddish rectangle off the right flank of the couch. The book passed cleanly through it, and slammed hard against the plaster wall, marking the spot of impact with a large, well-defined dent.

Now, the 'screensavers' began to move, first upward, and then toward him, slowly, taking a zigzag course, growing larger in size as they finally came within six inches of him. Mikie was now motionless. Frustration and fear had now been replaced with a feeling that somehow passed by panic as it raced to overtake his senses. Instinctively, he swung his arms at the rectangles, like a hiker trying to rid himself of July gnats and mosquitoes.

He choked as he swung, some emotion suppressing a scream that caught in the center of his throat.

Suddenly, the three images stopped in mid-air, began to glow brighter, and to change form. Their harmless rectangle appearance dissolved in stages, to form the outlines of three faces, the features of which no human mind had ever seen before. Runnion's brain, now literally on the edge of a stroke, still tried to label what his eyes told him were in front of him. It told him that each face resembled an animated set of huge razor-like teeth, jutting out six inches from a recessed skull, whose flattened forehead harbored eyes the color of its original 'screensaver' host. A black dot in the center of each eyeball burned with a blacker fire, twirling, spinning, creating a vortex that led to some unimaginable Hell deep within the shape it now took.

As each living nightmare moved and rotated, different parts of its 'anatomy' revealed itself to Runnion's fast disintegrating mental faculties. Two arm-like extensions shot out from the sides of each skull, flames the color of each thing's original screensaver, horribly licking gaping black pools of what seemed to him to be rotting meat that made up each arm. Runnion's mental violence was further quickened by the former screensavers' now sagging facial masses that took on the images of sad clowns, trying to escape their own agony, while starting to claw at him. What was left of his mental control forced him to turn toward the door, and attempt to run. But it was too late.

One arm of black distortion latched onto his designer robe's belt, and spun him back around with a speed that dizzied him. Before he could refocus his gaze, the yellow teeth let out a screech that resembled the cry a cat makes when its tail get caught in a door, and clamped down into the calf of his left leg, sending blood spitting onto the Persian rug and down into his boot slippers.

A scream whose contents contained agony, despair, and a fear that only a torture victim could know, roared from the money broker's gaping mouth, but not before the indigo-black facial outline locked its one extension onto his left arm, and with one, smooth pull, ripped it out of its socket, and flung it against the *Irises*. As he fell backward, screaming and throwing his remaining arm about him, the reddish face swelled to double its original proportions, and rammed its one extension through his bowels and out the back of his body, while its fang-like teeth ripped open his pectoral muscles.

In what appeared to be a coordinated attack, the trio continued to gnaw, rip, slash, and bite, while Runnion, still alive, mind gone, clawed and crawled toward the front door, screaming for Security. As though suffering some insult from its victim's clinging to life, the reddish mass flung the bastard onto his back, peered down onto his face, and with one snap of its blazing red teeth, bit through the blood-soaked face of Kate's ex, cleanly removing it from the rest of his head. The apartment then fell silent.

The neighbors couldn't take any more. What they knew of the Mr. Michael Runnion, they didn't like. Their New Yorker reputation for spotting a phony was as good as it was cracked up to be. But this wild party was uncharacteristic of him. It gave them a chance to get the little son-of-a-bitch in trouble, and they went for it. Standing out in the hallway as the noise was raging in the big shot's apartment, Mr. Edzkiel and Ms. Cadey rousted the other tenants on the floor from their late night activities.

The hallway was soon filled with a dozen disgruntled, older and old residents, all buzzing and aiming to teach the big shot a lesson, maybe.

"Maybe," Ms. Cadey grinned, "maybe we could even get that snip out-'ta here? What do you tink, Mr. Edzkiel?"

"Yes, we shouuld! We are ressspectaable people with a ressspectaable paassst, not like him and hisss generaation kind, aren't we, Ms. Cadey?" replied the old man, shaking his head up and down while looking at the others assembled, vying for approval and mutual agreement.

"I'll call the police maan, Mr. Edzkiel," reported Mr. Burnstein. "We don't hav' ta put up with such aasss him and hisss godlesss ssscgnaniganss!"

In four minutes flat, two Blues emerged from the elevator, wondering what all the commotion in the hallway was about. "What's the problem here? A disturbance of some kind was reported. Sounds dead quiet to me! What's going on?"

"Ohhh, you saahouudd have heard it a few minutesss ago, Officer 7438" she quipped, looking at his badge number. "In there," pointing to Runnion's front door, "All sssorts of terr'ble noissse coming from it! You came too laate aasss…" she stopped short of finishing her sentence, "…as usual."

Badge 7438 looked hard at her and the others, then turned to his partner. "All right, Frank, let's check it out. You people just go back in your places. There's nothing for you to see out here now. You called us, let us do our job."

Mr. Burnstein objected. "Don't tell usss ta go into our plaacesss, Mr. Policeman! We paay youur saalaary and have aa right to know whaatsss going on in there on thisss floor where we live and youu know it. We are New Yaaukers all our lifesss, and we gottt…."

Badge 7438 cut him off. "Look. It's real simple. Either you vacate the scene, or I'll haul all of you in for obstructing an investigation. Makes no difference to me. Either we take in one goof, or a dozen. Now, what's it gonna be?!"

Grumbling, the residents made their way to their apartments, and slowly closed the doors, leaving them opened just a crack, to watch what the cops were going to do.

Badge 7438 and Frank made their way to apartment 1426, and pressed the door buzzer. No answer. After several tries, Frank used his nightstick, making several sharp, short thuds on the door's surface. No answer. The older 7438 tapped Frank on the shoulder, and said, "Look maybe this bozo's out cold. A phone call just might roust him. Give 'em a ring while I call this one in to the station."

Frank walked over to the first cracked door, got Runnion's name from the lurker behind it, and called in a "Phone up" request to the Night Duty Sergeant at the Station. As the phone on the other side of door

1426 continued to ring, it was becoming apparent to the two cops that something might be wrong. Their suspicion grew, not simply due to their unanswered attempts to attract the attention of the occupant in apartment 1426, but from their instincts, developed from years of investigating such matters.

"Fra..." Badge 7438 broke off, looking down at his shoe. Blood was slowly seeping off the edge of the carpet that bordered the front door, and into the hallway. "Let's break it down!" Frank hollered.

Pushing Frank back, the older cop slammed his right foot hard against the door, directly beneath the door plate. It flew open, cracking and bouncing off the apartment wall behind it. Both men walked in cautiously, their hands on their service revolvers, ready to withdraw them if necessary.

A dark maroon stain was seeping down the middle of the light tan, tight knit carpeting that covered the fifteen foot length of hallway. Both cops shined their flashlights to the end of the hallway, and saw that it opened into the living room area. They saw no body, except for a large dark spot about midway down the hall—the source of the growing stain. They drew their weapons, each one taking up a sliding motion along either wall of the hallway as they approached the dark spot.

When they got to the living room, neither one was aware at first of what they were seeing. Badge 7438 found the light dimmer on the edge of the living room wall nearest him, and turned it up to full. The first words out of his mouth were, "My God, what happened here!" They were his only words before he began to vomit violently, coughing and turning red-faced as he choked on some vomit that caught in his windpipe.

Frank looked at the room. Parts of the bastard were strewn everywhere: an arm here, a piece of flesh there, with other body parts and organs draping the wall furnishings and furniture. The entire room was bathed in a shining, shimmering wet black-red liquid, that made the off-tan color of the plaster walls appear to be made up of streaks. It was Mike Runnion's blood. A slow, drip-drip-drip attracted Frank's attention to the white dished ceiling lamp. As he leaned his head back and looked up at it, he saw the open part of the bastard's skull. His face lay directly below it, staring up at the cop, as though it were trying to convey the unimaginable horror it had passed through. Frank looked at it coldly, and passed out.

Chapter 4

▼

Dead Reckoning

It was 3:30 P.M. when Kate walked through the large glass front door of *Say It With Pictures*. Something she could not put her finger on was beginning to get a foothold on her mind and emotions. Marcy and Peg, her two employees, were filing papers and talking to each other at the same time.

"Any calls?" Kate asked, expecting them to tell her Lasky called. "No, Kate, none from Mr. Lasky," replied Marcy, in a catty tone of voice. Surprised, Kate passed the two girls silently, briefcase in one hand and purse in the other, and went into her small private office.

"What's up with her?" complained Marcy "Oh, no!" as though now talking out loud to herself and not to Peg, "What if she didn't land that big cannery job! Things are lean around here the way it is. I wouldn't want this job to fold like the last three I had!"

"Well," Peg replied, "If you ask me, that big shot from the cannery calling her early this morning and insisting and insisting she come out there instead of him coming here as he was supposed to, sounds like he's pulling her strings already! Those types want everything for nothing, just because they bring their business to a little hick town like this. Maybe it didn't go too well?! Now what? Maybe one of us should go in to see her and ask. Hell, we have every right to know what's what; our paychecks depend on it!" The two girls' anxiety over the thought of losing their jobs if Kate's new business went sour, coupled to their normal small town views toward companies coming to Sunnberry and trying to take over, was mounting.

"You go, Marcy. You're the calm one. You ask her what's what."

"Me?! You go, Peg! You're the one who's all hot over Kate's mood. You're the one who's getting me all nervous about losing our jobs!"

"I got you all upset?!" exclaimed Peg, "You're the one who started thinking out loud and complaining and got me all stressed out! Tell you what. Let's both of us go and ask her just what's what," Peg volunteered.

Both girls put their work aside, and walked over to Kate's closed office door. They saw that she was staring off into space, a look of concern or worry on her face. Marcy gave a short, shy knock, that brought Kate back to the present.

Kate motioned for the two girls to come in. As Marcy pushed the door opened, she whispered to Peg, "This is not such a good idea after all!"

"Is there a problem, girls?" Kate asked, as though she was just awakening from a dream.

"Well, Kate," started Marcy, "Peg and I were wondering how the new deal went with the cannery job. We didn't mean to bother you, but you looked so concerned over something, that, well, being this is a new business, and jobs are so scarce here in town, and with all of our family expenses and all, well..." Kate cut her off, recalling how she was in the same position not long ago.

"Actually, girls," Kate said, "It went over much better than I ever expected. When I showed Mr. Lamour some samples of our work, and explained to him just what we are capable of producing here, he was very impressed. I didn't tell you because I didn't want you two to worry, but I did some legwork quietly, and found out quite a bit about Red Line Industries, Inc. I found out that the parent company is diversifying, and has a merger in the works that will not include the cannery operations scattered over the country. So the cannery division is going solo. And while it will have a corporate headquarters, it is setting its house in order by having each separate cannery provide for its advertising and trucking needs locally.

"This means that since we are the only graphics business in town, Mr. Lamour, the branch manager, does not have the upper hand he would like us to think he does. When I found this out, I prepared some copy especially for his plant here, and showed it to him today during our meeting. When he tried to push for a shorter contract with lowed pricing for our work, I casually mentioned what I heard about *Redline*. The result, ladies, is that we have, not a one year contract, but a three year contract with them, at the price I originally quoted him for one year, multiplied by three. We got it!" exclaimed Kate, momentarily forgetting the object of her real concern.

"Then we don't have to worry?" replied Peg and Marcy, almost in unison.

"Not one little bit. That is, providing we do our work!" This was Kate's friendly way of reminding them they had their jobs to do.

"Thanks, Kate! I, uh, guess we had better get back to it," Peg said with a broad smile of relief. As the two women closed Kate's office door behind them, Marcy turned to Peg and whispered, "Told 'ya! Nothing to worry about! She's probably worried over that guy she's seeing. You know how it is."

Marcy's remark was correct. Kate **was** worried about Lasky. It was 3 P.M. and there was no call from him. This was unusual, she thought. It was his habit to call every Monday afternoon after their weekend together, as though worried that he might have said something wrong to her, and might lose her. Yet he never expressed such concern in those calls, but rather, an attitude that Kate thought, at times, was rather flippant. But there was something more in her concern. She had a bad feeling that something was not right, not only with Lasky, but with things that were somehow part of her world in a global sense.

She argued with herself that he was probably becoming more relaxed about their arrangement, and got involved in that special work of his early on in the day, and forgot to phone. He was famous for that, but not on Mondays. Her attempt to quell her mounting anxiety was shattered as her telephone rang. "It's Mier! Thank God, afterall!" she muttered to herself as she picked up the receiver.

"Hello, Ms. Murphy? This is Mr. Lamour. I just wanted to say how happy I am with our new business association, and to tell you…" His words trailed off in Kate's mind as her sense of relief evaporated. Bringing herself back to her current reality, Kate deftly and politely handled Lamour's call, and hung up as soon as she could.

"Leaving early after all of that good news today, Kate?" Peg teased, as Kate hurriedly left her office and headed for the front door.

"Sorry, ladies, I have to. Got something to do that just won't wait. I'll see you tomorrow."

Kate returned to her own thought-world of anxiety as she moved unconsciously toward her car at a rapid pace. As she opened the door and got in, she caught herself. "Dammit, girl, what's wrong with you! You could have phoned him! No, that's no good. He keeps that answering machine on twenty-four hours a day, and never hears it when he's in his lab. At least that's his excuse. I'll bet he can't hear the damn thing! Sometimes I wish he'd lighten up a bit on his feelings about people in general. Always avoiding them until **he** is ready to talk to them. Goddammit, Lasky, you're infuriating sometimes!"

In minutes she was out of Sunnberry and on the road to Lasky's house. It was another beautiful early spring day. The lowering sun in the west and the still crisp temperature outside, gave the new green foliage along the roadside a mild frost-like coating that shimmered, producing tiny spectrums of color as she drove past it. Switching between her admiration of the spectral colors that shot from every direction and her growing apprehension over the situation, she became aware of how her nervousness caused the original twinkling colors to deaden somehow. Instead of bright and shimmering, they had lost their luster, as though now only mimicking their natural radiance.

"Damn him anyway! This time I'm going to be the forceful one! I think we have to sit down and have a serious talk about just where this relationship is going! Being casual is one thing, being ignorant and not keeping your own ritual of a Monday phone call is another! Especially after the weekend! Mier Lasky, if I'm good enough to help you think out your weird problems, I'd better be good enough to be considered also!" she yelled, as though in a face-to-face confrontation with him.

"I try my best to understand that man, but I need some understanding and consideration too! I'm beginning to think that if I don't put my foot down on some of these simple matters with him, our relationship will go to hell in a handbasket. Enough is enough!" Without realizing it, Kate had pressed her foot down harder on the gas petal and was hitting seventy-five miles an hour—a speed equal to her now raging temper.

Barely aware of the road and her passing surroundings, the forty-five minute drive to Lasky's house disappeared in a forgotten limbo of time. Suddenly, Kate became aware that his house was coming up quickly on her left. She hit the brake hard, slowing down her speeding auto until it broke into a series of jerking movements, and then evened out. Instead of her sense of apprehension breaking off as it did in other similar situations with Lasky, this time it shot through the roof of her emotional world, as though she was feeling something intuitively. Her heart began to beat faster and harder as she dropped her speed to ten mph, and began the entry from the road into the long driveway. Somewhere between her crests of anxiety and her now mounting anger, she expected to see Lasky emerge from the front door in defensive fashion to see who had entered his property. As she slowly and now cautiously neared the end of the driveway and approached the parking area, her anger disappeared. Only her anxiety remained, hitting a new high. Lasky was nowhere to be seen.

After she turned the car engine off, she blew the horn several times. "If he's still in bed, he'll go crazy. He's supposed to be working, not lollygagging around! 'No one comes here without an invitation!' he proudly told me long ago. So he deserves a little of the upset he caused me! And if he saw me coming and is playing one of his now-and-then childish games, well, we'll see who laughs last!" Her self-dialogue became more confused as her worry thickened. She blew the horn several more times, each shrill report lasting for ten seconds. There was still no sign of him.

Leaving her car, she peered into the garage window. Lasky's car was still there. There were no sounds coming from inside the house; no heavy footsteps to answer the banging she was making by hitting the garage door hard with her clenched fist. Kate felt an abrupt snap in her head. She realized that something was dreadfully wrong. All anxiety and anger immediately shut down within her, as though they were emotional luxuries for scares that have no substance. A calm of desperation immediately overtook her mind. Without calling out, in one smooth series of motions, she moved toward the front door of the house and took out her keys. Slipping the key into the lock, she gave a hard turn, and slowly pushed the door wide-opened.

As she stepped in cautiously, all of her senses were on red alert. She seemed to be perceiving with more than the five senses, as she took a firm foothold onto the landing midway between the first and second floors of the house. Nothing. No sound. No movement. As she started up the stairs to the first floor, she noticed that the front drapes of the large bay window were opened, as was the curtain of the glass doors leading to the back yard patio. "He was up at least long enough to open the curtains," she whispered to herself. "Maybe he went back to bed?"

Her heart was pounding so hard and rapidly now, that she started to gasp for breath. Reaching the top of the stairs, she called out in a subdued voice, "Mier? Mier, are you here?" No answer. Panic broke into her mind once more as she raced down the hallway and threw the master bedroom door open, only to find the bed empty, and no sign of Lasky. Her next thought of calling the police was short-lived, knowing that Lasky would consider this the worst breach of confidence he had in her. Now fighting to regain her desperate calmness, she checked the remaining rooms on the first floor. Moving back to the top of the stairway between the first and second levels, she caught the odor of something burning. "Oh my God!" she screamed, as she descended the steps to the lower laboratory level of the house in pole vault fashion.

Missing the last two steps, Kate lost her balance and slammed hard into the wall, seven feet across from the steps, and slid down to the floor, dazed. As she started to come to her senses again, she saw the laboratory door slightly ajar. A diffused white cloud was hovering near the floor, seeping slowly out of the laboratory. Having fully regained her awareness, she sprang to her feet screaming, "Mier! Are you all right!" as she pushed the heavy laboratory door aside, and looked inside. There on the floor, amid ebbing columns of white smoke, sputtering tesla coils and arcing transformers, she saw Lasky. He was lying on his back, motionless, his large chair knocked over from his fall, lying across his waist.

Kate ran into the room, continuing to scream his name. But there was no movement from him. As she made her way through the nightmarish scene, a stray, hot spark from the transformer nearest her burned its way through the stocking at her ankle, and scorched her flesh badly. But she took no notice of it as she lunged downward. With a burst of strength, she flung the chair from his waist, and grabbed him by the lapels of his lab coat. He was dead weight, heavy and rigid. Sobbing and choking from the smoke fumes, she dragged his body slowly to the laboratory door, repeating to herself, "Why, Mier? Why?" She was certain he was dead, but continued to drag his body out into the hallway, not knowing or caring what she was doing.

When Kate reached the short hallway outside the laboratory, she started to think clearly again. The calm desperation returned. Fumes were venting from the fully opened laboratory door now, and the formerly dispersed clouds of smoke were increasing in thickness in that small area. Remembering the access door to the garage off of the short hallway, she dropped Lasky's body to the floor and pulled the door wide opened.

Grabbing his lapels again, she struggled to pull his dead weight into the large open air garage, and laid him down gently by the rolling doors. With blinding speed she hit the electric control, and the automatic garage door rolled upward toward the ceiling, flooding the garage with fresh, crisp spring air.

In a moment she was on top of him, pumping his chest upward with stiffened arms and hands, trying to coax the smoke out of his lungs. He did not respond. She jumped from her sitting position and knelt beside him, giving him mouth-to-mouth resuscitation. Suddenly, he coughed hard, right into her open mouth. She then resumed her mounting position on top of his waist, and began to massage his chest once more. As she did, he began to cough violently, and gasp for breath. Lasky's dead-white color disappeared in a burst of bright red, his face becoming flushed with blood from the violent coughing. Fierce body spasms began, and coupled with the coughing and gasping, Lasky began to feel the presence of his own body once more.

Without realizing it, he pushed Kate backwards, knocking her off his waist. As she fell, he rolled around on to his stomach, and began to drag himself into the driveway. He began to gag and vomit as his head hit the full flush of onrushing fresh air. Kate sat on the concrete garage floor watching this, crying and sobbing. The conflicting emotions of relief at seeing him alive, coupled with a mounting rage over him nearly killed himself and of what he put her through, were too much for her all at one time. Her vision started to spin, and the last thing she remembered was the thought in her head, "Why, Mier? Why?" before she passed out.

She woke two hours later. The sun was setting, and the crisp spring air was now cold. A slight wind had started which made it feel like every bit of twenty degrees. Every bone in her body ached. She wondered what she was doing lying on a hard concrete floor. Within seconds, her memory returned, and she called out, "Mier!" As she looked around, she saw he was no longer sprawled out on the driveway where he had been. He had managed to pull himself toward the edge of the drive, where he had collapsed again, face down. She felt the wobbliness in her legs as she ran toward him with a jerking stride. When she got to him, she rolled him over, and saw that his normal color had returned. As though in a sound sleep, his breathing was slow and shallow.

This time her strength skyrocketed. Without thinking if it were possible to lift his full dead weight, she picked him up like a rag doll, and carried him back into the garage and up the stairs to the first floor, where she laid him on the couch in the living room. After she pulled his lab coat off, she propped his head up on two pillows, and covered him with a large, warm afghan, and began to rub his legs, then his arms, his chest, and finally, his face. Lasky began to groan, and move. Kate's conflicting emotions of a few hours ago resolved themselves into a flowing feeling of deep caring.

She looked at him with tears in her eyes, as a constellation of thoughts coursed through her mind in a split second. Their first meeting, the development of their relationship, his gradual confiding in her, her justified caution in romantic affairs, images of the bastard, her new business, how the money to start it came so easily, their weekends together, the intensity of the last one, her reactions of anger, worry, anxiety, rage at him not calling her today—all coalesced in that fragment of time the mind allows, to bring her to a final realization. She admitted to herself in between the tick of a clock, that the impossible had happened. She had fallen in love again, completely and hopelessly, with a very, very strange and difficult man.

To make matters even stranger, Lasky awoke briefly. He saw her sitting on the couch beside him, her head down, crying softly. He reached over and gently took hold of her right hand. Startled, she looked up at him, swallowing hard at the surprise of his touch. "Kate, don't ever leave me. I love you more than I ever let on. I mean it Kate. *I could never live without you.* And just now, I finally know it." Having said that, his hand slid off of hers, as he suddenly fell into a deep sleep.

She looked at him, stunned. What happened? This was not like him. As of a few moments ago, she had resolved somewhere between that same tick of the clock, that her love for him would have to become even more tolerant of his offish ways, and his inability to express his feelings for her. Now, even her anticipated need for understanding and tolerance was shattered with his telling her what she longed to hear. Staring off into space, she realized she should be happier at that moment than she had ever been before. Yet somehow, she was unsettled. Something was not right. She could feel that the reality of his expression of love for her of a few seconds ago, was a clashing contradiction with the essential man she knew him to be. A marked sense of disquiet and caution began to stir within her. She wondered if the event he passed through down in that room had done more damage than her eye could see. Pulling a chair across the room she positioned herself in it, and determined to spend the night watching over him.

The rising sun brought with it another fresh, clean spring day. The golden rays penetrated through the large bay window curtain that remain unclosed from the night before, filling the living room with a soft glow. A healthy and life giving warmth bathed the surroundings, and seemed to confer a silent peace on the two sleeping figures. Then, the peace of the setting was broken abruptly by the sound of Lasky thrashing around on the couch, his arms flailing this way and that. Kate opened her eyes, wondering if she had slept at all. It had been an uneasy night for her, spent in a pale sleep of fading nightmarish dream fragments. Moving from her chair to Lasky's side, she examined him carefully. He looked as though he were in a sound sleep, and nothing more. "Maybe it'll be all right," she said to herself. "Maybe all my fears and feelings of last night were part of the stress of yesterday. God, I hope so!" She then walked into the kitchen quietly, and looked at the wall clock. "8:15. Marcy and Peg will think I forgot about them," she mused, as she called her office.

"Hello. Marcy? Yea, hi. Listen. I'm all caught up in something, and won't be able to make it in today. Maybe not tomorrow, either. I don't know yet. No, there's nothing you or Peg can do to help. It's just one of those personal things, you know. Yes, it happens to all of us, I know, I know. Look. If Lamour calls, tell him I've been called away for a day or two, and that I'll catch up with him later in the week. Yea, that's right. His assistant, a 'Mr. Todd Glaser,' is supposed to start working with me next Monday, so there's still plenty of time for me to take care of these personal matters this week. Yea. Right.

"You and Peg know what to do to get the other two jobs done for the silk mill that are due next week, so you really don't need me hanging around all that much. Just go on with your work. A number you can reach me at? Uh, no, I'll be on the run. Wait a minute! Yes. Call me on my cell phone if you need me. Right. You can always get me that way. I'll be sure to carry it with me. Thanks, Marcy. I'll see you and Peg, if not tomorrow, then most probably Thursday. Take care."

After hanging up, Kate went down to her car, removed her cell phone, and brought it into the house. "Better to be safe than sorry," she reminded herself. "If they call, at least I'll be available while things get sorted out here." She determined to busy herself with cleaning up from the weekend, as Lasky had let everything go. The sink was full of dishes, empty cartons that were headed for the trash never made it there, the bed was still unmade, and a host of daily abandoned chores that Lasky never seemed to get around to, stood as silent reminders of his generally bad housekeeping practices. "He either needs a maid or a wife or both," she laughed, and started to giggle. It was only then that she felt the tension flow out of her, and a sense of relief began to fill her with a new warmth of hope.

It was 11:45 in the morning. Kate was finishing up with the household cleaning. As she stood by the kitchen sink finishing the dishes, she was humming softly to herself as she stared out the kitchen window onto the rolling, flat green lawn, that after a distance sloped up gently, only to suddenly cascade upward sharply and end in further terrain she could not see. A shadow fell across her right shoulder from a point somewhere behind her. The simple pleasure and quiet the outdoor scene gave her ended abruptly, as her mind tried to assemble an idea of what caused the change in lighting. She spun around to confront whatever it was.

There, standing in the kitchen doorway, was Lasky, a big smile on his face, clothes in complete disarray, with his hair standing on end. Not knowing whether to be relieved or frightened, she found herself laughing. "My God, you look like you just stuck your finger into an electric socket," she said, referring to the his hair. The remark went right past him, but she realized that her casual joking remark had been in poor taste, especially owing to the chain of events that led both of them to this point in time. She simply stood there and smiled at him, for what seemed to her like hours.

"What's for lunch?" Lasky asked, looking at her with a dazed stare, as though she were an object far away that he was trying to identify. Kate could not believe her ears.

"What's for lunch?! Are you crazy?! I mean, are you all right? Look at you! You look like something the cat dragged in, and all you can think of is food?!" The relief and happiness in her voice conveyed itself to him in such a way, that even in his weakened condition he understood the playful sense of her remarks. Reaching forward, Kate grabbed him by his left arm and put it over her shoulder. Unknowingly, Lasky had begun to slide down the door frame to the floor. "Here! Let me help you over to the table. You're still weak from the shock you had. Can you breathe all right? Are you going to lose your balance? You're not going to pass out on me again, are you?" A flood of questions, all of which she sensed the answer to in advance.

"I can breathe fine. Just hurts a little in my chest if I try to breathe deeply. Must still be carbon deposits in my lungs from all of that smoke."

"You knew the equipment caught fire?" Kate asked.

"Sure. After the jolt of current hit me in the head, I went down hard. I remember my chair falling behind me, and then somehow winding up on top of me. The smoke was coming out of the coils and transformers everywhere. Then I blacked out. But don't worry. I'm not going to pass out on you again. I remember the garage episode too, all too clearly, and know what I was feeling then. I can tell you, I feel a hell of a lot better now. Just weak. I guess I need some food."

Kate fixed him a light lunch of toast, scrambled eggs, apple juice and coffee. Lasky's appetite gave her a deep sense of relief, as she saw him consume four eggs, as many pieces of toast, two glasses of juice, and three cups of black coffee. "Well, if you can eat like that, you must be getting better!" she quipped, laughing easily as she teased him.

"I do," said Lasky. "I'm feeling much better…physically."

Kate caught the qualified remark. "What do you mean, 'physically'? Is there some other way you don't feel quite right yet?"

"Not sure," Lasky said, staring at a point above and behind her head.

"Mier, are you okay?" Kate asked him again for reassurance, as she squeezed his left hand gently.

" I guess so. It must still be the effect of that electrical shock. I read where a high-powered surge like that passing through a person's body, even momentarily, can make that person 'odd' in the head for days afterwards. If I remember correctly, it had to do with some actual physical brain changes that the electric current induced into the brain. The brain responds by producing an excess of different kinds of chemicals—neurotransmitters—that foul up the electrical pathways in the entire brain mass for awhile. After a few days, you return to normal, no worse for wear.

"In a few cases, the people who survived such accidents reported an increase in different types of mental functions, like abstract thinking ability or memory, and the like. So maybe that's what I'm feeling. All these brain and chemical changes the current produced. The trick, according to that paper I read, was to survive the initial shock. After that, the rest is pure gravy."

Kate's previous concerns were eased by his memory recall and speech pattern. She now felt certain that he did not sustain any serious permanent damage, and told him so. He too felt relieved at hearing this, since for him, he lived in his mind. Long ago he determined that if the organ for that mind was damaged in some irreparable way, he would put an end to it all. One of his greatest fears was becoming a "mental vegetable." He would have none of that. He explained this to Kate, as they sat quietly at the kitchen table, trying to bring themselves back to the normality of mundane, daily life.

Chapter 5

▼

The Portends of Things to Come

It was 2 P.M. before they finished their conversation at the kitchen table, a conclusion to a normally morning ritual marked by a growing silence between them, typical in so many married households.

"I'll clean up, Mier. You just go and sit down and try to relax a little. You may feel like you're one hundred percent, but I don't think you are yet."

"No, I'll help. Here. Let me wash the dishes. You dry."

"No, now listen to me. Go and sit down! See if that remaining few percent of you can come back."

"What do you mean, 'I'm not one hundred percent yet?' I feel fine."

"Did you hear yourself? Your usual response to something like that is 'I feel great.' Now it's 'I feel fine.' See? Even you know you're not fully recovered yet. Put that ego of yours away for today, and just do what I say, okay? I'm trying to help you get back on those big clodhoppers of yours, so you can get to retiring seriously, and I can get back to my work! After all, I did land that big cannery job as I just told you at breakfast, and right now, Marcy and Peg are trying to hold the fort down by themselves."

Lasky knew she was right. "Well, all right. I always think that if I 'act as if,' as the old saying goes, then I 'will become' as I act. Guess it's not working too well today. You know, Kate, actually, I do feel kind of tired."

"Then go and take a nap. It will do you good."

"No, it's not a physical tiredness. It's a slightly off-center type of feeling. Like I'm not aligned right inside somehow, and I'm losing energy from inside."

Kate passed it off jokingly. "Losing energy?! After a breakfast like that?! Get serious!" She closed her light-hearted remark with a smile. She felt herself beginning to relax completely inside, now. Her sense of self-assurance that disaster was averted was growing.

One of Kate's comments took hold. Lasky started to worry. "Kate, what am I going to do now? Everything is gone. Destroyed. I'm lucky the house didn't burn down too. Project T.A.A.C. is over. It's over…Unless…." There was a deafening silence between them. Kate felt an upsurge of fear and panic inside at his last remark and the emotional forces that nearly tore her apart that day converged into something she didn't know was inside her. In a frenzy, not realizing or caring what she was saying she turned to Lasky, grabbed him by his right arm, spun him around to face her, and screamed at him. Her normal composure had evaporated in a mist of complete uncaring.

"Unless? Unless what? Unless you go back to carrying out that idea and rebuild the lab? Now look, Mier, you put yourself through hell. You almost died, and would have, if it wasn't for my feminine intuition getting me out here. I saved you. A-Bomb is dead! That little animal never had a chance to live even a little life, and now it's gone. Gone because of your idea, and your carelessness. Gone because you are so continually wrapped up in yourself and your insane ideas, that you don't have one iota of concern for anyone, even a little animal that was trying to be your friend and companion. And your total oblivion of others and their lives and feelings included me, too, Mier!

"Do you know what I felt when I didn't hear from you today as usual? Do you know what I was feeling when I was racing out here to see what happened? Do you know how I found you, almost dead, in a scene that resembled something out of a Frankenstein movie? No, you don't! All you care about and can focus on is your own needs, your own craziness! We had better get something straight right now. I decided on the way up here I was going to confront you with this, but I didn't know how, or exactly when. But by God, I do now. I was going to wait until later in the week, after you fully recovered. But I can see that it can't wait.

"Mier, we are headed to something together. I am in love with you. I finally admitted it to myself today, in the midst of the hell on earth that I was going through trying to save your life. You told me, down in the garage when I dragged you out there from the lab, 'Kate, don't ever leave me. I love you more than I ever let on. I mean it Kate. *I could never live without you.*' Do you remember that, or was it a reaction from the shock? Look. I'm not pushing you. I never want you to feel I trapped you into anything. I'm not one of those types who does such a thing. But I need direction. **We** need direction, if what we have isn't going to die. And the part of **us** getting that direction is **you** starting to grow up a little, and open up to others who care for you and love you. And that means to me. To do that, you're going to have to take the time and make the effort to think of me and others besides yourself. You're going to have to consciously force yourself to realize—every day—that **you** are not the **only** one in **your** world.

"I'm not giving you an ultimatum. I'm making a statement. I resolved something only now. It must have all come together from the day's events, and from your uttering that sickening word, unless. So here it is. I won't hurt anymore. I mean I won't hurt for years again anymore. I've been through that with 'the bastard' as you call him. I'd rather hurt now for awhile by leaving our relationship, than get caught up in another long term hurt, which is still a hurt, but in a different way. In a way that has no room for me except when it's convenient for you, and which has me sitting on the sidelines in the meantime. I'm not like other women who use a man this way and that, and want to be fawned over twenty-four hours a day. And you damn well know that, Mier! But I am a human being, and I **need** to be **needed**, twenty-four hours a day. As a woman, I want to be appreciated now and then, and, yes, Mier, once in a while, when I feel like it, not just when you feel like it, I want to be fawned over. So what's it going to be? A life together eventually? I'm not pushing you for marriage now as I said, we have time to consider that given both of our pasts. Or a tiny man, with an even tinier mind, who has no room for anyone or anything, aside from his own greedy, self-serving ends? What's it going to be, Mier? And I want an answer, NOW!"

Kate could not believe what she had just done. A cold grim stare came over her face. It was not a physical punctuation to her demand for an answer. It was as though she was staring at herself in a mirror, and seeing the woman in that mirror as an evil twin. It wasn't supposed to happen this way. The talk with him about their relationship was supposed to be casual, seemingly impromptu, when both were relaxed, and Lasky was in a receptive frame of mind. With the speed of light all of these thoughts flashed through her mind. They spiraled down into a remembrance that some remarks cut deeply, and are never forgotten by the injured party. They last forever, and color at least the fringes of an otherwise good relationship. Combined with her knowing Lasky's ego as well as she did, for one frozen moment she held her breath, not knowing what he was going to do.

Mier Lasky stood still, leaning against the kitchen counter next to her. He was dazed. He heard every word she threw at him with such blinding speed, but did not reply. Instead, he just looked at her as though she was not there, and he was in some waking daydream state, paralyzed by an image he did not understand. Without saying a word, he turned from her, and walked out of the kitchen into the living room. Kate stood still, looking at the position of empty air he had just occupied, as though he were still standing in front of her, listening to her demand. She heard him walking almost clubfooted down the stairs. He was going down into his laboratory.

All of the energy left Kate's body. She fell against the kitchen counter, and slumped down a bit, assuming that no answer was an answer. By his leaving and returning to his lab, his actions told her he had made his decision. He was returning to his work. What she did no longer mattered to him. "It's all over, Kate," she whispered to herself. "Pick up your things and go." In an emotionally drained and physically weakened state, she collected her coat and cell phone, and walked down the first flight of stairs to the landing that separated the two floors of the house. She took the key to Lasky's house off of her keychain, and laid it gently on the carpet of the first floor directly above her head. Tears began to flow down her cheeks as she turned the front door knob. She knew that when she left it would be for good, and that she would never again be able to fall in love with anyone. Her emptiness inside was so vast, she could no longer feel pain, or relief, or anything. As she pulled the door open and started to walk out, she heard a voice.

"Kate! Kate! Would you come down here, please?"

She didn't know what to think. What was happening? Knowing him as she did, the conclusion she just reached upstairs had to be right. Lasky could never pass off such an insult, not after telling her only yesterday "I love you more than I ever let on. I mean it Kate. *I could never live without you.*" She had turned his feelings for her upside down at the very least, she thought, and the voice she just heard must have been from her own imagination, toying with the remains of her emotional wreckage. But the voice broke out again, piercing her introverted self-dialogue.

"Kate! Would you please come down here a minute?"

For a split second Kate knew she was standing between a life she *thought* she wanted, and one she already *had*. The first was filled with uncertainties and a man whose life and ideas she had made a mockery of only a few short minutes ago. The latter was a quiet life on her own, in her own business, with no emotional attachments. She was her own boss.

There was no need for understanding Lasky or anyone else beyond common courtesy. No need to have her mind divided twenty-four hours a day by those passing thoughts, wondering about him. No need to spend her weekends set to a fixed schedule with him. No need for anyone or anything but *Kate*. Between the last exhalation of the breath of his last call to her, and the first inhalation of his next breath, all these considerations pulsed through her mind. She made her decision in that same instant, and began to move, purposely, willfully, to what she knew in her heart she really wanted.

Lasky, standing in the center of the laboratory, turned around, and saw Kate standing in the outer hallway. "Well?! Aren't you going to come in?!"

Kate was numb all over, from body to soul. "You still want me after what I said to you upstairs?"

"What do you mean, do I still want you?! Are you kidding? I may have been out of it quite a bit yesterday and for a good part of today, young lady, but what I said goes, and always will. Kate, don't ever leave me. I love you more than I ever let on. I mean it Kate. *I could never live without you.* There, I've said it again. So, is that good enough?"

"But, I mean, what about what I said to you upstairs?"

"I had it coming, Kate, and I've known it for quite some time. In fact, in odd moments the thought of an inevitable confrontation with you would skate through my mind. But the ice was always too thin, and it would disappear somewhere inside of me. Now though, after the accident of yesterday, something has changed in me. I don't know what it is, but I feel more mellow. Not excessively compassionate or understanding or any such liberal nonsense, but somehow, just able to put things in a better perspective."

"But you were always able to do that, at least with little things that didn't upset you too much," Kate reminded him. "What about the bombshell I dropped on you a few minutes ago? Do you realize I pulled your ego rug right out from under you? I stopped short of calling you a wimp, and really bad-mouthed you and the work you've lived for all of these years.

What about that? Don't you realize what I said up there? Hasn't it hit home yet?"

Lasky looked hard at her and said, "Listen, girl, it hit me right between the eyes like a round from an elephant gun. And yes, I went down inside, just like you think I did. I understood every word of what you said. But it's like I just told you. Maybe that paper I read years ago was right. Maybe such violent electrical shocks change the brain configuration a little, and in my case, instead of affecting my memory or abstract thinking ability, it hit the emotional seat of my brain, and balanced it a little. But whatever it did, I feel that now I am what I always was inside, but just couldn't get out. It's as though the 'thing' inside my mind that's been preventing me all of my life from being more aware of others and their needs, has left me. See, I couldn't get that concern for others out! Whatever it was in me, kept refocusing me back to my concerns—my life, my this, my that—and always I knew better. It's as though this thing inside wanted me to *purposely* hurt others. But it's gone, and for God's sake, I hope that paper is right, and I remain like this!"

Kate dropped her coat and cell phone to the floor, and ran into the lab, flinging herself into Lasky's arms. She began to cry, but the tears were of joy and utter relief. "Oh, Mier! God, how I wanted to help you get to this point! I knew you had this in you all along. But despite what I said upstairs a few minutes ago, I was also prepared to accept whatever you were, and never planned on changing you if you couldn't or wouldn't want to change yourself. It had to be from you, and all I wanted to do was to help, if you wanted it. I love you, Mier, and I want to spend the rest of my life with you, whether we marry or not. I don't care anymore, Mier, I love you, and I want to be with you!"

Lasky held her tightly, reflecting in her warmth the harsh, cold attitude he had lived all of his life. The expression on his face had a melancholic draw to it, an irony that arose as the intensity of his past life had collided head on with each other at that present moment in time. He held onto Kate as tightly as he could for several minutes. As the feeling waned, he gently broke his grip on her, and looked around. Kate stood by his side quietly, as they both took stock of what was left of the laboratory.

Everywhere the mahogany paneled walls were pockmarked with tiny bits of shrapnel. The white drop ceiling was smoked over from the flames that began at the west wall where his apparatus was housed, while curling patterns of gray and black smoke stains covered the remainder of the ceiling in patchwork fashion. Only the fluorescent lighting in the center of the room and the east end still worked. Those that had provided the glareless light for the drama that ran from the center of the lab to the west wall, hung by frayed, burned wires, forming a twisted row of obstacles leading to his workbench, like soldiers in revolt that had broken their orderly formation.

The computers in the south, west, and north were shattered, their screens broken outwards, their sides pitted. The one on the bench at the east wall was the lone survivor, silently displaying the ever changing geometrical patterns of its Mystique screen saver. The wallrack tray cases of electronic components in the east were still intact. The blackboard on the south wall was beyond repair, its slate-like surface having been smashed through by a large chunk of metal that pierced it completely, and embedded itself into the wall beyond. The three shelf bookrack over the other half of the bench in the south had collapsed, scattering the books it housed. All of the test, measurement, and signal equipment on the bench in the north was ruined, with fire and smoke stains covering their surfaces, while holes from piercing shrapnel ended their usefulness.

The west wall—the place where Lasky had dared to play God—now seemed to him to be an entrance into the hellmouth itself, with the two charred, frayed tesla coils forming the columns of entrance into that region of darkness. All seemed to be completely destroyed: the capacitor banks, power cables, the two power transformers, frequency counters, signal generators, and the center of hell itself, the 'Thought Chamber.' Pyrex glass from the dynamited force had splintered it into thousands of jagged projectiles that were embedded in the walls, benches, electronic and electrical equipment, even into the books strewn here and there by the collapsed book rack. The heat and flames that erupted from the transformers, and the tesla coils arcing over to destruction, had burned the mahogany qualities of the paneling in that quarter beyond recognition. The workbench itself was a charred cinder of a form, somehow managing to maintain its upright stance. The tiny body of A-Bomb laid rigid against the side of the bench against the south wall. Its small form was burned beyond any recognition that it had once been a kitten. If they didn't know it was his pet, Kate and Lasky would have thought it a charred black rag.

The silence between Lasky and Kate was so deafening, neither could hear the breathing of the other if they had tried. Lasky's shoulders slumped forward, and his head dropped. Unconsciously, he was paying an act of final respect to what had been his way of life throughout all the years. Finally, in his characteristic verbal self-dialogue, his voice ripped through the empty silence of that dead room..

"It's all over. I can't believe it. It's all over. All those years. All that planning, learning, struggling, living like a hermit, scraping to get by while saving for T.A.A.C., building the equipment, fine tuning it, the loneliness,…it's all gone." Then he whispered, as though for Kate to hear it, "I'm so glad."

The odor of burned electrical equipment combined with the sharp smell of burning wood hung heavy in the air of the former laboratory. It began to irritate their eyes and noses. With a gentle tug, Kate moved him to the door, and without saying a word, began to lead him up the stairs, pausing only long enough in the hallway to pick up her purse and cell phone and sling them over her shoulder. As she did, she felt Lasky's body weaken somehow, as though a great current of energy had been drained from him in between the blink of an eye. Kate put this down to the stark realization that had just revealed itself to him when he faced the physical carnage in the laboratory. She gripped him about his waist, and helped him up the stairs.

Chapter 6

▼

The Reckoning

"Are you feeling better?" Kate asked, looking at Lasky who was now seated in his large Lazy Boy swivel recliner in the spacious living room.

"Yes, just a bit drained. I guess it was a real shock seeing all that damage up close for the first time. Know what I mean?"

"Of course I do," Kate replied. "Something like that is bound to have a hard impact on a person. Believe me, Mier, I understand. It's not as if your work was a hobby or a passing fad. It's what you devoted your entire life to. I'm only glad that I was here when you faced it's final outcome. I know how hard it can be to face broken dreams, honey. I had to face my own too. Everybody does. It's just that some are more devastating than others, I suppose." Her thoughts drifted back to the high hopes she had had for the bastard and herself. In a half-thought, she wondered how he was doing these days, but immediately dismissed the mental flight, realizing she didn't want to know.

They sat for a while and just talked a slightly strained talk—the type people use when filling in voids of time between pain, trying to nurse themselves back to a familiar reality. The afternoon sun was warm and comfortable, and its rays streaming through the large bay window in the living room began to relax both of them. Their conversation began to take on more meaningful tones, with the memories and feelings of the past day starting to slip from the corners of their minds. Gradually their discussion deepened and was eventually rounded by laughter, when suddenly, both of them heard what seemed to be a distant bell breaking in on their recently gathered sanity.

"That's my cell phone," Kate volunteered. "I'll get it. Probably the girls with another make-believe crisis. I swear, those two are the nosiest people I ever met. Anything to get a handle on where I am and what's going on," she objected, but with a slight smile breaking out at the corners of her mouth.

"Hello. This is Kate Murphy," she announced to the caller. Expecting to hear either Marge's or Peg's voice, she was stunned and taken off guard when the caller broke in with the strained, light-hearted greeting.

"Hello, Kate! This is Ronald Lamour! Why, I called your office but your employees told me you were out, and that they didn't know when you would return. They even said it might be a couple of days, and well, I'm not the kind to wait, so I pried your cell phone number out of them, and here I am!" Kate did not like the overly familiar ring in his voice. It wasn't only what he said, but the inflection in the way he said it, that stiffened Kate's back. She did not say another word, remembering the old business adage, "The first one forced to say something in a tense moment is the one who loses," and acted on it. Lamour's hand was forced by the lingering silence from Kate's end.

"Well, I guess you're wondering why I called like this, seeing we only summed everything up yesterday. First off, Kate, I can't say how happy I am that we will be working together, and that my company will be supplying you exclusively with our advertising business. I know that business in a small town like Sunnberry can be tough, especially for a new and struggling young company, and I have found that the best way for a young firm to really make headway is for the chief people involved in each company to see each other on a, oh, casual basis you might say, you know, besides the nitty-gritty work they have to do together during normal business hours.

"Coming from the big city as I have, and having been in the business-game a lot longer than you, I found out from experience that these little get-togethers are the guarantees that the young company needs to insure its future—not only with the business they already landed, but with the recommendations that those businesses make to other locals, and even to other companies thinking of coming into the area. So what do you say? I'm a stranger here, and would certainly appreciate it if we could get together tonight at, oh, say, 8 P.M.? You could shown me around a bit, we could have a few drinks, talk a little about starting my advertising campaign next week, and just, well, see what happens. What do you say, Kate? Does that sound good to you?"

Collecting herself as she listened to his veiled ultimatum, Kate nearly broke out laughing. The more Ronald Lamour went on, the more Kate was forced to make a serious effort to control herself. The clumsiness of this fifty-ish, balding, short, overweight chain-smoking minor executive in propositioning her, was like something out of a badly written romance novel. The thought rocketed across the screen of her mind that normally she would have felt sorry for someone like him, but that was about all. But his rudeness, arrogance, and the assumptions about her that had driven him to call, pushed her past this point of concern. In reality, his actions only served to deride him in her mind.

She started to whisper faint, vocal giggles when she thought of this unhandsome man who had managed to hang onto his job during his parent company's breakup, at the expense of being shipped to a place like Sunnberry. Taken together, his comments, insolence, and presumptions were more than she could handle at that moment. It was clear to her that he thought she was a local Sunnberry hick who had been born, raised, and grown up in that little town. Probably a cheerleader for the high school football team too, he would have figured, who had made good by getting her graphics education at the local community college or technical school, and who would do anything to keep the business bone, however meaty, that he had thrown her the day before, along with his promises for more. But Kate Murphy was a professional in every sense of the word, and her handling of the situation was a testament to that professionalism that any Fortune 500 top executive would have been proud to witness.

"Why, thank you, Mr. Lamour," she said with a mild gratitude in her voice.

"Yup! There you go again, Kate, just like in my office yesterday. Call me Ronald!"

"Thank you for that courtesy too, Mr. Lamour. But I'm afraid that my business courses in Graphics Arts Design at the University of Michigan taught me that a reasonable, respectful distance in business matters was best all around, and I certainly found that to be true from my years of working in New York City, handling some of the largest clients that used our graphics service there. Nothing personal, of course, it's just that it simplifies matters considerably, and prevents misunderstandings. All bad for business, as I'm sure your long career in the business arena has proven to you. It was a nice gesture though, and I will not forget it." There was dead air on Lamour's side of telephone, but Kate continued.

"It would be very difficult for me to accept such a gracious offer even if I were interested. You see, my fiancé might get the wrong impression. And he has been know to have such a bad temper; especially from the years he spent as a professional engineer in so many different countries, dealing with difficult people. Those kinds of experiences shape a man this way or that, and with him, well, he's rather suspicious and direct in all things. I'm sure you understand the situation now much more clearly."

Lasky caught the fiancé comment, and from Kate's struggle to suppress her laughter and general statements, figured out what was happening for himself. He started to laugh from his swivel recliner and shake his head. But what happened next threw Kate for a loop. Lamour cut in abruptly.

"Look, honey, it's this way. I don't give a goddamn where you worked when, or went to school, where. The fact is you're here, now, in this stink'in little town, and the place is dying on the vine. I'm the only big game in town, and for fifty-some odd miles around, and you goddamn well know it. And those other towns have their share of asshole companies like yours already, living from paycheck to paycheck, vying for any bone the companies there will throw them.

"Now let me tell you! The three contracts I gave you yesterday will keep your crummy little outfit going for the next three years, at least. But I'll tell you this too. Unless you and I become real good friends after hours whenever I'm up for it, baby, I'll cancel those goddamn contracts quicker than shit through a goose, and you can shove that little joke you call a business right up your sweet ass, because you know that's exactly what you'll have to do. I did my homework too, before getting shipped to this f—ing 'burg, and I know the score. The steel company, the silk mill, and a few mom-and-pops is all they got in this area here, along with some struggling forgotten about chainstores that could dry up and blow away any day…and some of them can't pay their employees now, let alone use your graphics shit. So get a grip on reality sweetheart, and get your ass over here to my office for eight sharp, or there'll be hell to pay, and you'll do the paying!"

Lasky's laughter stopped abruptly. He realized it was not due to Kate's radically changed demeanor, but to what he had abruptly perceived as a new ability to somehow feel the content of what Lamour had just said to Kate. It was as though Lamour's voice was passing through Lasky's mental ears before reaching the speaker in Kate's phone. But it passed through him in such a way that it was not an audible parade of sentences that he heard in his mind. Rather, it was a flow of thoughts—images of Kate that the cannery executive had drummed up in his fantasies, and which he was holding in his mind—that were being translated into word-pictures across the screen of Lasky's mind, as the fat business man spewed his venom at her.

In the few seconds between Lasky jumping up from his seat and grabbing the cell phone away from Kate, Kathleen Noel Murphy determined that no man would ever use or abuse her again, in any way. Her face grew hard and pale, as thoughts of the beatings she endured at the hands of the bastard exploded upwards from her memory. She determined to end the charade with Lamour at once, and in the only language he was obviously capable of understanding. Between the instant when Lasky tore the phone from her hands and began to speak, she accepted the fact that without the cannery account, her business had six months to live, at best. Lamour was right. He was the only big game in town, and she was about to call a raid on it, and destroy her own business. How would she pay back the note? What would happen now between her and Mier if he knew...all coursed through her as that instant of time ended, and it was now Lasky who was speaking to Lamour.

"Lamour, this is Mier Lasky. Kate's fiancé. I heard what you said, Lamour, and saw what you saw. Yea, that's right! Don't interrupt me again! I'm going to tell you this once, you little bastard, so I want you to listen carefully! Because if you don't I guarantee you we will meet up when you least expect it. It may not be today, or tomorrow, or next week, but we will meet. And when we do, I'll shove that filthy tongue of yours straight through the back of your skull, so it takes you and your fantasies with it on its way to hell where the lot of you belong. Now listen to me!" While he shouted on the phone, he stomped into the kitchen, with Kate following, as though his words of action required physical action as well.

"As of this moment, *Say It with Pictures* doesn't need you contract. And most of all, Lamour, it doesn't need or want you. Consider the contracts broken now. And before you open your mouth about getting all your lawyers in on it, know that I have my lawyers too, and will drag this out in the courts for as long as it takes. We'll see who has more money for lawyers and legal proceedings, Red Line Industries, or **us**." Kate caught the *us*, and looked up at Lasky with a blank stare.

"Oh. Don't kid yourself, Lamour, even though your parent company broke up and sent you cannery slobs packing to the 'burgs like this, their little corporate wants good relations with the locals. Count on it. When we publicize breaking your contract, on the grounds of your sexual harassment, I assure you, that you'll be out of there, quicker than shit through a goose, as you said to Kate, because no company wants a liability like you around. Not one."

Kate wondered how Lasky had heard the actual remarks Lamour had made to her. Her heart pounded in her throat, as she saw once again the old Mier Lasky, filled with a raging fire of emotions, and directing them at his target with surgical precision. She wondered if the brain changes they had discussed were only temporary after all. Lamour tried to cut in on Lasky's dropped ax, but the latter's mind was blazing with a white hot heat, and a mouth to match.

"Keep your mouth, shut, Lamour! I'm not done with you yet! Oh, yes, I can break this goddamn contract anytime I like, because I am the financial backer of Kate's company. I'm her silent partner. It's her call to get my opinion on jobs of any size, because that was our initial agreement when I underwrote her loan. She came to me about your job, because there was something about it that bothered her. Not about the contract, but about that little worm, Lamour, as she calls you. When she told me of your overly friendliness after signing the contract yesterday, I advised her to scrap it and you, on the grounds that you didn't make the first payment yet, as the contract specifies must be done, before it becomes binding.

"You see, Lamour, I have seen a thousand of you little twirps throughout my years in industry, enough to gag a maggot, and I predicted not ten minutes before you called that this would be your next move. It's always the way of your genetic cesspool kind. You and your lot should have been exterminated years ago. The world would be a hell of a better place if Nature, or someone, would have done all of us a favor and snuffed you out like the insect you are! Now don't ever dare to call her or me again. Or I swear to you, we'll have you in court on sexual harassment charges before the spit hits the ground! Remember that!" With that last threat, Lasky smashed Kate's cell phone down on the counter so hard it split the small phone in two.

Lamour sat behind his desk at Red Line Industries, with the telephone still in his hands for several minutes after Lasky ended the call. All he could do was stare off into empty space. He knew Lasky had him. There was nothing he could do. A sexual harassment charge, even if untrue, would have damned him in an instant, and forced him into an early retirement at best, or would get him fired outright, at worst. There were just some leftover attitudes from his generation that had no place in the cosmopolitan scheme of things today. Using his position to get sexual favors from company clients was one of those old leftover attitudes. He knew it all along, yet, he had always gotten away with it, since no one had ever forced his hand up until now.

He was worried. Who was this Lasky? Obviously he had money. "Will he try to get me fired anyway?" Lamour wondered. "Little sons-of-a-bitches with money always try to do that! Yea, that's what he'll try! Goddamn, trying to make extra points with that squeeze of his, that little whore! I'll fix them! No! Wait a minute, Ronald, get a grip on yourself! Don't send up a flare! Forget it! It's just their word against yours, and they're a couple. He's backing her business. Vested interest. She's his squeeze. No court would ever take his words for it. Yea, that's it! Just cool down! Be calm!

"Get your secretary in here now, and dictate a letter to that little bitch Murphy. Tell her you have changed your mind, and are not going to seal the contract with a first payment. Say you've been having second thoughts about all this advertising, and that you've decided to hold off on all advertising for awhile. No one can fault you for that! Get in the first shot. Don't give them a chance to undo you! Get that letter out now, today. And make it good. Nice and clean and professional. Yea, that'll do it! That'll take care of that f—, Lasky, too! By goddamn, Ronald, you're better than the two of them put together! Shove it right down their throats! Do it your way! Goddamn, I'm proud of you! Now get to it, and get that letter out today, now!"

Lamour reached for his intercom, and pressed the switch to his secretary's office. "Yes, sir!" erupted loudly from the plastic box.

"Mrs. Sallops, please come in here immediately. I have a letter to dictate, and I want it out in today's mail. Oh. Call the mail room and make a special point of it. I want this going out certified, first class, return receipt. I don't want any slip-ups on this one!"

With that, the fat, fiftyish, balding minor executive leaned back in his chair, smiled, and whispered to himself as Mrs. Sallops came through his office door, "Ronald, there isn't a f—er in the world who can get the better of you! Especially not some young more-money-than-brains snot like Lasky! Not a thing he can do to you now. Not a goddamn thing."

Kate and Lasky stood frozen in place. He was beet red. A rage whose intensity he had never quite known was coursing through his veins. In a few seconds it passed away abruptly, and completely. As it did, he began to recall what had just happened, and what he had said to Lamour. The only part he regretted was in telling the fat minor executive that he had underwritten Kate's note. Worse, the memory of that conversation was coming back to him in pieces, and when the piece hit that reminded him Kate was listening to his every word, the color drained from his face, quick and hard. He had gone completely white. His back was turned to Kate. His legs and feet felt like lead. He could not turn around to face her.

This time his uncontrollable ego had done him in. She now knew his secret. Her treatment at the hands of her ex had turned her off on men until she had met him, and in her way, she had placed as much trust and faith in him as she could muster. Now she knew he had betrayed it by going behind her back to underwrite her business loan. He knew she would take this as an insult to her determination, hard work, and life skills. He had treated her like an object he had kept in the corner until he felt ready to use her. She just learned that her very livelihood was due to his helping her covertly. Who knew what she now thought he had up his sleeves?! He stood there, fully aware of what had happened, and did not know what to do. A scratching sound behind him broke the silence.

"Mier? Are you all right?" Kate asked, as her fingernails gently rubbed the back of his sports shirt, producing the gentle scratching sound.

"I don't know what to do, Kate. I'm afraid to turn around. I can't look you in the face," was all he managed to say.

"Then I'll face you," Kate said in a serious tone of voice, as she stepped around Lasky's large frame and looked up at him. He thought that the tension in his head would burst a blood vessel. This was the moment he dreaded, and yet he somehow knew it would inevitably come. He could never succeed in living a normal, trusting, balanced life with a woman— any woman. Not even with Kate. It was just not in him. Now, this relationship too was about to end. All he had to do was listen to the tirade that was surely about to pour from her lips, and one he felt he justly deserved. Lasky did not speak. He had neither the strength nor courage to speak or to respond. But Kate had both, in abundance.

"I love you, Mier! I love you so much! What you did for me since we met, up to this moment, has been wonderful! We had our times of tension, yes. A good example of that was my flare-up a few hours ago. But do you know what, honey? Now I know that it's all part of the package deal. And that package deal is called Love. Not want, or sex, but the real thing. Love. The kind that keeps people going together when neither one of them could continue to go on alone. That, Mier, is what I have finally figured out from the events of these past few days.

"Don't you hear me? That is what you have shown me, and what I have been desperately trying to give you for the time we've known each other, ever since I found out you were the one who cared enough about me and my dreams to secretly make my business a reality! Didn't think I knew, did you? No! How could you! Judging from the look on your face now, I see I just gave you another shock. Well, come here, let's sit down and talk about it. It's about time." And with that brief confession and expression of love,

Kate lead a dumbfounded Lasky back to his rocker, sat him down, and began their long overdue conversation.

As the late afternoon faded into evening and then into night, they filled in the blanks of their early relationship for each other. Lasky explained his initial feelings for her, and that he was willing to gamble on her and her idea. Not only because of the romantic feelings he had for her, but also because he saw the opportunity to bring something new into what he considered to be a dull, lackluster little town in the middle of nowhere, as he put it. He then explained his unlucky and unhappy past with other women to her.

Kate told him of her impromptu visit to the Branstrome Bank to thank Alphonse Chinelli for the bank's financial help, only to see a file behind his desk that read "Lasky/Murphy." From there, Kate explained to him how she put two-and-two together, and in short order, figured out that he had really financed her. It was a mental hop-skip-and-a-jump for her to realize that his clandestine backing was due his uncertainty of her and any possible future relationship they might have. Yet his actions told her clearly that he was more than mildly interested in her, but that he did not want to strain their new relationship by having her know the truth. Kate explained to him how this enabled her to see what a man could be like. In turn, this new experience allowed her hate of men in general and hurt from her ex to subside long enough to begin a relationship with him.

Kate glanced up at the grandfather clock across the room. "Mier, it's eight o'clock. How about I make us some dinner? It's been an awfully hard day on both of us, and I'm hungry. How about you?"

Lasky thought a moment. He was trying to absorb what had just happened. This woman had just told him that she knew what he had done for her all along, and yet respected his wanting to keep it secret. And since she was now an independent business woman holding her own, and yet cared for him enough to spend all of her weekends and extra time with him, it was now clear to him that she loved him for what he was—emotional baggage and all. It dawned on him that he had found love, and was loved in return. With a great smile and twinkle in his eye, he looked up from the floor he was staring at while absorbing this realization and said, "Kate, I could eat a horse! Let's make that dinner together."

As he rose, he felt a wave of weakness overtake him again, this time knocking him back into his chair. With a second effort he pulled himself up to a standing position, but could not move. His legs had become shaky rubber poles he could not be sure of. He steadied himself against the chair and tried to walk, but it was no good. He couldn't move. Kate heard the scuffling sounds and came out of the kitchen to see what was happening. Lasky's head was down, his eyes staring at his now visibly shaking legs.

"What's the matter, Mier?" she puzzled.

"Nothing, Kate. Must still be a bit weak from recent events. It will pass."

"But you were fine a minute ago. Are you sure I shouldn't take you to the hospital? Maybe there is something wrong after all. That was a nasty shock. Maybe…"

Lasky interrupted. "Dammit, Kate, I'm okay!" He felt surges of hate and fury arise within him, but they were not directed at Kate. He looked down again, closed his eyes, and struggled for a moment to regain his emotional control.

"Sorry. I guess I'm still a bit unhinged from everything, that's all. I'm fine. How about that dinner? I could still eat that horse!"

Chapter 7

▼

Genesis

Ronald Lamour looked up at the clock on his office wall. It was eight at night. Although Mrs. Sallops had gotten his contract cancellation letter out in the mail before quitting time, he was still worried. His kind always are. He had called his wife and told her he would be working late.

"Running a new plant is not an easy job, Hon, and some problems crept up today that are still not straightened out, so I don't know when I'll be home tonight."

Marie Lamour had heard the story a hundred times before in their thirty year marriage, and knew what he was really up to. But then Lamour knew that she knew, and so the two kept their small pact between them, a subject never to be openly discussed.

"At least," Marie thought, "someone else will have to put up with him for the night!"

Lamour's side of the matter was, "Well, at least I get away from the old hag for the night, and get my fun in with a young one. Doesn't get any better than this!" In reality, Marie and Ronald were made for each other. They were just two different sides of the same tired, joyless, old coin.

"Goddamn that Murphy!" he squealed out between his thick, wrinkled lips, spraying saliva as he spoke to himself in a muffled voice. "She should be here right now, and we should be getting to know each other. Yes sir, we should be getin' to know each other real good! Goddamn her! I've got to find a way to fix her good! No little bitch can make an ass out of Ronald L. Lamour and get away with it! No sir! Not in a million years!" He began to fume, as his fantasies of them in a $40 a night room at the local motel vaporized just as the hard realities of the canning operations outside his office smacked in upon his dreams.

"What the…" was all he managed to say out loud before he found himself at one of the six windows that lined his office wall, and which allowed him to look down some thirty feet into the cannery operations themselves. A tow motor had skidded on some frozen peas that spewed out from the freezer shoot. Instead of the shoot operator sending the peas into a fifty-five pound box for shipment, he had missed the shoot, sending the pre-measured quantity of vegetables straight across the front of the factory floor. The slight slope of the floor needed for the drainage of excess water from thawed products, had sent the tow motor out of control when its rear wheels hit the peas. The loud thud that resulted set off the alarm, which frightened the shoot operator even more. In his panic, he lost his footing as he slipped on some of the peas, fell backwards, and pulled the shoot door completely out of the freezer.

Thousands of pounds of quickly melting green spheres were now pouring out of Freezer #2, and onto the factory floor, sending laborers, supervisors, other tow motors, and cleaning crew personnel in all directions, slipping, sliding, and falling down. Screams and cries of desperation went out in an uproar from the floor. The racket brought Lamour back to reality, as his brain registered what his eyes saw happening beneath him. He realized that the alarm meant a freezer had shut down automatically, and production would now fall behind schedule. Helplessly, he pounded on the windows of his "Boss's Fortress," as his screams of orders went unheard above the sounds of chaos that had taken over the factory processing area completely.

A second tow motor rounded a bend from the other side of the plant, its operator fancying himself coming to the rescue of his coworkers. As he rounded the corner at high speed, his front wheels met with the rising tide of the green sea, sending him and his machine streaking forward into Freezer #3. The front forks of his machine rammed straight through the sides of the freezer, knocking the twenty foot shoot completely off the freezer's front. A second alarm went off as the shoot collapsed to the floor, bringing with it thousands of pounds of frozen, sliced carrots. Lamour was frozen too. In absolute horror he saw his new plant being destroyed before his very eyes. Rotating yellow and red warning lights were also set off now by the alarm system of Freezer #2, in addition to another alarm wailing even louder than the first.

The tow motor's huge double forks had also pierced the freezer's massive internal ammonia cooling coils, which were now blowing off deadly ammonia gas into the factory. Workers choked and gasped as they rubbed their eyes, trying to find an exit to fresh air. Two men of the cleaning crew near the freezer puncture now lay dead on the floor, the first burst of gas hitting them directly in the face, filling their lungs with the poisonous substance. The tow motor operator also received a direct burst of the gas in the face as he tried to escape from his machine, which sent him sprawling to the floor. The heavy gas soon filled his lungs. It was a few brief moments before his death throes ended, and he joined the other two men in death.

The low temperature of the escaping gas leaked upward, freezing the heavy power lines that fed the freezer's electrical equipment. As though made of glass, the insulation of the power cables cracked, shorting out the high current wires they housed. Yellow, orange, and red sparks and lightning-bolt type flashes filled the air and fell to the floor, giving a scene of a mad experiment gone wrong. The operator of Freezer #2 had run to the rescue of his friend who operated the other freezer, and who was now sprawled on the floor, overcome by the gas. A sizzling power cable swept down in a large arc behind him as he ran, catching him on the shoulder just as he reached his fallen friend. Both men were electrocuted to death on the spot.

Lamour was still dazed. What he had witnessed had occurred in a little more than a minute. As the first traces of gas reached his "Fortress," he could not even smell it. His mind had introverted. He was in a state of mental shock. Partial realizations fell into his conscious mind like blocks of heavy cement, telling him that his life as a mid-management executive was being destroyed before his very eyes. No parent company would understand this. The destruction of a new plant, the massive loss of new harvest products, and dead employees! No company wants that type of publicity or the resulting image it will bring.

He would be the scapegoat. It didn't matter if he cut corners here and there on construction and safety measures. He needed the extra money. He always needed extra money. A few bucks more in his pocket were all part of the game. Everyone did it. Everyone knew how the industrial game was played. Even new corporate knew it. They did it themselves when they knew they could get away with it. It wasn't his fault. Throughout his career, he had set up five other plants just like this one. They had all succeeded. Maybe, just maybe, he would be pardoned for this. Maybe he could shift the blame on someone else. Sure! One of the dead guys down there! Who'd know?! They couldn't talk back! Who would? Sure! Accidents happen! That's why they're called accidents. And the fire that just broke out below among the cardboard boxes near the walls would surely reach his office! All he had to do was destroy all the building and safety plans first, and let the fire reach here, where it would do a proper job of any other incriminating papers he might forget. Then it was his word against anyone else's. That's it! That would do it!

As he turned to the file cabinet to get at the papers that needed destroying, he began to snap out of it. His coolness and shrewdness were returning. He now became aware of the growing presence of ammonia gas in his Fortress.

"Goddamn, Ron, get those papers and burn them! Do it now, and get your ass out of here before you keel over like one of those f—-offs in the plant!"

A white, pungent, paper-smelling smoke suddenly began to creep under his office door as he moved toward the filing cabinet. Ronald Lamour began to panic again, as the window on the door of his Fortress shattered from the increasing heat outside, allowing columns of smoke to pour into the room. His eyes began to burn badly, but he could still see the outline of the filing cabinet in front of him. He fumbled with his keys, trying to find the right one to open the lock.

"Goddamn, which f—ing key is it!" he cursed, as he began to cough from the accumulating gas. His recently returned coolness disappeared when he dropped the keys to the floor. Somewhere, below him, lost beneath the collecting smoke and gas, were the keys. He bent down, trying to find them by touch. Nothing. In his newly returned panic, he had kicked them away from himself. Frantically, he began to pound the cabinet with his fists, all reason leaving him. The filing cabinet would not open. He grabbed it by its sides, and began to scream and curse as he rocked it from side to side in a frenzied attempt to break it open. Finally losing his strength, he fell backwards against his desk, looking through the accumulating smoke and gas at the unopened filing cabinet.

In a second wind, he darted back to the filing cabinet. He pulled as hard as he could on the cabinet's handles, trying to spring the lock that kept him from his salvation. Cursing, screaming, pounding, and pulling, he continued, until the handle of the top drawer sprung off in his hand. The cabinet's theft-proof feature had just kicked in, sending a long, inner vertical bar down the cabinet's length, locking all the drawers up as though they were now all one. The key lock, normally depressed into its housing, had now withdrawn into its slot even further, as the vertical bar secured itself into position. Lamour realized what had happened to the cabinet as he cursed new technology. He sagged against the top of the filing cabinet, and began to cry and laugh hysterically. His only hope now was that somehow the heat would get to the papers in the cabinet and destroy them. But no sooner had this hope flashed across the screen of his mind, then he recalled the fireproof features of the cabinet, and realized they would prevent the documents from being destroyed. He began to cry bitterly.

Lamour's near-blindness caused by the smoke and gas was now added to by the sweat rolling into his eyes. Struggling to see through the blindness, in between his coughing spasms, Lamour blinked repeatedly, trying to make out the image behind what looked to him to be a bright pink line. It moved quickly and silently through the once normal atmosphere, and skirted alongside the filing cabinet he had declared war on. He forgot his mounting fear over the dangers of his situation, as he heard a crackling sound coming from the side of the cabinet.

"What the hell is that? Sounds like someone crinkling Glad Wrap!" was all he could get out, before a small set of three finger-like objects connected to a webbed center that resembled a tiny hand, crawled slowly around the cabinet, and came to rest on the cabinet's depressed key lock. The hot pink assemblage fingered the lock for a moment, and then ripped it from its cabinet housing with lightning speed. Lamour was mesmerized. He could not think. Whatever it was, it had just saved him. He now had access to the documents he had to destroy. Pulling hard on the top drawer, it flew open. He could not question. He could only act. Grabbing the papers, he turned to his office door, preparing to take them with him as he fled.

"I can always destroy them later. No one will ever know," was all he managed to say before he saw the hot pink colored line with the tiny hand emerge from the filing cabinet and block his escape route.

"Get the f—out of my way, whatever you are! Get out! I got no time for f—ing around!" Lamour spewed.

But the line with the tiny hand at one end did not move. Instead, it stretched itself into a rectangle, and began to shift its shape as the hand disappeared from it. The geometrical form grew to a two-by-three foot proportion, before it began oscillating between different geometries. After a rectangle, it became a square, then a loop, then a circle, then something like an infinity sign. As it changed, it began to make buzzing, hissing, and crackling sounds, changing shapes faster and faster. Lamour stopped dead in his tracks, watching in fascination. He had forgotten all about his flight to safety.

The changing hot pink shape gave birth to other forms that joined it in mid-air. From it emerged a green triangle, than a set of parallel yellow lines that connected with each other and grew into other shapes, and finally, a black human-like outline, blacker than black, with a monstrous face, took form. Its teeth and claws gave it the appearance of something that escaped from hell. It was caught between the forms of a huge lion, a snake, and a saber-toothed tiger with barred fangs. Its two eyes resembled pools of churning, swirling bright red masses of blood, sprinkled with black pits that oozed a yellowish substance into their bright red background. The cry it gave sounded to Lamour like a cross between spikes being drawn down a blackboard's surface, and a swallowed high pitch scream someone would make in their death agony.

Lamour went white. Whatever semblance of sanity he had managed to maintain throughout his life left him. His fear consumed what was left of his mind. Before he could utter a cry for help, the hot pink line brought back its tiny hand, and delivered a single poke to Lamour's left eye. For an instant, all he could feel was a dull thud, as if he was simply poked in the eye. Seconds later, he heard the faint sound of "drip, drip, drip." As he looked down, he saw the splatter of drops of blood on the floor and across his shoes. They were coming from the empty socket that was once his left eye. He was too far gone mentally to be able to understand all of what was happening, but for a fraction of a second he became aware that he was seeing out of one eye only. His left eye had not simply been punctured. It had been ripped from its socket, and was lying amid the spots of drying blood on the floor.

The green triangle took on the shape of a set of razors. Before Lamour lifted his head up from staring at his left eye lying on the floor, the razors began to slash his face and arms. Cold slivers of flesh fell from his face to the floor, while others chunked off inside his shirt. Screaming and cursing, Lamour beat at it furiously, but it continued to slash away at him. The yellow lines congealed into what looked like a large corkscrew, and bore itself in and out of Lamour's lower belly with one smooth, rapid motion. His body began to die, as the blood squirted from the hole in his lower stomach. But Lamour's sanity returned intact, a result of the desperate instinct to stay alive.

Still holding the documents that would damn him, he continued to scream and curse as he struck out at the ever changing colored shapes. They were now slamming him with terrible force against any wall of his Fortress that would have him. Broken bones in different parts of his body punctured his skin, leaving smeared bloody streaks on the walls at the points of impact. But Lamour was determined. He managed to get past the green triangle to the door, bolting off of his left leg. As he threw the door opened, he felt a crushing blow to the thrusting leg as he collapsed on the floor. The green triangle wavered in the smoke and gas, buzzing and crackling as it glided over the left leg that had once been attached to the screaming Lamour. Flaying his arms and papers about him, he tried to drag himself through the door. He felt a black coldness shoot through him as the bones in his ears delivered the sound of his spine being severed. Two enormous fangs had pierced his body, cutting his spinal cord cleanly in two.

There was no more pain in his body. Nor could he move. All he could do now was watch with a fear that only the damned could know, as the blacker than black beast picked him up. It stared at him curiously, tilting its massive head to the left and then right, eyeing him closely, before shoving two of its claws into his mouth. With a slow jerking motion, as if to lengthen the time of Lamour's mental terror and agony, the beast ripped the tongue from his mouth. As he hung like a puppet in the beast's one claw, the beast shoved the appendage back into his mouth. With another slow, jerking motion, it continued to pressure Lamour's once-foul tongue, until it broke through the back of his skull, and dangled in mind air.

The one eye in Lamour's head stared back at the beast, no longer knowing, not caring, nor feeling, yet still alive. A raging moan issued from the beast. Its high pitch, swallowed death throes sounded through the burning office and plant as it threw the helpless Lamour through the windows of his once-Fortress, sending him crashing onto the concrete floor, thirty feet below. There, staring up into the carnage of smoke, gas, fire, and dead bodies, his papers still clutched in his one hand, Ronald L. Lamour finally found peace. The darkness of death closed his one remaining good eye.

Outside, the flashing lights and sounds of fire trucks and ambulances were everywhere. The emergency help had arrived only minutes ago. The entire plant was now engulfed in flames, the billowing ammonia gas preventing the firefighters from moving in to do their jobs. The local hospital sent personnel to help tend the wounded, and volunteers to calm down those employees of Red Line Canneries who had managed to escape the destruction with only minor scrapes. Hysteria was rampant everywhere on the cannery grounds, as the toxic gas had produced symptoms of mania in the thirty people from the freezer section who had been exposed to large concentrations of the fumes. Police were running here and there, either fighting with those caught up in the chemically induced mania, or wrestling others down whose nerves had gotten the best of them. Onlookers had arrived on the scene, making the jobs of the cops and medical personnel even harder.

"Get those sons-of-a-bitches of a spectators out of here, Martin!" barked Police Chief Ruger. "We have enough problems here without those bastards screwing things up even more! Get them out of here now!"

"With what, Chief?! We don't have enough men on the force to contend with something like this! Look at it! The frigging building is going to collapse any minute now, and the vinershed behind it is on fire too! What's worse, I was told by one of the plant supervisors that made it out okay that there are three tanks of propane gas back there between the vinershed and main plant, each with twenty thousand pounds of propane in them! Goddamn, Chief, if they go, this whole frigging area of the town will go up with it! What are we gonna do? Evacuate the people in this section of the town? Or do you want me to try and round up some guys to get the crowd back? Friggin' hell, Chief, what are we going to do?" Sirens, screams of the wounded, curses from the cops, yells from the firefighters, surrounded the Chief and Officer Martin as they yelled at each other, trying to communicate.

"Look," Chief Ruger yelled, so Officer Martin could hear him. "Get in your car. Get to dispatch immediately. Tell them to call in the fire crews from Pleasant Corners. Tell them to send everything they got. Then tell dispatch to call in the State Police! We can't handle it all! We need more support! Go, Martin, go, go, go!"

As Officer Martin ran to his squad car, the Chief looked at the inferno, and the scene of human misery and confusion around him. He began to talk to himself. "Man, I'd hate to be the guy in charge of this plant! That son-of-a-bitch won't be able to get a job cleaning out shit houses after this! I wouldn't want to be in that guy's shoes for anything, and I mean, for anything!" Then he looked at his wristwatch. "Eight-thirty. Damn, it's going to be a long night!"

Chapter 8

▼

"Do Not Adjust the Keyboard Shelves!"

Miran Hicks was enjoying himself again. In front of him was Estel Knopp, a twenty-nine year employee of the Dundee Main Library of Penns University. For twenty-two of those twenty-nine years she had put up with this "Dictator of the Reference Room" as he was called by everyone: students, staff members, and strangers alike. Even though he was enjoying calling Estel on the carpet again, this time he was secretly troubled. Estel knew his game, and how he played it. Every other time she managed to cover herself on every charge he made against her, real or imagined. But now more was at stake for him.

If he could just get enough grounds to fire her before her thirtieth anniversary at the school, he would save the university her entire pension, and put another feather in his cap. Miran's boss, Al Chumpton, liked that too. Al would certainly give Miran another small raise for his efforts, and continue to look the other way when the Dictator would verbally abuse his staff, make their work hours a living hell in a thousand ways, and continue to fire younger staff members at his own discretion. "Let 'complaint' forms against Miran be damned as long as he saves the school money," was Al's policy. "Maybe he has the fastest employee turnover in the school's history. But each time he hires a new one, it's at minimum wage. As soon as they go up a bit in salary, bam! Good ol' Miran finds a way to sack 'em, and then starts new ones off all over again at the bottom rung of the pay scale. The school's lucky to have a man like him at the Reference Room helm."

But Miran had figured out a new way this time. Or rather, used an old way that others who were around a long time had no doubt forgotten about. A way he hadn't used since Tom Markowsky got the boot from him nineteen years ago. It was more than underhanded. It was also dangerous. Al Chumpton was not the ultimate authority in the firing of senior staff members headed for pension, although he benefited directly from their release. The matter had to be reviewed by the Library Board of Trustees, and that meant strangers who might look and dig a little deeper into the issue. That was the dangerous part.

Miran's staging and falsifying the event could be discovered, or at least, suspicions raised, and the one being fired saved from their fate. In such a case, the Board might review the other three cases over the past twenty-seven years, ever since Miran took over as Dictator. With enough evidence, they might even bring him up on charges and release him. His thirty-two years of service would vaporize in the same cloud he had sent the other three careers up in, leaving him without the thirty-five year pension he was homing in on.

From his seated position, swiveling around in his chair as though he were holding court, Miran Hicks stared hard at Estel, and in a voice loud and clear enough to be heard by the others staff members and some patrons nearby asked, "Well, Mrs. Knopp? What have you to say for yourself? This irregularity in the Donations ledger is striking! It shows that over the last six months $1,110 was contributed by donors for purchasing additional reference works materials. Of that we spent $652.39 on new books. That leaves a balance of $457.61. Yet your entry states there is only

$357.61 in the account. You were made responsible for the ledger. Where is the missing $100?"

Estel Knopp stood there, dumbfounded. She had no explanation. Over the past twenty-nine years she had learned the style and composition of every trap Hicks had devised. But not this one. All of his other tricks dealt with matters of efficiency, and could be handled, albeit carefully, if one kept their wits about them. Not so here. This was clearly a matter of her juggling the books, or at least, so it seemed.

"I can't explain it, Mr. Hicks. I keep that ledger locked in my desk at all times, along with the purchase authorization forms that only you and I have the authority to sign. That ledger hasn't left my desk. I checked all of the purchase orders myself that we submitted for the new books, and they add up to exactly what they should: $652.39. I distinctly remember checking last week, and the balance in the fund was what it should be: $457.61."

"Then, how, Mrs. Knopp, did it decrease by $100 in one week, if we didn't order anything, and the book was kept locked in your desk, to which only you have the only key? You will remember, Mrs. Knopp, that the last time I asked you to examine it, was on, oh, let me see my calendar here, oh yes! On the eighteenth of last month, which was five weeks ago? Can you explain this to me?" retorted Hicks.

Visibly stunned and nervous, Mrs. Knopp put her eyes down and responded, "I'm sorry, Mr. Hicks. I can't explain it. There is no way such a thing could have happened, and yet it did. I don't what else to say."

Hicks stood up. From his five foot ten inch height, he looked down on her five foot four inch, slightly heavy form, and squealed in a loud, obviously delighted voice, "Well, I know what to say! It's obvious you have tampered with the fund! Money just doesn't disappear from an account! The bank confirmed it today. The total in the special account that only you and I control is $357.61! I don't know how you did it and neither do they, but $100 is clearly missing! How could you jeopardize your entire career and pension for a measly $100, Mrs. Knopp?! But clearly, you did!

"Perhaps you 'borrowed' the money, intending to pay it back before it was discovered? Sorry for you, it was discovered before you had the chance! I've ordered the day time student staffers to begin an inventory of equipment, stationary, and books. Perhaps there is more that you 'borrowed,' all with the intentions of returning, but never got around to? Hmmm, Mrs. Knopp?"

The expression of joy on Hick's face was unmistakable. His pleasure was approaching an almost sexual excitement. His contrived escalation of her guilt by having a full inventory taken of the Reference Room assets was a ploy he devised and polished years ago. It would add to her 'guilt' by 'proving' that whatever other items were missing, all could and would naturally be blamed on her. A ballpoint pen here, a missing book there, an old pocket calculator somewhere else, all would add up naturally in the Board members' minds to damn her.

Estel fell silent. For a split second she wondered if she had taken the money, or overwrote a check she made out for their purchases. But she knew better. Her career at the school was over, and her pension…clearly gone.

"Well, Mrs. Knopp, I discussed the matter earlier with Mr. Chumpton. His investigation brought him to the same conclusions I reached. So, I am hereby suspending you without pay until the entire matter can be reviewed by the Library Board of Trustees. However, I should tell you that the information they receive will be the exact same I brought up to you this evening. Their review is simply a formality, but a necessary one. Since you are in my department and I am directly responsible for you, it will be my report, not one from Mr. Chumpton, that will be sent to the Board. It will go out in tomorrow morning's mail, first thing. I most strongly suggest, Mrs. Knopp, that you clean out your desk now, because surely you will receive your notice of termination from them within the month."

At that point Estel broke down into tears. There was nothing she could do. Hicks had gotten her after all. Her shoulders went limp as she turned around, still crying, and moved toward her desk, preparing to clean it out. The other staff members and few patrons who heard the episode looked at

Hicks with a hatred that fit the old saying, "If looks could kill," Hicks would have been nailed to the nearest wall. None of the staffers believed Estel did such a thing. To the patrons who did not know her, it didn't matter to them if she did it or not. They did know Hicks, and that automatically put them in her corner. The venom in the air was thick as Estel sat down at her desk, and continued to cry as she began to clean out her few personal possessions.

Hicks gave a wry smile that conveyed his sadistic personality to the others staffers, and said to Estel, "You can leave as soon as you are through cleaning out your desk. You are finished here, Mrs. Knopp. Just accept it!" As he finished, he turned around and glanced at the clock on the wall. It was 8:45 P.M. He motioned with his index finger to Mrs. Penel. "I'll be leaving early. You're in charge until closing time. Make sure everything runs smoothly, and above all, see to it that no one adjusts the keyboard shelves! You know how I hate that! I want to see them in their exact same positions tomorrow morning as they are now!" With that, Hicks flung his short coat over his left shoulder, picked up his attaché case, and swaggered out of the Reference Room.

As he moved through the computer catalog terminal area in the central hall, the female students at the terminals smiled and began to giggle. Everyone on campus knew him. They laughed at his strange gait—something between a feminine swinging of his hips and a strut that was overbalanced to the right side. His slim frame, bony face, and sloping forehead coupled to his swinging hip motion gave him the appearance of an effeminate Neanderthal on the prowl for a good time.

But Miran Hicks paid them no mind. He was used to the glances and giggles. He learned to protect his ego from them years ago, by reminding himself that he had the real power, not them. His mind was a stronghold unto itself, protecting itself from remembering too many details of his lonely life. No friends, no family, and an apartment as shabby and barren on the outside as he was on the inside. All that mattered to him was the power that he wielded in the Reference Room. It was not a job to him. It was his very reason for existing.

As he neared the guard's station on the way out of the library, the thought passed through his mind that maybe retiring after thirty-five years was a bad idea. Maybe he should stay on and go for forty years of service. That was better. He would have his power longer. It was good to have power. So good. Anything to hide from facing the life he made for himself that would come when he finally did retire, or was forced to. He blocked the latter thought out immediately. Such thoughts had no place in his life, now or ever. He felt better over the last self-lie, and smiled to himself wryly. The Reference Room was his kingdom. In it, he was all powerful, and it would stay that way as long as he wanted it to, or so he convinced himself.

He glided through the double doors and began to descend the long flight of marble steps leading to the campus grounds. Still smiling to himself, he started to laugh, when the one memory he could not tolerate in his thirty-two years of service broke in on him. "I can't wait until that snot comes back! That oversized little prick who caught me on one of the most difficult days in my entire career, and knocked me off my feet for a split moment! I wish I knew his name! I'd find a way to make his life so miserable, even get him barred from the campus by calling the campus police and drumming up something against him. Oh, how I wish I knew that snot's name and where he was! How stupid was he?!

"He saw the sign above the keyboards, "**DO NOT ADJUST THE KEYBOARD SHELVES**" and yet disregarded it and then jumped on me for admonishing him! Ohh, how I wish I knew who he was!" Everything to Miran Hicks was *I*, *me*, and *mine*. Part of this inferiority complex was his absolute inability to stand up in a confrontation to anyone who did call him to task in the truest sense of the word. He had to rationalize it away. The memory of Lasky's meeting with him head on in the Reference Room two years ago was the one cup of gall he could not swallow. It had festered in him since then and unnerved him when he thought about it.

He had to be the hero, or at least, the abused authority who was injured from simply doing his sworn duty.

His face began to turn red at the continued thought of that incident. As he rounded the bend leading from the library steps and walked down the campus, the scene of that night played itself over and over and over again in his mind. He squeezed his attaché handle hard, until his knuckles became as red as his cheeks. He forced himself to turn away from the closing scene in his mind. The scene in which Lasky brought the incident to an end by telling him loudly so everyone in the room could hear, "**Make sure you didn't, and make damn sure it stays that way!**" Hicks' eyes began to pulsate hard in their sockets. By an effort of will he changed the memory reel being played in his brain.

"Ah, well, Miran, you did it again!" he began to mumble to himself in a stifled voice. "Another pat on the back is coming from Chumpton, and no doubt, from some of the higher-ups, too! Knopp is done, and you're the genius who engineered it, as usual! That's going to save the school a lot of money, not having to pay an old bitch like her a thirty year pension! Deftly handled, old boy, deftly handled!

"All it took was a having the Donations account divided up into a 'mother and daughter' account, but arranging to have the balance reported for the 'mother' account only. Then I simply placed an advance order for a book that won't be published for six months under my own signature for $100, authorized an advance payment from the Donations 'daughter' account to get the discount, destroy the purchase order carbons, and $100 less appears in the 'mother' account. And the 'Knopp problem' is solved. Miran, you're a treasure! I wonder how this place will ever get along without you when you finally decide to retire!"

Mr. Hicks was feeling on top of the world now. The redness in his face and hands subsided. He became aware of the cool spring evening breeze, as he began to hum a made up tune. He was humming merrily as he crossed the central part of the main mall of the campus. The parking lot where he left his car was in sight. A series of low growing hedges shot off from the main mall area, each leading to a different part of the campus. The hedges bordered narrow walkways, forming a fence on both the left and right sides of the walkways. The landscape effect was one of a gigantic wheel, the hedges of which composed the spokes of the wheel. This gave a long, picturesque walk that led from the last stretch of the central mall area to whatever part of campus a person was going to.

As Miran glided along his path to the parking lot, he thought he heard a rustling sound. Something like the crackle of Glad Wrap. At first, he disregarded it. Then he realized that for some reason the campus was particularly deserted that night. It was early evening, and being the springtime, he was accustomed to seeing students everywhere. He quickly dismissed his observation and continued merrily along. The sound of the Glad Wrap became more frequent. Then it became louder. Miran stopped to listen.

"What the hell is that?" As he stood there, he strained his hearing. It was night, the campus was deserted, and unrecognized sounds were coming from the hedges on both his right and left side now. The crackling grew in volume, as though it was getting closer to him. His heart quickened. The crackling grew louder and became constant. It was all around him now. It was coming from inside the hedges. His heart began to pound hard in his throat. He could not feel it in his chest anymore.

The four walkway lamps lighting the remaining fifty yards to the parking lot began to buzz. The one closest to him exploded, followed by one further from him, then the third, and finally the last one at the end of the walkway. All shattered into a hundred pieces, and sent blue sparks into the air and to the ground, along with the exploding glass. The loud cracks and the sequence of their exploding frightened him badly. It was as though they were destroyed in a deliberate pattern in order to alarm him even more.

The coward that was Miran Hicks began to show through. His face broke out into a deathly white color, and his body became cold. Tiny beads of sweat formed on his forehead. He started to shake uncontrollably. In a timid, high-pitched voice he squeaked out, "Whoever you are,

I have a cell phone here! See?! I'm going to call campus security right now! Do you know who I am? I'm Senior Staff! I'm the Director of the Reference Room! Stop this nonsense now, or I'll have you fired if you're an employee, or dismissed if you're a student! Do you hear me? Stop this nonsense immediately!"

Waving his cell phone in the dark that now swallowed up his walkway, Miran began to fidget with the buttons of the device. He was calling campus security as he continued to threaten his unseen predator. "See?! I'm calling the campus police right now!"

The low level light of the cell phone's face was too dim. He could not see the numbers he was punching, but in desperation and terror, he punched in a series of numbers anyway. Somewhere in his fear frozen mind he hoped the electronic chirp of the buttons being depressed would be enough to scare off his would be assailants. He began to speak into the phone, trying to convince his tormentors that he had reached security.

"Hello! Police! I'm..." was all he was able to get out before a small, hot pink colored cylinder of light flashed out from one of the hedges. It went cleanly through Miran's left hand, and pierced his phone. The device made a brief wining sound, which stopped abruptly as he dropped it to the ground. Hicks was now genuinely terrified. His hand was bleeding badly. He could not see the blood, but he felt its warmth travel down his fingers before falling into the darkness of the walkway below.

All of his life he hid his cowardice behind the laws of the land meant to protect his kind. They were always there for him as he demanded they should be. "One must live and abide by all laws in a civilized society," he once told a coworker before destroying her possible career in his Reference Room, "there is simply no room or tolerance for any physical violence whatsoever!" The laws of his socially responsible, politically correct system had abandoned him, as his courage and manhood had many years ago. Miran Hicks was alone in the dark, with someone or something hiding in the hedges, closing in on him fast.

Unable to think, he reacted from pure instinct. Dropping his attaché case, he ran as fast as he could toward the end of the walkway that opened up into the parking lot. But his out of shape body, slight frame and peculiar stride prevented him from making any rapid progress. He tripped over his own feet, and sailed straight into the hard concrete walkway, skinning his face, good hand, and knees badly. The crackling was following him. It was not only around him now, it was in front of him, in the hedges, getting louder and louder. He struggled to get up on one knee, but as he was unaccustomed to any sort of physical pain, he collapsed back into the walkway. As he lay there, he looked around him. His head shot this way and that, still trying to identify the ever approaching crackling sounds.

But his tormentors had taken on a new dimension. Across his rapidly moving field of vision he noticed bright twinklings in the hedges. Hot pink, green, and yellow. Their twinkling seemed to keep in step with the crackling sounds. Suddenly, the twinklings were growing brighter, and the crackling they made was now on top of him. In a panic beyond normal fear, Miran Hicks lost all sensation of pain. He jumped to his feet and began to run down the final fifty yards of the walkway. His body now fell in step with his mind's demands. Even his strange gait gave way to his desperation this time, allowing him a normal running stance.

He was about fifty feet from the opening to the parking lot entrance, puffing, sweating, shaking from the terror that pursued him, when he saw bright twinkling lights on the walkway in front of him. Whatever it was behind him was now casting yellow, green, and hot pink reflections on the payment. He broke his stride long enough to look back over his left shoulder to see his pursuers. Instead of human beings with psychedelic light sticks, he saw three shapes floating in the air. All three had a luminous quality to them. The yellow one was changing its shape from a parallelogram to a rectangle, while the green one resembled a hypnotic spiral, swirling from its outer edge inward, as though it was flowing around ever smaller circles inwards toward a point. The hot pink shape contented itself to remain a simple rectangle, leading the pack.

He screamed as loud as he could, but there was no one around to hear him. The Dictator was alone in the dark, with three faces of evil hot on his heels. As he turned to face the entrance of the parking lot, he missed the curb and fell flat on his face, smashing his nose headlong into the lot's rough macadam surface. Blood poured out of his nostrils and down the back of his throat. In a wave of pain, he grabbed his nose, coughing, spitting and blowing out blood. He started to scream again, but the blood flowing down his throat made him choke and lose his breath. The fifty yard run had exhausted his out of shape body completely, and the emotions of terror had drained the last of his energy reserves.

The three geometries still floated in the air just a few feet behind him, as though they were corralling him toward his vehicle. Miran continued to stagger, trip, get back up and fall down repeatedly. He gave up trying to run. Instead he crawled toward his car as fast as he could. An expression that might have resembled the progeny of agony and the terror of the deathbed filled his eyes with an unholy madness. Somehow he found his keys in his pocket on the first try, opened the driver's door, and threw his failing carcass inside.

"You're safe! You're safe, Miran!" he heard his own voice tell him. "Lock the doors! Lock the doors now!" Losing the sense of the pain in his body, he slammed the locks on the driver's and passenger's side and began to relax. He started to calm down. As he did, the searing pain of his torn up hands, face, and punctured palm entered the field of his conscious sensation with brutal force.

"It doesn't matter, Miran! They can't get you now! You're safe! Safe!" He began to laugh and cry hysterically at the same time, as a man would who was crossing the boundary from sanity into the nightmare world of the mentally damned. He grabbed the steering column with both of his hands, and leaned his head forward onto them. The blood in his mouth was congealing, and slipping down his throat. He coughed and spit some of the larger chunks out on to the car's floor. The flow of blood from his nose had slowed, but the pain in his punctured left hand had a searing heat about it. He spent a few minutes catching his breath. He was now certain he would be all right. His wits were returning. All he had to do now was put the key in the ignition, start his car, and drive directly to the police station on campus. The law would help him. The law would deal with the thugs that attempted to maybe kill him. The law was there for him. It was always there for his kind.

He took a deep breath and leaned back against his car seat. The crackling sound returned, but it was outside of his car. It sounded more distant though, as if it were far away. Then he realized that the car's interior was muffling the three terrors that were right outside of his window. In returned horror, he watched as the three shifting geometries moved in front of the car. He could see their luminous glow directly through the front windshield. They were growing larger, larger, larger, until the three of them filled the space in front of his car. He began to blow his car horn, furiously smashing the horn button against the casing. Loud blasts of distress signal could be heard across the silent campus.

He screamed at the figures through the windshield. "Get the f—away from me! Get the f—out of here you f—s! Leave me alone! When I get to the police station and tell them about this, they'll get the lot of you little bastards and put you away for life! See how you like being the girlfriends of hardened criminals in the joint! That's what's in front of you, you little f—ers, and I'll enjoy my ass off thinking of them using yours for their nightly f—ing sessions!"

Miran Hicks was now convinced some students had staged this elaborate attack for some unknown reason, in an attempt to get back at him for something. Maybe boyfriends of some of the girls he had sacked. They deserved to lose their jobs anyway. Who cared how or if they could make up the money to stay in school? Certainly, not Miran. This was the only logical answer, because his world was ordered with what it should be— laws, society's rules, political correctness, and more laws, all designed to let him and his kind have free reign. As the horn continued to blow, the three forms slipped out of his view with a motion so smooth and quick, that for an instant he wondered if he hadn't imagined the entire episode. First they were there, and then they weren't. Nothing could move that fast, not in between the half-blink of an eye.

His heart was calming down. He could no longer hear it thumping in his throat. It was back in his chest where it belonged. It was ticking fast, but still, it felt better. He took his handkerchief out of his back pocket, and began to wipe the sweat and blood from his face and hands. His shaking stopped. His breathing was returning to normal. He looked out of the front windshield again, and then through the side windows of his car for any trace of the monsters that attacked him. They were gone. It was finally over.

With a loud sigh of relief, Miran leaned back against his seat, and put the handkerchief over his eyes. "Now, onto the police station." He gave one final sigh, leaned forward, and put the key in the ignition. But before turning the key, he did as all law abiding citizens of his caliber do. He adjusted the rear view mirror. As he did, he seemed to notice an area of blackness in the back seat that was darker than the surrounding blackness. He rubbed his eyes, but it did not dissolve. "Better get going, Miran. Your nerves are starting to get the best of you now!"

He started to turn the key in the ignition when a guttural, low pitch sound broke out from the back seat. "**DO NOT ADJUST…**" resounded from behind him, the words "**THE KEYBOARD SHELVES,**" being raised in tone to a cross between spikes being drawn down a blackboard's surface, and a swallowed high pitch scream someone would make in their death throes. An image of Mier Lasky and the incident in the Reference Room two years ago, emerged from the panicked depths of Miran's mind.

Past all emotional feeling, Miran swung his body around and peered into the back seat. A black line, blacker than black, sprouted outward this way and that, until it assumed a humanoid form. Its face began to rearrange itself before Miran's eyes. Its head became abnormally large, displaying the appearance of something that could be a hybrid between a lion, a snake, and a saber-toothed tiger with barred fangs. The blackness in the top of its skull banished, as its eye sockets took on the appearance of churning, swirling, bright red masses of blood, sprinkled with black pits that seeped a yellowish substance into their bright red background. Its gaping mouth opened and smiled wryly at Miran, through two lines of razor sharp, glistening teeth.

Miran's blood pressure soared, and he began to shake as he sat there motionless facing the black beast. In the next moment, the Dictator of the Reference Room lost control of his bladder and colon, and soiled himself. He could feel the warm wetness of his evacuation moving down his legs and up his belly.

Out of control, and seized by the human instinct to survive, Miran Hicks spun around and grabbed the car door handle with his damaged left hand, and pulled the lock up with his right. He flung the door open and got one foot outside on the ground. He might escape the hellspawn after all. As he pulled himself up to get out of his vehicle, he screamed so hard that his throat contracted violently, closing off his windpipe, stopping his cries in mid-stream. He was almost out of the car when a blacker than black arm-like appendage with three claw-like projections seized him by the back of his neck, and pulled him back into the car. Miran's left foot caught the door handle as he was being dragged back inside. The door closed with a loud "thunk."

Miran Hicks' muffled cries were not heard by anyone on the empty campus that cool, lovely, early spring night. If a passerby would have chanced upon the drama unfolding in the parking lot at that moment, he would have seen a 1992 Chevy rocking back and forth furiously, as muffled cries and pleas for help filled the outside air immediately around it. That same observer would have heard a "floop, floop, floop" sound, as Miran was mercilessly slammed against the sides of the car's interior. He would have the noticed the windows of the vehicle becoming fogged over with the splattered remains of the Dictator's body, as blood, vein, intestine and sinew slowly covered the inside of the windows. In two minutes or so the car stopped rocking. So did the cries and muffled pleas of Miran Hicks. Estel Knopp would be able to fulfill her final year of service at the Dundee Library in peace now, and collect her thirty year pension after all.

Chapter 9

▼

Shadow Man

Kate watched Lasky as he aimlessly rearranged the food on his plate. It was clear to both of them that he had lost his appetite. The thick silence filling the space between them grew even thicker over the past fifteen minutes. Kate reached across the table. She placed her fist firmly around his left wrist, and squeezed. "Hello? Is anyone in there?"

Lasky's hypnotic spell was broken. The dinner plate no longer mesmerized him. The task of rearranging its contents was now complete.

"Hum? Oh, I'm sorry, Kate. I just lost my appetite. It just vaporized. You know, like when you get bad news and the thought of food is taken away by the new worry."

"What's to worry about, Mier? You were fine an hour ago. You're still not quite yourself. It will probably take a day or two before you come back around to your old self."

Lasky gripped himself inside, as a man does when he sucks in his belly. "Old self, Kate? Let's not think about that. I am seeing with new eyes now, and I don't want that old self back. It stopped me from living too much life. If it wasn't for its influence, I could have shown you how I felt a long time ago, instead of holding back as much as I did."

He was oscillating back to his new self—the one Kate first saw down in the laboratory. With a movement that could have been read as one of disgust, he picked himself up from the table, walked into the living room, and sat down. Kate left him alone for a few minutes, and then followed. "Okay, there is something troubling you. Let me see if I can guess what it is," she said.

"For all the good it will do, go ahead," Lasky replied. His words had a cynical note in them.

"Well, for one," Kate said, "until the time of the accident you were your old self. We've been through that earlier today, remember?" her voice lowered as she gently reminded both of them of her explosion in the kitchen earlier that afternoon.

"Then the accident happened. You became the sweetest, most considerate man any woman could want. It was genuine, Mier, I could tell. But there was also something else in it. When you held me in your arms down in the lab, I could sense that you were aware of it and that you would call it weakness. A woman wouldn't, she would call it caring. But I understand this in men. That's just the way it is.

"Later, we talked all afternoon, trying to get past our numbness of the past recent events, and we succeeded. Then Lamour called. Your new self waned, and the old came back. But there was a difference this time. There was a rage that I never saw in you before, so I don't know where that fits. After you finished with Lamour, you couldn't face me. Literally. In your fury you spilled the beans about backing my loan. Something I knew about all along, but you had no idea I knew.

"You became this new self again, but there was something a little different about it this time. You seemed a little more caring or weaker, as you would put it. Remember what you said? 'I don't know what to do, Kate. I'm afraid to turn around. I can't look you in the face.' This was even more sensitive and caring than your holding me in your arms down in the lab.

As a result, dear, we resolved the one issue that was your stumbling block in our relationship! Now you are faulting yourself and feeling depressed beyond belief because you can't absorb all that has happened in such a short period of time. You probably feel like a piece of driftwood, floating in the open ocean, being buffeted about this way and that, as though you had no will of your own. Am I right?"

He was staring down at the shag carpeting as she gave her summation and analysis of the recent events, and her insights concerning them. He was listening intently to every word, waiting for her to somehow make everything all right by blending in the other sensation he was feeling. That other that was emerging from some hidden source deep within his nature, and which he intuitively felt he had to control. But Kate's epitome missed the other sensation, and Lasky was now consciously aware that he was struggling inside to suppress it from overtaking him.

"You're right on all points, Kate, but you missed one. But then, how could you know? Reading my behavior is one thing, trying to read my inner mind and emotions is quite another."

Kate looked at him intensely. "What do you mean, your inner mind and emotions? Doesn't behavior stem from what you think and feel? All the psychology I ever had said it does. Is there something more?"

"Yes and no," Lasky replied. "It all depends on who you want to believe, because in the final analysis, it's all a matter of belief. No one, and certainly not the psychologists, psychoanalysists, and psychotherapists know for sure. Because if they did, there wouldn't be as many schools of thought on the subject, and certainly so many different treatments and results…if you can call them that." Lasky's dim view of psychology was beginning to show again.

"I mean, the way the human mind works. Really works. How does the content of any one mind become part of that mind? Why does a given mind accept certain content and reject other content, or at least, act on some content while rejecting other material? What makes two kids who grow up in the same neighborhood, at the same time, with the same backgrounds, the same schooling, and types of family, shock the world in different ways? Like the one becoming a scientist and making a great discovery, while the other becomes a serial killer?

"What makes the mind tick? What is memory, and what are the roots of it? What about thought itself? Is it all due to the production and flow of chemicals through neural pathways as the textbooks all but outright say it is, or is it as I told you I suspect it actually is? That the forces that either made up thought or along which thought travels through the brain are electromagnetic in nature, and that the chemical basis of thought acts only as so many wires or conduits that simply allow the electromagnetic nature of thought to flow more rapidly through the brain. As I told you, my researches and experiments gave me the grounds to reject the idea that is still held today by modern science and psychology, that the chemical nature of brain secretions are responsible for thought, and are in fact, the very thought itself."

Lasky's outer demeanor was intense as he spoke, but there was an emptiness driving his words, and Kate sensed it. She watched him closely, and then broke in on him.

"You're going somewhere with this, Mier. Somewhere you haven't gone with me before. I don't think you should hold anything back now. We've come too far together after the last two days. It's all or nothing now. No more time for hidden secrets. What are you getting at? I want to know, Mier, and I mean it. You have me scared now, because I can feel a hollowness in your words. Also, there seems to be a hidden meaning.

"But even beyond that, you've lost your double edge of anger and control. Can you feel it? Are you aware of it? Where are we going with this conversation? Where is the meat of this going to take us in our lives together? Something is not right here, Mier, and I demand you tell me everything now. I'm not angry, just frightened, and the fear is increasing. It's as though we're linked at this moment, and the fear I'm feeling is not just my fear. It's *our* fear, because something in you has reached me, and our fears have added together. My God, Mier, what's happening?!"

Kate and Lasky became aware of the connection between them at that moment. It was a strong, blurred link that was only psychic in nature, and yet more real that a physical bond. Waves of energy were passing between them along that link, and both of them were now frightened. They both began to sweat.

"You're overloading me, Kate! Let me sort all of this out!" Lasky's voice was now shaking, and his words breaking up into a stutter. "Yes, I can feel the hollowness, or hidden meaning, as you call it. I call it an other sensation. Up until a minute or two ago it was just there, like a thought at the back at your mind you can't get out. Now it's struggling to come out, and I am fighting to keep it down.

"I don't know what it is, but it terrifies me. If it should come out, I don't know what would happen. Like maybe I'd lose control, and go on some kind of rampage. Maybe turn into some kind of monster, and start killing people. Maybe you'd better leave, Kate, because I don't know how long I can keep this thing down. It's me and yet it's not me, or else it's some secret part of me I never knew before. Maybe you'd better leave and leave now!"

She looked at him through the only eyes she now knew. All of her life she had sought the genuine emotion of human love, and in the events of the past two days she found it. Amidst the other sensation that was now threatening both of them, she found the core of this most fragile and yet most powerful of all human emotions. She walked over to Lasky, knelt down in front of him, put her arms around his neck, and said, "I'm not going anywhere without you! It's you and me fella, together, wherever this dream or nightmare of yours is going to take us." Tears began to run out of the corners of Lasky's eyes, as he leaned forward and embraced her, and struggled to keep the other sensation down.

They remained in the embrace for what seemed like an eternity to both of them. An eternity filled with the highest expression of human love, combined with an unknown terror that was slowly but surely embracing their lives, as they were embracing each other. Then Lasky broke the silence and the embrace. "I'm all right now, Kate. I've got it pushed down. Let me finish what I was saying."

Kate looked up at him, smiling, and replied, "I insist you do. I have to know." Like travelers refreshed at a desert oasis, a moment of calm now overtook their situation.

Lasky continued. "Throughout the years, this study of the nature of thought brought up other issues that are not a part of science. At least, not the science that is called science today. From what I have learned, there was a time when the dividing line between science and philosophy did not exist. What is now called the sciences of physics, chemistry, and biology, just to name a few, were at one time called Natural Philosophy. Things were studied as parts of Nature, not as some extension of man's cleverness used to study something out there, that he now labels as Nature.

"What I'm trying to say is that over the past two hundred years, ever since the industrial revolution, man became separated from Nature. Not just in his ways of living, but in terms of the way he thinks about himself and his immediate world. And this changed his behavior. Not just toward Nature, but toward his fellow human beings, and ultimately, toward himself. In other words, his psychic view of others and of himself underwent a radical and dangerous change. He and Nature were no longer one. Instead of being a part of the whole, as it were, he cut himself off, and became separate. Now man was intent on controlling the whole through his newly defined science, not to mention his new technology.

"What is worse, this newly emerging field of technology gave him the sense of added personal power. So much so, that he now thinks he can control and change Nature in anyway he chooses. And he just might be able to, at that. But again, in this process, he removed himself even further from his natural source, his inner connection with Nature. This is the price he paid, but one that most people do not recognize to this day.

"As I said, it started with the industrial revolution, but it escalated. This change did not occur in a precisely linear way. And that's what confused the picture of it even more. Enough time had to pass before the attitudes that caused the change, and the events that came about from it, could be viewed and put into some kind of order. Keep this in mind as I go along, okay?

"See, Kate, at the time of the industrial revolution, a firm belief in the dogma that humanity could save itself through science and reason took over. The guys who write the history books generally refer to this period as the Modern Age, and extend it from about the seventeenth century through World War II. Life was improving for larger numbers of people of all classes. Slowly and painfully, yes, but it was improving. And it was being accomplished by machines like the automatic loom, new ways to make metal, new knowledge of anatomy that improved surgical techniques, new food preservation techniques, the discovery of germs and antiseptics, optics that brought the heavens down to earth, the discovery and harnessing of electricity, motors, right down to rockets. And all were man-made. So the belief that reason and science, the products of the human mind themselves, could create a paradise for humankind on earth, became fixed in the human psyche.

"Never mind the wars and social chaos that were as prevalent and deadly in the eighteenth through twentieth centuries as they were in the fourteenth or seventeenth. They had taken on a new sophisticated face, one given them by improved weapons. Now they were seen as the inevitable price mankind had to pay for his new found goods and opulence. That is, until he learned to control his destructive urges.

"Then, at the end of World War II, something else happened. A new period began, one the historians are calling the Postmodern era. In it, the quantum leaps achieved in reason, education, science, and technology, gave rise to a belief that is now looked upon by more and more people as 'The Myth of Progress.' I mean, a myth arose that progress for its own sake was needed for human salvation. This myth took over society. The question of whether something was needed or helpful was no longer an issue. As long as something was invented or improved upon, it was enough. A use would be found for it, even if that use took away

something more from people—another intangible—like self-sufficiency, or the need to think and reason for themselves.

"It now became necessary to justify all new subjects in school and all
new technology, in order to prove their worth. In the process, the human
values, the attitudes that religion one time called the 'fruits of the soul'
and philosophy called the 'needs of the spirit,' were rejected. The 'need' for
'things' replaced peoples' need for inner peace and wholeness. 'Make more
money to buy more things' became the rallying cry of this new school of
thought, and a strange process for implementing this view came into
being. Don't build a better mouse trap, build a better mouse to justify the
need for a better mouse trap. Then build the trap, and keep improving it,
even though the new mouse was exterminated by the original, new trap.

"Things continued to change along this line until we have the situation we do today. Men and women still make babies, but day care centers
and public institutions like schools, raise them. Family time does not
exist, because dinner comes out of a box and into the microwave.
Computers solve all problems, until they break down, because the daily
user knows no more about them than how to turn them on. We have
become a nation of a "point-and-click" mentality, devoid of religion, philosophy, and the values of something more, like spirit. The kind of spirit
found everywhere in Nature.

"To soothe ourselves and prove we are more human than we ever were,
we have created government bodies and private foundations to look after
our human rights, while demanding them from other societies that don't
practice what we feel is good and right and true and noble. Then we
donate to these bodies and foundations to show how righteous and just we
are in our views. Yet, all around us, our society is falling apart.

"On the one hand, crime has never been greater in all of human history, and new diseases have never appeared as rapidly as they are now.
Children aren't children anymore, now they're young adults, with rights
all of their own. They have rights, but like their parents, no responsibilities
in the exercising these rights. Hell, like their parents, they don't even know

what their rights are! To them, their rights are their wants, not even their needs, and the society they created based on this concept, is trying to uphold their demands, by insuring they have more of the very things that caused the problems in the first place!

"Yet, on the other hand, self-help books are selling out as fast as the stores can put them on the shelves, while new cults rise up all the time, promising to show the one who will listen how to be saved, or at least find his or her way back to paradise. And if someone spouts what I just did, they're called a cynic or a crank, or ungrateful for the opulence all around them. Well, Kate, in my opinion, opulence lies in more than just new things.

"It lies in the intangibles that are a part of the soul, and that part is the most important. It's what lasts after we breathe our last, not the things we accumulate while we are breathing, and used to delude ourselves into believing we need. Because if we did need them, we wouldn't have to keep replacing them with more of the same, in order to reprove how happy they make us. These are all of the feelings I had throughout the years that I could not express, due to whatever it was in me that was holding me back. But now, after the accident as you call it, maybe the brain changes it induced have eliminated that part of me for good, and I can at last tell you and anyone else I feel like, just where I am coming from."

Kate listened intently, not making a sound. As Lasky sat there and continued, she finally saw the essential side to him that she loved. She had hints of it before, but never saw the mechanism that drove it. Now she not only saw his true nature, but the foundations of thought and philosophy upon which it was built. A warm feeling coursed through her body. Somewhere in the depths of her own soul, she knew they would live a long and happy life together. They were, afterall, just different poles of the same life.

"After I hammered all of this out and drew my own conclusions, I became totally discontent with society, and determined that I would use my inheritance to build the type of life that I wanted. To keep to that, I did as I told you, and worked for those years, saving my money, investing it, and all the rest. I also took to reading works that seemed critical in understanding the mess the world had gotten itself into. The medieval works were no good, since they were too close to the unfolding process, but works from the late eighteenth and nineteenth centuries seemed to have a message in them. As though their authors understood what was happening, and foresaw the shadow of the direction we were heading in as a civilization. Mostly, works by Jules Verne, Lewis Carroll, Charles Dickens, and W.B. Yeats appealed to me. They had the strongest and clearest messages.

"But one especially, seemingly written as a metaphor on the duality of the human condition, hit me hard. When I read the original, it became obvious that the label, metaphor or psychological interpretation placed on it by so called contemporary literary critics and psychologists, was not exactly correct after all. I can't prove it, but I have a feeling it was based on some experiment that either the author actually conducted upon himself, or more probably, knew of someone who had carried out such an out-landish experiment. I'm talking about Robert Louis Stevenson's *The Strange Case of Dr. Jekyll and Mr. Hyde*. You remember.

"Dr. Jekyll was the good medical doctor, and Mr. Hyde was the beast of depravity within him. When he injected a certain drug into his veins, one that he had created for the purpose of freeing Hyde, the doctor's physical appearance changed to accommodate the emerged Hyde. He became grotesque physically, and carried on, drinking, womanizing, and killing. Well, the physical transformation was the metaphor part, I figure. But the rest isn't. I came to think that each of us is composed of a good Dr. Jekyll and evil Mr. Hyde, and that the two could be separated. Or I should say, one could take over. That's the psychological interpretation side of it, except psychology did not take it far enough. They treat symptoms of cases like this, but don't really buy into their own theory that there are two sides to our nature.

"Since I was experimenting with thought and the mind, I became concerned that my work might produce an effect on me that was akin to the effect Dr. Jekyll's serum had on him, and release my beast of depravity. This was the central other issue that is not part of science that I spoke of earlier. Remember? Well, this drove me deeper into what I feel is the legitimate study of the human mind as far as science is concerned—psychoanalysis. Not psychology or any of the manipulative psychotherapies, but the real and original thing. The theoretical and experimental medical investigation of the human mind that psychoanalysis deals with directly.

"While this field is a science in one way, it is thought of as the last desperate straw by both the general scientific community and even the medical community today. Both of these communities insist that the somatic possibilities, those dealing with a possible physical cause of a mental disturbance, be exhausted first, before calling in a psychoanalyst. In short, in my opinion, this is another manifestation of the Postmodern era. Effects are dealt with as causes, while causes are treated as last ditch efforts.

"By studying psychoanalysis, I became convinced of two things. My two 'Final Conclusions' as I call them. They are composed of two postulates, assumptions that are held as being true. The First Postulate as I call it, is that what is termed the Id is a function of the mind, as the consciousness is. In other words, it is a process of the mind. It's not a separate part, nor can it act independently. The Second Postulate states that if what they call the super ego, or conscience is weak enough, the effects of the Id can manifest in the person, and produce such bizarre and destructive behavior as serial killing.

"What I'm really saying, is that this Id—the Mr. or Mrs. or Ms. Hyde in all of us—cannot come out of us physically, or dominate the average human personality, because of the conscience and general constitution of the human organism. This being the case, my concern that my experiments could produce some independent monster was merely that—a concern, generated by my own conscience. So while I have very little use for society as it is today, at the same time I did not want to do something that

would worsen it by creating some kind of horror film nightmare. After I
satisfied myself along these lines and felt assured, I then went on with my
experiments. And all was going well until the accident. Now all is gone.

"Who knows the good I could have produced through this work? I am
certain I would have created a new field of study that would have ennobled humankind greatly, showing it the beauty and power invested in it by
Nature. Maybe that one step of mine could have acted to help mankind
slowly turn it all around, and achieve that heaven on earth, or that salvation they all seem to be looking for. Such were my thoughts, Kate. Those
were my goals, and my motivations behind them. Now you know it all. I
wanted you to know everything."

Kate looked at him for a long time in silence. All along she did not
know what he was doing or why, and now realized that she judged him
wrongly. Her view of the accident was based upon incomplete information, and mentally she kept repeating this over and over again to herself.
But it wasn't working. Her reasoning was failing her. If she knew this man
as well as she thought she did, and having known of his kindness in
secretly backing her business venture and his gentleness toward her in so
many other ways, then she also reasoned that she should have concluded
that his private work was motivated from good, and not from some
twisted desire.

It was not until this moment that the final conclusion she harbored all
along dawned upon her. That he was operating out of some self-conceit,
itself based in an unnatural appetite for personal power over a society he
clearly despised. Yet his former aberrant personality traits made this initial
read of hers all too plausible, and so she tried to smooth out her now self-
beratement with this added consideration. With a sigh of both relief and
consternation, she finally spoke.

"Mier, I, I, just don't know what to say. All along I thought…"

"That's all right, Kate. I know what you thought. I thought the same
thing too at one point, and it scared me silly. That's why I began to look
deeper into myself and my own motivations, and why I undertook that

study in psychoanalysis. I just had to make sure, and had to know enough about myself, the me inside, that I could, before I went on with T.A.A.C. Don't feel bad. I think these concerns are all valid in any new frontier work. It's okay. We're okay, and that's all that counts."

The grandfather clock chimed once. It was 8:45 P.M. As they sat there quietly, Lasky felt a another powerful drain of energy, as though he was a sponge being wrung dry. His body went limp as he slumped forward in his rocker.

"Not again!" Kate said, leaning forward on the couch. "Are you getting weak again? You look terrible. Not white. Your face now has a gray pallor to it. Look, Mier, enough is enough. I don't care what you say. The shock you got from the accident has done more to you than that brain change you've been talking about. It's been a long time since you got jolted, and you're still being sapped of energy. It comes and goes without rhyme or reason. Can you imagine what would happen if you were driving a car, and this came on you?

"Enough is enough. Those articles you read on the brain change may have said it took time for the shocked person to come around fully and still be changed in some positive way, but it didn't go into any blow-by-blow coverage of the days it took, or the experiences the people went through during those days. I say this is not typical of those effects you read about either. Remember, those people didn't have some head band on and get hit directly in the head with some great blast of electricity when the jolt hit them. Who knows what it did to your nervous system? I'm taking you to the emergency room of the hospital. This can't continue. And I don't want to hear any arguments or complaints, because I'm not putting up with it! We have a life to get on with together now, you said so yourself. And if we are going to do that, you have got to get things in order. That begins now, with me taking the reigns for awhile. Like it or not, that's the way it's going to be!" Kate was worried. She was giving vent to her feeling of helplessness, and was determined to rectify the situation once and for all.

This time, Lasky did not fight her. He was too weak. His thoughts now hovered over her concern that perhaps the electrical shock did indeed damaged his nervous system. It did create a positive brain change in him, yes, but it may have done either irreparable, or worse yet, progressive spinal damage. That last thought filled him with a terrible panic. His gray pallor gave way to a dead white hue, showing the blood had drained rapidly from his face.

"All right, Kate, you win," Lasky replied weakly. "Help me up. We better get to the hospital fast, because I'm feeling worse by the minute. If I should pass out, call 911 and get them out here as fast as possible." Whatever bravado he had left in him, drained away in the same moment the blood left his face.

Kate struggled, trying to get his big frame out of the chair. Lasky tried to lift himself up at the same time. But each time he did he collapsed back into his recliner, pulling her down onto him. Finally, Kate stood behind the chair, and pushed against his back as he pulled himself forward. He got to his feet. She moved around to his left side, threw his left arm over her shoulder, grabbed him around the waist, and pulled him ahead as he lunged forward.

"Don't fall down, Mier. I don't know if I can muster the strength I did earlier when I carried you up the stairs," Kate pleaded.

"I'll do my best, Kate, but, damn, why am I so weak? I'm as weak as a…" He broke off suddenly. He was going to say "kitten" but didn't want to remind either of them of poor little A-Bomb.

The grandfather clock chimed nine times as they moved toward its wall. Together they were making good progress. All they had to do was get over the thick shag rug, and down the stairs to the landing. Kate intended to lead him out of the front door and prop him against one of the front porch pillars. She would get the car out of the garage, pull it aside the front steps, help him into it, and they would be off to the hospital. With a little luck, she figured, his diagnosis would not be as severe as he predicted, and proper treatment would give him a good prognosis. In a little while, they would be making their new life together. Such were the thoughts of Kathleen Noel Murphy as she pulled and continually re-balanced the weight in her arms.

A whaling sound arose all around them. It was sliced into sound segments by a pierce rising and falling series of high pitch, frantic tones.

"What the hell is happening!?" Lasky shouted, the suddenness and shrill nature of the chaotic noise unhinging him emotionally. He panicked, jerked backwards, and pulled both of them to the floor.

"Goddamn it! I've had enough of this!" Lasky blared, as he consciously resurrected the physical strength within him. He gabbed Kate by the back of her blouse, and yanked her to her feet. Both of them rushed to the big bay window in the front wall of the house. Lasky didn't even pull the cord. He threw its sides opened, and together, he and Kate peered into the surrounding darkness of his property. Flashing yellow and blinking red and blue lights broke through the curtain of noise, as they watched six police cars, four fire trucks, five ambulances, and as assortment of smaller medical vehicles stream past them on the road leading from Pleasant Corners to Sunnberry.

A chill ran through Lasky and he shook all over. "What's wrong?" Kate asked. You look like you just saw a ghost. You're still pale, but your color is coming back. Let's use your regained strength to get you into the car!"

"And do what, Kate? Get me to a hospital that just sent its emergency room staff to Sunnberry? A lot of good that place will do us now! No! Something is happening inside me, and something is happening out there, too, in Sunnberry! I don't know how I know it but I do. Somehow, Kate, I'm tied into it. Switch on the news!"

Stunned, unable to think past his logic and orders, Kate left him by the window and turned on the television set at the far end of the big room. "Turn on channel 8. That's the local one that covers only Sunnberry and Pleasant Corners, and the outlying areas around here." Kate did as he ordered.

When the picture formed on the screen, Kate turned the volume up. She and Lasky looked at the scenes coming across to them with dumb amazement. The reporter was screaming at the top of his voice into his microphone, trying to broadcast to a public he was not even sure was out in 'TV Land' anymore. Scenes of carnage were behind and aside of him everywhere. Long, coiled rows of firehose lay on the ground, spouting water everywhere from holes gouged in them by falling pieces of the cannery plant that were being thrown off by the burning building. Huge storage buildings on both sides of the cannery were burning brightly, sending small pieces of propane and ammonia gas tanks that were housed aside of them flying in all directions.

People in dazed states, wrapped in blankets, were stumbling and walking around aimlessly. Smoke drifted past the camera lens, temporarily blocking out the scene of fireman running and falling down, choking violently from the propane-ammonia gas combination, while police were fighting off or being trampled on by a frenzied public, determined to see what was happening. In the background, cries and screams of desperation poured through the microphone over the reporter's voice. The images fell hard upon Kate's and Lasky's mind as they watched in silence. Kate continued to turn the volume up to maximum, until they were finally able to hear the reporter.

"I repeat, we have a crisis here! About thirty minutes ago, Red Line Canneries' new installation that just began operations here two months ago went up in a blaze, apparently from a series of ammonia tank explosions inside the plant. A number of employees were killed during the first outbreak. We understand that more deaths followed before the main body of employees were able to clear the burning structure, but as yet, we have no numbers yet on those casualties. This reporter has also been informed by an inside source that there are three 20,000 pound tanks of propane gas on the property that are also being threatened by the blaze. I have also been told by Sunnberry's Police Chief, Paul Ruger, that help is on the way from Pleasant Corners. He has also called in the State Police, but the local barracks can't call in any of its fifteen officers fast enough to be of any immediate help. As you can see behind me, confusion and panic is everywhere. There is talk of evacuating the...."

At that moment, the television camera went blank, as Officer Martin put his hand over the lens and escorted its broadcasting technician away from the reporter. Chief Ruger's huge hand cupped the microphone in its grasp, and tore it away from the reporter. As he ripped it out of the reporter's hands, he screamed, "What the f—do you think you're doing, you little son-of-a-bitch! Can't you see what we have here?! The body count is piling up, and the entire situation is out of control! You broadcast something like a evacuation now, and we'll have a full blown riot on our hands! Goddamn it, we need help here, not people like you trying to make points with their boss for getting a scoop on a tragedy!"

The reporter marched up to Ruger's face, and yelled back. "Look you Nazi, the people have a right to know! That's what freedom of the press is all about! It doesn't matter if it's good news or bad news, they have a right to know! Or does your kind take to Mein Kampf better than it does the Constitution of the United Sates!"

Ruger pushed his face directly into the reporter's. "Get this straight! You can broadcast what has happened. Cover it all you like! Get the goriest pictures you can! But you have no authority to broadcast speculation that will—not could, but **will** cause more trouble and probably cost even more lives! That is not part of your goddamn First Amendment, which you parasites are the first to quote. Why don't you kind try to follow that other thing I once heard of. What was it called?! Oh yea! Responsible journalism!"

The reporter snapped back at Ruger. "The policies of journalism are not for you to decide. They're up to the journalist on the spot!" Twisting sideways to Ruger, the reporter pulled a vindictive sneer out of the corners of his mouth and said, "And this journalist has determined that what he decides to report tonight *are* the policies of this night's reporting."

Ruger reached around to the front of the reporter's coat, grabbed it by the lapels, and spun him around. With a fury in his eyes, Ruger smiled back wryly and said, "Oh, yeah, twirp? Got news for you! There's an old saying. It was true in the past, is true now, and will be true in the future. Thems with the guns, *make* the *rules*!" With that said, the reporter's eyes grew wide as his face waited to met with the Police Chief's fist. Blood and teeth flew out of his mouth as he hit the ground.

"Welcome to the real world! If I ever see you again, I'll make goddamn sure your piss-ass little carcass is one that gets a number in the final body count! Now get the f—out of here!"

The reporter tried to scramble to his feet, but slid on the water soaked ground and fell. With a lowered, hunched ape-like gait he finally managed to get out of the sight of the Police Chief, who had unknowingly placed his hand upon his weapon, and undid the strap that secured the cold blue .45 in its holster.

Officer Martin returned to Ruger's side. "Goddamn, Chief, I wish you wouldn't have done that! There's gonna be a hell of a problem from him after this night is over!"

"Forget it, Martin. I handled his kind before, and their bosses. I wasn't a Lieutenant on the Chicago Force for twenty-five years for nothing before coming back home to take this job! Some little snot nose punk reporter, probably a whole year out of journalism school, with all of his bleeding heart liberal laws on his side. Give him a couple of years. He'll find out like the others did just how to handle an assignment, without getting more people killed. Besides, there won't be any problem from him or his boss in this case. Bessy will make sure the mayor fires him before his mouth gets too loud or he talks to his boss."

"Bessy?" Officer Martin asked.

"Yea, Bessy Halfrick, the mayor's wife," replied Ruger.

"How is she gonna get that friggin idiot fired, Chief?"

"What are you talking about, Martin? You don't know? Damn it, son, you got a pile of stuff to learn yet, don't you? Sure, the mayor's wife will

insist that he's fired before the week's out! It's called family, boy! Bessy's my
sister, and that little prick's boss is the mayor's brother! Like I said. It's
called family, boy, family!"

Back in Lasky's home the picture and sound of channel 8 went dead.

"What happened?" Kate asked.

"Oh, probably Police Chief Ruger teaching responsible journalism to a
new kid the local television hired," Lasky explained with a laugh.

"You're kidding?!" Kate replied. "Does that actually go on here?"

"Go on here? Are you kidding me? It goes on everywhere, honey, in
small towns and cities everywhere. That's just the way it is."

Kate didn't say a word. She just started up at him blankly. Lasky's
energy began to fade again. Except this time, he felt a tingling throughout
his entire body. As though some low level electric current was passing
through him. He grabbed the swivel rocker next to him to steady himself.

"Hitting you again, isn't is?" Kate asked.

"Yea, but this time with a twist. I feel like everything is surreal, and I'm
tingling all over. Like when you were a kid and touched your tongue to
the positive terminal of a flashlight battery. Ever do that?"

"No," she replied. "I'm not that stupid!"

"Well, it gives you a little acid-like tickle from the current passing into
your tongue. Problem is, this is stronger, like I stuck my tongue to the terminal of a car battery."

"What do we do now? Maybe you're right. With all that trouble down
in the town the hospital will be short handed. But still, Mier, they'll have
emergency staff on duty to handle local problems. I still think we should
go now before the situation in Sunnberry worsens, and they pull all the
medical people from the Pleasant Corners hospital down there."

"You're not listening, Kate. Something is happening inside of me. I
can feel it. It's now a physical feeling. It's something in my mind, like an
enormous blackness opening outward that's bringing a hideous fright
and anxiety with it. I mean, the fear is moving up into my mind as the
blackness folds outward. That's how I see it in my mind. That unfolding

is also causing the physical tinglings. Taken together, it's telling me that I'm connected to the events that are going on down in Sunnberry. No medical procedure is going to correct this. I don't know what to do, because I can't quite make out the nature of this something inside, or exactly how it's connected. In other words, I don't know what to do. We're stalemated!"

Lasky's strength was not yet gone. He held on to the rocker and moved around to the front of it so he could sit down. As he did, Kate stood at the ready, holding her arms outward to either catch or support him. While he moved, she thought she noticed a faint outline of a luminous green line around his hands, and blinked several times to refocus. "This is starting to get to you too, girl! You can't fold up now!" she reminded herself in her thoughts.

Lasky had rounded the recliner successfully and was about to sit down when Kate caught an image on the dark mahogany wall paneling in front of them. She noticed her shadow, slightly bent forward, ready to support Lasky's movements. But what hit her next stopped her from speaking. Her mind went into a dialogue of doubt and disbelief, because such a thing was not possible. She was not a physicist, but she was a well educated and very intelligent woman. What she did not see could not exist, yet it did. Throwing her hands up to her eyes, she clenched her fists and rubbed them with her knuckles. The impossible was still there. Fighting through her disbelief and dismay, she collected her still-fading wits and grabbed Lasky by the shoulder. With a jerk, she pull him up to a full standing position.

"Mier, look at the wall behind you!" Kate yelled. The cry in her voice stunned him into a surge of strength. He turned around to meet the terror that overtook his girl's mind.

"What's the matter, Kate? What's wrong? That's just the wall there. What are you seeing?" Lasky said in a stuttering tone of voice.

"Look carefully, Mier," Kate whispered. "Look carefully."

"What? I still don't see anything!" Lasky's voice broke out, the stutter of some unknown fear now filling his throat.

"Damn you, Lasky!" Kate screamed, "Look, **Look**! Can't you see it?! Look, goddamn it, Look!" With that, Kate began to move her legs and arms in rhythm, like a child making angels in the snow. Her shadow on the wall carried out her instructions, performing her angel-making movements in exact step with her.

"So what, Kate? What's your point? Oh, no, please, Kate! Don't fold up on me now! If you do, we're both done for!" Lasky shouted, the fear in his throat having now moved up into his mouth.

"You!" Kate screamed. "You! Where is your shadow! You have none! You're standing next to me, but you have no shadow!"

Lasky's head was turned toward Kate. The frozen wave that ran through his body and mind bolted him to his spot. He could not turn around and look at the wall.

Kate lunged forward. With a strength she only demonstrated once before when she carried his body up to the living room, she grabbed him by the shoulders and spun him around to face the wall. Lasky looked on the mahogany surface. There he saw Kate's outline, the ends of her long hair still in motion as they fell silently back upon her shadow's shoulders. He could see her shadow's arms plainly, still extended, but running into empty air. They were extended into an emptiness of space where he was standing. The impossibility of the situation was rejected by his mind. A shadow is nothing more than a darkness created by a physical object intercepting rays of light. That's what physics says. His body was there, as solid as ever. He could feel it. So could Kate. Yet it was not blocking out the rays of light coming from the floor lamp behind them. Both of them stood there in silence for a few minutes, staring at something that could not exist.

"What's happened, Mier? Are you fading into nothingness? What's happening?!" Kate cried, each word being filled with dread.

Lasky did not reply. He moved closer to the wall, like a cobra in a trance-like state moves toward the sounds of a flute holding it in its power. When he reached the wall, he extended his arm, touching its surface with his hand. His second arm followed the actions of the first. In a moment, he was guiding both hands in a gliding motion over the surface of the wall, as a trapped miner in darkness might, searching for a way out. The tragedy of the scene caused Kate to break down. The only sounds that could be heard in the room were her hysterical cries, and the swishing sounds coming from Lasky's hands, searching for a way out of the nightmare he created.

After several minutes, the reality of his situation was accepted by his mind. He began to come out of himself. In the background, he heard Kate's sobs. Her hysteria had given way to the same reality, reducing her cries to an intermittent sobbing. As Lasky stared at his no-shadow, his eyes refocused onto a green outline that abruptly began to surround his hands and run up the length of both of his arms. He looked down at his body, and saw that his entire form was now covered with the green outline. He watched in dazed fascination as a yellow outline next emerged from the green, and after a few more seconds, a hot pink outline emerged from the yellow. A third sound had entered the room. It was the sound of Glad Wrap crinkling. Tiny jets of green, yellow, and hot pink light were darting off of Lasky's body into the air, and disappearing into some unknown ether several inches from him.

Kate became aware of the new sound, and slowly lifted her head up from its bowed, crying position. There, against the wall, she saw Lasky. The shadowless man was still without his shade. But now his form glowed with the three thin outlines, and the jagged streamers flew off his body into space. Kate swooned, and fell backward onto the couch. She passed into a delirium that neared unconsciousness. Her head fell backward, catching the back of the couch hard. The impact snapped her back into full consciousness. Lifting her head forward, she sat on the couch, looking at the man she loved standing in front of her. Thousands of thoughts raced through her clouded mind. But finally, she found her voice. "Can I touch, Mier? Are you electrified or something? What should I do?!"

Lasky moved toward the grandfather clock, and threw its front case open. He grabbed the metal face, testing for a discharge of electricity from his hand to the clock face. There was a fast, slight spark that grounded itself to the clock face.

"It's all right, Kate. Whatever this is, it's electric in nature. But something tells me that it has another side to it as well. It's fairly strong, but not intolerable. And I did feel a little extra tingling as I grabbed the metal face of the clock, but the clock is still working. It's not a real grandfather clock, you know. It's battery powered. Maybe I gave the battery a little recharge, but didn't short it out. That tingling I feel throughout my body is probably the electric component of whatever these colors are, but that's about all. At least their lower level charges. Otherwise, I'd go up like a cinder. Just like those cases of spontaneous human combustion you hear about every once in a while."

Kate moved off of the couch and approached him cautiously. "Can I touch you? What if you're the only one immune, and if someone else touches you, they get electrocuted?" Kate nervously asked.

"I don't think it works that way. Even electric eels have an inner insulating layer from their own charge. And unless this damn thing has generated an insulating layer inside my body somehow, I should fry if it is a high current." He extended his right forefinger in her direction. "Look, stand on one leg only, and extend one of your forefingers to mine. Standing on one foot will prevent you from making a good earth ground. In case I am highly electrified, you will get a shock but it won't kill you. It'll give you a jolt and knock you down, but that's about all."

Kate extended her right forefinger to his, and touched it. Nothing happened.

"Did you feel anything?"

"Yes. A very slight tingling ran down my finger, but stopped there. But I also have an acid taste in my mouth. Like the aftertaste from biting into a sour lemon," she reported. "That's it, then, Kate! That taste is due to electric current breaking down the saliva in your mouth into its acidic parts! This thing does at least have an electric component to it for sure! I knew it all along! Goddamn, why was I afraid to admit it to myself? Is this due to that brain change? Have I become so kind and considerate from it now, that I don't have the raw strength to admit harsh realities to myself?"

"What are you talking about?" Kate asked.

"No more time for explaining now. Get me a mirror!" She stood motionless for a few seconds, looking at him blankly.

"Go! Do it! Get me a mirror! Do it now!" Lasky shouted, knocking her out of her stupor.

Kate stumbled from her spot in the living room and raced into the bathroom. In a few seconds she was back in the living room, holding a hand mirror out to him. "What do you want it for?" she asked.

Without saying a word, he held the mirror up to his face and peered into his image. A grim look overtook his face.

"What's wrong, Mier? Oh, no, not something else?!" Kate blurted out loudly, clenching her fists and striking downgrade into empty air.

Lasky cleared the phlegm from his throat, and regained his composure. As he did, he dropped the mirror to the floor, and grabbed Kate by her shoulders, so her clothing would insulate her from his electric charge. "Listen to me! I want you to calm down. I have another surge of strength now, and I think I can control it somewhat. I say that, because I noticed that as soon as I faced the inevitable that I secretly knew all along, some measure of control and strength returned to me. Now, with that said, I'm asking you to get hold of yourself. Will you do that for us?"

"For us?!" Kate queried, her voice shaking.

"Yes, for us! All right?" he replied in a subdued tone of voice.

Lasky looked at her softly, and moved her in a semicircle so his face was not directly in the light. "Look into my eyes, closely. Keep calm, please. We can't afford anymore fear now from either of us. Brace yourself, and look into my eyes."

Kate tightened her insides the way people facing a crisis do, and looked up slowly into Lasky's eyes. He felt her fall backwards in his grip, but steadied her.

"What are they?!" Kate managed to say in a voice filled with muffled desperation. She continued to stare into his eyes now, having overcome her initial shock. She watched them as they moved, and changed form. Three tiny triangles, one yellow, one green, and the other a hot pink color, roamed around the periphery of Lasky's cornea. They were in both of his eyes, but the motion of the set in the right eye was followed by the dance of the other set in his left eye.

"I don't really know, but I have seen them before. A long time ago, when I was just beginning the experimental phase of TAAC. I didn't think anything of them then. And they weren't in my eyes, either. They were projections into the Thought Chamber. I had many such little successes, but they were all prefatory to my ultimate goal. One I never got around to telling you about, what with the accident and all the other things that happened."

"What ultimate goal? What are you talking about?"

"The ultimate object of T.A.A.C., Kate. To bring whatever I was holding in my thoughts into physical form. To bring it right out from my mind into the world, and give it a reality all of its own."

Kate stared up at him. She wondered if he were mad after all. A cold chill ran down her spine, as she struggled to put this new revelation into the perspectives she had hammered out throughout the past few bizarre days.

"There's no more time to explain. I now know what I'm sensing and maybe even why I'm sensing it, but I don't know how it works. I mean, I don't understand the mechanism that allows me to get glimpses of what's happening in Sunnberry now. But we have enough to go on. I'm sure of it! One other thing, Kate. About my two final conclusions. They were wrong. Dead wrong. Now I know that. I'll explain the rest as we work."

"You mean you are connected to that nightmare down in the town?" Kate screamed at him.

"Yes, I'm afraid I am! But we have to get to work now if I'm to stop it. If it can be stopped, that is!

"Work?" Kate asked. "Work at what? At making more monsters?" Her thoughts of his previous explanations, that he wanted to produce some good through this work that would have ennobled humankind, giving to it a beauty and power that was originally invested in it by Nature, now seemed like a hollow self-lie to her. "You lied to me! You told me all about ennobling mankind, helping people to see new horizons, and now at the eleventh hour you tell me your real, sordid goal of profit and gain! Mier, how could you deceive me like this!"

"Goddamn it, Kate, stop it! I didn't plan this! If I did, I would have unleashed this horror long ago on the bastards! But I didn't! In every new field, in every new exploration, there are dangers and risks. That's been the story of human history. Do you think Columbus knew that his finding a new world would result in a new country, but only after Indians in North, Central, and South America were exterminated by the explorers looking for gold that came after him? Well, did he know that or didn't he! Goddamn it, girl, it goes with the territory! Men know that! We do it not in *spite* of knowing it, but *because* we know it! That's the way men are! It's how Nature made us! It's the double edged sword I told you about! Now, are you going to help me or not! Because goddamn it, I have no more time for you if you won't! I'm fed up with having to justify myself to people! You're thinking with your glands! Start thinking with your brains, or get the hell out of here!"

A terrible, tense silence fell over the living room. It was plain to both of them they were at the final crossroads. Lasky didn't get to his final explanation of his project's purpose until it was too late, and Kate had assumed that what he told her earlier was the whole truth, and nothing but the truth. Somewhere deep inside herself, she found the final key, and it unlocked the final answer for her. She loved him no matter what, and was going to stay with him to the bitter end, regardless of what that end was.

"I guess we'd better get to work if we're going to send whatever they are back to where they came from." She moved over to him and put her arms around his waist. "I love you, honey. I love you no matter what."

Lasky wrapped his arms around her shoulder and pulled her close to his chest. "That goes double for me. I'm so sorry. I should have told you the final goal a lot sooner. I wasn't hiding it from you. It just didn't occur to me. You know me. I always have to give a long preface before getting to the point. But know this. I once told you I could never live without you. I still mean every word of it."

They stood there for a few silent moments. It was Lasky who broke the mutual embrace. "Help me down to the lab, Kate. I'm still a wee bit wobbly in the legs. But first, get the radio from the kitchen. Bring your cell phone too. Oh! In the bedroom closet you'll find an old dark brown wooden cane. I broke my leg six years ago and used it to get around with. Got pretty good with it, actually. I can use it to get around now, instead of leaning on your shoulders. Please grab that too. We have a lot ahead of us!"

Chapter 10

▼

Of Mice and Men

The foremen of Sunnberry Wire & Cable, Inc., were standing on the docks of the mills, watching the wavering blaze of light above the house-tops in the distance. The smell of ammonia gas had reached the steel company, and the laborers inside the mills were complaining. Like school children looking for an excuse to go home early, they started to threaten the foremen with complaints to their union if something wasn't done soon to protect them from the noxious fumes that were entering the plant. In reality, the fumes were not that bad yet. The air turbulence caused by the cannery fire met with the cooler night air and confined the winds to the west and north end of the town where the cannery was located, by forming a pocket. Once carried away from the inferno on the wind, the gas pockets sagged, and began to drift slowly, building up concentrations that drifted aimlessly into the east and south ends of the town, the areas of heaviest population, and to the steel mills.

The four wire mill foremen stood near the edge of the dock silently watching and smelling, until Tom Ferley, the Chief Foreman broke the silent tension. "It's a good thing we were the last of two industries the town allowed in this sector. Can you imagine if that new cannery was next to us? Our production schedule would be shot for months. You can't fall behind in this business. I've been here for twenty-six years, and I can tell you, it's a domino effect. Fall behind for more than twenty-four straight hours, and you'll lose half of your orders before the spit hits the ground. Every tom, dick and harry who uses steel cable waits until the eleventh hour to reorder what he needs to hold his costs down. And we take the short end of the stick for it. There's no lead time on reorders. They order it when they need it, and then they want it the day before they ordered it. That's how it is."

Rik Hubbell, one of the foreman under Tom, only smiled at his boss's tunnel vision. This problem was bad, and it was getting worse. It threatened more than the steel company, and he and the other two foremen knew it. "Well, Tom, I think there's more to worry about now than a production schedule. If that fire spreads, it could take the upper half of the town out with it. It might even reach here. Can you imagine what that would mean if it does? We all got family living down this end. Not like you and yours, with a house twenty miles further east of here. That's what we're thinking about, not just the job!"

"And who's fault is it that for you guys are living here in town? Damned if it's mine! Besides, don't be an ass, Rik! They probably have it under control right now, or soon will. The radio said they have reinforcements coming from Pleasant Corners, and at least they have it contained for now. That's what they said."

"Contained?!" Rik quipped. "With three 20,000 gallon propane tanks right behind the burning cannery? How long can they contain it before the fire hits one of them? The radio said the cannery illegally installed three 20,000 pound tanks of propane gas there. If one goes, it'll take the others with it! Sixty thousand pounds of propane going up? That will send fire, flames, and metal everywhere for a half mile around, and the west and north end will go up with it. If that happens, we won't be far behind. I think you'd better get the VP of Operations in here fast, Tom. A decision has to be made, a plan of some kind, in case we wind up with more on our hands than your logic allows!" Rick's tone and the volume of his voice rose. His own dialogue began to panic him.

"Look, Hubbell!" Ferley replied, "I'm the boss here, and don't you or any of the others forget it!" His voice showed signs of strained tension as he continued, while nodding his head toward the other two foremen who stood quietly beside Rik. "I make the decisions here, not you! I came up through the ranks! I earned this job through sweat, blood, and three hernias! I worked the machines like any of the guys running them now, but I had the brains to keep my mouth shut, take orders, and go the extra mile when the others were bitching about this or that, just like you are now! That's how I got to be Chief Foreman. And in those past ten years, production has never been higher and our costs lower!

"Oh, and by the way, the salary increases and bonuses have never been better for all of us as they have been the past ten years also. Or did you forget that? It's no coincidence. The company always shares its extra profit, but its got to have the extra to share. And thanks to me and the Chief Foreman in the cable mill, there's been extra these past years, plenty of extra, and you know it! Marv Eltmann works his mill the way I work mine, and we work together. That's why all of us have it so good now, including those assholes at the machines inside who are trying to get us to close down and send them home with pay! It's simple. The machines keep turning, and the wire and cable keep coming, or there is no pay!

"Now I want each of you to go in there and talk to your crews and make that goddamn plain to them! If any of them want to walk out, fine. Just tell them to make sure they keep walking though, because their job will be filled by some other grunt we pull in straight off the street tomorrow! It doesn't take a rocket scientist to run one of those machines, and we can train anyone in two weeks. Remind them of that! And screw the union complaints! That's why we have a Plant Superintendent. Frank Ketterman will handle them. That's his job! Besides, if you have to know, Walt Cotters is on his way in now. I got a phone call from him a little bit ago. What time is it, anyway?" The red in Ferley's cheeks could be seen clearly in the dock light. He took any questioning or even suggestions as threats to his authority, and was known to put them down, one way or another.

"It's 9:30," Rik replied in a subdued tone of voice. There was another violent rumble of the ground, and the flames across the housetops backdrop shot higher and brighter into the sky.

"Oh, no, there must have been another explosion! Damn! It sounded like one of those twenty thousand pound tanks of propane went up! Goddamn, now there will be big trouble for sure!" Ferley cut in, shaking his head "The VP will be here any minute now. He'll no doubt bring Frank with him. I'm going around to the front of the main office and wait for them. Walt said he wanted to see me and Marv as soon as he gets here. You guys just go on about your business. And fellas! Make goddamn sure the wire keeps spooling off onto those prepacks! Marv called an extra crew in tonight to beef up the wire closing operation. That big ski tow cable contract for that new resort in Colorado needs the cable shipped next week. And we're not only going to make that Friday ship date, we're going to beat it! Marv and I plan to get the flatbeds loaded by Wednesday, latest.

"Oh. And before you guys start talking about me behind my back when I leave, just remember. Come December, I'm going to remind you guys of this little bullshit danger when I hand you your Christmas bonus packs. Remember that!" Ferley turned away from them sharply, and with the cocksure strut of the only rooster in the barnyard, walked toward the steps at the back end of the dock toward the main office.

Rik Hubbell turned to the other two silent foremen. Both Pete Stenoski and 'Bluto' Trager were staring off in the direction of the fire. Rik looked away in the same direction, and said, "You know guys, I'm glad Lasky isn't here anymore. I liked him a lot, and we got to be pretty good friends, as you know. But seeing this tonight, and hearing Ferley's remarks, brings it all home again. He hated this place with a passion, and Ferley most of all."

Pete cut in abruptly. "He was none too fond of Ketterman or Cotters either! Man, I remember the three of them going at it in the wire testing lab that one day, when Lasky told them that goddamn Ferley had no business going into the circuitry and turning some knobs he knew nothing about! That son-of-a-bitch almost destroyed the 26 inch wire drawing machine! He told them straight out Ferley had no training in electronics and engineering, and just because the machine sat in his wire mill, didn't give him the right to go tampering with it. I walked in just as he said that, and Cotters stuck up for Ferley! Then Ketterman jumped in like the good stooge he is, and started in on Lasky. Man, what Lasky told the two of them isn't fit to print or say out loud! But he made it damn clear to both of them what he thought of them, Ferley, and, 'this half-assed run organization with clowns like you two at the wheel!' I though Cotters and Ketterman were going to explode on the spot! Man, the relations between them were none too good from that day till the day Lasky quit, what, some five years later?"

Bluto Trager finally broke his silence. "Yea, you know, it's weird how Lasky was always friendly with us foremen and the laborers in the mills, and stuck up for us. I never saw or heard of a member of management doing that before, at least, not to the extent he did. It's a miracle they kept him around here as much as they did!"

"Around?" smirked Rik. "They had that poor bastard on the road more often than not, setting up machine circuits at one of the auxiliary plants, here, there, or wherever. I think they only tolerated him around here until they could find another road assignment for him. What with all of the upgrading the company's been doing the past ten years, hell, they were able to keep him out of their hair pretty much of the time."

"Thing that gets me," Bluto inserted, "is that they didn't outright fire him. He's a good engineer and all that, but you figure, there's got to be others, just as good or even better, that will tow the company cable instead of causing all the trouble he did, while taking labor's part pretty much to boot!"

"I don't know," Hubbell replied. "He was a damn good engineer, and he also handled all the quality control procedures, the government audits, and actually wrote the entire Q.C. manual that we either live or die by to this day. That's a tough combination to get in any one man, and he did it for one salary. But whatever, he's gone now off on his own, and I wish him well. I'd wish anyone well that could get out of working anymore, period. Things sure aren't the way they used to be some twenty-odd years ago anymore, anywhere, these days. Well, I guess it's no use bitching, guys, we'd better get back in and see if we can calm the troops. The smell of ammonia is getting stronger now, and pretty soon, it will be all through the mills." The three foremen walked back into the wire mill, prepared to meet the anger of the work force.

Walt Cotters had arrived in his big Lincoln. Directly behind him, as Ferley had predicted, came Ketterman, his Chevy, its overdone body design trying to imitate a Chrysler, finally chugging to a full stop. In his characteristic peacock strut, Cotters emerged from his vehicle, and motioned to the waiting Tom Ferley and Marv Eltmann as one would motion to two fawning servants, to follow him into the main office building. Frank nonchalantly bounced along behind the tiny parade.

The four marched hurriedly down the narrow corridor of the first floor offices, and into Cotters' office in silence. As Cotters switched on the overhead light, he began in a low voice, as if what he was going to say was not to be heard even by distant ears. "Close the door," he told Ketterman.

"Gentlemen, sit down! We have a serious problem on our hands, and what we decide in the next few minutes here will may damn well determine the fate of our manufacturing facility in this town." Stunned, all three men sat down quietly, and placed their hands on their laps like schoolboys called in for an accounting of their actions.

Cotters continued, the volume of his voice now rising to normal levels within his now secure office. "I received private word from Chief Ruger that the cannery fire is more than they let out to the news people. It's like this. The body count has reached twenty-four already, and twelve people are still unaccounted for. The Plant Manager over there, Ronald Lamour, was also killed. Casualties from flying shrapnel, ammonia gas, burns, and general panic has claimed seventy-eight others, sixteen of which are critical. Ruger called me and Jim Hasbrow, the VP of Operations of the silk mills next door, because together we employ most of the people.

"They don't know if they can contain the fire. The explosions are the big part. Apparently, someone went ahead behind city council's back, and installed three 20,000 pound tanks of propane, instead of three 2500 pound tanks like they were licensed to do. The damn things are between the main plant—what used to be the main plant—and the vinershed that sends the raw product up to the plant for canning and packing. The trouble is, someone also went behind the council's orders and installed, apparently secretly, another 20,000 pound tank of propane underneath the vinershed. They were having it discreetly fed from well caps housed in the main plant.

"In other words, when the main tanks in the cannery were being refilled, they just routed an extra 20,000 pounds through some underground lines to refill the hidden tank. Carboscol, the propane provider, was happy over the added business, so they didn't say a word to anyone. And why should they? They're based in Pleasant Corners, and they didn't have to report anything to the Sunnberry Council, and so no one was the wiser. Whoever on the council took a kick back to look the other way on this one will have felony charges filed against him as soon as this mess is over, and they start the investigation. That's what Ruger told me.

"But all that aside, the hidden tank under the vinershed went up at 9:30. It's now 10:15. I can only imagine the nightmare over there now. Anyway, that explosion created a fire line right up to the three propane tanks between what used to be the cannery and vinershed. They tried to put it out, but other ammonia tanks by some other sheds also went up. Combined with the huge ammonia leaks from the cannery, and the ammonia tanks in the vinershed that exploded when the propane there ignited, and all of us have a real problem now."

"All of us?!" Frank broke in. "Why all of us! Hell, they're far enough away from us! The damn thing can't spread this far…can it?!"

"That's just it, Frank," Cotters explained. "Ruger has reinforcements coming from Pleasant Corners. Fireman, equipment, ambulances, paramedics, the whole nine yards. They should have arrived awhile ago from what he told me. But that fire line contains a trapped ammonia gas pocket. Damnedest thing he said he ever saw, as though something was holding it in there, even with the wind that kicked up from the fire-heated air all around. The firefighters he left couldn't get in at the tanks to foam them down because of the ammonia.

"What is worse is that they found out that bastard of a Lamour didn't buy just commercial grade ammonia. He bought something called anhydrous ammonia, which is supposed to be really bad, toxic stuff, because it's purified somehow. He paid more, but it lasts longer, and so he was saving money. Again, against the licensing regulations he had from the town council. Bottom line, gentlemen, is if they can't get in to foam down those three tanks and the fire line hits them, not only will the north and west end of town go up, but Ruger is worried it will spread fast because of the layout of this damn town, and our end will go up with it.

"There's also another part of this big worry for us. As you know, this end of town is on city gas. That's how things were thirty-some years ago when the plant started here. Same for the silk mill. The town needed the money, and so it forced the two of us to go to city gas. But the new zoning over in the north and west section made it too expensive for them to run the gas line out to it, so they decided that any industry coming into that newly zoned commercial area would have to go to a commercial source for gas, if they needed it. Problem is, if the fire spreads and comes to this end of town, there are just too many exposed pipes to foam down. Hell, we don't even know where all of the pipes we have here are anymore, after all of our expansion over the past ten years! Not only that, but the houses at this end are all on city gas too. Ruger told me that if the ground gets hot, or a main pipe breaks, any open flame will heat the gas until it breaks down. After it breaks down, the way the stuff acts, it will explode out of the ground piping used to channel it all over this end. If that happens and it hits the open air, it will take this end of town up in the biggest fireball anyone ever saw in these parts."

"You've got to be kidding, Walt!" Ketterman screamed. "You've got to have it all wrong! This is a hick town in a lot of ways, I agree, but it's not that stupid to not have thought of something like this happening! Ruger's got to be wrong! Nothing like this happens today, with all the checks-and-balances and safety measures provided by government regulation! You two have to be wrong, Walt, dead wrong!"

Cotters' always controlled temper, fanned by the heat of desperation of the impending situation, finally erupted at Ketterman. After controlling himself throughout the twenty-plus years of their professional relationship, he finally vented his pent-up hostility at him. "You're talking like you just got out of college, Frank!" Cotters screamed back at him. "Thirty years ago things weren't like the way they are today! This town—no goddamn town or city—springs up overnight! It's a product, Frank, not a sum of events, big and small, over the life history of the place! And there are screwups everywhere that no ones knows or cares about, until something like this happens. And yes, Frank, there are even goddamn stupid mistakes that were made legitimately, and which, at the time, looked like they were in everyone's best interest! That's called life, Ketterman, and you'd better start dealing with it now!

"Come to think of it, I have had my belly full of you all these years, hiding behind your desk, waiting for the free business lunch or dinner to roll around, and following me around like my second shadow! There's no more time for understanding or consideration of you and your asshole attitudes and incompetence, riding this corporate gravy train! This is it! Everything all of us worked for throughout all the years could incinerate tonight, and I just don't have anymore patience to put up with your wining demands and cowardice-in-the-face-of-reality attitude! Get your head out of your ass right now, Frank, or get out of here now! We've got a real problem here, and it's one I intend to address as best I can, with whatever little piss ass information I have! Now what's it going to be? Are you here to help, or not? If not, do as I said, and get the hell out of my sight now!"

The seething hostilities Frank had toward Walt from having to play second fiddle to him throughout the years finally erupted. The average size, somewhat stout man stood up slowly from his position on the couch and walked over to Cotters' desk. Tom and Marv looked down at the office carpeting. Both of them knew that the scene unfolding before their eyes was a long time overdue. They spoke privately of its inevitability at times, but neither expected that on this night of crisis and possible disaster, that inevitable confrontation would erupt along with the propane gas tanks on the other side of town.

Frank made his two hands into fists, and placed them down quietly on the front of Cotters' desk, bent forward, and began. "I guess it's true, Walt. What they say about a crisis bringing out the best and worst in people. You had your say, now I'm going to have mine. For over twenty years now, I listened to your double talk, excuse making, at every turn, and ran constant interference for you. I lied to the Board of Directors when you made any number of a dozen mistakes that cost this company hundreds of thousands of dollars. In the beginning, I figured that was my job, since I was directly under you on the corporate organizational chart. And yes what you're thinking is right. It's what I thought too. My loyalty is to you, since you were my immediate superior. I followed that road to hell, Walt, until it gradually ate away at my manhood.

"At first, I did what was best for you. My superior. Then, it turned into my doing what I though was best for us. Not what I knew was best for the entire company. After so many years, I took to justifying my actions in covering for you, and even becoming your lackey. That's right, Walt, all that union crap I had to handle was your idea, remember? I was supposed to be Plant Superintendent, not go-between for the company and the union grievances. I listened to you planning to cut costs here that wound up costing the company twice what the original plans would have run, and I lied for you there, when you got caught at it. I hid information from the Board for you, and destroyed even more.

"Pretty soon, I was as guilty as you are because I desperately needed this job to raise my family. I was afraid that if anyone found out I didn't have my degree in engineering like I said I did on my application form, I'd be fired on the spot. But you knew, Walt, and you let me know it. You kept it hidden all these years, and without threatening me directly. Just letting me know you knew was enough, you figured. You were right. I figured if corporate found out I'd lose my job. So I continued to play your game. I guess that's about the average reason for self-betrayal these days, and I'm going to have to live with it. Oh, and yes, I took plenty of advantage of the company too, on all those free 'business' lunches, dinners, and parties at the country club. And lied through my teeth on my expense account. Remember, Walt? But then sure you do, because you taught me how to do it, and then approved them for reimbursement! Remember those little perks, Walt? Well, I want these two guys here to hear it all. I guess they pretty well have, except for one thing."

With that Frank straightened up, and walked around the side of Cotters' desk, until he stood by Walter's side. He stood there a few silent moments, as everyone in the room held their breath. Especially Cotters, who swallowed hard, expecting Frank to physically thump him. Finally he spoke again.

"So Walter, you goddamn little maggot, this worm has now turned!"

Having said that, he reached out and grabbed him by the front of the shirt with one hand, clenched his fist tightly about the material, and dragged the pale Cotters up to his level.

"Effective, immediately, you little bastard, I resign! I was going to surprise you with this little bit of news in a year or two. But what the hell, now's as good a time as any! In fact, it couldn't have come during a better time for you, Walt. Right on the heels of what might turn out to be the destruction of this plant! Your sole reason for living! Oh. Whether or not this crisis passes, I am going to personally make a clean breast of everything to corporate in New York City. That's right, Walter, to the Board of Directors. Let them cancel my pension if they want! Me and the wife saved a good bit over the years, my old friend, to be able to retire decently to Fort Lauderdale as we wanted to all along.

"The pension would be nice, yes, but even nicer will be seeing them skin you alive when they find out what's been going on all these years. I even kept some records. Not many, but enough to hang you ten times over, and they'll have it as soon as things simmer back down to normal. Then, you little maggot, we'll see who has redeemed his manhood, and who is buried alive because he never had any in the first place!" Frank lifted Cotters up to face level, and with a jerking thrust, threw him back into his chair. Then he turned to the other two, who looked like men who had just grabbed a 220 volt electric line by the live ends, and got thrown across the floor by the jolt.

"And, uh, Marv, surprise, surprise! Ask this maggot if there is any truth to him firing you after your eighteen years of company service, to cut down on managerial overhead costs. Go into my office and open the top left hand drawer when you get a few minutes. You'll find your termination papers there, dated for May 25th of this year. Look at the 'Change of Management' report and the reasoning behind it, and look at whose signature is on it, recommending the change to the Board of Directors. Yep, good old Walt's. While you're at it, look at who your replacement will be. His cousin, Wile Cotters, who manages a coat hanger manufacturing company in Vermont. Not exactly wire rope and cable, is it, Marv?

"But that's okay, Walt will fix it, like he did your being promoted to Chief Foreman of both Strander and Closer Mills. Yep, good ol' Walt again. See, Marv, he didn't want you having so much power. He was afraid you could hide more from him, just as he has been hiding so many things from the Board all these years. So, divide and conquer is the rule, as he told me when he split that position into two. You over the Closer Mill, and Hank Stratum over the Strander Mill. Of course, to make it look like corporate did it, he downscaled Hank's power just a tiny, tiny bit, by having him report to you. And it worked, because you thought you were the real boss over both mills.

"Yet what you didn't know is that Hank came flying in here when that division happened, hell bent on leather on quitting on the spot. What did Walt do? Gave him a raise to keep him quiet. Did you know Hank makes $7,000 more a year than you do? And you're supposed to be his boss? Check it out. You knew something wasn't right, but swallowed it anyway, hook, line, and sinker, because you have no more guts that I did. Marv, you're an ass. You and this maggot deserve each other." Frank then turned to Tom, who was sitting as still as a stone statue, waiting for his turn to come. Frank continued.

"Ah, Tom. Tom, Tom, Tom. Walt's good old right hand man in the wire mill. Keeping everything going. Worrying about production schedules ahead of the men's health and safety, and about cutting costs at every conceivable and inconceivable corner. Tom, what a treasure your efforts were for corporate. That is, if they ever knew that you were the one behind them. Of course, they didn't. Walt took care of that. Like the new rod manufacturer you found six months ago that sells us the green rod for six cents a hundred pounds less than any other supplier. Did you know that saves us over two hundred grand a year? Know who got the reward for that discovery? Bet'cha do! He's sitting right behind his desk over there. Know what his reward was? Well, part of it, anyway. See that new Lincoln old Walt is driving these last couple of months? Got it, Tom! That was part of his reward from the Board! Plus, a $20,000 increase in salary!

"Tell me, Tom, what did you get? Hmmm? Embarrassed? Didn't know the Board paid off for saving it big bucks? Too bad. Well, let me tell you what you got for your reward, Mr. Ferley, because I can see you don't want to say it yourself. A 5% pay raise. And, you got it from…Walt, for your splendid research. That amounts to…what…about $2,000 a year, right? Yes sir, Tom, you're a good company man all right, and Walt made sure you were rewarded. He peeled the meat from the bone, and threw the bare bone to you. Stunned I know all about this, aren't you? Why, goddamn men, there isn't anything the VP of Operations hides from his lackey! He told me everything! There isn't one goddamn move either of you made or make that I don't know about first, middle, and last. And the two of us laughed at you two simple bastards all these years, and you never knew it. Uh...until now.

"So, gentleman, with that, I am finished here, and by design. I pulled my own plug. The three of you, though, deserve each other, and this goddamn company. As for me, this worm has finally turned."

With a rapid move to Cotters direction, Ketterman looked at him coldly and said, "You'll have my resignation in the mail tomorrow. That is, if this place is still standing. Either way, corporate will receive their packet of info too, and they will receive it a lot goddamn sooner than you want or expect, Walt. You may even have another surprise coming there! You know, Walt, if there is any justice in this world, the day will come when you'll see yourself for what you really are. A little man, with a tiny life and an even tinier mind. And you'll take that realization with you, right to your grave. That, Walt, is what I wish for you."

Frank Ketterman put a huge smile on his face. It did not hide the disgust and contempt he had for the three he left in the office as he slammed the door on his way out. He once hated himself as much as he hated the three behind the door. Perhaps more. But he finally vindicated himself, and was looking forward to making a new life for him and his wife in Fort Lauderdale. One both of them could be proud of.

Tom, Marv, and Walter watched the door slam behind Frank as he walked out of the office building for the last time. With their dirty linen hung on the line for each other to see, there was nothing left for them to say to each other. The embarrassment and humiliation heaped upon the three of them by the lackey they once laughed at, brought the ultimate disgrace each secretly knew he had earned throughout the years. Pushing it out of their minds would not work this time. Every secret requires the mistaken belief that its holder is the only one who knows it. That's what makes it secret. That's what makes it legitimate. That's what makes it worth a man's or woman's soul. But that condition was now shattered, and each of them were left to face the person inside that he created.

Tom and Marv stood up at the same time, and walked out of Cotters' office. They moved as phantoms, gliding silently across the thick green carpeting of the office. Tom turned to the left and walked down the hallway to the nearest exit, while Marv turned to the right to find his door out of the office building.

Walt sat behind his desk, staring off into space. His thirty years at the company would soon be over. All Ketterman had to do was fulfill his promise by sending the records he had to corporate, and Walt knew he would make good on his promise. Thoughts of the immediate danger to the plant left his mind. He couldn't think anymore. All he could do was feel. What he felt was the culmination of thirty years of deception, betrayal, and living high off the small and large miseries he had created for the workers of Sunnberry Wire & Cable.

Tom Ferley walked through the wire mill doors and called Rik Hubbell, Pete Stenoski, and Bluto Trager over to him. With the demeanor of a beaten animal, Tom looked at them and said in a hollow voice, "Sound the alarm for the men to close down all operations. Assemble them and tell them to go home. There's nothing more any of us can do here."

"But what about the furnace?" Rik questioned. "We can't just shut it down. It'll take three days to fire up to temperature again, and we sure can't leave it running with everyone gone! Once that fire over the other side of town is over, you and Cotters will be on our backs again to try and double production to make up for the shutdown. Dammit, Tom, what the hell are you thinking?"

Tom turned to Rik and gave a weak smile. The kind a man gives who has just lost his last dollar. "Just shut it down, Rik, and get the men out of here. I don't know what's going to happen with that fire over in the other end of town, but I just had it pointed out to me that there are other things that are more important than production schedules. This is one of them.

Please do as I ask." Rik, Pete, and Bluto looked at him and then each other in dumb amazement.

"Are you all right, Tom?" Rik asked.

"No, not really, but it's not important now. What is, is that we get these operations shut down and get the men out of here. According to Cotters there's a few real bad problems with this fire, and frankly, no one knows what will happen. Not just to the plant, but to the entire town."

"What?!" Bluto said, not believing his ears. "But the fire's all the way over in the west and north end. How can…" Tom cut him off.

"Look. There's no time to explain. Do as I said, please, and shut everything down. Then get the men out of here as fast as you can. You three leave with them. Not after them, but with them."

"What about you, Tom?" Rik asked.

"I'll just give a once around to make sure everything is battened down. Then I'll leave too. All right, men, let's get to it."

With that, Tom sounded the alarm and took charge. "Pete, Bluto, herd them over here. We have no time to lose."

The three foremen did as Rik ordered, and gathered the wire mill laborers and work crews into the center of the mill. Rik started.

"Fellas, listen to me carefully. I'm only going to say this once. The fire over the north end is either out of hand or pretty near it. No one seems to know just what is going on. We're shutting everything down as of now. Machine operators, close down your machines, and turn the power off at the electrical cabinets in back. Laborers, leave the prepacks where they are, and close all windows. Lock them down tight. Coilers, close and secure all bay doors on all docks, and close off the boiler room. Then shut the boilers down using the emergency shut down switch, open the ballasts, and let the water pour out into the drains. Assemble back here as soon as you're done. We're going to take a head count as you go out!"

In a frenzy, the wire mill personnel did as they were instructed, while the three foremen raced down to the furnace and lead bath. "Shut off gas valves 1 and 2 as I turn 3 and 4, Bluto," Rik yelled over the billowing noise of the forty foot long, 1200 degree furnace. They continued until all twelve valves were closed off.

"Pete, you get on the other side of the lead bath. There's fifty ton of molten lead in there. She'll take four days to cool, and it's gonna be a bitch to fire back up again, but we gotta close her down now. When I holler, we have to close off zones 1 and 2, 3 and 4, in sync, so we don't get a blow-back. You take zones 3 and 4. I'll take 1 and 2."

Working together, they finally closed both the furnace and lead bath down, and then ran back to the central area of the mill where the other men were gathering. After confirming that the entire mill was closed down, the three foremen took a head count as the men filed out the front door to their cars.

"Get home fast, guys! This is no night to be thinking of a cold one. I'm serious! Your families are going to need you!"

"Hey, Tom," Rik yelled. "We got it shut down! Where the hell are you, anyway?"

Tom Ferley emerged from his darkened office. "Good. Now you guys get out too. I'll follow along in a few minutes. Just a quick look around and I'll be off."

As Rik, Bluto and Pete filed through the front door of the mill and into the parking lot, Bluto looked at the two other foremen and said, "Fellas, I got a bad feeling about Tom. He sure isn't himself. I've never know him to care about anyone but himself all these years. And now this?! Maybe we should wait up for him."

"Never mind," said Rik. "I got a feeling too. This is the first time in years, maybe even since he was a kid, that Tom knows what he's doing. Let him be."

The three foremen got into their cars and joined the parade of cars leaving the plant property. Among them were the entire crews of the Closing and Stranding mills. In a few minutes the manufacturing plant was empty, except for Walt, Marv, and Tom. The last three ghosts sat alone in their offices, and simply waited for whatever was to come. It was

slowly dawning on Marv and Tom as it had to Walter, that their careers at
the steel company were over. The inevitable follow-up questions of what
each would do to earn a living after this did not enter their minds. Only
the cold numbness of facing themselves was their immediate concern.
None of them cared about the plant any longer.

Walter Cotters stared at the clock on his office wall. It was one of those
large, plain-faced business type clocks with the big, slow moving, red sec-
onds-hand, that insults the artificial ambiance found in any executive's
office. It was 10:45 P.M. His mind was still numb.

"How could everything fall apart so suddenly? How could my right-
hand man betray me like this?" he muttered to himself. Did the events of
the past half-hour really happen, he wondered, or was all this some type of
hallucination brought on by his anxiety control medication? Maybe there
wasn't even any fire at the cannery? Maybe he was having a bad drug
induced trip? Maybe…

His mind was fading in and out of reality. Thoughts of what just
occurred, the everyday appearance of his office, even the silence in the
empty main office building, now became surreal. As he tried to regain his
mental composure, Cotters noticed that the recessed lighting running
around the ceiling had started to flicker. He had them specially installed at
the east, south, and west walls for dramatic effect. During evening staff
meetings he would dim them so everyone sitting in the chairs and couches
set against those three walls would be sitting in shadow, while a single light
above his desk shone down on him brightly. It gave him the appearance of
a divine being calling souls to an accounting.

After flickering for a few moments, the coping lights dimmed and then
burst. All twelve recessed bulbs popped in order, beginning at the east end
of the ceiling, and finishing with the last one in the west. Glass and plastic
pieces blew outward in all directions, coating his office floor and desk with
their fractured remains. The single bright light above his desk switched on
by itself, bathing him in its divine light. Stray rays of light from the divine
source reflected off the scattered plastic and glass, suggesting the office had

just been coated with a layer of new fallen snow. After silence returned to his office, Walter uncovered his eyes. He shielded them with his arms to ward off the flying slivers.

The surreal state of his mind escalated, and he screamed out loud, "Goddamn you, Ketterman, you left me nothing!" as though Frank had somehow engineered the events of the past few minutes. "You'll pay for this, you son-of-a-bitch! I'm not beaten yet! You were *my* lackey! I wasn't yours! I'll have you discredited with the Board before the next sun sets! Then we'll see who gets the better of who! No one gets the better of Walt Cotters, no one, let alone you, you stupid lackey! Before I'm done with you, Ketterman, you won't simply lose your pension! I'll see to it that the Board brings you up on criminal charges for fraud and theft! Send some secret file to them that you've been keeping on me, will you! Well, we'll see whose file reads best and the most believable! Yours or mine! I taught you, remember? Before I'm done with you, you'll beg me to save your ass like I did a thousand times before over the years! But not this time, Ketterman, not this time! I'll run you so far into the ground..."

His mind now on the verge of nervous collapse, Cotters ranting was cut off in mid-sentence as the light above his head clicked off. No sooner did his mind register what had just happened, when the lights in the long hallway of the building also shut down. Walt was in darkness. The growing tension was too much for him. He began to sweat profusely, and pound his desk with his fists, screaming into the blackness that surrounded him.

"You f—er, Ketterman! You're behind this! I'll find you, you rotten bastard, and when I do, I won't wait to fix you with corporate! I'll kill you myself, right here and now! That's all you deserve, you filthy traitor! To die like the dog you are!"

As the lone voice continued to rant in the darkness, a crackling sound moved down the hallway toward his office. It wavered in the blackness, changing shapes, while gliding smoothly through the air toward Walt's open office door. As though it appeared out of nothingness, it emerged from the darkness in the hallway, and poked one of its hot-pink corners into the blackness of Walt's office.

Cotters' ranting stuck in his throat and ended there, as he heard a sound like Glad Wrap coming off of the luminous rectangle that glided into his office. The geometrical form took up a stance in the air in front of his desk, and froze itself into a stationary position. It no longer shifted its shape. It just hung in the air, motionless, in front of the dazed VP of Operations. The VP's mind finally waded through its surreal state and returned to reality. His heart began to pound hard in his chest, as he tried to make sense of the image in front of him. As he began to speak to it, Walt Cotters became aware of the strong smell of ammonia in his office. The fire was apparently spreading, and the winds were carrying the toxic gas to his plant's end of town.

"What are you?" he asked the rectangle that hung in the air in front of his desk. The form did not answer. It simply hung motionless in the air. Finally Walt panicked and screamed out, "Who are you?" The last emotion Walt Cotters felt was one of utter terror combined with the dismay of one who realizes his life is about to end, as a voice came out of the figure.

"From Lasky, with love!"

No sooner did the voice end its sentence, and the final thoughts of the trouble he had joyfully caused for Lasky pass through his mind, when a pair of long, hot-pink arms, each with three curved, claw-like projections, sprang out from the rectangle and fixed themselves to the side of the VP's head. With a rocking and pulling motion they began to exert an upward force against the executive's body. Cotters heard a popping sound in his ears. He began to scream from the onset of pain that followed, and then to gurgle, as his head moved upward away from his body and his windpipe constricted.

He grabbed the edge of his desk and pulled upward, while trying to slide his head down, through the powerful grip. He heard a cracking in his ears and skull, as the bones in his head began to collapse, and blood flowed into his mouth and down his throat. He coughed and spit up blood as the upward pulling continued, his body wiggling with the motion of a fish being brought out of the water. Walt Cotters continued to struggle until the arms of the rectangle tired of their game. With one short, abrupt upward pull, the arms finally ripped the head cleanly from Walt's body.

His headless corpse fell backward into its executive chair, and slumped down. The arms of the rectangle held the head in front of it, as though looking at it, and then turned it around so its eyes faced its body in the chair. Gently, the arms placed the head in the center of the desk. Blood from the gaping wound of the open throat flowed onto the desk blotter, while remnants of Walt's spinal cord made a slight clacking sound before coming to rest behind it. Even though the eyes were lifeless, they still bore a look of bewilderment and amazement at what they had witnessed and experienced. The divine light above Walt's desk clicked on again, bathing his head and body in its warm glow. Frank Ketterman got his wish. The day finally came when Walter Cotters was able to see himself for what he really was.

Marv Eltmann rattled the loose door knob of his Closer mill office as he closed it behind him. "Got to get that fixed someday" he muttered to himself, as he walked the six steps down to the concrete floor of the mill. Pausing, he looked out over the enormous expanse of space filled with closing machines. He pictured them running full throttle, forming the wire stands into the final rope and cable product. He turned to the south bay door and imagined the tow motors bringing the completed strands from the Stranding Mill across the way into his closing mill. His mind dwelled on the thought of better days, when he, Hank Stratum, and Tom Ferley worked closely together, providing the bread and butter for the two thousand families nationwide that Sunnberry Wire & Cable had provided for over the past four decades.

He turned back toward the vast expanse of mill space, and listened to the dead silence of closers that had stopped running. At the same time, he caught the smell of ammonia building up in the still atmosphere of his plant. "Well, I guess the fire is spreading afterall," he said to himself. "I expected us to get some whiffs of it down this end, but not this strong. Guess the fire kicked up the wind a bit and it's bringing the gas with it. I wonder if..." was all he managed to ask himself, when a loud series of reports tore through the mill, shattering several windows at the top of the mill walls, while shaking the entire building violently. Dust from the roof rafters fell to the concrete floor, sprinkling him in the process.

"Damn! I'll bet those three propane tanks Cotters told us about just went up! Shit, the whole town will go now!" Through the remaining windows along the top wall of the mill, Marv could see yellow and orange surges of colors light up the sky in the distance. He looked at his wristwatch by the dimmed ceiling lights of the mill.

"Naw, couldn't be those three tanks! If they went, I probably wouldn't be standing here," he joked to himself in the way a man with limited time left on earth might say. 10:55. Guess the reinforcements from Pleasant Corners couldn't get there in time to whatever else that bastard Lamour had hidden. It doesn't matter anymore. Get out of here now, old boy! Get back to the wife and kids as fast as you can! Forget any packing shit! Just grab all of them and herd them into the van and start driving south or east. Hain't gonna be nothin' left of this town come mornin' one way or another!"

With the last of his self analysis completed, Marv threw the breaker switch that turned off the remaining power to the ceiling lights in the mill, and slammed the doors to the plant behind him. He raced to his car as fast as he could, choking from the heavy concentrations of ammonia gas that now filled the air throughout the company property. In a few moments he was speeding down to the west gate, and then onto the road that ran past the mills. He would be home in ten minutes, and start his own little evacuation from the town.

Tom Ferley smelled the heavy breath of ammonia in his Wire Mill, but ignored it. The humanity he felt a few minutes ago was ebbing fast. He walked past the silent machines that once produced the noise and

wire that became his sole reason for living. Even his family was a secondary concern to him. The mill and his production quotas and schedules were all he ever thought about, until thirty-five minutes ago. After
the sound of the explosions some five minutes earlier, he smiled to himself, thinking that if he had to punch out now he would just make the
11:00 P.M. timecard stamp.

He realized that the last series of explosions were not the three 20,000
pound tanks of propane at the cannery going up in flames, but figured
that whatever they were, they had spread the fire. He reasoned however,
that the fire would not get to his wire mill for about another four hours,
unless those tanks went. If they exploded, time wouldn't matter anymore.
Too many houses between here and there, he mused to himself, and they'll
take time to burn. It didn't occur to him that those houses held people,
their lives, and all they had worked for. To Tom Ferley, those homes were
just a welcomed respite from the inevitable flames. Nothing more than a
man-made firebreak between the raging inferno and his reason for living.

He looked down at the cement floor of the wire mill, noting the deep
scrapes and scars it endured from so many years of heavy equipment moving over its surface, and two hundred pound prepacks of wire being
flipped onto it. He shuffled his right foot this way and that across the
floor, as if to kick the scars away. Maybe everything would be all right after
all, and in a day or two, production would resume, and all would return to
normal. The lighting thirty feet up on the ceiling was dimmed, part of the
final shutdown process his foremen implemented. The light faded into an
eerie silver-blue mercury glow the further it got from its source, and
finally ended in a greenish-black mist. Something like a shadow that
couldn't make up its mind if it wanted to be shadow or light, kept passing
between the boundary that separated the light from the darkness. Out of
the corner of his left eye, Tom caught a rotating glow, like a tow motor
flashing when it races across the floor. Tom turned to meet it.

As he peered into the greenish-black mist, he concentrated upon a space in
front of the big electrical panel and cabinet that housed the circuitry for the

26 inch wire drawing machine. His mind struggled to identify the yellow glow that faded in and out of sight, but his eyes could not resolve its form.

Finally he called out. "Is anyone there? Listen guys, if there are any stragglers here, get your asses out now! I'm shutting down the lighting and getting out myself. No more screwing around now, 'ya hear?"

No sound of an answer broke through the greenish-black mist to meet his ears. Still looking at the ever changing form, he began to walk slowly in its direction. The only sound he could hear were the light scuffles of his $19.95 penny loafers as he closed in on it. Now enveloped by the greenish-black mist, he stood only four feet from the panel's front door. The yellow glow he saw a few moments ago had disappeared, leaving him staring at the light green paint of the door.

"Must be going nuts, Tom," he laughed out loud to himself. "It's not bad enough your nose is filled with ammonia fumes, now your eyes are filled with gigantic yellow spots! Turn the damn lights out, throw the electrical master switches off, and go home yourself."

No sooner had he finished his private laugh, then the lights over the 26 inch machine came on with full intensity. It started up. All nine, huge metal blocks began turning, the one closest to the feed-in frame at the back of the machine pulling raw carbon rod from the frame. As the first block stripped the rod down to a smaller size, the next block coiled the wire up onto its front face, after which it passed it off to again to its die, which reduced its diameter even more. The process continued with lightning speed throughout the nine hole, block-die sequence, until the finished wire was taken up automatically by the spooler, and wound into a prepack of several hundred pounds.

Tom stood near the control panel in silence, some forty feet from the running machine, expecting to see its operator emerge at any moment from the shadows at the feed-in end. After regaining his sense of what was happening, he started to walk toward the machine, when the door of the electrical panel blew open and smashed hard against the concrete wall behind it. The loud crash of the door stopped his forward motion toward the running machine. In a single smooth movement, he pivoted around on his left foot, and began walking back to the control panel. In a moment he was back where he started, in front of the now opened electrical panel.

"Maybe the explosions loosened the locks and the door opened under its own weight," he said, as though talking to one of his foremen. "Those thumb-locks on these cabinet doors never were any good! Like I used to tell that idiot, Lasky. After you get this thing's circuits fixed, do something about those goddamn thumb-locks! I'm sick and tired of finding the panel door on this machine open! Someone could trip and go headlong into those fuse links, and get fried like a pig! But would that bastard listen? Who? Him? The great Mier Lasky? Not on your life! The bastard's gone now, and maybe I'll get the next guy who replaces him to listen to me!" The Tom that men hated had returned. His brief weakness caused by Frank's tirade had faded. All he could think of now was the hatred he had for Lasky, who treated him as the complaining pest he was.

As though waiting for an answer from the phantom foreman, he peered into the cabinet behind the panel door. There was no electrical sparking in the transformers, and the high current-carrying fuse block assemblies showed no burn signs from arc-over. The hum of the current through the cabinet was disrupted by another sound. One that came from somewhere directly behind him. The sound broke in on Tom's awareness gradually. It increased until it overtook the hum coming from the panel. But the crinkling sound also moved closer to him as it grew louder. Tom felt a burning sensation on the back of his neck, the kind one gets from a piece of ice that melts as soon as it hits the skin. Startled, he wrenched his body back into an upright stance, and spun around to meet the joker.

In front of him wavered the yellowish glow. It faded in and out, changing forms as it did. From glow, to rectangle, to square, to triangle, to a myriad of other half-forms before it engulfed Tom Ferley completely. Caught in its glow and changing shapes, Tom felt a stickiness in it. He screamed and cursed and struggled to tear free of the shape, but the harder he struggled, the more the stickiness grew, until it had the consistency of

Ocean City taffy. Unable to move, Tom went limp inside the yellowish mass. As he hung suspended in it, he felt a beating reverberate through it. It was as though the thing had a heart of its own. One that was beating madly over finally capturing its prey.

Looking through the yellowish glow, Tom Ferley saw what it intended for him. He managed one, last desperate cry, before the Ocean City taffy covered his mouth, turned him around, and slammed his body into the electrical cabinet. It pinned him against the high current-carrying fuse blocks and held him there, while the 200 amps of alternating current ripped through his body. Tom's tongue burned fast to the roof of his mouth, as his eyeballs popped from their sockets and dangled over his cheeks. Steam began to rise from his lifeless form, when the current heated his bodily fluids to a point above boiling. The 26 inch machine fell silent. The yellowish, ever changing shape reduced its size to a pin point, and vanished into thin air. Tom Ferley hung between the fuse blocks of the opened electrical panel, like the crucified would be savior of the wire mill that he fancied himself to be.

Frank Ketterman sped down Route 30 on his way out of town. He was making good time until he hit the police barricade. In an effort to control the crowd and manage the raging fire at the cannery, Police Chief Ruger cut two of his men free from crowd control and had them set up a road-block on the only road that led to the cannery. But it was also the only route to Pleasant Corners, where Frank and his wife lived.

"Damn," he said under his breath, "you should have known better! They were bound to close this road off! Man, look at the line of cars caught in all of that! Better find somewhere to turn off fast, or you'll be one of them!"

As he slowed his car, he noticed that the cars in front of him weren't caught in the roadblock. Instead, these cars were bringing in the curious who plague every tragedy, looking for some cheap and deadly thrill, while obstructing the authorities from doing their sworn duty. Further off, on the grass of the cannery property, he could see some other uniforms fighting with a group of men who were trying to break through to the fire area for a better look. Water hoses, fire trucks, police cars, and ambulances were everywhere. The flames in the background leaped higher and burned brighter with short upsurges of colors at times, indicating to him that the situation was far from under control.

"Got to find a way to turn around in the next twenty feet, or there'll be no turning around," he said to himself, as he hit his brakes harder. No sooner had he given himself these last instructions than he saw three men assault the two cops holding the roadblock. One cop manning the roadblock stood directly in front of the two police cars that were formed into a 'V' to form the barricade. Two men ran at him from the side, each man hitting him in the head with a piece of pipe. The cop fell to the ground and did not move. The second cop was attacked from the front by a mob and knocked senseless. In a few moments, the attackers stripped them of their sidearms, and began to ransack their vehicles.

Other assailants tore open the doors of three other cars caught in the roadblock. It was apparent to Frank that the three men and women in those vehicles were people trying to escape the burning end of town by fleeing to Pleasant Corners. The assailants drug the men from their cars and started to beat them mercilessly with their fists and small lengths of pipe. When the men finally collapsed to the ground, the mob began to rifle through their pockets, while six other male assailants forced the three women to the ground and began raping them. In those few seconds between applying his brakes and coming to a rolling stop, Frank Ketterman realized what he was witnessing. The society of the town had broken down, and rioting and looting had begun. Only one end of the town was now burning, as the wind had carried some of the flames to neighboring homes, and set them ablaze. In turn, they spread the fire to the homes around them, and a large scale destruction was on. But that one end on fire was enough to unleash the animal nature of the crowd, and that nature had gone wild.

Pulling himself out of his dazed state, Frank caught sight of a small mound in someone's front yard to his right. It sloped down sharply to meet the side of Route 30. He slammed the gas pedal to the floor, and gave a hard right turn on his steering column. The front tires of his car hit the mound with a thud, but negotiated the slope easily. In a moment he was on top of the mound, and speeding across someone's front lawn. He remembered that a side street paralleled Route 30, and continued on for a half-mile past the cannery. But it did not connect with the road that went to Pleasant Corners.

"No time to worry about people's property now, Frank!" he told himself. "Got to get home to Marilynn, no matter what!" In his own way, Frank had just become part of the mob.

He continued driving over the front of the lawn, then knocked down a fence, and raced over another lawn, gave a hard right, and tore down two more fences before his tires hit the curb of the street that paralleled Route 30. Sycamore Street was empty. Apparently all of the residents had gotten out, either to Pleasant Corners while they had the chance, or to the east and south ends of Sunnberry. Frank's car continued to rumble down Sycamore until he saw a cul de sack ahead of him. Sycamore street ended there. He slowed down, eyeing the yards on his left, until his sight landed on the last one before the cul de sack. It had a gentle slope that led up to its back edge. He gambled that the front of the yard gave direct access to Route 30, fences notwithstanding.

The smell of ammonia was heavy in his car, and he began to panic. Giving his steering wheel a sharp left turn, he ascended the slope and raced past the side of the house. In his panic, he didn't even turn the wheel to avoid hitting the side of the house. He sheared the drain spout completely from the corner of the home, and hit its side with a long, scraping action as his car traveled parallel along it. Aluminum siding panels flew off the house in all directions, coming to rest on different parts of the lawn. All Frank could see was the image of Marilynn in his mind, as he drove straight through a child's swimming pool, and knocked down a swing set

the parents had set up in their back yard. He finally saw the fence of the
front yard. It did border Route 30. Hitting his gas pedal solidly, the back
tires of his rear wheel drive Chevy dug deeply into the grass of the lawn,
and propelled Frank toward it with a jolt. In a second he burst through the
fence, and was on the far side of Route 30, past the cannery, past the fire,
past the mob, and past all danger.

He was not even aware that his heart was pounding hard in his chest,
only now slowing to a normal beat. His breathing was sporadic too, but he
put this off to the lingering ammonia fumes in his car. Realizing the crisis
was past, Frank pulled over to the side of the road and put the engine in
idle, while he wiped the sweat from his face and calmed down. He rolled
his window down, and breathed the cool night air deeply into his lungs.
Coming from the north, the wind had to pass him before it got to the cannery. It was a sweet night air. One that held safety, peace, and the vision of
a new life ahead for Marilynn and him. Frank remained there for ten minutes, calming down and collecting his wits, before he put the Chevy in
drive and started off down the empty Route 30 toward Pleasant Corners.
The last lingering sounds of chaos coming from the inferno behind him
dropped off into silence, the further he drove. He was now quiet and
thankful for his narrow escape, and only looked forward to seeing his wife.

Frank looked down at his wristwatch. It was only 11:10 P.M. His mind
went back to the incident in Walter Cotters' office, and he wondered how
so much could have gone so wrong in the past fifty-five minutes. He
recalled the good days he and Walt had had together. The genuine good
days, when neither of them were taking advantage of the other, posturing
for the employees and government inspectors, or building kingdoms of
lies and deceit by covering up for each other's mistakes, and for their own.
In those days, Frank thought, both of them were equally afraid of the
plant expansion and increased production demands being made. During
those days, they worked together as a real team. Those were the days of
real growth that taxed them to the limit, ones which they handled effec-
tively at first.

But the screen of his memory began to tarnish over with the images of the mistakes and problems that came up, and how badly they handled them. The Board should have understood they were still young men with a lot on their plates back in those days, doing the best they could, and that mistakes were bound to be made. Instead, corporate understood nothing but the bottom line. Only the profit-to-loss ratio was important to them. Demand upon demand, one increased production quota after another, errors in judgment, false reports to corporate, cover-ups, more mistakes, compounded cover-ups, and soon, both of them had sold their souls for their paychecks. Frank fumed and smashed the steering wheel's central hub of plastic as he blamed the Board for everything. If only he and Walt had had a little more time to grow into their jobs back in those days. If only corporate had been a little more understanding. If only...

Frank's mind was not on Route 30. It remained back in the past, suffering from regrets that could never be made up or corrected. He made up his mind though that he would do nothing to destroy Walt's career with the company. He had stashed away incriminating evidence as he told Cotters, yes, because in later years he no longer trusted the Vice President. But he figured that the tongue-lashing and physical assault he made on his former colleague and friend would do almost as much damage to Walt's reputation and position of power, as would a report to the Board. Frank smiled to himself, as he speculated how Tom, Marv, and Walt would get along after the incident less than an hour ago. In the end, Frank felt vindicated. He was the better man. He could destroy Walt with a single report, but he wouldn't. He was a good man after all, and mentally patted himself on the back for the gracious humanity he would extend to Cotters.

He did not drive Route 30 late at night very often, and did not notice how badly it was lit. As with most small, Pennsylvania two-lane roads, only the intermittent lamp of a garage, or the mercury vapor property light of one of the houses that dotted the long roadway, broke the vast expanse of blackness that covered the distance between Sunnberry and Pleasant Corners. He had been driving for ten minutes in a pitch blackness knifed

through only by his car's headlamps, when he suddenly became aware of
something lying across the road in front of him. His brain, unable to put
the image it registered into a category, signaled his right foot to slam the
breaks on immediately. In a few seconds, his car came to a screeching halt,
some twenty feet from the obstruction.

Frank peered through the front windshield at the huge green rectangle that stretched across the entire width of the road. His headlights
shone through it, so he could see the road surface on the other side of it.
As he stared at it, he first thought that it was a large plate glass with a
green pane around it, that must have fallen off a truck. By dumb luck it
fell on its edge, and somehow balanced itself on the flat road surface.
But as he continued to stare at it, he couldn't see any reflection coming
from it. If it were a large section of glass, certainly there would be some
reflection from different points along its length. He then considered that
perhaps it was some kind of barricade device that the reinforcements
from Pleasant Corners were rushing to the cannery scene, and that one
of them had fallen from a truck and landed upright. But strain as he
might, he could not figure out how a hollow green pane could be used to
stop oncoming vehicles.

Finally, he decided that it was some kind of trap laid by looters that
had worked their way this far past Sunnberry. He rolled up his car window quickly, locked his door, and began to blow the car's horn as he
drove slowly up to it. No one emerged from the shadows on either side
of it to try and car jack him, or slow him down. When he was about five
feet from it, Frank decided that if there were would be assailants hiding
along the roadside in the darkness, a quick turn to his right while hitting
the gas pedal would send him past the obstruction and into the field
next to it. He figured he could then easily cut a hard left, and get around
the rectangle before anyone could leap out at him, and be safely on his
way to Marilynn.

After another two feet of travel, Frank cut his wheels a hard right, and
hit the gas. He bordered past the empty front of the rectangle, his front

wheels just digging into the earth of the field, when the rectangle shot past his path, meeting the driver's side of his car with a loud thud. He stepped on the brakes and came to a full stop. As incredible as it seemed to him, this empty green obstruction had just damaged the side of his car. He could see straight through it, but somehow, it had substance. Hard substance, that brought his car to a halt. Losing his temper now, Frank popped the door lock, and jumped out of his Chevy. He spun around quickly, reached down to the floor of the back seat, and emerged holding a tire iron.

"What the hell is going on here?" he screamed, as he approached the green rectangle. Marching toward the obstacle, his fear had vanished. All he wanted was someone to vent his frustration and anger on now. "All right you rotten sons-of-a-bitches! Any of you hiding in the bushes can come out now, because I'm good and mad, and would love nothing better than to wrap this tire iron around your skulls! Come on you little bastards, I'm waiting for you!" But no one came out of the darkness. Waiting and listening for what seemed to be an eternal minute, Frank heard and saw nothing. All he was aware of was a gentle, cool, sweet spring breeze.

He stood there for another eternal minute, eyeing the green pane carefully. He was right. There was no substance to it. He could clearly see the road on the other side of it, and even watched as a tiny field mouse darted across the road behind the seemingly empty green rectangle. Finally, he reached out with the pointed end of the tire iron, and moved it through the space in the rectangle. As soon as the tire iron came into contact with the empty space, the green pane turned a bright luminous green, while its former empty space became filled with twinkling, luminous points of green light. A crackling sound that grew steadily in intensity now came from the obstacle. Frank pulled the tire iron out of the green twinkling lights, and jumped back. The cracklings grew louder.

"Sounds just like that plastic wrap Marilynn uses around the kitchen," he said to himself. "What the hell is this thing anyway?" His fear had given way again. Only this time, to curiosity, instead of anger.

Frank dropped the tire iron to the ground and approached the crackling, glowing, and twinkling rectangle. Slowly, he placed the open palm of his right hand against the twinkling surface. It gave a curious, gentle tickle. Frank started to laugh. "The damn thing is tickling me! I wonder what it is, anyway?"

He pulled his hand away, and scratched his palm. "Maybe I can just drive straight through it. I probably hit the corner of the pane with the car," he muttered to himself, "and that's what damaged it. Probably cost me a couple of hundred to fix the Chevy now. And all over some weird nonsense thing standing in the road! If I could put the tire iron through it, I sure as hell can drive through it. One more test though. Just to make sure. I wouldn't want to damage the old Chevy anymore. I have no intentions of buying a new one for a couple of years, so this old girl will have to last."

Frank moved closer to the twinkling green lights in the space of the rectangle for the final test. Cautiously, but without fear, he put his right hand through the obstacle's space, to the other end. There was the same gentle tickling he felt over his palm, now gliding over the entire surface of his hand. He looked at his hand through the green twinkling on the other side of the rectangle, made a fist, opened it, closed it again, and repeated the process several more times until he was comfortable there was no danger.

"I don't know what it is, but it sure isn't anything to be afraid of," he said out loud to himself. "Ah, what the hell," he laughed, and with that, shoved his right arm up to his elbow clear through the empty space within the rectangle. The same reflected light from his Chevy's headlamps that had showed his open and closed fists a few seconds ago, now showed that his forearm was missing. He could feel his arm on the other side of the green obstacle, but he could no longer see it. Panicked, he pulled his arm backward, but it would not come. Something was holding it fast on the other side of the rectangle. He was still able to clearly see the road on the other side through the green twinkling, but his arm had disappeared, and he could not remove it.

Panic gave way to terror in Frank Ketterman now, as his right forearm began to feel like ice. He began to scream for help, but there was no one to hear his desperate cries. The cold in his right arm soon made room for a second sensation. A searing pain now peeled down the length of his invisible right forearm. He screamed and jerked his arm backward repeatedly, trying to remove it from the green twinkling, but it would not budge. Instead, long, white strips tinted red in places, came flying back out of the green twinkling, and landed at Frank's feet. He stared at them until his mind was finally able to identify them. They were strips of meat from his right forearm. In agony he pulled and pulled on his right forearm, desperately trying to free it from the tiny green lights, but he could not. As he pulled, more thin slivers of meat came flying back at him, landing at his feet. His cries of pain intensified, as small chunks of bone were thrown back as well, adding to the grisly collection of meaty bits lying on the ground.

As he started to weaken from loss of blood and shock, Frank felt a pull. He was being pulled through the green twinkling to the other side of the rectangle that had no other side. He could still see the continuation of Route 30 on the other side of the green obstacle. Slowly, an inch at a time and with a jerking motion, Frank Ketterman was pulled through the green rectangle. As more of him entered the green twinkling, larger slivers of flesh and bone were thrown back on what used to be his side of the obstacle. After awhile, Frank disappeared completely inside the green rectangle, and silence returned to the quiet spring countryside. In an instant, the green triangle stopped its glowing and twinkling, and withdrew its four corners into one central point and vanished into nothingness. The same field mouse that ran across the road a few minutes before returned by the same path, being careful to avoid the headlights of Frank's Chevy, which just purred quietly by the side of the road.

Chapter 11

▼

The Burning

Chief Ruger eyed his wristwatch absent-mindedly. Finally the hour and minute hands registered upon his besieged senses. It was 11:15 P.M. The holocaust around him was beyond his control. Everywhere he looked there was violence. From the crowd fighting with the fireman and his own police officers, to ambulances being overturned, to the screams of men and women in cars trapped at the road block. He was thankful the road-block was beyond his vision. He didn't want or need to see what was causing their terror and agony.

Paul Ruger was a man well fitted for his work by his very nature. He had a strong sense of balance and justice. One that would not tolerate the contrivances and constitutional interpretations made by reporters on the scene of a tragedy to suit their sensationalist needs. "Those so-called 'journalists,'" he often said, "are like dogs fighting over a filthy old rag. They sell their human misery by the pound, like a grocery store sells bread. You can tell. The size of their rags increased in weight over the years. But one thing they won't do, is fill their rags with the suffering I'm here to prevent or stop. That's just the way it is."

But tonight, *he* was one of those suffering, over his inability to control the savage human events happening all around him. Soaked in sweat, his normally clean and well ordered uniform disheveled, he was again unaware that his right hand rested itself on his revolver, and had undone the strap that secured it in its holster. He was near the breaking point, when a voice behind him broke in on his fury. It was Mayor Halfrick.

"Paul, what the hell is happening here? I got a report from that twirp I sent to cover the fire that you belted him. Is that true?" the Mayor asked.

"Belted him?!" the Chief turned and replied. "You're goddamn lucky I didn't kill him! Do you know what he tried to do?"

"Yea, I know. The cameraman filled me in. But you shouldn't of hit him, Paul. There's going to be trouble over that," the Mayor insisted.

Paul Ruger had enough. He grabbed the Mayor by the front collar of his windbreaker, and pulled Jim Halfrick's face forward. "Look, Jim! Look! You're telling me there's going to be trouble from my putting that little bastard of yours on the ground where he belonged? Want trouble, Jim? Take a goddamn look around you! **Here**, is trouble. Here is the body count going out of sight from the dead of the cannery explosion and from the people of this glorious little town, rioting, looting, raping, and killing each other. Here, Jim, is trouble!

"The way it looks now this whole goddamn town may go up in flames tonight, because the entire situation is out of control! Everything! From the fire to crowd control! And you're worrying about the first Amendment? All that rights shit only works as long as everyone stays in their little holes and lets society do to them whatever it wants, as long as it's done peacefully. But put a night together like this when the beast inside each of us breaks free, and you can shove your goddamn rights and constitutional amendments right up your ass, Jim, because none of them mean a thing!

"And you, Jim, are goddamn old enough and smart enough to know it's all true. Every stinking word I just said. So if you want to report on real trouble, old pal, get those lazy good-for-nothing journalists of yours out

here, now, and let them report on this! Or have they abandoned the sinking ship, Jim, or maybe some of those dead bodies lying out there on the
lawn are some of your defenders of free speech! Well, what's it going to be,
Mr. Mayor, are you and what's left of your people going to help, or are you
going to stand there with your thumb up your ass, defending a constitution that only works for the guilty and the dregs of this stinking society all
of us created!"

Mayor Halfrick's head could not move in Ruger's grasp. He was forced
to see the events happening around him. For some reason, he had looked
at the carnage on his way into the cannery grounds, but hadn't really seen
the devastation. Especially, he had not seen the bodies scattered in nearly
every quarter of the cannery's well manicured front lawn.

"All right, Paul, you can let go now. I get your point. I'll talk to my
brother. I'll tell him that little bastard was interfering with your rescue
efforts, and in the heat of the battle he got thumped," the Mayor said, in
an almost reverent, apologetic voice.

"Better do more than that, Jim. Tell your brother to get that punk off
the paper. Because I swear to you, Jim, if I see him again, there will be
real trouble. The kind that's laying on the lawn all around us!" Ruger
snapped back.

"Consider it done, Paul. Consider it done," the Mayor finally replied.

Chief Ruger released the Mayor from his grasp. Jim Halfrick saw how
close the Chief was to going over the edge, and why. The realization suddenly broke in on Jim's mind that Ruger was not overreacting. As he
looked around him, the full impact of the situation hit him. His heart
skipped a beat as he saw for himself that things were way out of control.
Grabbing the Chief by his arm, he pulled him into the shadows, and
began to speak to him as quietly as the screams and sounds of chaos surrounding them would allow.

"What's the full story, Paul?" the Mayor asked, with a shaking voice.
"I've got to know."

"The cannery is beyond saving. But that's not our problem now. At 9:30 a twenty thousand pound tank of propane that Lamour had secretly installed behind the vinershed went up. It laid a fire-line to three other tanks between the vinershed and the main plant. Those tanks have turned out to be twenty thousand pounders, Jim, not the twenty-five hundred pounders they were licensed to install.

"When this is all over, there will be a state investigation for sure. And whoever on the town council took a kickback to look the other way while Lamour installed those illegal tanks will face felony charges. His or their asses will be grass, because the destruction and death caused by it is beyond calculation right now," the Chief quipped, looking at the Mayor with a questioning eye as to his possible role in the situation. The Mayor put his head down and coughed. Ruger read his hacking for what it was. It wasn't due to the ammonia gas that still hung heavy in the air, but to his guilt.

The Chief continued. "The reinforcements from Pleasant Corners got here at 9:30 exactly, just as that one tank behind the vinershed went up and took the shed with it. The metal frags from the tank and the wood and metal from the shed blew outward into the fields behind the plant, and spread to the woods behind them. From there the winds kicked up and carried the flames to homes in the north end first, and then the west end. The result, from what I heard a few minutes ago, is that now both ends of the town are lost. We don't have enough firefighters between us and the Pleasant Corners force to be able to handle a quarter of this carnage, let alone to control it all.

"The fire is spreading. My concern now is that it will spread to the west and east ends of the town, and hit the city gas lines. If that happens, there won't be anything left of Sunnberry. I alerted Walt Cotters of the wire mill and Steve Marconi of the silk mill to evacuate their shifts, and lock everything down tight. I got resistance from both of them. You know, nothing but complaints as to why we can't control it, why are they paying taxes, et cetera. To top it all off, at 9:30 we had a body count of twenty-four, and twelve missing. That was from the fire and poisoning from the cannery explosion alone.

"Since then, something has happened to the minds of the people in this town. I never saw anything like it. Not even in the Chicago riots of the '70's. They've all gone mad. The citizens of this town are killing each other. Surely you saw what was going on at the roadblock? From what I heard from Martin, it's a grisly scene up there. And the raping. Look at the bodies all over the lawn here. I don't know if they're all dead or not, and I sure in the hell don't have the manpower to find out. That's not to mention the rampaging and looting that one of my other officers reported is raging downtown. There isn't a store left intact.

"Pleasant Corners sent all the manpower they could. Even volunteers came. Made no difference. Their firefighters, police, and medics were attacked by the crowd too. We don't know how many of them were killed. But it wouldn't have mattered. Once that huge hidden tank went up, we were outgunned. I have our remaining police force and the Pleasant Corners cops under my jurisdiction now, and have set up a defensive perimeter against the crowd. It begins at the flagpole, since the pole divides the cannery lawn into two sections. That's the official outer perimeter...the flagpole. The outer section fifty yards further back from it is held by the crowd. Our inner area, our fire-line, is twenty yards behind the outer perimeter, down toward us as you can see. It's divided off by the squad cars and fire trucks. It's manned by my last twelve officers. Anyone who breaks through the plane formed at the flagpole will be shot dead on the spot. I didn't order it just that way, but told them to use whatever force was necessary to keep the mob back. I think the time has come, though, when I'll have to give those orders directly," Ruger coldly reported to the Mayor. Jim Halfrick listened in dumb amazement, unable to utter a word in response.

"So, your honor," the Police Chief continued, "the situation is like this. We are trapped between the burning cannery and a citizen mob that is totally out of control. And behind them half the town is burning, with a damn good possibility of the other end going up with it, either from the flames or a city gas line explosion. Martin called the gas people and ordered the gas mains to be turned off. They finally got to the main valves outside the city at 10:30, and closed them down."

"Then the east and west end should be all right, right? I mean, there shouldn't be any gas explosions then, right?" the Mayor desperately pleaded, expecting at least some good news on this point from the Chief.

"Wrong, Mr. Mayor! The gas is cut off, but they can't drain out what's already in the lines under the town, and in the pipes of the homes! All that gas is just sitting there, waiting for a flicker of fire. Then that will be that," Ruger snapped. The Mayor fell backward against Ruger's police car, which was angled into a defensive position on the cannery driveway, half in and half out of ever-changing shadows thrown by the burning cannery.

After a few minutes of silence between them, Ruger began speaking again. "There's something else you should also know, Jim. Our Fire Chief told me there was no reason our gas masks should not have worked. They should have allowed our own firefighters to get in and foam down those three illegal propane tanks, but they didn't. We took out four men from their first attempt to get in at those tanks, and three from their second attempt. Three of those seven men died from asphyxiation, and two are in serious condition.

"It's like something has gone wrong with the laws of Nature itself. The Fire Chief told me the gas mask filters just melted in the mask cylinders. There was heat in the area from the fire, yes, but not that much. Not enough to melt gas filters inside the metal cylinders. We figured that they were defective or old from age…hell, they never had to use gas masks before this. When the crew from Pleasant Corners got here, they sent in four men immediately, to foam down the tanks. Same thing happened to their filters! Two of those men died. The other two are in serious condition as well. And with all the other wounded we have pulled back here in our barricade, we can't get them out because of that insane mob out there. So we are losing more people as I speak. Some of the wounded, I mean."

"Didn't you call the State Police in? I mean, we need all the help we can get in here, and we need it now, Paul!" the Mayor asked, with a look of fear on his face.

"Jim," the Chief went on, "I didn't start being a cop yesterday. Of course I had Dispatch call them first off when I got here. They told me their fifteen man force was scattered here and there on patrol, and it would take time to call them in. That's the last I heard from them. And if you're thinking of why didn't I call in for state help, the answer to that is simple. I got here at 8:30. The only problem then was a burning cannery. Take a look around. It's now 11:25. Not three hours have gone by, and look what we're facing. The situation developed too fast. I used every thing that was at hand, and that was that. We're in the middle of nowhere, Jim. We're three-and-a-half hours from Pittsburgh, and five-and-a-half hours from Phily. No help could get here that fast. And there are no other towns of even half our size, except for Old Furnace, and that's fifty-some miles away, and they only have three cops and a six-man volunteer fire company!

"So we're stuck with our problem, Jim, and right now, I don't know what the hell else to do. If you have any suggestions, let me know them fast. Because either that mob will get to us, or those three 20,000 pounder tanks will go up sooner or later. And if they do, all of us on this side of town will be blown from here to hell in an instant. Those tanks are directly behind this burning cannery building right behind us, Mr. Mayor. Not like that one that went off way down behind the vinershed. That structure took the brunt of the force, and being some three hundred yards away, we were lucky. There's nothing left of the cannery to shield an explosion like the one coming if we don't foam those tanks. Add to that they're only a little over a hundred yards away from us, and you'll get some idea of the problem. Start thinking, Jim. Start thinking, hard!"

The pupils of the Mayor's eyes were dilated, as though he popped a couple of amphetamines only a few minutes ago. His mouth was drier than desert sand in mid July, and he coughed intermittently as the rising and falling ammonia fumes skirted past his nostrils. "I can't believe any of this is happening, Paul! I don't know what to tell you. What happened? We were such a friendly little community. We had our problems like any other, but what happened here doesn't make any sense! What do we do, Paul? What do we do?" the Mayor replied, his voice trailing off into nothingness as his last few words fell from his lips.

The screams of agony from people being beaten and murdered off in the distance out of their vision finally reached their ears. A roar went out from the mob that was still cloaked in the blackness of the night beyond their eyes, but the sound was ominous. Like a pack of beasts gone wild over the smell of a fresh kill. The Mayor felt his blood chill, while the Chief's began to boil. He grabbed the bull horn and shouted through it to what was left of his combined police force.

"Listen up men! The situation behind us, the fire I mean, is uncontrollable. We have nowhere left to retreat to. That means that you twelve men on the fire-line are holding the last line of defense we have. I have another six armed men with me back here. We've established an inner perimeter as a course of last resort, some thirty yards behind you. But if you don't hold the outer, we sure in the hell won't be able to hold the inner.

"So listen to me carefully. These are my official orders, and I'll stand behind them. The Mayor backs me up in this. He's here with me now. Mayor, you tell them!"

Jim Halfrick was dumbfounded, but took the bullhorn from the Chief. He knew there was no other way, and so he blurted out his approval of the Chief's orders, before he even heard them. "This is Mayor Halfrick! Listen to me carefully! I will back our Chief of Police in whatever orders he is going to give you men. I'm adding my orders to his. Follow his commands to the letter, and do what he tells you to do!" Having said that he handed the bullhorn back to the Chief of Police. Paul took it in his right hand, threw the switch to the 'on' position, and continued.

"These are my orders. The first sons-of-a-bitches that come through the outer perimeter—that cross the plane of the flagpole—are to be shot dead. There will be no warning shots. It doesn't matter who they are. Kill them on the spot. Something has gone very wrong with this town tonight. Friends are killing friends, neighbors are killing neighbors. Take no chances. Anyone that breaks past the outer barricade of cannery chain fence onto the lawn and gets past the flagpole is to be shot down. Those are my orders! Carry them out! Any man who abandons his post or refuses to fire at point-blank range on anyone that gets past that flagpole will be shot by me!"

The twelve police who were manning the barricade on the cannery grounds didn't even turn their heads to look in the direction of the Chief as he spoke. In fact, each man there had already reached the decision to shoot down anyone who crossed into the barricade area. It was just that now they had a clear line of demarcation given to them by the Chief. The flagpole.

The Chief moved past the Mayor to the trunk of his squad car, opened it, and handed the Jim Halfrick a .38 caliber Police Special with holster, and a box of cartridges. "Strap it on, Jim, the time for talking is done!" He bent down into the trunk a second time, pulled out a rifle, and handed it to the Mayor as well. "Take this too. Know how to load it?" he asked in a stern voice.

"Yea, I know how. A .30 caliber carbine. I guess we are in for a hell of a lot more trouble, aren't we, Paul?" the Mayor wheezed out.

"It's like I said to myself a little over three hours ago, Jim," the Chief replied back dryly. "It's gonna be a long night."

As Chief Ruger turned to take his position over the hood of his squad car, he spotted some firemen from Pleasant Corners sitting behind the inner perimeter. He left Mayor Halfrick to level his carbine in the mob's direction along with the others who backed up the inner perimeter, and walked over to the four exhausted men.

"Fellas, I don't want to be a hard ass, but you just heard me over the bullhorn. Our situation is even worse because of those three propane tanks behind what is left of this cannery. I know you men are beyond bushed, but I got to ask you. Can you give it one more go and try to get those tanks foamed down? From what I understand, the foam is stored in underground containers. Those containers have nozzles pointed in all directions at the tanks, but it takes two men, one on each of two chicken switches to pull them at the same time. The Fire Chief from Pleasant Corners told me that when those switches are pulled, the foam will jut out and seal off the tanks off from that ring of fire that formed around them. If we don't get them foamed down, that fire will inch its way in toward them and they'll blow. You know what that means. I don't see any other firemen here, so you guys are elected. I got to ask you to go in and pull those chicken switches."

All four men had their heads bowed. They were dazed at the events of the night, and their inability to do their jobs. None of the four seasoned firefighters had experienced anything like this before. Finally their Crew Leader spoke.

"Chief, we'll go back in, but I don't know what good it will do. That ring of fire isn't acting like any normal fire. It flares up ten feet and burns near white hot when we try to cross it to get in at the tanks. It doesn't matter what point we try to cross it, or even if we try to cross it from four different points at the same time. It's like the goddamn thing is alive! The ammonia pockets were melting our mask filters before, but that gas cloud has finally drifted up high enough to allow us to get in at the fire-circle. But at least we can breathe, and that's something. Let us have five more minutes to catch our breaths, and we'll go back in. Good enough?"

The Chief looked down at them. His heart sank as a memory from his days in Vietnam surfaced. He saw four men in the same position as these four were in now. He was the Platoon Sergeant in those days, and had to order those four men to knock out a VC pill box that had cut half his platoon to ribbons, and had pinned the rest of them down. His eyes dilated as his mind turned inward to that hot, late day attack in September 1967, when those four men went up the hill. He saw the scene all over again, as three were killed before the fourth tossed a grenade into the enemy bunker with his dying strength, and knocked it out. From a distance Ruger finally caught the threads of a voice that began to pull him out of his spell.

"Chief? Chief? Do you mind if we 'take five' before going back in?" the Crew Leader of the fire team asked again.

Ruger was not yet back to normal. In a subdued voice he answered the Crew Leader. "Not at all, not at all. Just take real good care when you go back in. Keep your head down, and your powder dry."

The Crew Leader looked at the other three firefighters. They were too young to know what Ruger was talking about. He wasn't aware of what he said to them, either. In his mind, Paul Ruger was back with his platoon in Quang Tri on that hot September day in 1967, and he was sending those same four men back up that hill.

His eyes still glazed over from his post traumatic syndrome attack, Ruger turned from the four firefighters and began to walk back to the Mayor, when a deafening roar went up from the mob a hundred yards away behind the chain fence. He knew instantly what had happened. The rattle of chain and metal followed the roar, until it dinted hard in his ears. The mob had broken through the fence, and was running out on the lawn toward the flagpole, screaming out unintelligible sounds. Gunfire erupted from their ranks, pelting the squad cars and fire trucks that formed the fire-line, while whizzing past Ruger and the others at the inner perimeter.

As the gunfire from the mob increased, one of the twelve officers holding the fire-line took a round in the forehead, and flew backwards from his position behind the squad car. A raging fury now filled the other eleven officers on the fire-line. Seeing one of their comrades lying dead on the ground was all the license they needed. The mob had not yet reached the plane of the flagpole when, acting in unison, the officers laid down a deadly volley of return fire, directly into the advancing crowd. The single action rifles of the mob were no match for the automatic weapons of the officers. Bodies dropped out of the advancing crowd by the dozen, as the police continued to hammer the mob with murderous replies. Ruger and the Mayor, along with the six other men holding the inner perimeter, leveled their weapons across the car hoods, ready to fire on any members of the mob that broke through the fire-line.

"Be damn careful you don't hit our own men," the Chief called out to his troops. "They're directly in the line of our fire! Mark your targets as they break around the ends of the barricade, and fire-at-will!"

Out of the corner of his eye, the Chief caught sight of the four fire-fighters. Their five-minute break over, they were heading back behind the burning cannery, into the propane tank area. "Well, Jim, this is it. If they can foam down those tanks and we stop the crowd, we can still rescue this situation. If not..." Ruger broke off there.

At first, the heavy casualties the mob took slowed them down. They halted almost exactly at the flagpole. But a renewed frenzy shot through their mass mind, and they began to run the last fifty yards toward the fire-line, screaming obscenities and firing their weapons. Three more police officers were hit by their fire, decreasing the effectiveness of the firepower the remaining seven poured into the crowd. The last seven police officers knew they would be overrun in a matter of moments, and began to drop back toward the inner perimeter. Two of the seven stayed at the fire-line, setting up a rear guard action to allow the remaining five to reach the outer perimeter safely.

As the five retreating officers reached Ruger and his team, the two officers at the fire-line were overrun. One was shot in the head several times, while the other was bludgeoned to death by what looked to Ruger to be five teens, no older than sixteen or seventeen years old. The mob halted at that point and examined the bodies, making sure all five men were dead. They then turned in the direction of the outer perimeter, and resumed their run toward it, screaming and firing their weapons as they advanced. They moved across the last thirty yards to the waiting Ruger and his tiny squad of defenders.

Ruger gave out a shout. "Everyone! Open fire!"

Another deadly series of volleys tore through the advancing crowd. The body count of the mob grew more rapidly then before. In addition to the fire of automatic weapons coming from the perimeter defenders, explosions now ripped through the crowd ranks from all directions. This new sound of death stunned them, bringing them to a full stop some fifteen yards in front of the perimeter. Ruger made sure they paid with their blood for every inch of ground they took.

"I've been saving these beauties since Nam," Ruger said to the Mayor, as he lobbed another grenade into the crowd. "I knew they'd come in handy some day! And by damn, Jim, this is the day!"

The surreal image of the events unfolding around them drove Ruger and his small squad into the same blood lust as the mob. He was no longer the Chief of Police. He was back in the bush in Nam, fighting the VC and NVA regulars that got past the kill zone of his fire base, and who were now coming over the wire directly outside of their stronghold. Nothing mattered to him except the body count. The more of the enemy he and his squad could kill, the better their chances of living through the night. That's how it was back then. That's how it was now. There was no difference on this night. "Charlie" was everywhere, Ruger thought. Or was it Sunnberry residents. It didn't matter. The business at hand was killing. Somewhere in Ruger's and the defenders' minds, the line that divided the citizens of Sunnberry from the VC and NVA disappeared. Whoever they were, they were the enemy, and had to be stopped. They needed killing, and they needed it just as fast as Sergeant Ruger and the remaining members of his platoon could manage it.

Ruger threw his last grenade. The shrapnel it scattered in all directions killed another four of the mob directly, and wounded another six. "Not bad," Ruger thought. "Not bad at all!"

As though someone had just broken through with news of an armistice, both the mob and the perimeter defenders ceased their hostilities. A hush fell over the battlefield of the former cannery lawn. Only the sound of expanding metal being scorched by the last flames of the cannery fire could be heard in the background. Both aggressors and defenders looked up in amazement. Their war had been intruded upon by a threat greater than their two armies combined. A threat that the soldiers of each could feel, but which they could not understand. As battle weary eyes from both warring sides looked up into the air above the cannery, a loud crackling sound filled the air, replacing the grim near-silence of a few moments ago. As it became louder, the warriors of both sides dropped their weapons.

They watched in awe as three enormous rectangles, one a hot-pink in color, another an emerald green, and a third bright yellow, floated up into the air. They rose to a height of three hundred feet, and took up a position above and behind the former cannery, and above the propane tanks. The crackling noise they made suddenly ceased. With it came a silence that is only experienced in a graveyard at night. A still, hanging silence that wraps such a place in an unnatural stillness. A stillness that seems to be hiding some terror ready to break forth from the blackness surrounding it. Chief Ruger, the Mayor, and all of the combatants watched as the hot pink rectangle angled one of its corners to a point directly beneath it.

Ruger realized that the thing was pointing its corner to an area on the ground that housed the three huge tanks of gas. As they watched, the floating rectangle fired a series of short bursts of hot pink cylindrical bolts at the tanks on the ground. The cylinders of light-energy hit the three propane tanks simultaneously. The explosion that resulted rocked the entire town violently, throwing hot metal, fire, flame, concrete, and scorched sections of earth upwards and outwards in all directions. An orange and red fireball filled the night sky, rising upward, collapsing back into itself in layers, until it resembled a mushroom cloud. Chief Ruger, the Mayor, all of the combatants, along with the north and west end of Sunnberry, were gone.

Out of the raging fireball, three geometrical forms, still assuming their rectangular shapes, emerged. Each began to glow brighter in its character-istic color, giving off a colored light that was painful to look at. The three forms rose higher up into the red-orange filled night sky, and grew even larger. The hot-pink shape took on the form of an enormous diamond, while the green geometry collapsed its four points and changed into a cylinder. The yellow form turned into a wheel, its numerous spokes extending outward beyond its circumference. Between the blinks of an eye, the hot-pink diamond took up a position over the south end of the town, while the yellow spoke-wheel took a stance and hovered several hundred feet above the east end. The green cylinder set itself between the other two forms, as though to cover the immediate territory between these two compass points.

Acting in unison, the hot-pink geometry began emitting bolts of pinkish-red light energy from the edges of its diamond surface, while the yellow figure emitted hot yellow bolts from the spokes of its wheel-like shape. Both objects began to spin furiously, sending hundreds of light bolts per minute in a scattered array over the town below. As the energy bolts of light hit the ground, whatever stood in their way exploded with a violent report, sending fire, flame, and debris for hundreds of yards in all directions. Homes, office buildings, merchant stores, gas stations, park statues, all were obliterated from the face of the earth, as though they never existed. Screams and cries of panic and terror tore through the now smoke-dense, hot, dry night air of what had once been the town of Sunnberry.

Residents were being killed by the thousands, by either the light bolts or flying debris. No one escaped the fury of the geometries. They seemed to not only seek out groups of people running for cover, but zero in on smaller bands of residents trying to escape the devastation. In one instance, a family of four had just been herded into the family car by the father. As he started to drive off, the yellow spinning wheel turned itself slightly to cover the family's escape route, and directed a short blast of light bolts at the fleeing vehicle. It seemed to notice as the car exploded into flames, and the four occupants burned to death before being able to escape.

The green cylinder paused, as though watching the rampage being visited upon the small city by its two comrades. Without warning, it suddenly broke from its sentinel position, and drifted slowly to a point high up the sky. Once there, it situated itself midway between the silk mill and Sunnberry Wire & Cable. In an instant, it went from a full stationary position to one of a furious rotation, angled itself backward on its central axis, and began firing a stream of bright green bolts of light energy at manufacturing facilities on the ground below. The explosions, fire, and hurtling chunks of metal from the huge manufacturing machines ripped through the furnace-like night air, as the buildings were consumed in the energy of its light bolts.

As Chief Ruger predicted, the remaining city gas in the pipes of the homes of the residents on the south and east side of the town was ignited by the fires. As though a finale to the devastation and butchery was engineered by the glowing invaders, a series of light bolts from all three geometries were fired at the gas capping station on the outskirts of the town. Their energy penetrated the ground, and detonated the huge volume of gas still feeding the fires in the burning homes of Sunnberry. With one enormous sigh, the earth on which the town stood pushed upward and exploded outward in one violent burst. The entire town and the remaining residents not killed in the earlier attacks, now disappeared in the inferno of mushroom-like fireballs that popped up everywhere. It was exactly midnight. The town of Sunnberry ceased to exist.

As the flames and smoke leapt upwards, the three geometries assumed their normal rectangular shapes, and became motionless once more. Silently, they hovered in the air, as though examining the fruits of their labor. They satisfied themselves that no structure built by human hands remained standing. They seemed to survey the burning wreckage carefully, until they were content that no human being had escaped their wrath. As far as they could tell, all 150,000 residents of the city of Sunnberry were now destroyed. Their motion suggested a questioning though. Like a man that expects to find something that he is looking for in a certain place, but cannot locate it there. Again, as though upon some silent command given by one of them to the other two, the three figures moved together and took up a position on Route 30, just outside the former town. Ahead of them lay a thirty-five mile stretch of night time highway, the route to Pleasant Gap, and to other things between it and them.

The night air behind them was still filled with intermittent explosions and the sound of falling metal. Creaks from collapsing wooden and steel beams could also be heard, followed closely by the sounds of thuds, as parts of the structures finally collapsed to the ground. As if following some secret instruction issued by their unseen Master, the three rectangles moved outward from each other and formed a gigantic circle. Without warning, a formless void, blacker than black, appeared in the center of that circle, growing larger and larger. Assuming the form it took during its killing of Ronald Lamour, its teeth and claws gave it the appearance of something that had clawed its way out of the bottomless pit of hell.

It was caught between the forms of a huge lion, a snake, and a saber-toothed tiger with barred fangs. As in the brutal murder of Lamour, its two eyes again resembled pools of churning, swirling bright red masses of blood, sprinkled with black pits that oozed a yellowish substance into their bright red background. Once again, it took on a human form for its body outline. One that encased the lion-like body and saber-toothed tiger features in one face, attached to a broad, bloated snake-like body with tail. Two leg-like appendages extended downward from a point underneath the tail, giving it a firm stance. As its unnatural form took shape, steam began to rise from its body. A strange hissing sound, like air escaping through a thick liquid, accompanied its transformation.

Having reached a height of a hundred feet, its broad body appeared to jut out to a width of about twenty-five feet, when its contortions suddenly stopped. The phantasm's shape shifting to the form it wanted, was completed. With a circular sweeping motion, it stretched out its two arm-like appendages with claws, and brought them over its head. As it did so, the three rectangles moved toward it, until all three were absorbed into its dead black mass. As it stood there, it began to give forth a baleful, mournful howl that set the trees and leaves in the surrounding countryside into a terrible vibration. Lifting its head slowly, it peered into the night...up Route 30, to the object of its final attack.

Within its massive chest-like area, the three rectangles assumed smaller dimensions, and quietly began to rotate in opposite directions, burning brighter than ever in their characteristic colors. With one loud "thud," the Black Beast lifted and slammed its right foot down on the ground, and began its journey up the highway. This latest merging of the four geometries had given birth to a new creation. The Black Beast was taking on substance. Its fearful body was taking on matter, and becoming real. As it moved slowly along, howling and moaning, it destroyed everything in its path. Every house that Lasky had looked at on his drive home on that last day of his working life, was destroyed by violent, deep blue electric arcs that the Beast projected from the ends of its claws. As each home exploded and burst into flames from those currents, and its occupants died, the Beast grew darker in its blackness. It was becoming more real with each destruction. Somewhere in its nature, it knew that one special death was needed. One single death that would give it full substance, and the life of its own that was its instinct to win.

Chapter 12

▼

The Mind Mell

Lasky made his way down the flight of stairs to his laboratory by himself. As he turned down the short corridor leading to the lab, he saw the door was still opened. A pungent smell of burned plastic, wire, ceiling paneling, and electrical equipment hung heavy in the air around him. He stopped to consider just what had happened. He was weakening again, and was afraid to reenter the lab.

"What's wrong," he muttered to himself under his breath. "That new self of yours…the more caring self as Kate called it…starting to rear its ugly ahead again? My old self was all right. I felt more human. This other is like a degraded version. Can't let this happen now! This thing is far from over. If anything, need me the way I was. There's no time…" His self dialogue was cut short as a resounding sound of thunder shook the ground and the very air he breathed. "Kate!" He cried out. "What was that? Did you feel it?" he shouted up the stairs.

"Yes I did! It sounded from up here like an explosion of some kind! But from where? We're thirtysome miles from Sunnberry, and about twenty from Pleasant Corners! It would have to be a terrible explosion to carry this far!" Kate yelled back to him from the kitchen. "I'll be right there!"

In a few moments she caught up with him in the short hallway leading to the laboratory. "Here's the radio, cell phone, and your cane. I had a little trouble finding the cane," she said. "But that explosion. What could it have come from?"

Lasky fell against the wall, and seemed to go into a trance-like state. In his mind's eye he could see a violent explosion. It was a large, white tank situated between two buildings, both of which were on fire. The writing on the side of the tank read "Propane," in bright red letters. As he watched the events unfold in his mind, he saw bodies lying on the ground, chaos everywhere, and firefighters trying desperately to control the flames of the larger of the two burning buildings. In the background, he saw police wrestling and fighting with people who were trying to break through a protective barricade they had established. There was panic, fear, and death everywhere. He could smell the powerful, toxic smell of ammonia heavy in the air, and for a few moments, he began to gasp from its fumes, as though he was actually present at the fire.

He continued to watch the events occurring in Sunnberry unfold in his mind. Amidst the chaos unfolding at some point below his field of view, he saw the image of a red-orange fireball rise up out of a darkness that was patched with glowing yellow light. The light of a fire. In a few seconds the fireball took on a new shape. It had become a miniature mushroom cloud, rising upward into the sky, layer upon layer of its burning clouds streaming downward, and folding themselves under in a precise pattern.

"Something is happening inside of me, again!" Lasky blurted out. "I can feel it now as I did upstairs a while ago. It's that same physical feeling, and something in my mind, like before. But this time the enormous blackness opened outward into a scene of total destruction. Wait! I can see it clearer now! Yes! It's the cannery fire! There is no mistake about it! What else could it be?" Lasky continued to describe the sights he was viewing in his mind to her, as though he were the reporter on the scene.

"The fire and the destruction in the area of the cannery is hideous! That explosion was a big propane gas tank exploding! All around there are dead bodies. They're everywhere! The place is like a madhouse! Wait! There is smoke drifting across my vision, a gray-green smoke, but I can see through it in patches. People are stumbling around in dazed states, some are on fire, others are wrapped in blankets, fireman are running and falling down, choking from the ammonia gas fumes, and the police are fighting off people in droves! The people are becoming violent! A couple of men are beating a cop with pieces of wood and metal that was blown off from the explosion! I can hear sounds coming from the background. Cries and screams of panic! There's fire everywhere now from the propane tank explosion! It spread to the fields behind the cannery, and from there into the woods!

"Kate! Waves of anxiety are moving up from somewhere inside me as I watch this! I mean, a fear is moving up into my mind as the blackness folds outward onto the scene! There's no doubt about it now, I'm connected to the events that are going down! I can see everything! In the distance beyond there are more people gathering. Like a mob of some kind, but I can't see what they're doing! There's something else. My other self, emerging from somewhere inside of me, is drawing energy from me—from my body and mind. I can feel it! Upstairs I just knew, intuitively, that I had to control it. But now it's no longer a hunch. I now **know** I have to control it. I've got to push it down, or else it will suck my insides right into it, literally. There's a pulling sensation coming from it, like I'm being sucked from inside my guts down into some kind of black vortex!"

As he spoke, Kate looked into his tranced-over eyes. In his pupils, she saw the three rectangles glowing brightly, pulsating, and growing larger. She spoke to him sternly. "Can you hold on?"

"I have to! There's no choice. I sense these things are growing, but they're only the advanced guard of something much, much more terrible and frightening! It's as though those three glowing rectangles are its soldiers, and it's the General, waiting to come out on the battlefield himself.

Kate, give me that cane! I've got to see just how much damage was really done to the equipment! Really check it out, and see if there's the slightest chance to get out of this. I have an idea."

As they made their way through of the open door of the laboratory, Lasky put his right arm across Kate's path and halted her advance. "I forgot about A-Bomb. I'm so sorry, Kate. Let me go in and remove her. I don't want you to have to see that again," Lasky said to her in a low, hurting voice.

"No, you wait here, Mier. Please, just turn around. I know how badly you feel about this. Please, do as I ask." Kate replied. Lasky did as she asked, shaking his head sideways as he turned. He was coming to grips with the damage and destruction he had created. Not simply the life of one small animal that his work had taken, but all of those human lives down in Sunnberry that were now on his conscience. Tears began to stream down his face as Kate walked over to the small body, placed it in a rug that had been under the bench at the south wall, quietly moved behind him, and disappeared into the garage. In a few minutes she returned.

"Later on, when all of this is over, we'll bury her in the backyard, if that's all right with you," she suggested.

Lasky looked at her and then put his head down. All he managed to get out was, "Of course not. That's where I intended to bury her."

Kate grabbed him by the shoulder and turned him around to face her. She looked into his eyes. The three rectangles were still in his pupils, changing into different geometries as she watched, but they were not as bright as before. "You're weakening again, aren't you?" she asked.

"Yes. I'm falling back into my new, other self. The one that has so much weakness of character and personality to it, as opposed to the simple compassion of my old self."

"Can you control it," Kate inquired. There was a slight note of desperation in her voice. Lasky caught it. He knew he could not afford any weakness now. Not with what he felt was a coming showdown between him and the things he created.

"Yes, I can," he told her in a clear voice. A grim expression came over his face, and his jaw jutted out as if in defiance.

"How?" she asked. "I think I should know in case I have to help you."

"Don't worry. I'm in control. You needn't worry about how I do it. All that matters is that I do it."

The sharpness of his reply met her head on. She stiffened her stance, as she realized she was now talking to the old Lasky. That arrogant, sharp, curt self that had little or no concern for anyone's feelings, and at times, not even hers.

"Okay, then, you control it! But be damned certain you do, Mier, because now I'm twice as scared as you are, and I don't know what the hell is happening or what we are going to do, or what the f—will come out of this, or if we will! And I sure in the hell won't put up with any more of your shifting between selves. This is totally ridiculous, and I've had my belly full of it!"

Kate's sharp reply, carefully designed to either reinforce his old state or encourage it to the surface in case he was just pretending a few moments ago, accomplished what she intended. Lasky's abruptness was reinforced. "All right then, let's get on with this goddamn job! And since when did you take to cussing like that! I don't like it! It's bad enough when a man does it, but damn it, lady, it stinks when a woman takes to it!"

Both of them cut off their verbal encounter at that point, aware that further words could bring about another argument that neither could afford at that moment. "Well, we'd better get to it. First off, do you mind if I use your cell phone? There's someone I have to call. I don't even know exactly what I'm going to do or how to do it or if it can be done, but I have one of those feelings that things are gelling together in my mind, and I'm going to need another man to help pull it off. No offense, but I'm going to need another guy," Lasky told Kate abruptly.

"No offense taken," she replied in an equally abrupt tone of voice. She was offended he would not take her into his confidence at this late point. Especially since everything hung in the balance of his maintaining the control he assured her he now had.

After the last onset, with the personality weakness emerging, Lasky asked himself what would be needed to resurrect his old self. That self of egotism and determination to succeed at any price. Images of Kate's ex flowed into his consciousness in unbroken waves in response. From that point on, he continued to imagine scenes of Mike hitting her. That brought about a resurfacing of the self he knew so well and needed so desperately now. "I trust the bastard gets his someday," was all he muttered to himself as he gritted his teeth when the images first began flowing into his mind. Unknown to Lasky, the bastard had received his just desserts. Ironically, in death, Mike Runnion was finally serving a useful purpose.

"Can I have that phone? I've got to call that other guy," Lasky repeated his request. Without a word, she took it from her handbag, and gave it to him. He moved off from where they were standing in the middle of the lab, to the east wall, and began dialing.

"Who are you calling anyway?" she asked him, walking toward the damaged equipment at the west wall.

"Old John. You remember. I told you quite a bit about him. He's the one man at the plant I truly liked and respected. Sort of like a father figure for me. Always there when I needed him, good news or bad. Always listened, and helped in every and any way he could. The way I left him last week has me somewhat upset. He deserved better than that, but I was too callous to see it. I meant to give him a call. But one thing led to another, and well, here we are now."

Kate turned and looked back at him from her position near one of the exploded transformers. Lasky returned the glance, knowing what she was fearing, and quickly cut her worries off.

"Don't worry, I'm not reverting. Surely I can have *some* concern for the people I care about. Don't worry. I'm doing fine." With that Kate gave a sign of relief, and turned back to examine the damaged equipment.

Old John was standing on the back porch of his house watching the raging fire from the propane gas tank explosion. A thought of self-congratulations skirted around the corner of his mind, as he recalled how his wife had insisted they get away from all the new industrialization coming to the town, and buy a house on the very edge of the east corner of the city. He put his head down and sighed deeply but quietly, as he recalled her. How he missed Ann. It was some nine years since she passed away. The void in his life was ever with him, and he frequently smiled at thinking the time would not be far off when they would be together again. He had faith in such things. A simple, abiding faith, that rose above the doctrine and dogma of contemporary disbelief in such superstitious matters.

He looked down at his wristwatch, and in the afterglow of the fire, could still make out the time. "10 P.M." he whispered to himself. "A whole half hour since that big explosion. I'll bet it's like Ben told me. The cannery people put in those blasted big tanks of gas, and now one of them went up! Got to be somethin' like that, cause a regular fire don't burn this long, this bright.

"I hope he's all right. He didn't like having to take that supervising job on second shift. Said it would be nothin' but trouble, because the head man, that new manager, was really crooked, and was doing things behind the town's back. Like putting in those oversized propane tanks and ammonia backup tanks right next to the freezers in the production area. But then again, like he said, maybe someone on the council knew after all, because the plant passed the local inspection before firin' up. Who knows? I wonder though if the blaze will catch up with us folks up in this corner? Maybe…"

John's self speculations were cut off as he caught the distant sound of his telephone ringing. Without giving the matter a second thought, he raced through the back porch door, through the kitchen, into the living room, and picked up the receiver.

"The Naller residence!" came his almost singing, merry greeting to the unknown caller.

"John?" Lasky queried. "Is this John Naller speaking?"

"None other!" came the equally singing, merry reply.

"John, this is Mier Lasky calling. I didn't think I'd be talkin' to you again so soon. Not after leavin' the plant only last week, but I must speak to you. Do you have time to talk?" Lasky warily probed, keeping his fingers crossed that the older man had not written him off in the ensuing days since his retirement.

Old John was surprised to hear from Lasky so soon, but somehow, he was not shocked. Somewhere in the depths of his psyche, Old John was feeling things that his everyday self didn't want to know. Things that revolved around Lasky, the difficult younger man that he had come to like. Old John understood that his feelings for him were fatherly ones, and put it down to Ann and him not having any children. But his everyday self continued to push the feelings of the past week down, because somehow last week was not the real Mier Lasky he cared about. Last week was a young man who was monstrous in a hidden, nebulous way, only wearing Lasky's face. None of it made any sense to the routine, honest, linear nature of the older man, and so his mind continued to ward them off by the simple action of suppression.

"Mier? That you?! Well, it's good to hear from you! How have you been? Guess ya' heard about the fireworks down here in town. I've just been out on the back porch watchin' them maself, and boy, about a half-hour ago, somethin' really went wrong there! One heck of an explosion! You shoulda' seen it! There was a fireball that stayed in the sky there long 'nough for me to get to the porch and see it after I heard the explosion! All red and orange like. The thing looked like a tiny mushroom cloud!"

Lasky froze to his spot in the lab. Old John was describing to him the same image he had seen in his mind. There was no doubt now. Through an unknown law of the mind, he had direct sight-at-a-distance, and, most probably, he reasoned, an equal, direct knowledge of the monsters causing the destruction. But his mind was shielding him from the latter. It threw up an automatic protective mechanism to save his sanity. He was afraid of losing control. He was afraid of going on a rampage himself, killing as freely as the geometries that he was now certain were his own mental creations.

He finally admitted to himself that the first time he saw the ever-changing triangles in the Thought Chamber during the early days of his experiments, something deep within him sent up a warning. One he chose to ignore, because of his hatred for people in general. This realization surfaced from the hidden depths of his nature and anchored itself into the ebbing tides of his awareness at that moment. He swallowed hard, finally admitting to himself that he knew this to be true all along.

He was wrong about a part of his theory. He could feel the war raging inside his own mind. Maybe his superego was now weak enough to allow the Id to take over completely, sending him off on the killing spree he feared was in his nature after all. A killing spree all of his own, just as is heard of in the news, when an apparently normal person acts berserk. He now knew all of this consciously. His entire body broke out into an intense cold sweat as fear of turning into a savage killer bolted him to the floor. It could happen if he gave up his conscious control. But with this last insight, it was also now apparent to him that it would be necessary to take that risk. To abandon that control if only for a moment, in order to gain an insight into the exact nature of these geometries, and learn what they intended to do. But it wasn't time. Not quite yet.

"I know, John. I know," Lasky replied, the grimness in his voice being clearly detected and interpreted by the older man. "John, I need your help, and I need it desperately. The cannery fire…the general destruction going on in Sunnberry…maybe other things I'm not aware of but which I feel I brought about on this night…John, I'm responsible for all of it. I can't tell you now, here, over the phone just how, what, and why, but I do know what I'm talking about. I created a living nightmare, John, through that work of mine I was so secretive about. You used to tease me about it, remember? What did you say my last day at the plant? '...yer not gonna make some kind of Frankenstein monster or do something crazy, are you?' Remember that, John? Do you remember my reply to you? 'Don't talk like an ass, John!' Well, my friend, I'm the ass, not you. And I need your help right now, because what I started won't end with what I feel will be the complete destruction of Sunnberry. That's just the beginning, John, unless I...*we*...stop it here, now, tonight."

Old John listened intently as Lasky's desperate voice trailed off into silence. A constellation of thought raced through John's mind as he listened to the young engineer bare his soul to him. Thoughts of how his own intuition had helped him in his life through a thousand and one episodes, major and minor alike. Now, as during those other special times of intuitive insight, the older man's mental faculties were merging bits of knowledge with pieces of intuition, producing a combination of feelings and ideas that presented themselves to his conscious mind as a framed picture to be acted upon. Old John broke his silence and replied in a heavy characteristic long drawl. The kind he would fall into when the situation was serious, and he wanted to do what he could without hurting the other people involved.

"Ya know, Mier, I was kiddin' and I wasn't on yur last day at the mills. All along I kinda had the feelin' that you were up to somethin' that was, well, no good, ya might say. I never figured ya to be the kind to do no good on purpose, but I got to tell ya, if ya don't mind too much, that sometimes yer head is too big fer yer hat, and ya wind up losin' the hat and bangin' yer head. That last day ya left. Well, remember what I said to ya? 'Ya know somethin', Mier? I got a feeling yer not done here yet. No, yer not gonna come back to work or anything like that, but because of...well...I don't know what, but I think yer just not done with things back here. I feel bad, *real bad*, about the 'why' behind it all. Like somethin' in a pitch black corner that's hidin' and waitin' to bring all of this about. But ya know, somehow, I just *know* you, this plant, and this town ya despise so much, are gonna meet head on...one more time.' Looks like I was right, but I didn't figure I'd be this right this soon. Ya know what I mean? So now yer fat's in the fire but good, and ya need my help to pull it out, huh?" John was not being vindictive in his closing comments. It was his way of punctuating a thought, while waiting for its verification to come.

"No, John," Lasky replied in a deep, monotone voice. "it's no longer just me. How I wish it was that simple. Now everyone's involved. And I mean just that. It's not only the people in Sunnberry, and the small communities between there and Pleasant Corners, it could be everyone, John. I mean all those that lie way, way out beyond this little corner of the world of ours. I don't understand it all myself, yet. But with each passing minute, things I sense and somehow know, are coming together more rapidly, and in living color, and what the probable outcome from what I know up to right now, up to this minute, is as I said. Everyone's fat is in the fire I made. I can't tell you anymore now. There isn't time. I got to know, *now*, John, will you help me or not?"

The monotone feature of Lasky's voice disappeared in the last few sentences, and was replaced with a shaking note of terror that was increased by the depth in his voice. This quality added the dimension of life to the framed picture that presented itself to Old John's mind. The picture he knew he had to act on. Without a further questioning comment, the older man turned himself over to his intuition, and acted on the sum total of the portrait that now stood before his mind's eye. "What do ya want me to do, Mier?" was his only reply.

Lasky breathed a heavy sigh of relief that John heard clearly over the telephone. "Get in your car, and drive up here to my home just as fast as you can. There is no time for anything else. What I'm feeling now is that we are on the edge of hell itself, and it's going to tear wide open before too long. Get out of town, John, and get up here as fast as you can! All right?!" The desperation in his voice was now renewed.

"I'm on my way now. Kin I bring anything with me? I don't know why I ask that but I do! Is there anything ya need?" The tone in Old John's voice was now rising, betraying an increased level of fear in him even to his own ears.

"No. Whatever we have here will have to be enough. Just get out, John, start driving now! I don't think the situation down there will hold out much beyond an hour or so. It's going to get a lot worse!" was Lasky's frightening comments to his friend.

"I'm headin' out the door now! I should be up there in what...about forty-five minutes?" John both answered and asked.

"If you're lucky," Mier replied. "Just one thing. But listen to me carefully. Route 30. There's trouble there, and it's growing. There are crowds—mobs—forming, and there's a police barricade being set up. It's 10:30 now. I can see it. Everything is falling apart there. This mob that's formed is about to go wild. Maybe I didn't like the bastards in that town, but their mood is being made for them, these things of mine...these creations of mine...are influencing the Ids of all those people!"

John cut in. "What are you talking about, a mob forming, police barricades, an Id, creations of yours? Mier, what the hell is going on? What do you mean you can see everything. How can you from yer home? There's nothing on the TV. Some kind of blackout's been put on. No doubt by our beloved Chief Ruger from what that reporter was jabberin' about tonight. What are you talking about anyway?"

"Never mind, John, there's no time left for talk. Just get in your car, work your way around Route 30 for a few blocks before it passes by the cannery, get back on it where it continues past the cannery property, and get up here as fast as you can. Kate, my fiancé, is here with me. Maybe together we can stop this nightmare. I'll see you soon."

As Old John hung up the phone, his confusion over the remarks about the problems accelerating in Sunnberry overtook him for a moment. Then John smiled to himself as he grabbed his coat and walked through his front door to the car.

"Well, looks like the young fella finally got somethin straight after all! A fiancé after bein' retired for a few days?" he laughed. "These young ones sure move fast! They really do!"

Kate was at the north end of the laboratory, looking closely at the damage. She did not pay particular attention to Lasky's conversation, but did catch parts of it. The one part she didn't miss was the word fiancee.

"So it's fiancee now, is it, Mr. Lasky? Where did that one come from! Is there something I don't know about? I don't recall you asking me to marry you! The last thing mentioned on the subject was something to the effect that the matter was still up in the air. Well, is it or isn't it? " Kate teased, smiling slyly from across the room.

Lasky was wrapped up in the mental leftovers of his conversation with Old John. He would have missed her comments completely, had not that one word stuck out.

"Hmm? Fiancee? Fiancee?" he repeated, as though trying to grab hold of the meaning of the word, and what it meant to both of them. After changing mental gears, he realized what he had said. "Uh, yes, I suppose I meant that," was the only response that seemed to fall from his lips.

Kate looked at him hard, her smile fading rapidly into a blank expression. "No, no, I'm not pushing you. I told you I would never do that. It doesn't matter if we continue along like this or not, as long as we continue on together. All right?"

Her gentleness and consideration for him was the straw that broke the camel's back. In that frozen moment, in which he figured both of their lives were hanging by the single thread of a chance that he was about to take, Mier finally caught the first clear glimpse of Kate, himself, and their relationship as a couple. She had turned away from him, directing her attention to the damaged equipment. Without a further self-absorbed thought or analytical reason, he moved quickly and silently across the distance separating them.

He spun her around, grabbed her by the shoulders, and said, "Kate, this is the wrong time, I know. It shouldn't be this way. Not under these circumstances. I have to be frank with you, honey. I don't know if my idea will work. I really mean that. We could be living our last few hours on this earth, together, now. In fact, I'm not so sure this idea I have for stopping these monsters I created will work. The odds are we won't live to see the morning. I never really thought about it before, at least, not seriously. I mean, about us getting married. I just didn't have the time. But I'm asking you now, amid all of this destruction, danger and uncertainty…will you marry me? If we get out of this situation alive Kate, I want you to be my wife. I'm tired of talking and thinking of me only. I want this to be a *we*. An *us* from now on. So, what do you say, young lady? Will you be my wife?"

Kate looked up at him. Her expression of surprise at being spun around so abruptly melted into a broad, gentle smile that showed the perfection of her well-formed mouth. Without a moment's hesitation, she threw her arms around his neck, and pulled Lasky's neck down to her level and whispered, "Of course I'll marry you! I wouldn't let you go for the world, not even with all of your strange ideas and weird ways. I never wanted a boring life, and I'm sure with you, we'll never have that problem!"

Lasky pulled his head away from her grasp, and complimented her smile with a broad one of his own. "Then I guess that's that!" he said to her in a smooth, even voice. "From now on, it'll be just the two of us against the world."

Kate put her right index finger up to his lips and said, " From now on it'll be just the two of us. Period. We don't need to think about the rest!"

Lasky's face flushed, as the impact of his growing awareness of this loving and understanding woman hit the deepest recesses of his mind. Without another word, they embraced and kissed a long, passionate kiss, and it became apparent to both of them that their bodies were responding appropriately as nature intended. It was Kate who broke the impassioned embrace.

"Well, I think we'd better get back to work! Hopefully, we'll have plenty for time later on to be together."

In a disappointed, low tone of voice he replied, "Yes, you're right. But darn! It's always something!"

They began to laugh hysterically over the situation. They might have hours left to live, standing in the destroyed laboratory, with creations of Lasky's closing in on them, a town not far from them destroyed by the monsters he somehow let loose, and yet both of them were becoming excited after he proposed marriage to her. But the hysteria of their laughter brought a release that both of them needed. A release that recentered them, and allowed them to refocus on the dangerous and improbable job at hand.

As they turned to examine the burned and exploded equipment at the north wall of the lab, she reminded him of his earlier promise. "Upstairs you said you didn't have time to explain what you were sensing and why, that you didn't know how it works. Well, you said you didn't understand the mechanism that allows you to get glimpses of what's happening down in Sunnberry. But you said you have enough to go on. You also said your theory was partly wrong, and that you'd explain it to me as we worked. Will you? Tell me what you figured out."

Lasky took her by her hand and sat her in the insulated chair at the experimental workbench, and began to explain. "I think we'll have to let our examination of the equipment go for a few minutes, Kate. You're right. I should piece all of this together. But for both of us now, not just for you. Everything hinges on the conclusions I've reached these past few hours, and I'd better get it all straight in my own head before we go any further. It'll help me to hear myself, because that's how I can see the big picture. I talk to myself out loud a lot, as you know. So, let's get on with it."

Kate smiled as Lasky entered his lecturing mood. She expected the frantic pacing to begin any minute. It did, as soon as he began.

"All right. Let's take it from the top. Remember I told you about the inner mind and emotions, and that behavior is believed to stem solely from what we think and feel? You said this is what you were taught too, but asked if there is something more to it that I was basing my work on? Remember that? I then explained that, in my opinion, the thinking-feeling-acting basis of behavior was a matter of debate. It really depends on who you want to believe, because in the final analysis, it's all a matter of belief.

"Then I said that in reality, no one, and that includes the psychologists, psychoanalysists, and psychotherapists themselves know for sure, because if they did, there wouldn't be as many schools of thought on the subject, and certainly so many different treatments and results. I told you that my study of behavior got me to questioning how the human mind *really* works. How does the content of any mind become part of that mind? Why does a given mind accept certain content and reject other content, or at least, act on some content while rejecting other material? What makes two kids with the same background, turn out differently? What makes our minds tick? What is memory?

"What about thought itself? Is it all due to the production and flow of chemicals through neural pathways, or is it as I suspect? That the forces that either make up thought or along which thought travels through the brain are electromagnetic in Nature, and that the chemical basis of thought acts only as so many wires that allows the electromagnetic nature of thought to flow more rapidly through the brain. I told you before that my researches and experiments gave me the grounds to reject the idea that is held today that the chemical nature of brain secretions are not simply responsible for thought, but are in fact, thought itself.

"My preliminary experiments, especially the ones in which I saw those constantly changing geometries in the Thought Chamber, convinced me that the accepted theories on the nature of thought are completely wrong. Remember I brought up other issues to you. That once a division between science and philosophy did not exist. What is now called the sciences of physics, chemistry, and biology, for example, were at one time called Natural Philosophy. Things were studied as parts of Nature, not as extensions of man's cleverness. I believe human perspective changed when humankind moved from having very little to having excess, which occurred over the past two hundred years. In short, mankind has separated itself from Nature. Not just in his ways of living, but in terms of the way he thinks about himself and his immediate world.

"This changed his behavior toward Nature, his fellow human beings, and ultimately, toward himself. In so many words, his psychic view of others and of himself underwent a radical and dangerous change. He and Nature were no longer one. Instead of being a part of the whole, as it were, he cut himself off, and became separate, now intent on controlling the whole through his newly defined science. The new technologies have added to the sense of personal power. So much so, that now mankind thinks it can control and change Nature as it chooses. But in this process, man has removed himself even further from any inner connection with his natural source. This is the price he paid, but one that most people don't recognize to this day.

"Then, as I see it, a myth overtook society, one that states that progress for its own sake is needed for human salvation. The question of whether something was needed or helpful was no longer an issue. As long as something was invented or improved upon, it was enough. A use would be found for it, even if that use took away an intangible, like self-sufficiency, or the need to think and achieve. The need of the spirit or the soul has been replaced by the need for things. 'Make more money to buy more things' has become the slogan of this new school of thought, and a strange process for implementing this view came into being. Remember the mouse trap metaphor? 'Don't build a better mouse trap, build a better mouse to justify the need for a better mouse trap.' Then build the trap, and keep improving it, even though the 'new mouse' was exterminated by the original, new trap. The psychic split deepens, and the result is the crime and other irreparable social conditions and individually personal longings for meaning that we have today.

"Since I was experimenting with thought and the mind, all of these speculations and insights caused me to became concerned that my work might produce an effect on me that was akin to the effect Dr. Jekyll's serum had on him, and release my beast of depravity. This drove me to study psychoanalysis. Not psychology or any of the manipulative psychotherapies, but the real and original thing—the theoretical and experimental medical investigation of the human mind directly. I eventually arrived at two conclusions or postulates. The first postulate termed the Id as a function of the mind, as the consciousness is. In other words, it is a process of the mind. In and of itself it's not a separate part, and it can't act independently.

"The second postulate states that if what they call the super ego or conscience is weak enough, the effects of the Id can manifest in the person, and produce such bizarre and destructive behavior as serial killing. In other words, the Id, the Hyde in all of us, cannot come out of us physically, or dominate the average human personality, because of the conscience and general constitution of the human organism. This being the case, my concern that my experiments could produce some independent monster was merely that—a concern—generated by my own conscience. And yes, while I have very little use for society as it is today, at the same time I did not want to do something that would worsen it by creating and unleashing some kind of monster. After I satisfied myself along these lines and felt assured, I then went on with my experiments. To make a long story short, after all that study and consideration of the problem, I reasoned that the psychic split in each of us was just an aberration of the original function of the Id, but no more. So my work continued.

"But after the events of the past few days, I now know that the reason I am able to see-at-a-distance, have these colored rectangles in my eyes, now have a new self and a weaker second new self, is because my first postulate is **wrong**. Apparently, the psychic split in all of us moderns is so severe that under certain circumstances...as in my experiments...the Id can become separated from the body-mind reality of the individual. Not the entire essence of this part of the mind, but enough of it that feeds off a central source of energy. Me. That's why I become weak at times. It's drawing psychic energy hard from me during those episodes.

"But the separation also enables me to have a new self. One that is more compassionate and understanding, because all of my hates and feelings of the personal injustices done to me throughout the years were projected out of me, and are roaming around, doing what it is their nature...what is my nature...to do if I could get away with it. Destroy all those I hate or have something against. And that second new self, the weaker one, manifests when the energy draw is greater than normal. It must be when it needs enormous amounts of energy to execute its own, natural will, which is to destroy. First, I figure, it destroys those I have a personal grudge against. Like Lamour, who must have gone up with his cannery. Then, it destroys those I have a general grudge against, like the town of Sunnberry.

"I figure the colored rectangles in my eyes are evidence that it is growing stronger, and now, taking on a **will of its own**. This is an independent will, and here's the real problem, Kate. Unlike all of the horror flick films that deal with such a topic, it doesn't need me anymore. I don't know how I know this. I also know it is becoming **self-existent**. I have no objective proof for this, other than a sense I have. One that is growing stronger by the minute. This aberration is taking on a life of its own, with a will of its own, and a purpose of its own. Destruction and immediate self-gratification in whatever it wants, which is what its nature is all about. This aberration, this psychic split that I originally thought it was, is now becoming a full-fledged living entity, capable of drawing energy it needs from other sources. Like from the minds of others. I can sense this too at times of the greatest energy drain. It literally feeds off the terror it creates in its victims.

"While I don't know for certain, I think it toys with its prey...terrifies them and induces enormous pain...before it destroys them. And in the process, it—they—absorb the enormous energy coming from their psychic states of fear and pain, growing stronger in the process. That would account for all the hysteria in Sunnberry, and probably for a lot more destruction and killing it has done that I have no direct knowledge of. The ultimate goal of T.A.A.C. was to bring about the object of my thought out from my mind into the world, and give it a reality all of its own. Well, Kate, I succeeded. The only problem is, that *because of the accident*, the wrong thing came out."

Kate listened to his every word. She too sensed in some way, that their mutual understanding of the situation was critical if they were to survive. Finally, she spoke.

"Mier, it now seems to make sense, but I have a few questions. Do we have time for them?"

Lasky looked at his wristwatch. "It's 10:45 now. We'd better...uhh!" His voice broke off, as a wave shot through him, and a delight, almost sexual in nature, rose up into his mind from some deep hidden source. He fell backward, but broke his fall with the cane.

"What's wrong!" Kate screamed, as she jumped up from the insulated chair.

"Something just happened. Someone I had a special dislike for has just been killed by those things. I can feel it. Ohh! It was Walter Cotters! The Thing tore his head from his body, and sat it on Walt's desk, facing his body! I can see it all...clearly! The terror before his death was horrible! But it was also exciting, Kate! I can feel waves of excitement pouring through me! It's what the Thing I created is feeling! Oh, Kate, what have I done?" Lasky muttered, his eyes filling up with tears.

She helped him over to the insulated chair and sat him in it. "Now look! Now's not the time for other selves! I need the old you! The one that still has enough of his Id in him intact, and has the guts we both need to end this nightmare! Dammit, Mier, snap out of it!"

In desperation, Kate struck his face hard. His tears gave way to shock at first, until he got hold of himself. He then went back in his mind to his control mechanism, and thought of the bastard beating her. In a moment his old self returned. He looked up at Kate and said, "Thanks, honey! I needed that!" with a wry smile, and began to laugh. "Let's get on with those questions of yours."

"So then," Kate began to question, "this Thing, as you now call it, that is roaming around killing and destroying both your known enemies and anything or anyone you have any type of beef with, is actually a part of your own mind. It is still connected to you, and is effecting you by drawing energy from you, while yet allowing you to see through its eyes as it were, just what it is doing. And now, it's allowing you to even feel some kind of pleasure it gets from killing? It's not real in the sense of any solid or anything like that, but it's a kind of energy that can think and feel for itself, and has an agenda of total destruction? At first, it only went for your known enemies—all those you had something against—consciously? Then it broadened that agenda to include anything or anyone you even remotely disliked? Now, it had broadened that agenda even further, to include its own agenda, which includes killing and destroying for its own sake, and it does this because that is its nature? Its instinct, as it were? And for some reason, it is now letting you feel what it is feeling, seeing what it is seeing, and think what it is thinking, with increased clarity? Am I right?"

"Dead on target, Kate," Lasky replied.

Kate continued. "Then it's not acting on instinct any longer, Mier. That's as clear as the nose on your face. Somehow, this Thing has learned to think for itself. It may even be coordinating its attacks on Sunnberry, in an effort to absorb as much terror from its victims as it can, so it can grow stronger, faster. The picture of Walt Cotters you just described seemed like a designed attack, one meant to produce as much fear as possible. That's not instinct as I understand it. That's purposeful, planned cruelty of the most animalistic sort! Correct?"

"All too correct," he commented. "I am certain it is not using my rational, my thinking, faculties though. This whole damn thing is so subjective, yet its effects—what the Thing does—are so objective. So real in terms of its destruction. But I am certain it is not taking from me in this respect. I don't know how it managed it, but in the short space of time since the accident, it has managed to *evolve* a type of thought process of its own. Its thinking may be crude, but it is damn sly in its operation. All I can say is..."

Lasky's words were cut off in mid-sentence as he sat motionless in the chair, and entered what seemed to Kate to be a trance-like state. His eyes glossed over, his expression took on a blank, mask-like quality, and he began to mutter something just above an audible level.

"I'm in the wire mill at Sunnberry Wire & Cable. It's Tom. Tom Ferley, the Chief Foreman of the wire mill. He's watching a yellow glow that formed by the panel of the 26 inch wire drawing machine. The machine he used to tamper with against my orders, purposely, more than any other, to get me going. There's something happening now! It's something sticky, all over him! Aaagh! It shoved him into the electrical circuit! He's being electrocuted to death! His body is literally shaking, and coming apart. His eyes have popped...!" At that point Lasky stopped his narrative. He caught himself and stopped the weakness of excessive compassion from overtaking him again, by recalling a scene from Mike's treatment of Kate.

"I'm all right. It's over. Ferley got his too. There is no doubt about it in my mind now. This Thing *can* think and plan. But it hasn't evolved a way of thinking by itself. It not only gets its energy from me, but it gets terror and pain from its victims before it kills them. And there is something more! It takes energy *from their deaths as well! It feeds off their life as it passes from their bodies*! I just had a distinct impression of that as his killed Tom! For all I know, what is called the spirit in a person *is* their life force.

"One thing I now know for certain though, is that their life force is absorbed, along with the psychic energy from their terror and pain. If there is an afterlife, from what I just felt, this Thing even robs them of that. It literally makes their life force a part of it. Maybe that's how it learned to think, by assimilating the many minds that it absorbed at the moment of their deaths. Yes, I am feeling something from it this very moment. Kate, I am right! It does absorb the very spirit of a person after it kills them, and uses their minds to mimic its own thought processes! The poor sons-of-a-bitches can't even rest in death!"

A terrible frozen shudder flowed slowly through Kate's body as she heard his words. It was as though the very human desire for an existence after death were sucked out of her. The coldness of the grave took on a new meaning for her and Lasky, who was shaking uncontrollably at the realization he had just had.

Neither of them spoke for a time. Kate rose quickly from the seat she had taken on top of the bench against the west wall, walked over to Lasky, and stared into his eyes. The three tiny triangles were still in his eyes. But they were no longer skirting around the periphery of his corneas. They now occupied the central positions of his eyes, continuing to oscillate and change shape.

"Are they still there?" Mier asked calmly.

"Yes," Kate returned the reply. But they are now in the center of your pupils, and are very bright. Much brighter than before. Can you see all right? I mean, I thought something in the center of the pupils would block your vision?"

"No, I can see perfectly. I'm not even aware of them. At least not physically aware of them. I can't even feel their movements or shape-shifting. Try touching me directly on my skin with one of your fingers, and see if it still tingles as it did before, and if you get that acid taste in your mouth." Kate did as he asked, and jumped back with a start.

"From now on, I'd better only touch you by your clothing! I got a bigger shock this time, and the taste of acid in my mouth is much stronger. Your level of energy is going up too, right along with theirs…the things in your eye…or whatever this Thing is, as you call it. Are *you* feeding off their energy increase somehow?" Kate asked, the desperation in her voice being apparent.

"No, it wouldn't work like that. I am the unwilling recipient of *some* their increased energy. At least, the electric component part of it, since those rectangles are still connected to me. The question is, if they grow too strong, could this electric charge in me build up so much that it could electrocute me? That's the question I have, and one I have no answer to," he said to her grimly.

"You mean that if they continue to grow they could kill you by some type of remote electrocution?" she asked, the panic in her voice rising to a higher level.

"Yes, I think this Thing can do that. But I don't know just how much energy they'd need to be able to transfer that much across space without wires, to fry me to a crisp. I'm banking that this Thing isn't that smart to have reasoned this out, or that there simply aren't enough people in this area for it to kill to be able to do me in that way. It has plans for me, but not just yet. Not at this moment.

"In the meantime, we'll have to put the plan I have to stop them into effect as soon as we can. That's our only chance. I don't even know if it will work. The idea started to come to me yesterday, but I couldn't put it together because I didn't have all of the facts. Today I do, and I think it makes sense. As soon as Old John gets here, we'll have to go to work. But there's no more time for talking now. You understand pretty much all that I do, and it will have to be enough. We'll all learn more as we go along. Just like research. Isn't that something!" he said, the last remark being directed to himself. "It's 11:05 now. We better get to work!"

"Not before you know one more thing," Kate cut in. "You still have no shadow."

Lasky got up out of his chair with the aid of his cane, and began examining the experimental equipment at the west wall carefully. He knelt down to examine the oversized transformers, when he was knocked backward onto the floor. Kate caught his fall out of the corner of her eye, and turned to him.

"Not again!" she said in a shrill voice. "What are you seeing this time!"

Lasky did not reply immediately, but sat on the floor and watched the scene unfold in his mind, as slivers of Frank Ketterman's flesh and pieces of his bones were ejected from a green rectangular pane situated in the middle of Route 30. He watched with an unconscious smile, as the green twinkling lights in the rectangle grew more intense in color as the stripping and boning operation proceeded, and Ketterman's pleas for mercy and cries of pain grew more fervent. As he watched the drama unfold within his mind, he sat, mesmerized at the reality of it. It was as though he were in a movie theater, sitting in the front row, gazing up in awe at the big screen as it tantalized and gratified his sense of empirical, cold justice. In a few minutes he spoke to Kate.

"It's all over for him, too. Frank Ketterman, I mean. He was another guy at Sunnberry Wire & Cable I detested. But you know, he wasn't really all that bad compared to Cotters and Ferley, and a few others I could name. For him to have met that kind of end…" He broke off his conclusion as he became aware Kate was looking at him as though he were a laboratory rat under examination. "Yea, I know it doesn't put me in a good light. But things are as they are, and I can't do anything about the present, or the past. All I can do is trust that my idea works, and that we will see the sunrise. I'll just have to live with what I've done for the rest of my life. Maybe, in the end, that will be punishment enough."

She did not reply. The look on her face was one of anger blended with compassion. No matter how hard she tried over the past few days, she was still not able to separate these two conflicting emotions when she thought of what his experiments had done. At this moment, a thought broke across the field of her mind like a meteor. She wondered if she would ever be able to understand him, and the complex reasons for what he had done. Lasky looked down at his watch. It was 11:15 P.M. Five minutes after Frank Ketterman disappeared into oblivion. Lasky continued.

"Old John left at 10:30. He must have beaten that green triangle I saw in my vision by a few minutes, if at all. Ohh, how I wish he did! I need him here, now, because there's not much time left. Those things, or that Thing, is gearing up for some kind of fury. It's getting ready for a big kill. The feeling of delight and power is growing in me, and it's coming from it."

She looked at him in her retained silence. The expression on her face became harder, as the corners of her mouth tightened, and the veins in her neck began to stand out. At that moment, both of them heard something. A car's wheels screeched as it rounded the bend coming off of Route 30, and started down the long drive leading to the house.

"That's him! It's got to be him! Go open the garage doors, honey, and let him in! I can't hobble around too well on this cane."

Without a moment's hesitation, Kate walked across the laboratory floor, through its door, and down the short hallway leading to the garage. As she entered the garage, she saw the headlights of what looked like a medium size car flashing through the garage door windows. She pressed a switch on the side of the wall, and the large doors rolled up in unison, leaving her silhouetted against the oncoming headlights.

Old John saw her immediately. "Wow! That is some young lady Mier found! My goodness, maybe he does have some common sense afterall!"

As he strained his eyes to see her more clearly, Kate moved from the shadows of the garage interior onto the macadam driveway. Old John's headlights fell on her fully, illustrating her tall, slender, and well figured body. Her long auburn hair, draped across her shoulders and over her chest, sparkled in the flat yellow of his headlights, creating the impression of a close golden aura surrounding her head and shoulders. Kate's purposeful motions directing him to the parking area at the end of the driveway highlighted her from different angles, while demonstrating a purposefulness and quiet determination that added to her physical beauty.

The older man was impressed, and smiled to himself. "She's a lovely woman," he thought. "I'm happy to see that Lasky found her. I think these two will do all right together. Yes sir, I think they're goin' to be all right."

Somewhere in his mind, he was recalling the days when he and his wife, Ruth, first met, and the thirty-two years they spent together before she was taken suddenly by cancer. The remembrances surfaced into his consciousness gently, bringing some tears with them, that trickled easily down the furrows of a face hardened by years of loneliness. As he approached Kate, he slowed to a crawl, and turned into the small parking area on the left. After quickly wiping away the tears from his face, he turned the engine off and got out of his car slowly.

Kate approached him hurriedly, extending her right had to him as the distance between them became smaller. "Mr. Naller?" Kate asked in a tone of voice that tried to conceal a very real anxiety within it. Old John picked it up immediately, but kept his insight to himself.

"Why, you must be the young lady Mier told me about! Glad ta meet ya! Let me congratulate you too! Mier told me over the phone a while ago that you and him are gonna get married, and I want to wish the both of you the very best. I keep thinkin'…"

Kate's suppressed anxiety overtook her otherwise polite personality. "Forgive me, Mr. Naller, but there just isn't time! We have a very serious problem here, and according to Mier, all hell is going to break loose sooner than any of us want! Please! Let's go inside. He's waiting for you!"

The eruption of her anxiety, and its increasing levels as she spoke, brought Old John's survival instinct to the front of his mind. The hairs on his back bristled, and he could feel tiny beads of nervous sweat begin to roll down his spine. As he looked at her in the diffused glow of the garage lights, he saw a terror in her eyes that he had seen only once before. On Iwo Jima during World War II, when the Marine Corps forces he was a part of made an amphibious assault on that Pacific island fortification. He saw that same look of terror in the eyes of his fellow Grunts, as they were about to die in one of the most violent and costly military actions of that war. The cold chill that ran through his entire body stiffened him up now as it did then, doubling his interior resolve to do his best in this 'action,' as he did in that one. With some clear thinking and a bit of luck, he thought, he would make it through this hell as he made it through the one the history books call 'The Inferno of the Pacific.' He looked at Kate coldly now, all trace of smile gone from his face, and all cordiality gone from his voice.

"All right, young lady. Let's get on with it. Take me to Mier."

"Follow me," she replied, in an equally grim and determined voice.

She led him through the garage, down the short hallway, and into the laboratory. Standing in the middle of the floor, now nearer to the center of the room, was Lasky, propped upright by his cane. It was 11:23. In the few minutes since Kate left him to welcome Old John, Lasky's appearance had changed drastically. Old John's vision of the engineer last Wednesday had become a reality. Lasky had undergone a terrifying transformation. As both he and Kate stared, the younger man seemed to fade in and out of their present reality. In this reality-shift, the younger man was now dressed as Old John had seen him. Now, as in that earlier image, he was almost unrecognizable in appearance, a withering shell of his normal self.

He resembled a phantom, desperately trying to cling to life and sanity. Lasky's face had taken on an ashen hew, and his eyes had sunk deeply into their sockets. There seemed to be no difference in color between his brown pupils and the white matter surrounding them. His bulky appearance had changed. His mass was still there, physically, but somehow, it looked slimmer and hanging down. Somewhat like a muscle builder who gives up his training and allows the muscular tissue to degrade into sagging flesh. Saliva was drooling out of the corners of his mouth, wetting the front of his shirt. They rushed over to where he was standing.

The older man grabbed Lasky by the shoulders, and shook him hard.

"Hey, Mier! Listen to me! Remember your last day at the mills when I saw ya' off? I saw you then just as you are now! It was a premonition! Listen to me, boy! Can you hear me! Snap out of it! This lady of yours here tells me there's a world of trouble comin' down on all of us sooner than any of us wants! This is no time ta fold up on us! Damn you, snap out of it!"

Lasky heard every one of his friend's words, but was unable to respond. Naller's voice seemed to come from some far away point in space and time, circling around in tube-like fashion until it finally reached his ears. Something had a grip on his mind that he couldn't break. A thought floating across what was left of his mind told him it was the Thing. It was growing stronger, getting ready for its ultimate kill. *He* would be that kill, the vagrant thought told him, but none of it mattered. Lasky's mind was following a vortex, spiraling downward into some bottomless black pit that emptied into the extinction of death.

Acting from pure instinct, Old John did what he had done to a few of his comrades on Iwo Jima, when they turned inward so much that they lost themselves in the heat of battle. Pushing Kate away from him so he would not hit her, he opened his right hand, drew his arm upward in one quick motion, and with a fierce downward stroke caught Lasky across his face. The slap crackled though the laboratory with a deafening noise, and threw Lasky backward. Only the older man's grip on the engineer's shirt collar prevented Mier from flying backward into the bench at the north wall. Kate looked on in amazement, but kept out of the action. She sensed that this was some brutal ritual engaged in by men when facing desperate conditions, when the luxury of understanding, or a kinder approach, was neither called for nor effective.

The slap in the face jolted Lasky's consciousness. His downward spiral into some death-like state halted abruptly, as he began to become aware of himself again. Kate and Old John looked on, as his internal struggle threw up physical signs they used to gauge his return to the world of the living. The ashen pallor started to fade, and the separation between brown pupils and the white-matter of his eyes became distinct. But Lasky was unaware of the changes, as he grabbed onto his returned awareness of himself with all of the mental hold he could muster, and concentrated on images of Mike beating Kate. After two minutes, he shook his head repeatedly, and broke his trance-like stare that was formerly fixed on his own spiral into oblivion. He stared at them as though dazed, and spoke.

"John! It's you!" Grabbing the older man weakly by his shoulders, Lasky continued, the color returning to his cheeks, and his grip on John's shoulders becoming stronger. "It really is you, John! I can't tell you how glad I am to see you! Are you all right? Did you manage to get out of

Sunnberry without any trouble? Did you see anything on Route 30 outside of town on the way here?"

"Whoa! Wait a minute, young fella!" John replied, now wearing his characteristic lazy smile. "One thing at a time! First I got some questions for ya! What the heck has been goin' on down here in this room of yers, and what did ya mean when you told me over the phone that what's happenin' in the town was due to some creations of yours influencin' the people there somehow, so's they were goin' crazy. I gotta know if I'm to help ya," John insisted.

Lasky looked at his wristwatch again. "It's 11:40 now, John, and my insides are churning away like butter now. There just isn't anytime left to te..."

His words were cut off in mid-stream as they all felt a tightly compressed shudder of the ground. It was immediately followed by a powerful shock wave that broke through to the air in the lab, and threw the three of them against the north wall of the laboratory with violent force. Old John was thrown across the bench that ran the entire length of the wall. He hit the paneling with a magnum force that sent him sliding across the bench's surface. As he slid across the bench top, he tried to grab its surface to stop from sliding to the floor. But the force of his impact with the wall and bench weakened him too much. He gradually coursed across the bench, and descended to the floor. Kate was slammed full face into the wall a few feet from John. It was as though she was picked up by some invisible force and hurled against the wall above the bench top. Unconscious, she fell backward onto the floor. Her petite nose was damaged badly, blood flowing from it profusely.

Lasky was thrown upwards onto the bench top. His heavy body landed hard on top of the destroyed equipment. As he lay there, he felt blood flowing out of his mouth and nose, while pieces of test equipment gouged his body in dozens of places. Slowly, he threw his legs into the air above the floor, and moved himself off the bench's surface and onto the floor. As he did, sharp pains grabbed him in his rib cage. He could feel he had broken ribs on both sides. From his scant knowledge of medicine, he breathed in slowly and deeply, and then spit hard onto the floor. "Good!" he muttered to himself. "It hurts like hell, but the lungs aren't punctured." He repeated the process several more times to convince himself that his lungs were indeed intact.

No sooner had he regained full control over his body and mind, then his mind was propelled into another state of emotional euphoria. Unlike the other times however, this state was one of supreme ecstasy. The smile that broke out over his face was one of crystallized evil. It was a response to some hellish pleasure that told him tens of thousands of lives were just lost in the town of Sunnberry, many miles away. The Thing that was still in contact with his mind had delivered this knowledge to him by a telepathy not yet understood. He began to howl and laugh loudly, his face turning a deep red, a reflection of the terrible human destruction that had just been visited upon his former foes in that small city he despised so much. His howls of delight and ecstasy grew louder and more animalistic, as Old John and Kate began to awake from their unconsciousness and pass into a twilight stupor.

As Kate and Old John regained their senses, they became aware of the howling. Unaware of her own injury, Kate looked at Lasky. He was hunched over on all fours, howling, laughing hysterically, and clawing at the tiled floor like an animal. Saliva fell from his gaping mouth, making pools on the tile. She was beyond the feelings of horror, or terror, or anger, anymore. Kathleen Noel Murphy was used up emotionally. The scene in front of her eyes gave the word insanity a new definition. One her mind refused to recognize or accept.

As she sat on the floor watching the animal actions of the man she loved, John came to his senses fully, and jumped up. Grabbing an extension cord from one of the benches, in one Herculean effort he pulled the receptacle end off, exposing its raw, bare copper wires. With lightning speed, the older man rammed the plug end into a live electrical outlet, and jumped on Lasky. The force of Old John's weight knocked both of them flat onto the floor. Old John scrambled to his knees and hit Lasky square on the jaw, knocking him senseless. In one final lightning move, the older man slammed the bare copper wires of the extension cord into the flesh of Lasky's right arm, sending 110 volts of house current into the stunned mad man. Lasky wiggled and squirmed, trying to pull the wires from his arm, but Old John secured them by clamping his left hand over the wires that were now drawing blood from the younger man's forearm. For a full five seconds the electric current passed through both of their bodies, until both men collapsed to the floor, unable to move.

Exhausted, Kate crawled on all fours over to the two men. Old John was unconscious. His breathing was labored. Lasky's eyes were opened, and transfixed. She thought this last shock may have been the one that finally killed him, but she just could not feel anything beyond this questioning curiosity. Instinctively yet calmly, Kate leaned down and began to give Old John artificial respiration. In a few moments he began to cough, and opened his eyes. His heart was fluttering, but assumed its normal rhythm after he hit himself hard in the chest a few times with the edge of his closed fist. Finally, he spoke.

"How is Mier?" he asked in a raspy voice.

"I don't know," came her dull, matter-of-fact answer.

Old John had seen such battle fatigue before, and recognized it immediately. Without saying a word, he crawled over and examined him.

"He's alive, Kate. I take it yer Kate, Mier's fiancee. Ya know, we was never properly introduced," John said with a smile. "I know you know who I am, but fer formality's sake, let me introduce myself. I'm Old John as Mier calls me, though I don't think he knows I know that's his pet name for me. John Naller is my given name. I'm real happy ta meet ya, Kate, even if these aren't the best of all circumstances to meet under," he said with a cackling note in his voice.

That small bit of very ill-timed humor was the secret ingredient that brought Kate out of herself, and back into her emotional world of feeling. She started to laugh, but the blood from her nose dripped into her mouth, cutting her laughter short. After wiping it away, she looked at Old John and said, "Mr. Naller, it is I who am happy to meet you! Mier told me a lot about you over the past several years. I can tell you, there is not another man alive he admires and respects more than you. The truth is, you're a father to him in many ways. And as you know, that big jerk lying there is one bad kid to have at times!"

With that said, both of them broke into a laughter that was so out of place and time with the desperateness of their situation, that its appearance caused them to laugh harder. The ice between them was broken. It was as though the older man and Kate had been friends for years.

"Well," John finally managed to get out after their bout of laughter ended, "I guess we'd better get this bad kid up and movin', 'cause it seems to me that this situation's got to git a lot worse ba'fore it gets better!" Working together, Kate and John resurrected Lasky one more time, got him to his feet, then sat him in the large insulated chair.

Lasky looked up at John, half angry, half relieved. "What the hell was all that about, John! Dammit, I was almost electrocuted once from my experiments! What were you trying to do, finish the job? First it's a hard, cold slap in the face, next a belt in the mouth, and then electrified wires in the arm? What gives!"

"You mean ya remember all that?" John asked, puzzled.

"Damn right I remember it! Who wouldn't!" Lasky retorted.

"Then why the heck didn't ya do somethin' about controllin' it yerself?" the older man asked, a sharp rise in anger filled his words.

"You don't understand, I was out of control, John. I was not experiencing feelings that made me act like that. I *was* those feelings. There was nothing to control, because the feelings and I were one and the same. Do you understand?" Lasky asked, searching John's now hardened expression for the glint of an early answer.

"I suppose so. I saw things like that on Iwo Jima. In combat, and on the medical ship after the battle. One guy went crazy—just like you did—and a young medic used an electric cord to shock him back to normal. That's where I got the idea when I saw you goin' crazy. Just experience is all," was John's toned down reply. An understanding smile then broke out over the older man's face.

"Ya didn't tell me 'nough though, Mier. Over the phone I mean. And hey! A few minutes ago when I was checkin' to see if ya were dead or alive, I got a shock from yer skin. I don't remember that medic saying anything about no leftover shock from that guy he zapped with live electricity! What's goin' on, and what do you have to do with that mess in Sunnberry? And there's somethin' else. Maybe I'm the one that's goin' crazy here, and not you. Leastwise, not you alone, cause I see little bright colors in yer eyes, movin' right across them, changing shapes. What is goin' on here, anyway?" The older man's insistence to know became a serious issue, as the smile fell from his face, and his voice took on a harsh, demanding tone.

"Kate, I'll fill him in on the situation generally, and you take it from there. Don't forget about telling him about my not having a shadow now, either. But first, if you will, John, under the table there, pull out that brown box. In it is a medical kit. It's pretty complete. I suggest we patch ourselves up as best as we can and fast," was Lasky's reply to Old John's demands.

Old John did as Lasky asked, and produced the medical kit from the box. Kate's nose stopped bleeding, but was starting to swell badly. Old John put a portable ice patch on it, to keep the swelling down. Together, he and Kate then wrapped Lasky's ribs with layers of tight strapping tape to hold them in place. He grunted as the older man applied the necessary pressure to hold the broken bones intact. Kate put alcohol on his numerous bleeding cuts, made by his collision with the test instruments on the bench. As they tended to him, he spoke quietly.

"That shock wave that hit us, John, was three 20,000 pound tanks of propane gas exploding at the cannery in Sunnberry. My insane behavior was the result of an ecstasy that the Thing I created in my experiments felt as it absorbed the terror, fear, and life force of tens of thousands of Sunnberry residents killed by that explosion. I know this to be true, because I'm in communication with it right now. I can see through its eyes, a sight-at-a-distance, and I can feel its feelings and sense in my mind the process it mimics that produces something like thoughts. Kate will explain in detail all of it to you after we finish here. While she does that, I'm going to take a better look at the equipment over there by the west wall. That was where the Thought Chamber was, and where I brought this Thing out from the most secret recesses of my own mind.

"It's me, John, or part of me. The worst part. What psychoanalysis calls the Id, the center of all instinct, instant gratification and buried rage in all of us. Unknowingly, it was separated from me by an electric shock that nearly killed me, while I was trying to bring into existence whatever object I held in my thoughts. In other words, John, my special project dealt with turning my thoughts in concrete things. I succeeded a number of times, in a way, until the big experiment a few days ago. Something unforeseen—a little kitten Kate gave me for a retirement present—crept into the lab when I began the experiment, and shorted out that burned out equipment you see over there.

"In the process, it separated a large part of my Id from me. That Id, that Thing, grew in power and independence, until now. But unlike any of the sci-fi movies, this Thing doesn't need me alive in order for it to exist. I know this from feeling its thoughts, such as they are. Now it has one mission. To kill me. In doing so, it will be free. It will have an existence and will of its own, and an enormous amount of a peculiar energy that is a kind of living energy that cannot be destroyed by conventional means, nor any I am aware of. That's the long and short of it, John, in a nutshell. Kate can explain the rest to you, and answer any of your questions. In the meantime, I got to get back to work." After delivering this matter-of-fact dissertation to a stunned Old John, Lasky turned and hobbled over to the burned out bench, and began to rifle through the damaged transformers and oil-filled capacitor banks.

Kate and Old John went over to the bench at the east wall and spoke quietly. After she had filled him in on some of the details of the recent events, and answered his questions, the two of them went over to Lasky. He was managing as best he could. The broken ribs and his generally depleted physical condition had taken its toll. John was the first to speak.

"Kate explained quite a bit to me, Mier. Looks like none of us 'ill get out'a this unless that idea of yours she told me about works. Think it's high time ya filled both of us in on it. How about it?"

"Well," Lasky replied in a monotone voice that indicated his absorption with inspecting the damaged equipment, "it's really not that complicated. The funny thing is, the theoretical basis of T.A.A.C. is very complicated. But not the reverse of it. At least I don't think so. And if I'm wrong, then none of us will be around too much longer to do anything about it. I should tell you, John, that the electrical shock you gave me with the extension cord did the trick. It was only 110 volts of regular alternating house current, which itself can be lethal. But it was a far cry from the 220 volts that drove each of these two transformers that produced two million volts of what's called radio frequency or, RF current. That's what the 50,000 volts of the transformers' outputs produced, when they delivered their output to the tesla coils. Those coils, together, produced the RF current that went through the electrode band I had attached to my head during the experiment. I figure that the lower 110 volts, delivered over a longer period of time…probably five or more seconds from what it felt like…moderated and stabilized the brain changes Kate might have told you about. Did you tell him?" Lasky asked.

"That and a bit more. He had to know as much as we do, without all of the trimmings," she replied, her voice showing the cold, analytical attitude she now took toward the situation they were in.

"Good!" Lasky snapped. "He does have to know. So. Those brain changes were oscillating…varying my brain cells in size and changing shape over time, and being pushed this way and that by the connection I have with the 'Thing' out there. But that last electrical jolt shocked the brain cells again and changed them—both physically and chemically, I think—so that they have assumed some type of idealized and permanently modified new shape. That's what must have caused the positive changes in other people who underwent a bad electrical shock as reported in the journal articles I read on the subject.

"Now, I feel like a 'third new self.' Neither the 'first new self' of compassion, or the 'second new self' of weakness. What I'm saying is that now I'm aligned with the way I have always felt inside, and wanted to express in thought and deed, but never could in a manner that captured my intent. To put it bluntly, I couldn't 'be me' from thought to act. I would always sabotage my intentions so that what I did—the way I acted—was not in keeping with what I was thinking and feeling. I was inconsistent, if you will. I can tell that now my old self is gone. I'm now the way I wanted to be all of my life, but the price to others has been terrible. I wanted both of you to know this in case we don't make it through the night.

"Maybe, at least in some way, some good came out of this nightmare, even though it was at the high cost to so many people. I know how that sounds. But at this moment, I have to try and find some good in all of this. I'm not trying to justify anything. Forgive me if it sounds that way. We have to go on and try to destroy the Thing for our own sakes, and I need all the inner strength I can muster. 'What is past is prologue' is an old saying, and no amount of guilt or anger will stop what I created. We have to do it, and to do that, we will need every ounce of physical, mental, and moral strength we have. All right? Agreed?"

Kate replied immediately. John's approval and agreement took a few seconds longer. His was from an older generation, steeped in a Judeo-Christian ethic that held to a ten commandment view of life. But in the end he had to agree with Lasky's final conclusions, and so added his agreement to Kate's.

"So, Mier," John asked coolly, "Just how do we destroy this 'Thing' you created or separated from you, or whatever."

"As I started to say, " Lasky explained, "it's a lot simpler than the theory behind my work to create what I was thinking about. Here's what I figure." He extended his bare, right arm out to both of them. "Touch it. Tell me what you feel," he said with an insistence. Old John touched the flesh on the engineer's arm first, followed by Kate.

"What do you feel," Lasky asked.

"A heck of a tingling, like little needles," John replied.

"And you, Kate?"

"It's a much greater electric charge than I ever felt before when I touched you. It's growing in intensity. Do you still think it will burn you to a cinder like you said it might earlier?" she countered, questioning.

"No, it won't! Here's a surprise for you. One that I've been holding back on until I was sure. Now, I am. My brain cells were not the only cells of my body that underwent a change. *All* of the cells in my body changed, both physically and chemically. I have no acid taste in my mouth as you did when you first touched me upstairs a few hours ago. I didn't tell you, but I had that lemony-acid taste too. As time went on, it lessened. And after John gave me that jolt with the electrified extension cord, it stopped. Which means that my body has developed an insulation to its own electric charge, much like an eel's body develops against its body's charge-generating ability.

"What's more, this insulation is protecting me from sharing the Thing's rapture when it kills, and from taking me over so I degrade to a primitive animalistic state akin to its own nature. The charge is only still in me because I'm still in contact with it. Of that I am certain. I can feel it. What all of this means, is that the Thing is some strange kind of living electricity as I suspected. But that's all we need. It's like a house of cards. Remove one from the base, and the whole structure collapses, no matter how stable the top layers are. And electricity is one of its bases.

"Right now, I am seeing-at-a-distance again, even as I speak. I am seeing through its eyes at this moment. Yet, I am in control of my own mind now, and my physical strength is returning. The Thing out there now consists of three rectangles that are hovering over the east and south end of Sunnberry, destroying the town and killing the remaining population. They are firing energy bolts of some kind at buildings and people. The geometries are destroying all in their path. And with their firing of those energy bolts I can feel an upsurge in the electricity levels in my own body, yet they are not effecting me or my mind, but each of you felt the electric charge increase when you touched my arm just now. All of that destruction is occurring, right now, down in Sunnberry, and yet I'm not wrapped up in some ecstasy, or crawling on the floor, howling like some kind of rabid animal. And why? *Because now I am fully insulated from their effects*, thanks to John's memory and quick thinking. So that's the key."

"What's the key?" the other two asked in unison, sounding irritated with Lasky for saying half of what he was thinking, but believing he was being obvious.

"*Electricity!*" He burst out, the joy of discovery filling his word. "It's *electricity!*"

"Ya got me there. I don't understand the stuff," John confessed. "Just what do you mean? I mean, how do we use electricity to kill it?"

Kate cut in. "Me too. I use the stuff just as much as anyone else, but don't understand one bit about it."

"Do you see all of this equipment? What's left of it, I mean!" Lasky replied, using a cautious sweeping motion of his right arm to impress them, while favoring his aching ribs. "All of this equipment was used to take a very, very tiny electrical current that was traveling around in my brain, *magnify* it millions of times and *regulate* it, so that a *thought boundary* as I call it could be overcome, and the object I was thinking about would *jump* from my mind into the world of our reality. That is the how behind Project TAAC. I wasn't *creating* what I thought about in the strictest sense of the word, but rather, I was bridging a gap between my thoughts and the real world! *That* is what Project TAAC is all about, and was my ultimate discovery about the nature of thought, and my ultimate secret. On that single discovery, I designed and built all of this equipment, and brought, not created, the Thing into existence when the accident occurred. You would be right to say I separated it from my mind—a part of my Id—or that I brought it into the reality. But technically, I was just bridging a gap between the two worlds. The world of thought and the world of reality. That is the theoretical basis of my work."

Kate cut in abruptly. "Yes, yes, that's all well and good, but how do we stop it?"

Lasky flashed a disapproving glance at her, and replied, "By first understanding what we are dealing with, and how it came about. That's why I just gave you that fifteen second lecture that took me over twenty years to discover. Unless all of us have some knowledge as to the nature of the Thing, we'll get nowhere. One thing I learned in all of this. When the human mind has facts to go on—even facts it may not understand at the moment—it has an ability to form ideas that uses those facts in a correct way, so those ideas work. That's why I wanted to carefully explain this to both of you. Maybe one or both of you will do something without knowing it that will be based on those facts, and in the process, help us win the day. That's why I wanted you and John to hear what I just said. Understood?"

Kate's impatience subsided. She smiled back at him. "Understood."

"Now, here's my idea. We work in reverse. By that I mean, we use the electrical component of its nature against it. We treat it just as though it were any other electricity, and in the process, bring its house of cards down. We can't effect the living part of that electricity, because no one knows what life really is. But we do know about electricity, and I think that's all we need to know. Here's what we do. But first…"

He looked at his watch again, but his collision with the wall and the test equipment had crushed it. Turning to Old John he asked, "What time is it?"

The older man glanced at his timepiece. "12:15 A.M."

Lasky continued. "Then it makes sense. A few minutes ago while we were talking, I saw through its eyes again. There were four triangles. Yellow, green, hot-pink, and black. Acting together, they gave birth to a monstrosity outside of Sunnberry after they finished destroying the town. A new form has emerged. It's a deep, jet-black outline, some kind of monstrous being right out of hell. It's coming this way right now. We'll all see it sooner than we want to. It's coming straight down Route 30, destroying every house it passes, by firing some dark blue arc that I'll wager anything is electricity. A few minutes after its birth, it began taking on substance. Matter, somehow. It's not just some simple outline in the sky anymore. I know this too. It's coming. To find me. It has to kill me to establish a complete independence of its own. Then there will be nothing to stop it because there is no way to destroy energy. It can't be done. It's one of the laws of physics."

"How long before it gets here, do ya think?" John asked.

"The damn Thing is probably a hundred feet tall, and very broad. Its gait is huge, but slow. I can see it now. Its feet produce a pounding sound as it walks. We need that! It will alert us. I'd say, maybe forty-five minutes before it gets here. It stops to destroy any building it sees, and then has to break its inertia that comes from taking on matter. The fact that it's now taking on matter, coupled with its slowness in breaking its inertia and the time it takes to destroy, are probably the only things that will buy us the few extra minutes we're going to need."

"Then let's get to it!" Kate countered, pulling him out his habitual tendency to think things through too much. "Now what do we do, and how does it work! See? I am listening so I get the knowledge you were harping about a few minutes ago."

Old John laughed out loud, thinking they'd make a perfect couple. He knew the balancing value of laughter, especially at times of extreme danger.

Pointing to the two large, damaged transformers, Lasky began. "These transformers are shot. Luckily, when I was equipping the lab, I bought backups of almost every piece of equipment that could blow from one reason or another. There are two more of these things in the garage. John, I need you and Kate to lug them in here, remove these two dead ones, and set the new ones in their place. You'll find the new ones against the west wall, in the corner. They're under a brown tarp, on a wooden skid. They're very heavy. I wish I could help, but my ribs are killing me."

Without a further word, the two raced through the lab, down the short hall way, and into the garage. They found the tarp and pulled it back. John grabbed a crowbar from a wall rack, and used it to unpacked both transformers from their wooden crates. Slowly, they lifted one of the transformers. But the weight of the transformer was too much for Kate. Her end slid through her hands, and hit the floor with a thud.

"Wait! I got an idea!" John yelled. "That wheelbarrow over there! Bring it over here!"

She raced across the garage, and wheeled the old piece of garden equipment over. Together, they lifted the transformer and dropped it into the barrow. Old John pushed, but the wheelbarrow collapsed, spilling the transformer out onto the floor.

"The darned thing is too big for this old wheelbarrow. It won't push right!"

"Oh yes it will!" Her voice rang out in determination. "You push, and I'll steady it!"

Working together, they succeeded in getting the first transformer into the lab. Lasky disconnected the power cables from the two burned out transformers in the meantime, and cleared the wooden platform they rested on, in preparation for the new power units. After removing the two burned out ones, Old John and Kate returned to the garage, and in a few minutes, brought the second unit into the lab.

"Good!" Lasky shouted. "Now here's what we do, and why. Move the new transformers onto the platform, and over the holes, and bolt them down. That's it, line them up, one behind the other. But turn them around, so the red lugs of each transformer are toward the back, and the blue lugs are toward the front. I'll explain in a minute."

Working as fast as they could, Kate and Old John walked the transformers onto the wooden platform, and after considerable struggle, got their mounting holes directly over the center of the holes Lasky originally drilled into the platform. Kate stood back after the holes were aligned, while John bolted the power units down solidly to the platform.

"There!" John said proudly. "Those darn thinks won't move if they took a direct hit with a mortar round!"

"Good!" Lasky replied. "They have to be stable. Now, do both of you see those red and blue lugs?" Both nodded. "Here's how my idea works, the whole thing being the reverse of what I did to bridge the thought barrier, and it's all based on simple electrical laws.

"We know this thing has an electrical component to it. How much is another matter, but it must be huge. The laws of electricity tell us that if something is *grounded,* the force of the electrical current can be grounded literally. That is, sent into the earth and made harmless. At the same time, an earth ground stabilizes the current flow in whatever else that current is flowing through. Any sudden discharge, or a short in the circuit sends the current to earth, protecting the circuit and the object the current is flowing through.

"Now, the earth acts as a giant spherical capacitor. That's a device that stores electrical charges. Our earth has a negative charge to it. My experiments showed me that the charge associated with thought is positive in nature. This means that that Thing out there has a gigantic positive charge, and is pretty much shielded from being drained into the earth because of two things. The air, which itself has a positive charge and insulates it from the ground, and the fact that it still comes from me, and I am insulated from ground in any number of infinite ways. For instance, just by wearing shoes, or standing on any insulator, likes rugs, for instance. Even the floors of a house are not earth grounds, or at least not good ones." Lasky continued to talk as they worked, pulling the power cables from the tangled debris, and testing them to see if they were still useable.

"Negative charges," he went on, "particles called electrons, are responsible for current flow. They flow from negative to positive. But these negative charges produce a current that flows in the *opposite* direction—from positive to negative. And that's how we destroy it. We get its positive current to flow through me while I am heavily insulated from the earth, and I assimilate it. Its content. Bottom line, I take that part of my Id back into me, by using the electrical characteristics of its nature to engineer the reabsorption. Then we direct the positive charge into the earth ground, thus neutralizing its excess positive power. I will suffer some type of electrical shock, to be sure. But I'm banking that my trickle drain of its energy will be enough to prevent me from being electrocuted by its enormous power…that, and my complete insulation from earth ground should protect me."

"Wait a minute!" Kate interrupted. "Are you crazy? If this thing has the amount of power—current—that you say it does, no amount of insulation in the world is going to protect you from being electrocuted! I'm no engineer, but even I know that!"

Old John cut in right behind Kate. "That goes for me, too, Mier. I saw enough in the steel mills where they used hundreds of amps and thousands of volts to run those machines, and I watched and talked a lot with the guys from maintenance. What Kate says is pretty much on the mark, if ya round it out, so to speak. Yer gonna git yourself killed in the process, if ya try somethin' like this. Then what? You'll be dead, and the thing won't have no one to take it back into 'im, and it'll go on some kinda rampage forever, and all of us will be join' ya, sooner or later!"

"What you and Kate say," Lasky replied in a cold voice, is quite true…ordinarily. But hear me out. That trickle current can save my life, even though I'm not certain, and allow me to take those monsters back into my mind. Here's how it works. See the red lugs on the transformers? Those are the secondary sides of the transformers. That is the part that provides an increased current output from the current that is placed into the primary sides…through the blue lugs. Normally, you put a smaller current in through the primary and get a stepped up voltage and current out of the secondary. What we are going to do is *reverse* the electrical logic! By putting the power of that Thing into the secondary, it will be stepped *down,* not up, so that I will be receiving a much smaller current through the electrodes taped to my head. And remember, I will be fully insulated from earth ground.

"By grounding one side of the secondary, I think the trickle current will weaken the charge enough to allow me to survive. After the current passes through me, it will then be earthed on the primary side which will also be grounded, right into the earth. The Thing I separated from myself should then just be a part of my mind, as it is in all humans, unable to harm anyone directly. Remember too, it gets its positive energy from the atmosphere and from the life force of the people it kills. As long as there are people to kill, and an atmosphere, it will have power of its own. That's why it doesn't need me, and wants to destroy me. Because I can take it back into my own mind, the center of positive power where it came from, and it instinctively knows this. That's the theory. That's what I think will happen. Besides, it's all we have. There's nothing more."

Kate and John looked at each other, not knowing what to say. "Now let's get the transformers hooked up, because we have yard work to do," Lasky said with a smile.

John and Kate connected the power cables to the transformers as he directed, while he readied the insulated chair. Stacking layers of wooden blocks and Plexiglas sheets on top of each other in alternating, Plexiglas/wood, Plexiglas/wood fashion, he produced a sturdy stand that stood two feet off the floor, one which would fully insulate him from any ground connection. Although the bench at the west wall was badly damaged, it turned out to be more stable than he thought. He used it to hold the heavy cables that connected the electrode headband to the secondary of the transformers. With Kate's and John's help, the three of them then lifted the heavy, insulated chair up, and situated it on the Plexiglas-wood stand.

"What time is it?" Lasky asked.

"12:40," John replied. "Do you think the Thing is anywhere near us yet?"

"No. I can still see through its eyes, but I can't make out the territory. But since the ground isn't pounding, I'd say we have about a half hour before it gets here. Let me check the connections to the transformers and the electrode headband one more time. Then there are three more connections I have to make before we go outside. That will be the last part of our preparations. If we're lucky, we just might finish before it gets here."

Lasky picked up three large power cables. He connected one to a red lug of the transformer closest to the wall, and hooked its other end to a one inch thick, solid copper rod that ran through the ceiling of the laboratory, and down into its floor. Then he did the same with the second power cable, connecting it to a blue lug of the transformer. Its other end was then connected directly to his electrode headband assembly. Finally, he connected the third power cable to another electrode on the headband, and the other end of the cable to the second copper bar in the other corner of the west wall.

"What's that for?" John asked.

"These are the ground connections that will provide the trickle current and final grounding to earth ground that I told you about. There are two solid copper rods that run straight through the upstairs walls, and up through the roof. This one, and that other one over there," Lasky explained, pointing to the second rod in the northwest corner. "Each of them have a four foot section sticking up in air on top of the roof, but you can't see them because they're hidden by the chimneys. The guy who owned this house before I bought it was a Ham Radio Operator. He was so petrified of lighting hitting his equipment, he sunk these massive copper rods through the house, drove them six feet into the earth, and connected the ground connections of his Ham equipment directly to them.

"But there's more. This guy was absolutely fanatical. He went even further. During the summer months of sudden, bad electrical storms, he used to string a copper screen, fifteen foot high and thirty yards long, from the copper bars coming out of the roof, and connect them to a third copper rod driven into the ground by that big oak tree up in the west end of the property. When lightning struck at any point near the copper rods or anywhere near the house, the rods or screen caught it. The lightning strike was then earthed either through the rods and into the earth, or into the third rod up by the oak tree, and straight to ground. I was going to scrap the screen when I bought this place, but just never got around to it. Now I'm damn glad I never found the time! It's laying alongside the house against the south wall, wrapped in plastic sheeting to protect it from the weather. That's the yard work we have to do."

As they hurried out of the lab and down the short hallway to the garage, he gave them instructions. "John, grab some hammers, large nails, and a crow bar. You'll find everything on the bench by the garage door. Kate, please run upstairs and turn on the floodlights for the backyard, and bring a couple of flashlights from the hall closet on your way back. We're gonna need all the light we can get. I'll get some rope."

While Kate did as he instructed, the men got the equipment they needed, and opened the garage doors. To their surprise, a power gale had started up. The wind blinded them with its force, but Lasky countered by running back into the lab. When he returned, he gave each of them a pair of safety goggles to protect them from the biting winds and flying debris.

"This is going to be tougher than I thought," he said grimly. "That Thing has thrown up this wind. I can feel it. I wasn't sure before, but I am now. The connection I have with it is a two-way street. In other words, it can tap into my mind as I can tap into that nightmare it calls a mind. It knows we're up to something. But I'll bet you a dime to a donut, it can't read my mind as completely and clearly as I can read its. And it can't reason either. If it could, we wouldn't have gotten this far. But we better get this job done while we can, because I can sense it's just increased its speed now. We'll be lucky if we have twenty minutes left before it gets here."

"Wait a minute!" Old John screamed, trying to be heard over the howling winds. "You didn't tell us everything! All that theory and stuff, but you didn't tell us how you're gonna connect this Thing to that ground yer talkin' 'bout! Yer not gonna walk up to it and stick some copper screen into it or no copper rod or nothin', so how ya gonna short the thing out?"

Kate jumped in immediately. "Dammit, Mier, why don't you tell us everything at once! The suspense is killing me! If this was a horror novel,

I'd be biting the corners of the damn book by now! I can't take anymore! We have to know how you intend to ground that monster!"

"All right. Last time!" Lasky, shouted back, his words breaking hard on the winds. "We're going to string the copper screening between the house at that old oak tree. *Not* to that third copper rod near the tree, because that would be too good of an earth ground! I need the current that drives the Thing to pass through me *first* so I can re-assimilate it. If I don't, and we just short it out, I don't know what would happen. Its electrical nature would probably just short to the true ground, leaving a living part of it floating around. Somehow, I'd wager it would find a way to still make trouble, and I'd be an incomplete human being. I suspect both of us would just die, but only partially, because It and I need to complete each other.

"That oak tree's the answer. Its ground will take a little of the monster's dangerous electrical edge off. That's what I want. When we unpack the screen from its plastic covers, we'll roll it up there, and lay it lengthwise between the house and the oak tree. Then we'll unravel it on the lawn. Next, John, you and Kate hammer the edge of the screen nearest the oak tree into the tree. Use plenty of large nails, because it has to stay put. After it's secured there, we'll tie a rope through the opposite edge, and throw it up to the roof. John, you'll get up there and fix the rope to a small pulley assembly you'll find at the southwest edge of the roof near the chimney. I can't climb with these ribs, or I'd do it myself.

"When you get the screen fastened to the pulley, hoist on the rope, and the screen will lift up and stretch between the house and the tree. Just like the guy who owned this house before me used to do. We'll have a fifteen foot high, thirty yards long, copper screen between the house and the tree. Like a giant tennis net. On your way up to the roof, John, grab a power cable from the lab. After the screen is set up across the lawn, hook one end of the power cable to it, and the other end to the copper rod in the southwest corner, nearest the chimney. Then we'll have the special ground I told you about. I'll go back into the lab and do what I have to do. That's it.

Let's go outside and unwrap the copper screen, and get to work. I'll fill you in on the rest as we set things up."

The 'Force of Three' moved out into the yard. The winds were stronger than a few minutes ago. As they struggled to pull the long cylinder of rolled up screen out from behind some hedges alongside the house, Kate broke in.

"All right, Mier, what about us?" she asked. "What are we supposed to do while you're back in the lab trying to ground it?"

Lasky continued. "I was getting to that. The two of you will have to divert the Thing toward the screen. It must come into contact with the screen. Just once. Just for one second. The effect of the grounding will then freeze it in the screen, and allow me to do my work. How the two of you are going to attract its attention, I don't know. I don't even know how it will react if and when it sees both of you, because, one, it's so damn tall, I'm not sure it will be able to make out the two of you in the darkness, floodlights or not. There are no highway lights outside of my house, so my property is very dark.

"Two, it has one, single purpose that I can feel is intensifying the closer it gets. That purpose is to kill me. Here's the last little bit of agony. Even if it sees one or the both of you, I don't know if it will care about destroying you. Its survival instinct knows it only has to kill me, and it will be free forever. It can't reason as we know it, but it does have a powerful instinct for what's important to it, and for doing what it has to in some order of priority that it has established. At first, it did what I secretly wanted to do to my enemies. Now it does what it wants. The bottom line of all of this, is that one way or another, you've got to get it into the screen, or it's over for all of us. That's the last fly in the ointment, and to be frank with you, I don't have the answer to it."

Kate and Old John said nothing. Each became wrapped up in their own thoughts and fears, as the three of them continued to unpack the copper screen. As they rolled the long cylinder up to the central part of the lawn behind the house, the winds increased sharply. Struggling, they silently unraveled the screen, using large stones from a small abandoned rock garden to secure the screen on the ground. When the screen was laid out, Lasky attempted to give verbal directions for setting it up. But the winds became even fiercer. The Thing was getting closer.

Each of them wondered just how long they had before the monstrous form appeared, and perhaps sent all of them to oblivion, in whatever priority it had. As the winds increased in speed and intensity, one gale blew Kate off her feet, sending her careening across the lawn. Old John ran after her and grabbed her by her arm and pulled her back to their work area. Bits and pieces of loose dirt and small stones began to pelt them, stinging their faces severely. A few larger stone fragments cut the mens' faces and bare arms, while slivers of wood buried themselves in Kate's longsleeve blouse. Others sliced her cheeks and ears before becoming tangled in her long hair.

The winds continued to grow in strength, as they struggled to maintain their balance and continue working. Old John maneuvered Kate in front of him, using his body as a backstop to prevent her from being blown away. Lasky yelled to Old John, wanting to know the time. But even though the older man was only ten feet from him, Lasky's words were soaked up by the winds, the way a dry sponge soaks up every drop of water. He finally pointed to his wrist. John ran over to him, pulled out a flashlight and shined it on his wristwatch. It was 12:50. With desperate swinging arm motions, Lasky signaled for him and John to grab the edge of the screen nearest the oak tree, and to pull it toward the tree. Using more hand motions, he mimed for John to bring a hammer and nails. The older man motioned back, pointing to his belt and pocket, telling Lasky he already had them on him. Lasky then motioned to Kate to lie down flat on the ground and shielded her head, while the two of them fastened the screen to the tree.

With a see-saw dragging motion, the two men moved the screen up to the oak tree. Fighting against the winds, they managed to stand it upright, and hold it in place while each of them took turns nailing it in place against the tree's large, rock-solid trunk. John motioned for Lasky to run down to the center of the screen on the lawn, and stabilize it while he held it upright in place. After Lasky secured the center of the screen, Old John lifted his end up into the air. As he walked toward Lasky, he pushed the screen up into the air. When he rejoined his former boss at the center of the screen, half of the trap was set. The first half of the screen was standing up, fifteen feet into the air.

Together the two men lifted the last half of the screen, and walked it toward the southwest corner of the house. Old John took the crowbar from his belt, and punched two holes, one in the top and one in the bottom corner of the screen. Using his pocket knife, he cut two lengths of the rope he brought from the garage, and secured them through the holes. He and Lasky fastened the end closest to the ground to a steel rod the builders of the house used as foundation markers. The wind had not increased beyond its last deafening roar, allowing them to scream at each other when separated by only a few feet.

"Where's the ladder, Mier?" the older man yelled. "I gotta get this other end tied up through the pulley on the roof!"

Lasky shouted back, "Over on the north side of the house, John! It's lying on the ground against the wall!"

With that, the older man bent his body at a low angle, and worked his way to the other side of the house, leaving Lasky to struggle in keeping the second half of the screen upright. In a few minutes, he returned with the ladder.

"All right, John! Get up the ladder! Watch the wind so it doesn't blow you off the roof!"

"Don't worry about that," John shouted. "I hain't goin' nowhere but up, and I'm stayin' put til this thing is set up right!"

John dug the ladder's heels deep into the soft farming soil at a low angle, and scurried up to the roof. When he swung the pulley over the edge of the roof, Lasky threw him the rope end that jutted from the screen holes. The older man cranked the winch end of the pulley, until the second half of the copper screen stood erect. He then tied the rope's free end around the chimney of the south side of the roof, wrapped the last part of the rope through the pulley wheels, and knotted the end. As he pulled on the winch handle one more time, he heard a 'pop' as the screen became taut, and the knot jammed in place.

"This screen hain't goin' nowhere but up, and she's gonna stay that way now!" he shouted down.

"Stand back!" Lasky threw the final power cable up to the roof. John grabbed it, and connected the one end with its alligator toothed clamp to the screen, and the other end to the copper rod hidden behind the chimney. The trap was set.

"Time, John! Time?" Lasky yelled to his confederate, after he returned to his side.

"It's 1:10!"

Lasky hollered. "I didn't think we'd have this much time. Maybe..." His comment was cut off in midsentence. Suddenly, the ground began to shudder. A low level vibration started through the earth.

"It's coming!" Lasky shouted.

Grim expressions overtook the faces of both men. They were numb to the pain that racked both of their bodies, and to the blood running from the numerous cuts caused by the flying debris. Lasky motioned to Kate who was still lying on the ground, to now join them. As she made her way slowly through the winds, Lasky turned to Old John.

"John," Lasky said into the older man's ear, as he pulled him downward toward him, "This is a hell of a time to say this, but it's got to be said. You were like a father to me in many ways. My dad and I never got along. We were always at sword's point. Just one of those things. But when I met you, something clicked inside. You gave me the emotional support and strength to carry on in a job I hated, and you taught me to tolerate people I couldn't stand. You taught me to accept responsibility for my actions, and to live more honorably then I ever would have if I didn't meet you. And in all of that, tonight included, you gave me some of your wisdom. I never showed my appreciation and gratitude to you, and maybe, now it's too late. But I had to tell you how I felt, and let you know just how much I owe you. If we don't make it…"

Old John pulled his head away from Lasky, and cocked the engineer's head downward, so he could speak into his ear.

"I knew you were grateful all along, Mier. But I'm glad you finally told me. It makes me feel good inside. Every man wants to leave a part of himself behind in some way. A legacy sort of, so some of him still lives after he's gone. Maybe none of us will get through this night alive. If we don't, the kind of man you turned out to be in these last few hours, Mier, well, it'll be 'nough for me. Ya see, young man, me and what I learned throughout my life will have made a difference afterall. And I'll settle for that."

The two men looked in each other's eyes, and a warmth as ancient as the human race passed between them in that second. Both knew that whatever the outcome of this night would be, their lives counted. If to no one else, then at least to each other. And that was all both of them needed. The ages-old tribal male ritual of asserted masculinity was complete.

Kate finally made her way over to them. "What now?" She yelled, trying to be heard above the winds. "I feel the vibration in the ground! It's coming, isn't it?"

"Yes!" Lasky cried. "The vibrations are getting stronger now! It's got to be close! Look! Here's what we do! As soon as we get sight of it, I want you and John to drop back, beyond the screen, and move to the north! Use your flashlights to attract its attention! Run around, holler, for all the good it will do, but do anything to attract its attention! Pull it into the screen! I'll head back into the lab and get ready. Once it hits the screen, if my idea is right, the nightmare will end in a few seconds!

"If I'm wrong; if I'm wrong, then Kate, I want tell you again what I told you a few days ago. *I love you more than I ever let on. I mean it Kate. I could never live without you.* I mean *every* word of it! If there is a life after this one, we'll meet there, and in some vastness none of us understands now, we will find our happiness together!"

As Lasky spoke to Kate, he grabbed her by her slim shoulders, and pulled her toward him. Old John, recalling his younger days with a broad smile, turned his head away as the engineer kissed Kate passionately. Their embrace was shattered by a enormous pounding in the ground. It seemed that the earth's shaking went from a state of vibration to one in which it was being hammered violently, some intermediate steps in the process being missed.

"Look! Look!" John screamed. "In the south! Look at it!"

None of them could believe what they saw. Moving with a fury equal to the winds it started, the Black Beast broke into their field of view. As it approached, its features burned into the dead blackness of the surrounding night. It's human-like body outline was every bit of the hundred foot height Lasky had envisioned. The Beast's enormous claws caught their attention, as they radiated a dark blue light into the darkness that surrounded its blacker-than-black color. The nightmare's humanoid form was still trapped between the figures of a huge lion, a snake, and a saber-toothed tiger with barred fangs. The two eyes in the center of its makeshift head remained as before—pools of churning, bright red masses of blood, dusted with black pits that oozed a yellowish substance into their bright hot-pink background.

Something happened. The Beast's outline began to change before their eyes. Its lion-like and saber-toothed tiger features incorporated themselves into a well defined upper body and face, and attached themselves to a now well defined broad, bloated snake-like body with a tail at its lower end. Two leg-like appendages extending downwards from a point underneath the tail, gave it its great stride and firm stance. As it grew nearer, the strange hissing sound it made gave way to a growl, which soon turned into a long, drawn out baleful howl. It threw up its two arm-like appendages with claws, and began to swing them about wildly as it continued its deep, graveyard-like howl. Lasky, Kate, and Old John became transfixed for a few seconds at the horror approaching them. The three of them could now see the three rectangles quietly rotating in opposite directions in the

Beast's massive chest area, each burning brightly in its characteristic colors. Lasky broke their spell.

"Quick!" he screamed, "Kate! John! You go around the back, and start yelling. Use your flashlights to attract its attention! Do whatever you have to, to get it into the screen! I'm going into the lab!"

With that, Kate and John went off, struggling against the powerful winds and flying debris, until they fought their way to the lawn in back of the house. Lasky disappeared from sight, and raced back into the laboratory. For a moment he stood silent, looking at what was left of his years of work, and now, ironically, the new apparatus setup designed to destroy the monstrosity that came from that work.

"It doesn't matter anymore," he said to himself out loud. "All my work is gone. There is just one last duty to perform. It's now or never."

He moved quickly to the west wall and the new transformers. Not wanting to take any chances, he inspected the wiring and connections to the transformers and power cables one final time, and then took up his position in the insulated chair on top of the Plexiglas/wood stand. After he sat down, he placed the electrode band around his head, and began to stare off into the space of the burned west wall.

"It's now or never!" he repeated to himself. "Come on, you bastard," he screamed, as though the Beast could hear him from his laboratory. "I'm waiting for you! Come and get me if you've got the guts, you son-of-a-bitch! Because one way or another, you won't take another human life…not Kate's and not John's…not if I have to take both of us to hell to stop you! Come on you goddamn bastard, I'm waiting for you!"

Outside, the Beast had stopped its forward advance. It was surveying the area, looking for something it could feel was very close. It was searching for the mind of Mier Lasky, its Creator. The object of its next, critical attack.

John held Kate by her arm to prevent her from being blown away by the furious winds. The appearance of the Black Beast changed the winds' contours, driving them into a spiraling, tornado-like pattern.

"Hold on, Kate!" Old John screamed above the winds. "Hold on! We have to get beyond the screen! When we do, we separate! You move up the lawn to the northwest. I'll move to the north! Stay put, hunched down so the wind doesn't git ya, and start holerin' and waving yer flashlight like there was no tomorrow, because there won't be any if we don't git that thing inta the screen! We'll confuse it by you just stayin' there hunched over screemin' and wavin' yer flashlight, and me runnin' back and forth between the north and northeast, doin' the same thing. It's bound to git the critter's attention! Mier better be darned ready, because it looks like that thing sure is ready to raise some cane! Let's go!"

As the two souls struggled against the winds, flying debris continued to pelt them. But now, it came from all directions because of the tornado nature of the winds. Their bodies were numb to the new black-and-blue marks being heaped upon earlier damage to their bodies, and to the small streams of blood that flowed silently from cuts and gashes. John pulled Kate with him. Together they made their way under the copper screen, and to their positions in the back yard.

"Now you stay put here, and wait fer my hand signal! Then, turn the flashlight on, and start wavin' it and screamin' fer all yer worth!" Old John took to the north, turned to Kate, and began waving his arm. The two of them switched on their flashlights, and began screaming and yelling. Their flashlights shown into the sky, directly into the Beast's face.

The monstrosity aborted from Lasky's mind whipped its freakish head in the direction of the lights. The sounds made by the two distracters fell faintly on its instincts, but annoyed it enormously. Its nature to destroy took over its original attempt for the moment. Lasky could wait another few seconds. A sneer of contempt and overwhelming hate came over its face, as its howl grew louder and louder, while it threw its massive head from side to side. With a slow, reaching motion, it stretched out one of its arms, and ripped two telephone poles from the earth. It hurled one at Kate and the other at John. But its anger and uncontrolled strength caused the poles to overshoot their marks. Both smashed into the ground behind the two decoys.

The howls and thuds told Lasky that Kate and John were at work, trying to attract the Beast into the screen. He focused his mind on the thought of bringing the Beast and its geometries back into his mind. With his entire will he concentrated on a scene of the three of them merging into one being—him. As he did, he gritted his teeth and braced himself for what was to come.

Once Old John and Kate got the Beast's attention, they would not let it break its focus. Kate waved her flashlight wildly, while John ran from the north to the northeast of the grounds, frantically shining his flashlight into the air in all directions, and screaming for all he was worth. The wasted effort of the Beast to kill them with the telephone poles, combined with their openly taunting it, drove it wild. It threw its enormous head backward, and gave out a wailing sound that sent chills up Kate's and John's spines, while alerting Lasky that their plan was working. Its fury sent it over the edge of its ability to control its own actions.

As it stood motionless over Route 30, it looked around for another missile. Grabbing a thirty foot length of hedging it tore from the ground, it snapped it in two, and hurled the pieces of tangled growth at the decoys. The shorter length of hedge landed a few feet in front of Kate, hiding her from the Beast's sight. Old John turned to see if Kate was still safe. But in that instant, he failed to see the monstrosity hurl its latest deadly projectile at him. As he turned back to the Beast, the hedge was almost upon him. His aging reflexes gave out. He could not clear the projectile's path in time. He was hit hard by the green mass, and went down under it.

Kate saw what happened. Throwing all concern for her tenuous safety aside, she jumped up from her crouching position to run to Old John's aid. But the tornado-like gusts seemed to reflect the fury of the Beast, and grew even stronger. The impact she felt from them as she stood up slammed into her with solid brickwall force. She collapsed to the ground with a thump. Shaking her head to regain her senses, she started to crawl along the ground to the tangled pile of hedge that buried Old John, when she saw a hand emerge from the green mass of leaves. It was John. As she crawled toward him, he pulled himself out from the projectile, and made his way to her. He was cut and bruised severely, and was losing blood from a large gash that went clear across his forehead.

"John! John! Are you all right?" Kate asked in desperation. "Are you going to make it? You're losing a lot of blood! Pleeaassee don't die or pass out on me now, John! Are you going to make it?" came her combined frantic questions and pleas to him.

"I'm none the better fer ware, young lady," John screamed at her as the two finally came together midway between their original positions. "But don't ya worry none, I'll make it! Head cuts like this always bleed a lot, but it don't mean nothin'! It'll stop in a awhile. This isn't the first one I had in my seventy-two years a' life, so's I know what I'm talkin' 'bout!"

Relieved, she put her head down, and then lifted it up again. The look of desperation on her face told the older man she was near panic. "What are we going to do, John? What are we going to do now?" she pleaded.

"Hain't but one thing to do!" John yelled back to her through the gailing winds. "Continue to do what we were a' doin'! We got it's attention fer sure! Look at it! It's just a standin' there eyein' us over right now, not knowin' what to make from its last barrage! We can use that!"

"Use it how?" She yelled back in a failing voice, tears now streaming down her face.

"You stay right here, but hunch down. Don't lay down like ya are now! I'm gonna git up, and run over to the hedges it hit me with, and take up a stance behind 'em, and start makin' a darned fool of the thing! If I'm right...seein' that thing came from a man...showin' it up like this and makin' fun of its last try to kill us will send it right over the brink of hell, and it'll come after us up here!"

She looked at him blankly for the first time and screamed, "And then what?"

"Then, we gits it into that screen. One way er 'nother!"

Old John picked himself up, and ran back to the hedges. Signaling Kate again with an arm wave, the two of them switched their flashlights back on, and continued to shine them in the Beast's face, while they yelled as best as they could above the winds.

For a moment, the Thing from Lasky's mind could not decipher what it was seeing. It thought it had destroyed its latest victims. Its instincts for destruction played back its history of dealing with human beings. Up to this moment, all of the others ran in panic and fear, feeding it with their emotions of terror and their life force, as it snuffed out their existence. Something was wrong here. It was picking up panic and fear, but not terror. And there was no life force to absorb. The sight of these two humans escaping its last attack, coupled to their renewed taunting with lights, motion, and screams, drove the instinctual nature of the horror to some unknown realm beyond sanity. Its head resumed its sideways thrashing movements, while it resumed its spine-chilling wailing sound.

Flailing its two leviathan-like arms in all directions, it picked up its feet and smashed them into the ground. The living nightmare was doing what they wanted it to—move away from the front of the house to the back of the property, where Kate, Old John and the copper net were waiting.

As it pounded the ground moving in on their positions, John yelled.

"Keep crouched down and make yer way back to the northwest! Then keep mocking it with the light and yer screams! It hates motion of any kind!"

She did as she was told, while John ran back to the pile of hedge in the northeast. Once more, the two resumed their attack on the Beast with their flashlights and shouts. As the freak from the mind closed in on them, it saw the copper screen stretched across its path. It knew it could fire its blue arcs of energy at them and destroy them from where it now stood. It was aware that it could have destroyed them using its electrical current streams all along. But something deep within its nature prevented it from doing that. Instead, it desired to mangle them with its own claws. To do that, it knew it had to cross the barrier to get at them.

It started to move toward the screen, but then...suddenly stopped. It was reading something from Lasky's mind. It was aware that the engineer was waiting inside the laboratory, but for what? Lasky jumped in his insulated chair. He could feel the Thing probing his thoughts and memory. Kate and John continued to shout and flash their lights into and out of its face, but to no avail. It drew an image from Lasky's mind. In that image, it saw itself passing through the screen and vaporizing into nothingness. The Beast had sensed the trap. But it could not understand the rest of the mental image. It could not understand him hiding in the house, or how touching the screen would end its separate existence. It could not reason. But it did sense the end of its own existence if it touched that screen, and froze to its spot, wailing, and thrashing its head and arms in all directions.

Suddenly Kate caught motion out of the corner of her left eye. John was running toward the northwest corner of the house. The gale winds and flying debris prevented her from making out what he was up to, so she continued to taunt and mock the Beast.

Old John got to the edge of the house and bent down. As he picked up a coil of wire rope, he started to talk to himself out loud.

"This is it! I thought I saw a piece of cable on the ground when we made our way back here before! I was right! A good ol' piece of aluminum aircraft launching and arresting cable! That Lasky! Probably stole this from the company! It'd be a funny thing if this piece a' cable turns out ta save all our necks! I jest wish the darn thing's long enough!"

As he worked to unravel the cable, he realized that the Thing might realize that it could either step over the net with its gigantic gait, or just walk around it! When he unraveled the small diameter cable, he found it was a sling, set with aluminum eyes at each end. "Perfect!" he said to himself. "Sometimes things do work out fer the best after all! Not much. 'bout twenty feet. Guess it'll have to be enough!"

He knelt down, and pulled the hammer and crowbar from his belt. He grabbed one aluminum eye of the sling and used the hammer to drive the curled end of the crowbar through it, and then pounded the eye into a shape that wedged the crowbar in place. Working intently, he used the wedged crowbar as a lever to open the second eye of the sling and force the metal head of the hammer through it, jamming it in the aluminum eye. Finally, he used the crowbar as a mallet, pounding on the aluminum eye to jam the metal head of the hammer into the sling's eye as tight as he could. Suddenly, he heard a faint cry break on his ears through the winds.

"John! John!" Kate was screaming, "Look! Look! It's coming over the net!"

As John's eyes focused through his sweaty safety glasses, he saw the Beast had taken one huge step over the net. It railed and howled as though in victory. Its instinct for survival at any cost had forced some type of reasoning response in it, and now it was on its way to destroy its enemies. First the two in front of it that had refused to give their life energy, and then, its Master, whom it knew it must destroy. Inside the laboratory Lasky felt the pounding of the earth as its foot hit the ground. His reason told him the Thing he brought forth had figured a way out of the trap. He stood to jump off the Plexiglas/wood stand and run out to join the fight, but a force from deep within his mind told him to stay at the transformers.

"John! What are we going to do!" Kate screamed. "Help, John! What should we do!"

Without answering her, Old John ran out through the winds. Larger rocks and other debris now hit him squarely in his face and body. His head wound began to bleed again, red stains of blood cascading down the surface of his safely glasses. Finally he made his way to the middle of the grounds, and took a stand about thirty feet from the towering nightmare. Stretching out his right arm until it was at its full length, he began to swing his aluminum cable, hammer-crowbar weapon assembly. As he swung it, he fed it more cable length from his other hand, until the weapon made huge circles in the air. The 'whoosh' sound it produced as it ripped through the wind stood as a symbolic gesture to the opposition this band of three had taken to a horror whose time had come. Even at Kate's distance from him, she could hear the 'whooshing' sound. Goose

3

pimples ran throughout her body, as she watched the older man standing face to face with the Beast. Her mind went back to her Sunday school days. She was recalling the story of David and Goliath, and how now, as then, one seemingly insignificant man stood between their ultimate defeat, or victory.

As the weapon's speed increased, the Beast looked down at John with a sneer of contempt and hate upon its twisted face. It started to grin as it lifted its second leg from the ground. In a few seconds, it would be over the screen, and the defeat of the three defenders would be assured. At that moment, Old John let the weapon fly from his hands. The crowbar flew upwards toward the Black Beast, and struck in the trunk of its snake-like, bloated body. The other end of the cable with the hammer hit the copper screen seconds later. Both ends embedded themselves in their targets. The Evil had been brought into contact with the copper net. Moans and screams went up from the horror, as it thrashed its head from side to side and flailed its arms in all directions. Its graveyard howl returned, louder than any of them had heard before. Something was happening. The Beast was transfixed. It could not move. John and Kate stood speechless, watching the drama unfold before their eyes. Its body began to smoke, as a stench arose from it, and the ferocity of the winds decreased.

In the lab, Lasky was hit by the first jolt from the Beast's contact with the copper screen. The electrical current passing through his body was greater than he expected. He began to shake and squirm in his chair, trying to endure the shock. The moans and cries of the Beast crashed in upon his ears, and he knew that he and the part of his mind out in the yard were now in contact. Ever expanding circles of every color of the rainbow broke upon his consciousness. In his mind, he saw an enormous black form with three, colored, rotating rectangles becoming smaller, and moving toward his mind with the speed of light. They were in agony, screaming, fighting the pull of his mind on them. Lasky continued the process of reabsorption, his will fighting theirs in order to bring about their final reunion. As he struggled, he heard the sound of liquid hitting his chair, and something warm flowing down his chest and ears, and into his mouth. He was hemorrhaging. Blood was draining out of his body due to the intense electrical shock he was maintaining. Finally he saw wisps of smoke rising from his body. The electrical current was heating his body fluids, and driving them out through his pores. He was dying, and he knew it.

"There isn't time to continue the process at this pace," he managed to mutter to himself through the blood coming out of his mouth. "There just isn't time. The trickle current is too slow. It's not enough. But I've got to take it back into me before I die. Not another human being will take my place. Not one more!" His consciousness and memory fading, Lasky continued the battle of wills between himself and the Beast, as he struggled to remember something about earth grounds. His mind was filled with circles of light that now seemed to burn the inside of his skull, and a cloudiness that kept his memory from him. But he continued the struggle to remember. Then the memory he was searching for hit like a bolt from the blue.

"One more power cable. That's all I need."

As he looked around, he saw a badly burned cable with large alligator clamps on each end lying by the south wall. Now operating purely on instinct himself, Lasky tore the electrode headband off his head, jumped off of the platform, and staggered to the south wall. The odor of his own burning flesh nauseated him. Grabbing the cable, he picked up a utility knife from the bench, and sliced out the insulation from the center of it. Still staggering, he made his way back to the transformers and grounded copper rods. He connected one of the alligator clamps to the copper rod that was attached to the red lug of the one transformer's secondary winding, and the other alligator end to the second copper rod attached to blue lug of the other transformer's primary winding. The two rods were now connected directly to the earth. Without missing a beat, he climbed back on his insulated chair, and fixed the electrode headband back onto his skull.

"This is it!" he said to himself, as he pulled the old cable attached to the headband away from the blue lug of the one transformer. "When I connect this clamp to the middle of the cable that has shorted the two rods to earth, all three of us...the two rods and myself...will be shorted out directly to earth."

He looked up to the ceiling. A sadness overtook him that he never felt before. He knew his life would be over when he made the final clamp connection, and that he and Kate would have to wait for another time and another world to be together. As he leaned forward and connected the last clamp to the cable connecting the two earth grounds to each other, he whispered, "I love you Kate. I could never live without you." The clamp locked onto the cable connecting the two copper rods.

"John! Look, John!" Kate screamed, now in a voice of wonder and joy.

The Black Beast began to shimmer in the darkness of the surrounding night. Its howls ceased, while the three geometries in its chest stopped spinning and lost their color. The Beast's two eyes clouded over. Their swirling, churning pools of bright red blood, sprinkled with black pits oozing a yellowish substance, ceased. Gray clouds now filled its once horrendous eye sockets. As they stood, now holding onto each other, Old John and Kate watched in amazement as the outline of the monster stopped its shimmering vibration, and came to an abrupt stillness. Before their eyes, its gigantic body drew itself inward from all directions, became a single point in the early morning air, and then simply vanished.

"Looks like Mier's idea worked after all! But I got a bad feelin' about this whole thing yet young lady. You'd better wait out here while I go and check on him."

"Mier's idea worked, John, but not without your courage and resourcefulness. It was a terrible experience. Are you all right?"

"Well, I'm alive, and that's somethin', although I have to tell ya, I've seen a whole lot better days, and nights, for that matter," he teased with a smile.

"Like I said, I'll go check on Mier. Just in case. You know."

"No," she countered. "No, it's him and me no matter what. We've come too far together for me to abandon him now, no matter what has happened. We'll go in together."

The night was calm and serene, as the two defenders made their way down the lawn and into the garage that led to the laboratory. Neither was aware of the stillness, or the evening stars that had just broken through the drifting clouds of smoke from the former town of Sunnberry.

"Calling Dr. Gordon, calling Dr. Gordon. Please report to room 436," the overhead public announcement system of Pleasant Corners Community Hospital called out, as Old John and Kate made their way through the halls of the fourth floor. Both of the former defenders wore reminders of the battle. John's forehead was wrapped all the way around with a turban bandage, and his right arm was set in a cast. Somewhere in the battle, he had fractured that arm and never knew it. His face and other arm displayed smaller bandages, meant to heal the many cuts and bruises he received from the flying stones and debris.

Kate was bandaged considerably too. Her face was patched with several surgical type dressings, while both of her arms were completely wrapped from the wind-tossed debris that cut through her blouse. She walked along slowly with Old John, as she was not accustomed to using the cane the hospital gave her. Her left leg was badly bruised and swollen from her part in the war-like action. Both of their eyes were black and blue, and their faces swollen. They did not speak to each other, but walked quietly into room 436. There, in a hospital bed, was Mier Lasky, wide awake. As they entered the room, a smile broke over his withered face. The electrical energy that surged through him during the fight had driven out many of his body fluids, giving him the appearance of a slightly wrinkled prune. Intravenous lines feeding fluids, blood and antibiotics were sticking out of him everywhere. He was fortunate to be alive, and he knew it.

"Well!" he said to his two confederates as they approached his bed, "where have the two of you been?"

"What da ya mean, where have we been?" Old John teased him back. "Yer finally awake, and hollerin' already for an accountin' of where we've been! That's some gratitude fer a guy who's been unconscious fer three days I'll tell ya', and who should be just plain dead from all he went through!"

"Three days?" Mier asked, an astonished look on his face. "I've been out of it three days? I just woke up and figured it was the day after our combat with the Black Beast! You mean I was unconscious all that time?"

"Shhhh!" Kate reprimanded. "Keep your voice down! We'll explain everything in detail when you get out of here. But that's going to be a few weeks from what the nurse told us! So just keep your voice down, and listen to what we tell you in case you're asked. The hospital is bound to want to confirm our story with you, so listen carefully!"

"But I have a million questions," Lasky broke in. "What about Sunnberry? What do they think happened to the town? Is there any of it left standing anymore? Are there any people still alive from it? What about the steel plant? Did we really succeed in sending the Thing back...into my mind, I mean? And not least of all, how are the two of you? I have a million questions..."

"Keep yer voice down," Old John cut in. "Now listen ta me careful! Ronald Lamour got the blame fer the whole thing. The whole destruction of the town. Those illegal tanks of propane were what done him in as far as gettin' the blame goes. One thing led to 'nother in a situation like that, that the town wasn't prepared fer, and the next thing ya know, things spiraled out a' hand and then out a' control. The ammonia gas got the blame, too. The authorities said, it poisoned peoples' minds so they was hallucinatin', and thought they saw rectangular things above the town that destroyed the propane tanks and killed thousands of people. But the authorities said no such things as those rectangles can exist, so it was the people hallucinatin'. The fire spread, so the authorities say, through the propane gas lines in the east and south sides a' town, and everything then went with it. Town, people, the works. They also found the bodies of Walt

Cotters, Tom Ferley, and a few others from the plant that you and I knew. They found 'em dead in the plant buildings. But the explosions that tore the plant apart and the fire messed them bodies up somethin' bad, so they're just victims of a bad situation gone out of hand.

"As to any people left, well, a few thousand who had the good sense to git when the gittin' was good made it, and are comin' back. Looks like with the government's help and peoples' home insurance, they're gonna rebuild Sunnberry. That's about it. We'll tell ya all bout it when yer out a' here. OK?" the older man said with a big smile, and a fatherly look in his eyes.

"Yes," Kate continued. "That's about all there is to the story. Now about yourself. We told them you are an electrical engineer, you retired early from the steel company, and you were playing around with high voltage electricity when a lightning bolt from a stray electrical storm hit one of those copper rods that run through your house. We happened to be with you at the time, and that's how you were saved. John, being your friend from the steel company, made it up to your house just in time as the town was going up in flames and smoke. And since I am, uh, your fiancé, well, no more explanation was necessary on that point.

"That explained the massive burning of your body, your loss of fluids, and your hemorrhaging. Those broken ribs happened earlier that night, we told them, when you fell down the stairs, and we bandaged you up. We tried to call an ambulance, but were told none was available due to the burning of Sunnberry. They bought all of it. John and I also disconnected your cables from those rods and transformers, and said we were upstairs when the lightning flash hit your lab. The force of the strike destroyed all of your other equipment too, because a fire broke out. They said they expected that would happen from a direct strike. So be grateful to your best friend and your woman, Mier Lasky, because you nearly fried all of us, in one way or another!

"As to reabsorbing the Thing. Well, how do you feel?" Kate asked.

Lasky thought a moment and then replied. "Better and more whole than I ever felt in my entire life. Yes, I can feel it. I have successfully taken the Beast back into me. It's all right now."

Kate then added, "And look at the floor. Guess who's got his shadow back?"

Lasky looked at her and broke into laughter. Every part of his body ached as he laughed, and he grimaced, but kept laughing. "Looks like I'm marrying one hell of a woman, here, John! I'll bet she keeps me in line after this! You know something, my friend," he said as he looked him straight in the eyes, "a man couldn't be any luckier than this. That luck includes having a friend like you." Something passed between the two men at that point. Something that is private to men, as other feelings are private to women.

Old John flashed a warm glance back at Lasky and replied, "Yer in good hands son, yer in good hands with Kate!" John turned to her and said, "I'll tell ya what. I'm gonna take a little walk outside. I kinda feel you two need private time together." As John left the room, Kate turned back to Lasky.

"Were you serious, Mier? Are you absolutely certain you want to marry me? Maybe what you're feeling is gratitude, and you're confusing that with love. We've just been through some very strange times together, and you might be misreading the situation. I don't want to be forcing you into anything that you or maybe both of us will regret later. Maybe…"

With her last word, Lasky reached up and pulled her close. His long, gentle, delicate kiss answered her doubts, and she gave her consent in the returned gentleness of her kiss.

He spoke softly. "Remember. I will always love you. I could never live without you. I still mean every word."

She stood by his bed for a long time, quietly, while they held hands, and basked in the warm glow of life, and their future together. Quietly, imperceptibly, memories of his experiments surfaced. He reviewed his laboratory setup, the theory behind his work, and A-bomb's fateful action that brought about so much destruction to so many.

Still he wondered. "Don't be a fool," he told himself. "You created hell on earth for so many with your insane idea. Maybe it was doomed from the start. Maybe that kitten putting its paw into the discharge was an action sent by someone or something greater than you. A sign that your work should not continue. Maybe it was doomed from the start,...UNLESS...

The End?

9 780595 154654